MOONBLOOD

MOONBLOOD

Alastair MacNeill

VICTOR GOLLANCZ

LONDON

First published in Great Britain 1996
by Victor Gollancz
An imprint of the Cassell Group
Wellington House, 125 Strand, London WC2R 0BB

A catalogue record for this book is
available from the British Library.

ISBN 0 575 06296 7

Typeset by CentraCet, Cambridge
Printed in Great Britain by
St Edmundsbury Press Ltd, Bury St Edmunds, Suffolk

96 97 98 5 4 3 2 1

The culture of the Yanomamo Indians of northern Brazil is steeped in myths which have been passed down the generations. One of their myths on the creation is known as the 'Moonblood' legend. It maintains that one of their ancestors shot Moon in the belly and His blood fell to the earth where it turned into men. Where the blood was thick the men were ferocious and all but exterminated one another, but where only a few drops fell, or where it became diluted with water, the men were less warlike and did not kill each other. But because Moon's blood was spilt, the Yanomamo now regard all men as fierce and combative . . .

1

Donald Brennan was beyond physical exhaustion as he fled through the jungle, kept going only by an overwhelming sense of fear. He was drenched in sweat, his face and arms covered in scratches from overhanging branches. He'd long since lost his bearings. Not that it mattered any more. His only concern now was to stay alive.

A sudden movement caught his eye. He turned sharply, to see a startled white-tailed deer scamper into the bushes, lost his footing and fell heavily to the ground. The machete spun from his hand, landing in dense undergrowth. He could hear the tracker dogs barking excitedly – quite close now. His pursuers were gaining on him. He had to keep moving.

Then he heard rushing water. A river. If he could just reach it it would throw the dogs off his scent. He struggled to his feet and went in search of the machete – a waste of valuable seconds, he knew, but without it he'd be lost.

He found it and set off towards the water. A short time later he emerged into a clearing, which ended abruptly with a sheer forty-foot drop to the river below. Brennan peered down: the river was in full flow and he knew how treacherous the undercurrents could be, even to an experienced swimmer like himself. He'd have to jump and take his chances. He couldn't turn back and the river represented his last chance of escape.

He took a couple of steps back and was about to launch himself over the edge when he heard an ominous rustling from the bushes behind him. Before he could move an Alsatian burst from the undergrowth and lunged at him. He stumbled backwards in terror and lashed out wildly with the machete. The dog howled in agony as the blade sank into its neck. The full weight of body slammed into Brennan's chest, toppling them both over the edge of the ravine.

He never saw the partially submerged log but felt a hammering blow to the side of his head as he struck the water. He was dragged under by the powerful currents but, barely conscious, managed to propel himself to the surface. He tried to make for the riverbank but the surging currents swept him on downstream. Again, his head dipped under the water. He knew then he was going to die. Suddenly in his mind his son's face appeared like some celluloid illusion, then began slowly to fade, until there was only darkness . . .

Those who knew Kelly McBride had always suspected she'd come to the Amazon from her native Ireland to escape her past. That had been ten years ago, yet no one was any the wiser. Any questions about her past were met with silence. She knew it infuriated people, but it also kept them at a distance – exactly the way she wanted it.

It was common knowledge that she'd spent the first two years at a mission outpost, close to the Venezuelan border, working among the pockets of Yanomamo Indians who inhabited that area of northern Brazil, and that while she was there she'd discovered an abandoned forty-eight-foot tramp steamer in an overgrown inlet a few miles from the mission. With the help of some Indians and passing river traders, she'd got the boat operational and converted it from steam to diesel, which had cost the last of the savings she'd had transferred from her modest account in Ireland. Then she'd renamed it: the *Shamrock Gal*.

Over the next few months she'd pestered the traders to teach her how to pilot the *Gal*, and when she'd become confident enough to go solo she began to collect supplies for the mission from neighbouring ports, until they closed, when she'd decided to go into business herself as a river trader.

That had been eight years ago. Now the *Shamrock Gal* was a familiar sight on the Rio Branco where she did most of her trade with the Yanomamo villages along the river. In the last few years, though, the area had been swamped with *garimpeiros*, miners, in search of the deposits of gold, diamonds and tin ore that lay beneath Yanomamo land. And with this unwelcome influx of prospectors had come roads and airfields. Like many of her fellow traders, Kelly had found it increasingly difficult to compete with trucks and light aircraft, and now her business came mainly from those areas that were still only accessible from the water. She knew, though, that it was only a matter of time before more of the forest was destroyed to build more roads and airfields to accommodate the demand for a quick and effective supply route. It was necessary expansion in the name of progress, or so a visiting politician had told her. Kelly, however, saw it only as wanton rape of sacred Yanomamo land in the name of greed, which would only get worse as more money poured into the area from powerful international organizations.

She had problems of her own too: she was already in debt to unscrupulous suppliers in Boa Vista, the main river town, with her business tailing off every month, the future was looking bleak. But she'd never quit before and was determined to fight on to the bitter end . . .

'Rasha!'

The agitated voice brought her out of her reverie. She put her hand to her forehead to shield her eyes from the fierce overhead sun and squinted at the Indian standing on the bow of the *Shamrock Gal*, one of the two Yanomamo who'd worked loyally for her ever since she first began to trade.

Rasha was the unflattering name the Yanomamo had given her when she'd first arrived at the mission. A *rasha* was a fruit with the pasty texture of a boiled potato and the term had referred to the then pallid colour of her skin. She'd since acquired a rich golden tan but the name had stuck. It never failed both to baffle and amuse any Yanomamo when they first met her.

'What is it?' Kelly called from the wheelhouse in the centre of the boat. She was fluent in their language.

'There's a body in the water,' came the excited reply. 'It's a *naba*.'

9

Naba was Yanomami for someone not of their tribe, and Kelly's first thought was that it was probably a *garimpeiro* who'd drunk too much cheap liquor and fallen in the river. It wasn't an uncommon event, with several *garimpeiro* settlements along that stretch of river.

She manoeuvred the *Shamrock Gal* towards the bank. The body was floating face down in the shallow water, trapped in a mesh of tangled roots. The second Indian emerged from below deck with a pole and tried unsuccessfully to prise it free. He jumped into the water and swam over to it.

Kelly called out to the other crewman to drop anchor, shut down the engine and crossed to the rail. When the body was turned over in the water her hand flew to her mouth in horror. She'd known Donald Brennan well from his anthropological trips to the region to study the Yanomamo and their culture. Although she'd never much liked him, she knew that his journals had been a major factor in helping to bring the increasing plight of the Yanomamo to the attention of the outside world.

She watched as the body was disentangled from the roots and brought to the boat. A rope ladder was unfurled down the side of the hull and the two Yanomamo hauled the body on board. Apart from the livid skin, the only other external indication of death by drowning was the film of white foam, a mixture of air, water and mucus, around the mouth and nostrils. Kelly also noticed that the palms of the hands were wrinkled, suggesting that the body had been in the water for some time. One of the Indians threw a tarpaulin over it.

'Are you going to take him back to Boa Vista?' he asked.

Kelly didn't reply. Earlier that morning supplies, mainly of fresh produce, had been loaded aboard the *Shamrock Gal* to be delivered to several villages up-river. Now it would have to wait until the authorities in Boa Vista had questioned her about the discovery of the body and by then it would have gone off. She'd have to sell it to a rival trader at a knock-down price after she'd docked at Boa Vista. She wouldn't even be able to cover her costs, which would only add to her mounting debts.

The Yanomamo sensed what was going through her mind. 'We can throw the *naba* back in the water, Rasha.'

'It's a tempting thought,' she muttered, through clenched teeth, then sighed and walked dejectedly back to the wheelhouse. 'Weigh anchor. We're going back to Boa Vista.'

2

Ray Brennan had always wanted to be a cop. He'd joined the police straight from school and had earned his detective's shield by the age of twenty-six. That had been twelve years ago, and for the last ten he'd been stationed at Precinct 40 in the crime-ridden borough of the South Bronx in his native New York.

His partner for those ten years had been Lou Monks. The two men had contrasting personalities: Monks was a staunch family man, Brennan a confirmed bachelor. Monks relished the company of his friends; Brennan shied away from the limelight and only socialized under protest. Monks took little interest in his health; Brennan kept himself in condition by working out at least twice a week at a gym on the Upper East Side.

Even their methods of detection were dissimilar. Monks was methodical and used a combination of logic and common sense; Brennan relied strongly on gut feelings, a sharp, intuitive mind, and obtuse methods of deduction. Yet they invariably came to the same conclusions.

'That's the hotel over there,' Brennan announced, pointing to a run-down building on the corner of the next block. 'Let's hope we're not too late.'

Monks parked the unmarked police car in the only available space on the opposite side of the street then switched off the engine and got out. At six foot, Brennan was the taller of the two by several inches. He had a strong, charismatic face with cold, mesmeric, pale blue eyes and thick black hair, greying prematurely at the temples. Monks was twelve years Brennan's senior; his thinning brown hair was combed away from a craggy face dominated by a bulbous nose, which had been broken several times during thirty-one years' service with the NYPD.

The two men surveyed the exterior of the hotel with distaste. Scabs of cracked paint were peeling off the drab grey, graffiti-covered walls and only the letters 'A' and 'H' in MAJESTIC HOTEL – spelt out in a yellow neon sign directly above the entrance – were illuminated in a forlorn attempt at welcome.

'I can't believe anyone would stay at a fleabag like that.' Monks snorted disdainfully.

'Nobody does stay there,' Brennan replied, as they crossed the street towards the hotel. 'It's just a convenient place for the local hookers to take their johns. That's some turnover if they rent the same room a dozen times in a day.'

'You'd think with money like that they could afford to give the place a lick of paint.'

'If you were coming here to get laid, would you really care what the décor looked like?' Brennan asked.

Monks ignored him and the drunk slumped against the wall, mumbling incoherently to himself – pushed open the door and stepped into the lobby. The walls were papered in a garish floral design of lilac and turquoise. The threadbare carpet was purple. A stuffed elk's head with only one antler was displayed prominently on the wall beside the empty reception desk. He tapped the bell with his palm.

'I'm on the phone, I'll be through in a minute,' a male voice called.

Brennan's eyes went to the television set on a table behind the desk, which showed a repeat of the previous night's interview with the new Vice-President on *Face The Nation*. It had been ten months since the Republican Party had been swept back into power in a landslide victory for the right and the Vice-President was widely regarded as its standard-bearer. Decorated for bravery during the Vietnam War, he had lobbied relentlessly in favour of the Constitution's controversial Second Amendment – which gave every individual the

13

right to bear arms – although he had been quick to distance himself from the fanaticism of the right-wing paramilitary groups and their anti-federalist views. A devout Christian with the looks of a choirboy, his vitriolic speeches had brought disillusioned conservative voters back to the polling stations. But many had serious misgivings about men like him with their moralistic views on subjects like abortion and homo-sexuality. They regarded politics and religion as uneasy bed-fellows. Ray Brennan was one of them.

'Your buddy's on TV, Lou,' Brennan said, stabbing a finger at the flickering screen.

'I voted for the President, not for him,' Monks replied defensively.

'C'mon! They came as a package. Vote for one, and you get the other too.'

'At least I made the effort to vote,' Monks said tersely. He thumped on the bell again. 'Hey, you! Get out here now! We haven't got all day.'

Moments later, an unkempt middle-aged man appeared. He took a long drag on his cigarette as he eyed the two men suspiciously. 'What do you want?'

'Police,' Monks said, holding up his shield. 'I'm Detective Lou Monks. This is my partner, Detective Ray Brennan. Are you the manager?' A cursory nod. 'We're looking for a girl called Tina. She checked in here about ten minutes ago.'

'Don't know her,' the man said with a shrug.

'We're not Vice,' Monks assured him, then took a photo-graph from his pocket and placed it on the counter. 'We have reason to believe this man was with her. His name's Chico Nunez. Recognize him?'

'I don't remember.'

Brennan grabbed the man's wrist as he was about to tap the ash off his cigarette. 'Then I'd suggest you start to jog your memory otherwise you're going to have Vice crawling all over this rathole by the end of the day.'

The man stared coldly at Brennan, then ground out his cigarette in the ashtray. 'Room twenty-eight. Third-floor.'

'I'll take the bedroom door,' Brennan said to Monks, 'you

get up on the fire escape and cover the window in case he tries to duck out that way.' He gestured to the manager. 'I'm sure Conrad Hilton here will be glad to show you which window it is.'

'Give me a couple of minutes to get into position,' Monks replied, then followed the man across the foyer and out into the street.

Brennan headed for the elevator but when the doors parted he was struck by the overpowering stench of vomit and decided to take the stairs. Once he found the third floor, he walked slowly down the corridor until he found the room. He took out his revolver. Like those of his colleagues who had resisted the lure of the automatic, his preference was for the stainless steel Smith & Wesson M66 .357 with a four-inch barrel. It wasn't ideal for concealed carrying, but it had never let him down. And, as far as he was concerned, that was a powerful argument in its defence.

He briefly considered knocking at the door and announcing himself but if he did Nunez would have time to take the whore hostage. Best to go in unannounced. He took a step backwards then drew up his knee sharply and kicked the door close to the lock. The wood splintered. A second kick and the door flew open. 'Police!' he yelled, and leapt inside, into a narrow corridor, then moved cautiously along it pausing at the corner before swinging round, the revolver extended at arm's length. Nunez, dressed only in a pair of torn jeans, had an arm locked around the woman's neck, a 9mm Astra automatic pressed into the flesh under her chin.

'Put the gun down, cop, or I'll kill the bitch,' Nunez threatened as he forced her, naked, out of the bed, holding her tightly to him as he backed up against the wall.

'And give you another hostage?' Brennan retorted. 'You've been watching too many movies, Chico.'

'Do it!' Nunez said, and pressed the barrel harder into her neck. The sight nicked her skin and a trickle of blood ran down her throat. 'You don't think I'd kill her, do you? Well, you're wrong, man. She don't mean nothing to me.'

'You're not that stupid,' Brennan replied. 'You were only a

passenger in the drive-by shooting over on Grand Concourse last night. We've already got the gunman in custody. I'd say you're looking at one to three at Riker's. Maximum. With remission, you'll probably be out in twelve months. But you kill the girl, and I'll drop you where you stand.' He shook his head as Nunez glanced towards the window. 'My partner's out there. He won't let you past him either. Face it, Chico, there are only two ways you can leave this room. In cuffs or in a bodybag. It's your choice.'

'You can guarantee me that I'll be out in twelve months?' Nunez asked.

'You know I can't make any deals. All I can do is put in a good word for you with the DA, but only if you drop the gun and let the girl go.'

Nunez swallowed nervously as he stared at the barrel of Brennan's revolver. He had no doubt that Brennan would kill him if he shot the hooker. But he had never intended to harm her. He'd never shot anyone in his life. He'd only grabbed her as a hostage, but that had been a futile gesture. 'OK, I'll put the piece down,' he said.

'First let go of the girl,' Brennan ordered, and Nunez removed his arm from around her neck. 'Step away from him and cross to the window,' he told her, without taking his eyes off Nunez. She did as she was told and crouched down against the wall, her arms wrapped across her naked breasts. 'Drop the gun on the bed then put your hands on the back of your head and interlock your fingers,' Brennan ordered.

Nunez raised his free hand towards Brennan, then let the gun fall. He didn't move.

'I said put your hands on your head and interlock your fingers. Do it now!'

Monks, who'd been on the fire escape close to the open window, clambered into the room and trained his revolver on Nunez as Brennan removed a pair of handcuffs from his belt and snapped them round the man's wrists. He pushed him up against the wall and frisked him – he was clean.

Monks retrieved Nunez' automatic and as he handed the tearful woman a sheet to wrap around herself a familiar figure appeared in the doorway. 'Hey, Raoul,' Monks called out in greeting. 'What brings you here?'

Detective Raoul Garcia, the youngest man on the squad, entered the room. 'I was sent over to relieve Ray.' His eyes went to Brennan. 'You're to get back to the station house and report to Captain d'Arcy.'

'What does he want?' Brennan asked, a hint of irritation in his voice.

'No idea,' Garcia replied. 'That's all I was told.'

'Whatever it is, you'd better get going,' Monks said, then took the car keys from his pocket and held them up towards Brennan. 'You know d'Arcy doesn't like to be kept waiting.'

Brennan plucked the keys from Monks's fingers and left the room.

'Come in, Ray. Close the door behind you.'

Frank d'Arcy was a former body-builder who'd won a number of competitions at both state and national level and his trophies were displayed prominently on the shelf behind his desk. Now in his mid-forties, it had been fifteen years since he'd last competed but he kept himself in shape with a strenuous workout every morning. His muscular physique and cropped blond hair gave him the appearance of a tough, uncompromising cop. It was an image he did little to dispel, although those who worked with him knew him to be a man of integrity whose door was always open to them. He'd been the station commander at Precinct 40 for the past four years, and although in that time most of his men had felt the full force of his wrath, he was also fiercely loyal to them – even when they occasionally bent the rules in their pursuit of justice. And there was one detective on his squad who'd crossed that line more times than any of the others: Ray Brennan. But Brennan also had the highest clear-up rate on his squad, and that's what really counted . . .

'Sit down,' d'Arcy said, indicating the chair in front of his desk.

Slowly Brennan did as he was told, without taking his eyes off d'Arcy's face: it was obvious from his grim expression that something was amiss. 'Has there been more flak from upstairs over the way I handled—'

'No, this has nothing to do with work,' d'Arcy cut in quickly. 'I only wish to God it had.' He prodded the closed folder in front of him, then sat back in his chair and rubbed his hands down his face. 'I've done this hundreds of times, but it never gets any easier. Especially when it's one of your own. I received a telephone call from your aunt. Gloria Hardcastle. She was calling from your mother's house.'

'What's happened?' Brennan asked sharply, sitting forward in the chair.

'It's your brother, Donald. His body was recovered yesterday morning from a river in northern Brazil. An autopsy confirmed he'd drowned. That's all your aunt told me over the phone. I'm sure she'll be able to tell you more when you see her. Of course, you'll have immediate compassionate leave. Garcia can work with Monks until you're ready to come back.' D'Arcy sat forward and clasped his spade-like hands on the desk. 'I'm very sorry, Ray.'

'Thank you, sir,' Brennan said, and dropped his eyes to the carpet. It was several moments before he spoke again. Then he said, 'It's the kid I feel sorry for right now.'

'The kid?' d'Arcy replied, with a frown.

'Donald's son, Jason,' Brennan replied. 'His mother was killed eight years ago in a head-on collison with a drunk driver on the Queensboro Bridge.'

'Who'll look after him?' d'Arcy asked.

'My mother, I guess. He always stays with her whenever Donald goes off – went off on one of his Amazon expeditions.'

'He was an anthropologist, wasn't he?' d'Arcy said, recalling that from Brennan's personnel file.

'And a damn good one, by all accounts,' Brennan replied, then raised his head to look at d'Arcy. 'Donald and I were never close. Not even as kids. We fell out completely ten years ago. I doubt whether I saw him more than half a dozen times after that. And then it was only for Christmas or Thanksgiving at our parents' house. We'd become virtual strangers.'

'What caused that?' d'Arcy asked.

Brennan got to his feet and crossed to the door where he paused, his hand resting lightly on the handle. 'A woman, what else?' he replied, then left the room.

Her name was Gillian Price, and she was the most beautiful woman he'd ever seen. At least, that's what he'd thought when he first laid eyes on her at the art gallery on Madison Avenue where he and Monks had been called to investigate a break-in. He'd persuaded her to have a drink with him that night, and the relationship had snowballed from there. With hindsight he'd realized they'd been incompatible from the start. She had a degree in contemporary art, spoke several European languages fluently, and lived in an expensive apartment overlooking Central Park – but the sex had more than made up for the social differences. Three months later they'd got engaged, much to her parents' displeasure. His own mother had been more receptive to the idea, but he knew now that beneath the façade she had been already planning to sabotage things. She'd always known Gillian was the wrong girl for Ray – but perfect for Donald. She waited until he had returned from one of his trips then, with Ray safely out of the way on night shifts, she took to inviting Gillian to dinner then leaving the two of them alone afterwards. Gillian was drawn to Donald's intellect and two months later broke off her engagement to himself. She and Donald were married at the eighteenth-century church of St Luke-in-the-Fields. Ray had refused to attend the wedding.

Brennan could still remember the blazing row he'd had with his mother shortly after the wedding when he'd learnt of her part in it. Since then his relationship with his mother had remained cold and distant, even though all the fight had drained out of her after his father had died of cancer four years ago. He knew in his heart he'd never be able to forgive her.

He swung his car into the driveway of the family home in Southampton, one of six fashionable towns on the island's South Fork, known collectively as the Hamptons, where many affluent New Yorkers had their summer retreats. The two-

19

storey house was on the beach front with a breathtaking view of the Atlantic. He drove up the tree-lined driveway into the courtyard and pulled up beside the grey stone steps. He switched off the engine. The front door opened and a sombre-faced man came out on to the steps as Brennan climbed out of the car. Haskins, the butler. Brennan had never had much contact with him – he'd already left home when the man had replaced Jennings, the previous family retainer. Jennings had lied frequently to get the young Ray out of trouble with his mother and the two had been close. When Jennings died shortly after Brennan left home, he'd been the only member of the family to attend the funeral.

'Good afternoon, sir,' Haskins said. 'Mrs Brennan is expecting you. If you'd care to follow me, I'll show you to the conservatory.'

'I lived here for eighteen years, Haskins,' Brennan said acidly as he stepped into the elegant hallway. 'I think I can find my own way to the conservatory, don't you?'

'As you wish, sir,' Haskins replied, and closed the door behind him.

Brennan had always hated the affluence that surrounded his family. His father had made his money as one of New York's most successful corporate lawyers, and his mother, who had an arts degree from Harvard, had worked for twenty years at the Metropolitan Museum of Art as their expert on post-impressionist art, and then as an evaluator at Christie's on Park Avenue. Brennan didn't know how much his father had been worth at his death – he hadn't attended the reading of the will. It hadn't interested him. He was his own person, with his own life to lead, and he'd always been determined to do that on his own terms.

He reached the conservatory and paused in the open doorway. His mother was sitting in her favourite wicker chair by the window, staring out across the freshly mown lawn, which led down to the diamond-shaped swimming pool. She was a graceful woman in her mid-sixties who'd always taken a pride in her appearance – the clothes, the hair, the make-up, always immaculate. Even now, in the depths of despair, she was still the epitome of refinement and elegance. Brennan knew it wasn't so much vanity that dictated her image, rather what she felt was expected of a woman of her standing. His eyes went to the only other person in the room – his aunt, Gloria Hardcastle, his late father's eldest sister, now in her late seventies and suffering from rheumatoid arthritis. She was the only relative he still visited regularly.

She hobbled towards him, leaning heavily on her stick, and hugged him. 'Oh, Raymond, I'm so sorry about Donald. I couldn't believe the news when I heard it. Only last month he was telling me how much he was looking forward to going back to the Amazon.'

'Do you know exactly what happened?' Brennan asked.

'Well, from what the Brazilian Embassy told your mother this morning, Donald's body was discovered in the Rio Branco in northern Brazil. An autopsy confirmed he'd drowned. He had a gash above his ear, probably from striking something solid in the water. Perhaps a log, or a boulder. That's what the pathologist said.'

'Who identified the body?' Brennan asked.

'From what I can gather, the river trader who found it.'

Brennan looked across at his mother. 'How's she been?'

'You know what Shirley's like,' his aunt said resignedly. 'I don't believe she ever shed a tear in front of the family when your father died. Certainly not at the funeral. It's exactly the same now. It's obvious that she's been crying, but she's hardly said a word to me since I arrived.'

'Thanks for coming, Gloria. I know she appreciates your being here, even if she doesn't show it,' Brennan said.

'Oh, don't be silly. I'll stay with her as long as she wants. I know you and your mother haven't always seen eye to eye over the years, but . . . well, she's always been very good to me, especially after your uncle Malcolm died. I don't think I could have made it without her support.' She looked over at Shirley Brennan. 'I'll leave you two alone. I'll be in the lounge if you need me.'

'Thanks,' Brennan replied, then crossed the room towards his mother's chair.

'Hello, Ray,' she said in an emotionless voice as she watched his reflection in the window.

He perched on the edge of the chair next to hers. He didn't embrace her – it would have been an empty gesture and they both knew it. 'I'm sorry about Donald,' he said softly, almost as if he were an outsider. Yet in many ways that is what he was, especially when it had come to the special closeness Donald had always shared with their mother. As a child Brennan had resented it, but as he'd got older he'd come to accept it, albeit from a distance.

'I can still remember you and Donald playing Cowboys and Indians out on the lawn,' she said, a distant look in her eyes. 'There was never any argument about who'd play who, though. You were always the cowboy and he was the Indian. But, then, he always was one for the underdog, even as a boy.'

'Except that he always insisted on winning,' Brennan reminded her. 'And, being the older brother, he invariably got his own way.'

'Donald was the gentlest child I've ever known,' was the sharp reply. 'He never laid a finger on *you*. *You* were the aggressive one. You even punched him in the face once and broke his nose.'

'At least the bullying stopped after that,' Brennan replied.

'He never bullied you,' she said bitterly. 'It was just another of your efforts to get all the attention.'

He checked himself before he said something he'd regret. When it came to Donald, she only ever saw what she wanted to see. When it came to him, she only ever saw what she didn't want to see in Donald. It had been that way since they were kids. And nothing he could say would ever change it.

'Have you told Jason yet?' he asked.

'How do you tell a nine-year-old boy his father's dead?' she replied, then shook her head slowly. 'No, I haven't told him. He's gone to the movies with a friend. I'll tell him when he comes home. God knows what I'm going to say to him, though.'

'Do you want me to do it?' Brennan offered.

22

'Why the sudden concern for Jason's feelings?' She bristled. 'You never cared about him before.'

'That's not true—'

'You know very well it is,' she interrupted, as the tears welled in her eyes. She regained her composure quickly and continued, 'Giving him a present on his birthday, or at Christmas, hardly constitutes being a caring uncle, does it? You never tried to get to know him, did you? Donald had to raise him alone after Gillian died. It wasn't easy, and you certainly didn't help any. How often did he call you up and ask you to look after Jason while he was away? But you were always too busy doing something else, weren't you?'

He said nothing. She was right. He'd always kept his distance from Jason. His excuse had always been the same, he wasn't comfortable around children. Which was true, up to a point. But Jason reminded him so much of Gillian. And, ten years on, Gillian was still the only woman he'd ever truly loved and he doubted that he'd ever get over her. But he was damned if he'd give his mother the satisfaction of knowing that.

'I'll talk to Jason,' Shirley Brennan said, in a more placating tone. 'Anyway, you'll be too busy packing.'

'Packing?' Brennan said, eyeing her suspiciously. 'And where am I going?'

'Some years ago Donald left specific instructions with me that if he were to . . .' her voice faltered '. . . to die while he was in the Amazon, he wanted to be cremated, according to Yanomamo tradition, in the village he's been using as a base ever since he first went there. I don't know why, but he specifically asked that you carry out his last wishes.' She took a sealed envelope from her handbag and held it out to her son. His name was written across the front in Donald's familiar scrawl. 'Take it. It only says what I've already told you.'

Brennan took the envelope hesitantly from her, slit it open and removed the single sheet of paper. 'Why wasn't I told about this before?' he demanded, after he had read the handwritten note.

'When were you around to discuss it? The only time you and Donald were ever in the same room in the last ten years was when you dropped by for a few hours on Thanksgiving or at Christmas. And even then you hardly spoke to him.'

'Which makes this all the more incomprehensible,' Brennan said.

'It's what he wanted. I don't know why. But if you have a problem—'

'I don't,' he interjected.

'Good, because I've already booked you on a flight to Miami tomorrow morning. You'll have a couple of hours to wait there for a connecting flight to Manaus. You'll be able to collect both tickets at the United desk in the morning. Unfortunately Varig only run two scheduled flights a week between Manaus and Boa Vista – where Donald's body is – so I've arranged for you to get a lift aboard one of the light aircraft which fly cargo to the mining settlements in the area. The pilot's name is Salinas and he's agreed to act as your interpreter while you're there. He'll meet your flight at Manaus.' She took a sheet of paper from her handbag and handed it to him. 'Those are your flight times. You'll also need a visa. I've spoken to the Brazilian Embassy and they'll give you priority treatment when you go there this afternoon. Also, you'll need to be inoculated against tetanus, typhoid, hepatitis, and diphtheria, as well as starting a course of anti-malaria tablets. Dr Robson's agreed to see you at short notice. Your appointment's for three o'clock.'

'I'll be there,' Brennan said, slipping his instructions into his shirt pocket.

She pointed to an envelope on the table. 'There's two thousand dollars in that. Take it, for expenses.'

He picked it up, then looked at his watch. 'I'll have to go. I've still got a lot to do this afternoon. Do you want me to ask Gloria to come back again?'

'No, thank you,' she said softly. 'I'll call her if I need her, but right now I'd like to be alone. Close the door behind you when you leave.'

Brennan said goodbye to his aunt and was about to make

for the front door. Instead he doubled back to the conservatory to check on his mother.

Shirley Brennan's hands were over her face, and her body shuddering. She was sobbing uncontrollably. He didn't go in, knowing she would only let down her guard when she was alone. And she needed to get it out of her system. He looked away, feeling as if he were somehow intruding on her private grief just by being there.

Had she seen him? He hoped not. But an uneasy sense of guilt lingered in his mind as he left the house.

3

Brennan was one of the last passengers to disembark from the Lockheed Tristar once it had landed at Eduardo Gomez airport in Manaus. Shortly before their final descent, the captain had announced that the ground temperature was 31° Celsius and Brennan had expected to be engulfed in the stifling humidity when he stepped out on to the mobile stairs. He was pleasantly surprised to discover that a recent shower had cleared the air and, although hot, it wasn't muggy.

He slipped on a pair of sunglasses and followed the other passengers across the tarmac to the terminal building where he joined the queue at passport control. His passport stamped, Brennan slipped it into his shirt pocket and emerged into the main concourse where he scanned the sparse crowd congregated around the arrival gate.

A man he estimated to be in his mid-thirties, with straggly, shoulder-length black hair, was holding a piece of battered cardboard above his head, the word BRANAN scrawled across it in black letters. Brennan approached him. 'Salinas?' he enquired.

The man grinned. '*Si* . . . I am Salinas,' he said hesitantly. 'You are Bra-nan?'

'Brennan,' he replied.

'You have luggage?' Salinas asked.

'Just this,' Brennan replied, indicating his holdall.

'We can go. The plane is ready.'

'How long will it take us to fly to Boa Vista?' Brennan asked, falling in line beside the other man as they walked towards the departure lounge.

'Two, maybe three hours. Not more. You have friend in Boa Vista?'

'Friend?' Brennan replied with a frown. 'No. I'm going to collect my brother's body. You know that.'

'I not know,' Salinas said quickly.

'Wait up,' Brennan said, stopping abruptly and grabbing Salinas' arm. 'What do you mean you don't know? You've already been paid up front to act as my interpreter once we get to Boa Vista.'

'Int-er-per,' Salinas said with a helpless shrug. 'What is this word?'

'Interpreter. My translator.' Brennan cursed when the blank expression remained etched on Salinas' face. 'I don't speak Portuguese and the people in Boa Vista don't speak English. So you'll be talking for me and telling me what they say back to you.'

'Ah, *si*, inte-perator, I understand now. But I not paid for this. I only paid to fly you to Boa Vista.'

'I don't fucking believe this!' Brennan snapped. 'This was all supposed to have been fixed. OK, how much is it going to cost for you to act as my translator?'

'I not do it,' Salinas told him, and took a step back when he saw the fury in Brennan's eyes. 'I have full cargo on plane. I leave some in Boa Vista. I take rest to other towns. If I do not, I not get paid. I make bad name, then other pilots, they take my business. This is why I must deliver tonight. I come back for you . . . four days.' He held up four fingers to make sure Brennan had understood him. 'That is when I next in Boa Vista. I not know when I there again. I not wait for you. Too much business.'

'In other words, if I'm not ready to leave Boa Vista in four days' time, you'll go without me?' Brennan demanded.

'*Si*, this is right,' Salinas said.

Brennan breathed deeply to calm himself. 'OK, so you can't stay in Boa Vista. Do you know anyone there who'd be able to help me out?'

Salinas pondered for a moment then shook his head. 'Some, they speak little Yanomami. But not English.'

'What about the taxi drivers?' Brennan asked. 'Surely some of them must speak English?'

'Maybe little, but I not know them,' Salinas replied. 'I know only pilots. They not speak English.'

'Can you help me find a taxi driver who speaks some English before you leave?' Brennan asked, desperation edging into his voice.

'I not have time. I must go to other towns.'

'OK, how much?' Brennan asked, removing his wallet from his jeans' pocket. He opened it and peeled off five twenty-dollar bills. 'Is that enough?'

Salinas stared at the money in Brennan's hand. American dollars were always in demand in Brazil, and he could make a handsome profit by exchanging them on the black market. His avarice got the better of him and his eyes went to the wallet in Brennan's other hand. 'You pay two hundred dollar. I speak to taxi drivers at airport.'

'For two hundred dollars you'll *find* someone who can act as my translator,' Brennan told him.

'*Si*, I find you man,' Salinas agreed, and reached for the money.

Brennan pulled back his hand and tucked the money into his wallet. 'I'll pay you on delivery. Not before.'

'You not trust Salinas?' the Brazilian said, clasping his hand theatrically to his chest.

'You're damn right I don't,' Brennan said.

Salinas gave him a wide nicotine-stained grin and patted him on the arm, as if he were now an old friend. 'I like you. You not take shit.' He picked up Brennan's holdall. 'Come, we go now. I show you plane.'

The plane was a dilapidated single-winged Mooney M.22. It had been a five-seater but a previous owner had removed three of the seats to make more room for cargo.

Brennan initially kept a wary distance as he eyed the battered fuselage with a distinct uneasiness, reluctant to venture inside, but he relented when Salinas started up the engine, oblivious to his passenger's trepidation. He climbed

28

in through the passenger door and, after pulling it shut, tested it was secure by pushing forcefully against it with his shoulder. He stowed the holdall under his seat.

Salinas gestured for him to buckle up and, after contacting the control tower, he was given clearance for take-off. He gave Brennan a thumb's-up and taxied down a small ancillary runway.

Brennan's disquiet about the plane's airworthiness was heightened by a succession of ominous metallic creaks and groans as it rose slowly into the cerulean sky. He cast an anxious look at Salinas, but got no response. He shifted uncomfortably in his seat: there was no turning back and his fate lay in Salinas' hands. In an attempt to take his mind off that worrying thought, he turned his attention to the scenery and within minutes had become immersed in the sheer magnificence of his surroundings.

To the west, the muddy, discoloured waters of the Rio Negro cut an unsightly furrow through the verdant carpet of lush forest as far as the eye could see. To the east lay the mighty Rio Amazonas, whose daily flow would amply supply New York with water for ten years. The jungle was punctuated by areas that had been cleared either by a tribe to build a new village or, more deleteriously, by logging companies, or ranch owners in search of pasture for their beef cattle.

He recalled an incident some months earlier when Lou Monks's youngest daughter had turned up at the precinct and, much to her father's chagrin, distributed leaflets on behalf of one of the city's environmental groups. That night he'd taken time out to read a copy. It told him that an acre of South American tropical rainforest was destroyed every second. An area the size of Central Park would disappear in fifteen minutes. He'd never thought much more about it until now, but as he looked down to where huge areas of forest had been laid waste and abandoned, he felt ashamed of his apathy.

As they neared Boa Vista, Brennan could see a rugged stretch of mountains rising up into the clouds that hung on the distant horizon. Many regarded the mountains as the unofficial border between Brazil and neighbouring Venezuela.

This was the heart of Yanomamo country and as Salinas began the final descent towards the airport, Brennan found himself wondering how many times Donald had made the same journey since he'd started coming to the Roraima region of northern Brazil to work among the Yanomamo.

Salinas executed a near-perfect landing and came to a halt close to a pick-up truck parked at the edge of the runway. Brennan climbed out of the plane and, within seconds, sweat was streaming down his face.

He was surprised by the number of armed soldiers on duty inside the terminal building. Salinas explained, as best he could, that Boa Vista was used by cocaine smugglers and suggested that Brennan should let him do the talking when they reached passport control. Brennan didn't argue: he'd explained on the plane about the circumstances of his brother's death. They had no trouble clearing passport control but Brennan's holdall was searched thoroughly at customs.

They were besieged by half a dozen taxi drivers the moment they came out of the building but Salinas waved them away. Then, he singled one out and beckoned him forward. They spoke briefly and the man gestured to a driver sitting in his taxi, the door open, reading a newspaper.

'He only driver here who speak little English,' Salinas told Brennan. 'Come, we talk with him.'

As they walked across to the taxi, the driver spotted them, folded up the newspaper and tossed it on to the dashboard. He got out of the car and reached for Brennan's holdall. Salinas snapped at him angrily then led him a short distance away. A brief discussion followed, then Salinas turned back to Brennan. 'He say there is boat in harbour . . . called . . . eh . . .' He trailed off with a frown in the driver's direction.

'*Shamrock Gal,*' the driver announced. 'Captain . . . speak English. Call . . . Kelly.' He tapped his chest then pointed to Brennan. 'American, I . . . take you . . . Kelly?'

'Yeah, you take me Kelly,' Brennan replied, then took Salinas to one side and pushed the two hundred dollars into his hand. 'You said you'd be back here again in four days. What time?'

'Morning,' Salinas said, then looked at his watch. 'We meet here, at airport. Ten o'clock.'

'I'll be here,' Brennan told him.

'I go now. Much work.' Salinas hurried back towards the terminal then looked round fleetingly, his hand raised. *'Tchau.'*

Brennan waved absently then turned to the driver. 'How much will it cost to go to harbour?'

'You . . . have dollar, American?'

'I can pay you either in dollars, or in your own currency,' Brennan replied.

'No. Our . . . money . . . bad. *Muito problema.* You pay dollar.'

'How much?' Brennan asked.

'Five dollar. I take you . . . boat.'

'Deal,' Brennan said, opened the back door, tossed in the holdall and climbed in after it.

'Where you from, American?'

'New York.'

'Yankees,' the man replied with a grin. He started up the engine and drove the two miles into Boa Vista. Brennan was struck by the size of the town, with its tree-lined boulevards and endless string of roads that branched off from each other in every possible direction. But there was also an unmistakable air of desolation about the place. Many of the hotels and general stores, which had sprung up with the gold rush back in the early eighties, were now boarded up, and the signs of poverty were everywhere, among the locals and the Indians, many of whom had been forced to venture into this concrete wasteland after losing their homes in the name of progress. Under-age prostitutes huddled together in small groups in the streets close to the harbour and every time a car slowed down one of the girls would hurry over, hopeful of turning a trick to feed her empty belly.

The taxi continued on past the main harbour gates for another few hundred yards before turning off on to a dirt road, which brought them into the section of the harbour

31

where the river traders moored their vessels. The driver pulled up beside the *Shamrock Gal*.

Brennan peered at the dilapidated tramp steamer. The white hull was desperately in need of a fresh coat of paint and the boat's name, in green italics on the bow, had faded from years in the sun. The thin funnel, unused since the vessel was converted to diesel, was badly rusted and had corroded in several places. An Indian, dressed only in a pair of shorts, was sitting on the deck, his legs dangling over the side of the hull, idling whittling a lump of wood with a penknife. He looked up when Brennan got out of the taxi, then yawned and returned to his whittling.

Brennan paid the driver, who drove off. He stared after the vehicle until it had disappeared from sight. When he turned back to the boat he saw two men standing in the shadow of a pile of crates further down the quay. They weren't locals and, with their cropped hair and muscular physique, their appearance was military. He estimated the taller of the two to be in his early forties, the other in his mid- to late-thirties. Both wore black mirror sunglasses and the shorter one was wearing a flak jacket over his black vest. They walked slowly towards him.

'You from the States?' the taller man asked. The accent was American, but Brennan couldn't place the state of origin.

'Yeah,' he replied.

'What brings you down here?' his companion asked, in a strong southern drawl – Brennan guessed Alabama.

'I'm looking for a guy called Kelly. Is that either of you?'

'I'm Kelly,' a female voice called down from the deck of the *Shamrock Gal*. There was a faint, but distinctive, Irish brogue in the voice. 'Kelly McBride. What do you want?'

Brennan looked up at her in surprise. He estimated her to be in her early thirties. She had a strikingly attractive face, devoid of make-up, and her shoulder-length blonde hair was tied in a ponytail, which she had slotted through the hole at the back of her black peaked cap. The unflattering dungarees and white V-neck T-shirt did nothing to enhance her slender figure.

'So, do I pass inspection?' she asked sarcastically, her eyebrows raised questioningly at him.

He hadn't realized he'd been staring until her voice shattered his thoughts. He gave an embarrassed laugh. 'Sorry, I didn't mean to . . . well, it's just that . . .' He trailed off.

'It's just that you didn't think I'd be a woman?' She finished the sentence for him. 'You still haven't said what you want.'

'My name's Ray Brennan. I'm here to collect my brother's body.'

'I was the one who found him, about a hundred miles upriver,' Kelly said, her voice softening. 'I'm sorry.'

'Thanks. Did you also make the ID?' Brennan asked. She nodded. 'You must have known Donald well.'

'Well enough,' she replied. 'I do a lot of my trade with Yanomamo villages along the river. I used to bump into him whenever he was out here.'

'We all knew Donald around here,' the taller of the two men added, then extended a hand towards Brennan. 'I'm Tom Caldwell. My condolences.'

'Thanks,' Brennan said, gripping Caldwell's hand.

Caldwell indicated his colleague. 'This is Bobby Dixon.'

'So what brings you guys out here to this backwater?' Brennan asked.

'We're security consultants for Eduardo Silva,' Caldwell replied. 'You may have heard of him.'

Brennan shook his head. 'Can't say I have.'

'He's one of the largest cattle breeders in the country,' Caldwell said. 'He's a bit of an eccentric, though. Lives a reclusive life, somewhere near São Paulo I believe. I've only met him a couple of times since we've been here. We're based at the largest of his ranches. It's about three hundred miles west of here.'

'What about you?' Dixon said.

'I'm a cop, with the NYPD.'

'I remember Donald saying that,' Kelly said. 'Not that he talked about you very often.'

'Yeah, well, that was Donald for you,' Brennan replied tersely. 'Look, as I said just now, I'm here to collect his body.

33

Problem is, I don't speak the lingo. The taxi driver brought me here so I could find someone to interpret for me. It shouldn't take long to complete the formalities.'

Caldwell gave him an apologetic shrug. 'Sorry, can't help you there. Bobby and I are due to fly back to the ranch in the next hour. We've got a meeting scheduled there for eight o'clock. But Kelly speaks Portuguese.'

She glowered furiously at Caldwell but forced a smile when Brennan looked up at her. 'I'm waiting for a delivery from one of my suppliers. He should have been here twenty minutes ago.'

'I'm more than prepared to pay you for your time, Ms McBride,' Brennan told her. 'In American dollars, if you'd prefer. They seem to be a pretty popular currency around here.'

'That's because the Brazilian economy's up to shit.' Dixon snorted.

'We've got to get going,' Caldwell said. 'We can give you a lift to the mortuary if you like. It's on our way to the airport. But you'll have to come with us now.'

'That depends on Ms McBride,' Brennan replied.

'OK,' she said after a moment. Her eyes went to Caldwell. 'I'll need to have a word with my crew before we leave, in case my supplier turns up while I'm away. Tell them what to do.'

Caldwell gave her an acknowledging wave before she disappeared. 'She's quite a character, that one,' he said. 'You wouldn't think it to look at her, but she can drink most men under the table. And these river traders can drink. Their favourite hit's *cachaca*, a rotgut made from rum and sugar cane. *I* can't drink much of it but it doesn't seem to affect her.'

'You'll often find her in one of the harbour bars when she's in town,' Dixon said, as he pushed up his sunglasses and rubbed his eyes with his thumb and forefinger. 'She'll take on any challenger. Does it purely for the money. I've never known her to lose.'

Brennan scanned the length of the *Shamrock Gal*. 'What

brought her out here in the first place?' he asked. 'There must be a stóry behind it somewhere. How long's she been here?'

'Ten years,' Kelly said, from the top of the boarding ramp. 'Eight of those as the skipper of the *Shamrock Gal*. Any more questions?'

'I'm sorry,' Brennan said. 'I guess it's just instinct – comes with the job.'

'You aren't in New York now, Mr Brennan,' she said coldly, when she was on the quay. 'I've no intention of prying into your life. All I ask is the same courtesy in return.'

Caldwell smiled fleetingly at Brennan's discomfort, then went after Dixon who was already walking towards a black Mercedes parked a short distance away in front of a derelict warehouse.

Brennan put a hand lightly on Kelly's arm as she was about to go after Caldwell, then withdrew it when she looked at him pointedly. 'We haven't got off to a very good start, have we?' he said ruefully. 'I didn't mean to offend you, and if I have, then I apologize.'

'Apology accepted.'

'How much do I owe you?' Brennan asked as he took out his wallet.

'Put it away,' she replied, and waited until he'd slipped it back into his pocket before continuing. 'I don't deny I'm usually first in line when it comes to making a fast buck, but only where business is concerned. I wouldn't insult Donald's memory by taking money from you at a time like this.'

'Thanks,' Brennan said, then followed her into the back of the Mercedes.

Dixon drove them into town. The mortuary was a two-storey building with a drab grey façade and the words NECROTERIO DO BOA VISTA etched into the stone blocks directly above the arched entrance. Faded blinds were drawn discreetly across the windows that faced out over the street.

Caldwell shook hands with Brennan, then nodded to Dixon who engaged the gears and drove away. Moments later the car disappeared from view around a corner.

'They all look the same, don't they?' Brennan said, staring at the building.

'I guess you must have seen your fair share of these places.'

'Too many,' Brennan replied, then climbed the steps and pushed open the front door. He found himself in a black-and-white tiled foyer. An elderly woman sat alone in the reception area, staring blankly at the floor. It was a look Brennan had seen all too often over the years: the numbness that invariably comes before the onset of grief. He followed Kelly to the desk where a nurse smiled blandly at them. Kelly explained why they were there and the woman gestured to the plastic chairs against the opposite wall then reached for the telephone. A couple of minutes later a middle-aged man appeared, wearing an unbuttoned white coat over a T-shirt and a pair of baggy trousers.

Kelly spoke briefly to him. 'He's the pathologist on duty,' she told Brennan. 'He says the paperwork's been done. All you have to do is sign a release form for Donald's body.'

'Tell him I'd like to see the body first. And ask him if he carried out the autopsy.'

After consulting the pathologist, she said, 'No, he didn't.'

'Then I want to see a copy of the report as well,' Brennan told her.

They followed the man down an ill-lit corridor and through a set of swing doors, which led into a bland, impersonal room with whitewashed walls. Brennan became instantly aware of the overpowering smell of formaldehyde that hung in the damp air. The pathologist pulled open one of the metal drawers that lined one side of the room, to reveal the outline of a body, covered by a white sheet. He lifted back the sheet then left the room to get the autopsy report.

Kelly noticed the uncertainty in Brennan's eyes as he took a hesitant step towards the drawer then stopped. 'Are you all right?' she asked.

'Yeah, sure,' he said gruffly. As a cop, he'd learnt how to deal with anguished relatives. The secret was to keep a distance, and never allow himself to become involved in their grief. Now he knew how difficult it was to take those few steps

36

to where the body lay. But it wasn't as if he and Donald had been close. Hell, he'd been closer to colleagues killed in the line of duty and never had any trouble keeping his emotions in check. So why this sudden conflict? Was it simply because Donald was his brother? Or was it guilt – that Donald had died in the knowledge that his younger brother had refused to accept the olive branch he'd held out so many times since Gillian had died? Suddenly Brennan felt both angry and uncomfortable. Angry because he wasn't in control of his own emotions. Uncomfortable because he knew he'd struck a raw nerve in himself. He pushed these thoughts from his mind – this was neither the time nor the place for self-recrimination.

The pathologist was standing at the door, watching him. Kelly was holding a copy of the report. Brennan asked for a pair of surgical gloves then, taking a deep breath, crossed to the open drawer. The face showed appreciable signs of bruising, which would have occurred within a few hours of death when the body struck any submerged objects as it was carried down-river. He felt no emotion as he looked at his brother's discoloured face but, then, that didn't surprise him. He'd already reverted back to the role of an impartial New York cop. This wasn't his brother; it was just another body in a mortuary. It was the only way he'd get through it.

He tilted the head to one side where the scalp had been shaved around a laceration above the left ear. 'What does it say about the head wound?' he asked.

'A depressed fracture of the skull, causing a . . .' Kelly trailed off. 'Sorry, but I learnt my Portuguese on the river. It doesn't stretch to medical terminology.'

'I'd guess an extradural haemorrhage,' Brennan said, taking a closer look. 'It's usually caused by a violent blow.'

'It mentions a violent blow to the skull,' she told him. 'It also says the impact would have initiated internal bleeding, which normally causes temporary unconsciousness. And that if he'd hit his head when he was already in the water, that would have caused him to drown.'

'It's one theory,' Brennan said, as he pulled away more of

37

the sheet. 'Another being that he was hit before he fell in the water.'

'You mean he was murdered?' she said in horror.

He didn't reply as he examined the arms. They were bruised, too, but what caught his attention were the numerous small cuts on the hands and forearms. He asked Kelly what the pathologist had made of them.

'That they were probably caused by his hands and arms brushing against undergrowth, maybe as a result of him falling down an embankment into the water,' she replied.

'Possibly,' Brennan said. 'What does the report say about the lungs?'

'They were swollen and water-logged with large areas of purple blotches under the . . . sorry, I don't know this word.'

'It'll be the pleurae,' he said. 'It's the membrane that covers the lungs. Purple mottling of the pleurae is consistent with drowning.'

'It says that water was also present in the oesophagus and the stomach,' she added.

'Does it say whether a diatom test was carried out?'

'I don't even know what that is in English, never mind in Portuguese,' she told him.

'Diatoms are algae found in water,' Brennan replied. 'They would be circulated by the blood through the body of a drowning person as long as their heart was still beating. So if diatoms were found in sensitive areas like the liver and the brain, it's pretty conclusive evidence that the person drowned. But if they were already dead when they were put in the water, the diatoms would probably reach the lungs by passive percolation, but nowhere else, because the blood would have already ceased to circulate.'

'For a cop you know a lot about pathology,' she said.

'I've attended enough post-mortems,' Brennan replied.

'I'll ask him,' she said. The pathologist took the report from her and found the relevant section. She read it quickly. 'They did a test. Tissue samples taken from the kidneys, liver, brain were found to contain diatoms.'

38

'Then I agree with his findings. Donald drowned,' Brennan said, as he replaced the sheet over his brother's face.

She spoke to the pathologist, who then left the room. 'He'll have the release forms brought to reception.'

'Let's go,' Brennan said, peeling off the gloves and tossing them into the bin by the door.

'You think there's more to this than meets the eye, don't you?' she asked.

'Probably not,' he replied. 'It's just the cop in me taking over. Even if it was foul play, there's no real evidence to go on. The cuts on the hands and forearms *could* have been caused by him grabbing on to branches as he fell down an embankment, as it says in the autopsy report.'

'What about the head wound?'

'He could have hit his head on a log when he fell into the water. It makes sense, especially as it was the subsequent haemorrhaging that led to his drowning.' Brennan pushed open the swing door and followed her into the corridor. 'And even if he was struck on the head before he hit the water, do you really think the Brazilian police are going to send a team of investigators into the jungle to chase after statements from the Yanomamo on that kind of flimsy evidence? If this were New York, it would have been put down to accidental death.'

'So what happens now?' she asked. 'Are you going to have Donald's body flown back to America?'

'No,' he replied. 'How would you like to make some extra money? Say, five hundred US dollars. In cash.'

'I'm listening,' she said warily, but before he could elaborate the pathologist appeared with a folder. She watched Brennan sign next to the other man's pencil crosses. Then the pathologist handed him the documents and told Kelly they could make arrangements with the nurse to have the body removed from the mortuary. 'So what exactly *are* you going to do?' she asked after the pathologist had left. 'It must have something to do with the five hundred dollars you just offered me.'

He gestured to the two nearest chairs. They sat down and he told her about Donald's last wish to be cremated, according to Yanomamo tradition, at the village where he'd stayed when he came to the Amazon. 'I'm prepared to pay you five hundred dollars to take the body there. I've got the name of the village—'

'I know its name,' she cut in sharply. 'I do a lot of trade there.'

'Do I take it that there could be a problem getting the body there?' he asked.

'No,' she answered. 'It would take the *Shamrock Gal* between two and a half and three hours to reach the village. The problems would only start once we got there.'

'What kind of problems?'

'You'd have to get the *tuxuana*'s permission to hold the ceremony at his village,' she replied. 'He's the village chief.'

'You don't sound very confident that he'd give it.'

'Donald may have lived among the Yanomamo, but he was never regarded as one of them. And in the ten years I've been here, I've never known the Yanomamo to hold a traditional funeral for a *naba*. The *tuxuana* may agree to make an exception in Donald's case. But I wouldn't count on it.'

'Which would mean bringing Donald's body back here again, then arranging for it to be returned to the States,' Brennan said wearily.

Kelly got to her feet and began to pace the floor as she contemplated his offer. Five hundred dollars. The money would cover her outstanding debts. And having had a visit earlier in the week from a couple of unsavoury *pistoleiros* after she'd failed to meet a fortnightly repayment she knew that next time they wouldn't just let her off with a verbal warning. Five hundred dollars was a good price, but . . .

'Seven-fifty, and you pay for the fuel as well,' she announced. 'The full amount up front. But if the *tuxuana* refuses to allow the funeral to take place at his village, it'll cost you another two-fifty to have Donald's body brought back to Boa Vista.'

'And would that two-fifty include the price of the fuel for the return journey?' Brennan asked sardonically.

'Naturally. I wouldn't want to appear unreasonable,' she

40

replied, tongue-in-cheek. 'Those are my terms, Mr Brennan. Take them, or leave them.'

'Do I have much choice?' He paused. 'Can you arrange to have Donald's body taken to your boat?'

'I'm sure I can figure something out,' she said, adding, 'It'll cost you, of course.'

'Why doesn't that surprise me?' he muttered.

'The money's not for me,' she said. 'We'll have to bribe one of the mortuary drivers to take the body to the *Gal*.'

'And how much are we talking about this time?'

She shrugged. 'Fifty dollars should cover it.'

He took out the money and handed it to her. 'Do you want the seven-fifty now?'

'You can pay me on the boat,' she replied, then spoke to the nurse before turning back to Brennan. 'There's a couple of drivers here tonight. The nurse says they're in a hut at the back of the building. We can use a side entrance.' She crossed to the front door then stopped. 'Well, are you coming?'

'Whatever you say.' Brennan went after her.

Kelly saw there had been trouble when the ambulance's headlights picked out the broken crates scattered across the quay in front of the *Shamrock Gal*. She was up front with the driver, while Brennan was sitting beside his brother's body.

She told the driver to open the back door for Brennan then stepped out on to the quay. She could feel fruit from the crates squelching under her feet as she hurried across to the boarding ramp. A movement caught the corner of her eye and she wheeled round to see two figures creeping out of a corroded metal container, which had been left on the quay-side some months earlier. Her heart missed a beat but then she exhaled in relief when she saw, in the reflection of the deck light on the boat, that it was her crew.

The two Yanomamo glanced at the ambulance. 'Are you sick, Rasha?' one asked anxiously.

'No, I'll explain later,' she replied, then gestured to the wreckage around her. 'What happened?'

'The supplier arrived after you'd already left with the *naba*,

41

but when he tried to unload the crates the *pistoleiro* broke them all,' the other man told her. 'We tried to stop him but he has a gun. The supplier was frightened and drove away. The *pistoleiro* just laughed at him then went on the boat. He said he was going to wait for you. We came ashore to warn you.'

'And who is this *pistoleiro*?' she demanded.

'One of the men who was here before.'

'What does he want? The next payment's not due for another week.' Kelly stared around her. 'I've already paid for this. Now look at it.'

The Indians exchanged bewildered looks – they hadn't understood a word she'd said in her native tongue.

'Trouble?' Brennan asked behind her.

'Nothing I can't handle,' she said defiantly.

'What is it?' he pressed.

She explained briefly, then said to the nearest Indian, 'You say he's on the boat?'

'Yes, Rasha. He had a bottle of *cachaca* with him.'

Brennan grabbed her arm as she was about to mount the boarding ramp. 'What the hell do you think you're doing? This goon's obviously mad at you, and you're just going to march on board and confront him on your own? Why don't I go first?'

'I can look after myself,' Kelly said, jerked her arm free and strode up the ramp and on to the deck. She went into the wheelhouse and took down the modified 12-gauge shotgun she kept beside the wheel, crossed to the open hatchway and silently slipped down the wooden stairs. She paused at the bottom to contemplate her next move. To her right was the storage area, to her left her own quarters. She went left to the cabin, which was partitioned off by a single sheet hanging loosely across the doorway. She pulled it aside. He wasn't there. Wood creaked behind her – a footstep on a loose board – but before she could turn she was grabbed roughly from behind, her arms were pinned tightly to her sides, and the shotgun clattered to the floor. She could smell the cheap liquor on his breath as she struggled furiously but his grip was too powerful. He forced her past the sheet, down on to the single bed, and pushed her face into the pillow. He eased the pressure on her arms and she twisted her head to the side, gasping for air. She cried out as he pressed his knee agonizingly into the small of her back. His fingers dug painfully into her skin, but much as she struggled, she couldn't break free. Then she felt one of his hands fumble under her body for her breasts. Desperately, she kicked backwards but he laughed contemptuously, grabbed hold of a breast through her dungarees and began to squeeze it.

Suddenly she felt him pulled off her, then heard a dull thump, followed by a howl of pain. She turned over to see Brennan standing above the man, who was now on his knees, blood streaming through his fingers from his shattered nose. Brennan retrieved the shotgun from the floor and slammed down the butt on the back of the man's head. He crumpled into an unconscious heap at Brennan's feet. He frisked the man, relieved him of the automatic tucked into a holster at the back of his trousers, and asked, 'You OK?'

'Just about, I think,' she said weakly.

Brennan turned the shotgun around in his hands. 'Where did you get this?' he asked.

'I traded it for some supplies with the Yanomamo a few years back. I don't know where they got it from, though. Probably a *garimpeiro*.'

'This is a Wilson. It's a specialist weapon, used by the US Marshals' Witness Protection units.'

'I'll take your word for it,' she said. 'It doesn't work. It never has. I've kept it as a deterrent. Not that I've had much call for it, but it feels good to have it on board.'

'I'd say this was stolen from a federal marshal back in the States. That means you've been handling stolen property – which, in the eyes of the law, is a felony,' he said, with a half-smile and handed it back to her.

'You're the cop, arrest me,' she retorted, then looked past him at the two Yanomamo, who appeared at the foot of the stairs. 'I'm all right,' she assured them.

Their eyes went first to the unconscious figure on the floor, then to Brennan. Then they broke into wide grins of approval. 'Do you want us to throw him into the water?' one asked Kelly.

'Leave him on the quay,' she told them. 'Then get the body from the back of the ambulance and bring it on board.'

'Body?' one said.

'Just do it, I'll explain everything once we're under way.'

'We're leaving tonight?' the Yanomamo asked, surprised. 'You said we wouldn't go until tomorrow morning.'

'I know what I said. But there's been a change of plan. I'll explain it all later. Now get rid of this *lixo*,' she said disdainfully, referring to the *pistoleiro* as garbage.

Brennan stepped aside as the two Indians struggled to half carry, half drag the unconscious man up the stairs and on to the deck. 'You certainly have some interesting friends,' he said.

'He caught me by surprise, that's all,' she replied defensively. 'He'd have made a mistake though. Then I'd have made my move. I can look after myself. I've done it successfully for the past ten years. Just remember that.'

'Yeah, I sure will next time some drunken bastard tries to rape you,' Brennan said, then walked towards the stairs.

'Ray, wait!' she called. He stopped at the foot of the stairs, caught off-guard by her use of his first name. She fiddled uncomfortably with her gold bracelet. 'I found out quickly when I first became a river trader that it's the survival of the fittest out here. Nobody's going to help you if you get into trouble. That's why you have to learn to look after yourself.' She pulled off her cap and tossed it on to the bed. 'I guess what I'm trying to say is that I'm not used to having to rely on someone else to get me out of a tight spot. But that doesn't mean I didn't appreciate what you did for me tonight. Thanks.' She slipped past him and disappeared up on deck.

After she'd gone Brennan remained at the foot of the stairs. He'd caught a brief glimpse of vulnerability in her, and he could see something of himself there too. Now he wasn't as defensive as she was – but he had been once, in those first few years after Gillian had left him. His barriers were still up and

44

only now he knew when to let them down, who to let in, who to keep out. Yet Kelly didn't have that choice. Not if she was to survive in this male environment. It wouldn't have been easy for her over the years, which was why she'd chosen to trust no one. That way there could be no misunderstandings.

So why had she allowed him beyond *her* barriers? That intrigued him. Or was it deeper than that? The thought surprised him. He'd only known her a few hours, but there was no denying she was attractive. He found himself thinking of the women he'd slept with since Gillian. Attractive women he'd known only for a few hours. More often than not he'd never even discovered their surnames. It was better that way. They'd all been perfect one-night stands with no strings attached. Carnal satisfaction. Nothing more. Yet with Kelly it was different.

He chided himself for even having these thoughts when he should be mourning his brother. Or was this his way of blocking out the emotions that had threatened to surface since he'd first seen Donald in the morgue?

He felt isolated and confused, all these jumbled thoughts spinning out of control. He didn't want them to make sense. He just wanted them to go away. But he knew they wouldn't. They couldn't. Suddenly his once impenetrable barriers seemed brittle, ready to crumble at the slightest touch. He felt very vulnerable indeed . . .

4

Brennan kept to himself for most of the journey but his solitude hadn't been entirely of his own choosing. Kelly had remained at the wheel, even though both Yanomamo could have relieved her.

Seated on the wooden bench that ran the length of the stern railing, he'd focused his attention on the passing scenery as the tramp made its way slowly through the coppery waters of the Rio Branco. He'd half expected to see semi-naked warriors suddenly burst out from the undergrowth and rush to the water's edge, their faces hidden under elaborately painted war masks, and hurl spears at the passing boat – something like one of those B-movies of the forties and fifties he saw as a kid. But he spotted only a couple of naked children frolicking at the water's edge while their mother washed some clothes in the river. They'd shouted to Kelly, in the wheelhouse, and she'd waved back at them. He'd waved too, but they'd just stared back at him expressionlessly.

Once he saw several caiman stretched out languidly on a deserted stretch of the riverbank, basking in the last hours of daylight. They didn't stir as the *Shamrock Gal* went past. The occasional scarlet macaw, or sulphur-breasted toucan, would appear in the sky above the boat, then disappear over the towering canopy of green on either side of the river. But the multifarious sounds emanating from within the jungle made up for not seeing more wildlife: the dissonant yawl of a howler monkey, the raucous shrieking of an orange-winged parrot, the throaty roar of a prowling jaguar.

It was only when he first smelt the food cooking on the bow

that he realized how hungry he was – his last meal had been a light lunch at thirty thousand feet over the Atlantic. He wasn't sure what to expect when one of the Yanomamo brought him a plate – certainly something spicy and exotic, but not chicken, rice and beans. Known as *feijoada*, it was easy to prepare and regarded by many as the national dish of Brazil, yet it seemed out of place in such surroundings. But this didn't diminish his appetite and he ate ravenously, wiping up the last of the sauce with a thin slice of corn bread. This was followed by a mug of *cafezinho* – a strong but sweet black coffee. Although he took coffee with a dash of milk and no sugar, he drank it anyway and, to his surprise, found it quite palatable.

He was surprised at the speed of the tropical nightfall. One minute the dying embers of the day illuminated the distant saffron horizon, and the next a murky darkness descended. With the night came a new symphony of sounds – and the onset of the mosquitoes. After he'd squashed a couple on his arm he went below deck for his insect repellent spray.

When he returned topside he crossed to the open wheelhouse. Kelly didn't take her attention off the dark river ahead. 'Mosquitoes, eh?' she said, detecting the chemical on him.

'Yeah,' he said. 'They don't seem to affect you, though.'

'They sucked me dry a long time ago,' she said. 'You become immune to them after a while. Not that I take any chances, though. I still take antimalarials, particularly during the warm season. That's when the mosquitoes are worst.'

The silence that followed was broken by one of the Yanomamo calling to his colleague. 'We're not far from the *shabono* now,' she told Brennan. 'Another few minutes and you should be able to see it.'

'The *shabono*?' Brennan queried.

'The village. Although it's more like a large, communal house where each family has their own living quarters. You'll see what I mean when we get there.'

The two Indians hurried to the bow where they began shouting and waving their arms. Moments later silhouettes appeared in a clearing on the bank a few hundred yards up-river. Some were carrying flambeaus, and the flames flickered uneven shadows across their dark faces.

'I think you can safely assume the whole *shabono* now knows we're here,' Kelly said.

'Does your crew come from this village?' Brennan asked.

'No. Theirs is further on. There's friction between the two villages at the moment. A couple of weeks ago a warring party from the other *shabono* came here and abducted two girls. Since then things have been tense, although there hasn't been any violence. At least not yet. But I've heard there's a lot of pressure on the *tuxuana* to lead a reciprocal raid to get the girls back.'

'Will he?' Brennan asked.

'More than likely, when he feels the time's right,' she replied. 'The tribe's honour's at stake. And honour's important to the Yanomamo.'

'Will *they* be safe here, then?' Brennan asked, as one of the Indians ran to the stern ready to drop anchor.

'Those two clowns are accepted wherever they go,' she said, with a half-smile, 'and the *Gal* is their home now.'

Kelly manoeuvred the boat close to the bank and Brennan heard a muffled splash as the anchor hit the water. One of the crew lowered the boarding ramp and were joined immediately on deck by some of the men who had been waiting on the bank. They all began to talk at once, chattering and gesticulating as they caught up on the latest gossip.

Brennan watched as Kelly went down the ramp with ease. He didn't feel so confident – it had no protective rails and he could feel it rocking gently beneath his feet. The only way to do it was to bow his head and run. It all went well until he slipped on a wet patch, and had to stamp his foot in the water to stop himself landing face first in the mud at the river's edge. There was a chorus of laughter from the cluster of Yanomamo standing behind Kelly and he cursed under his breath as he lifted his sodden foot out of the water then jumped nimbly on to the bank.

'That's one way of trying to break the ice,' she said with a grin.

48

'And my leg,' Brennan muttered. He saw that the men were studying him closely, though careful to keep their distance. Two had red pigment painted on their faces and chests and carried hand-made spears. The other three held the torches. They were all naked, apart from a length of thin cotton string tied around their waists and secured to their foreskins.

'Stop staring,' Kelly hissed.

'Was I?' Brennan said, startled. 'Is it as uncomfortable as it looks?' ·

'I believe so,' she replied.

'Does it ever . . . come loose?' he asked.

'Sometimes, but not often. It's a major source of embarrassment when it does happen, though. That's why most Yanomamo men now wear loincloths, or shorts if they can get them through the missions. This is one of the few remaining *shabonos* which keeps to the traditional roots of Yanomamo culture. Most of the others have become westernized over the years. It's the main reason Donald chose to live here. It gave him an insight into a way of life you seldom encounter any more.'

The four Yanomamo disembarked from the *Shamrock Gal*. One of the crew was carrying Brennan's holdall, which he placed on the ground in front of him. Instantly the others, who until that moment had kept a respectful distance, set upon it like a bunch of kids opening presents on Christmas morning. Within seconds one had removed Brennan's spare jeans, another his Walkman, a third a couple of T-shirts. The autopsy report was discarded in the mayhem and Brennan frantically scooped up the sheets of paper as they spilled across the muddy ground. He saw Kelly remonstrating with them but she was pushed aside by a man who removed Brennan's toiletry bag and tipped out the contents. Brennan waded into the crowd to retrieve his holdall, but a man jabbed at him with the tip of his spear. Brennan clamped a hand around the decorated shaft, twisted it violently, forcing the man off-balance, then wrenched it from him and flung it into the water.

49

Kelly grabbed his arm and pulled him away from the Indians, who had suddenly formed a threatening semi-circle around him. She spoke to them quietly, and they finally backed away. 'What are you trying to do? Get yourself killed?' she asked. 'This is their *shabono*. You have to abide by their customs.'

'And it's one of their customs to help themselves to the contents of my bag?'

'It's their custom to exchange goods with any visitor,' Kelly told him. 'They were a little over-zealous but, then, that's their nature.'

'You could have warned me this would happen,' Brennan said. 'It's just as well I didn't put the gun in there I took off that goon back in Boa Vista. Anyway, I thought you said they were traditionalists. What the hell do they want with a Walkman – or a pair of jeans for that matter?'

'They'll use them to trade with other *shabonos*,' Kelly replied.

By now several more Yanomamo had appeared and were hovering in the background. There were children among them, clinging to their mother's arms. Then he realized that a couple of the men who'd raided his holdall had gone, taking their booty with them. He was about to mention this to Kelly when he saw them returning with a third man. They joined the other three and the man berated them furiously. At one moment he pointed to Brennan, although without looking at him. They shrank backwards as the tirade continued, their heads hung in shame. When the man had finished they placed Brennan's possessions carefully on the ground beside the holdall before skulking back towards the *shabono*.

'That's the *tuxuana*,' Kelly told Brennan. 'He's furious with them for having shamed him in your eyes. They took from you, but didn't offer you anything in return. He's already punished them – they won't be allowed to trade with you once you've been invited into the *shabono*.'

Brennan had been expecting the *tuxuana* to appear resplendent in a crown of multicoloured feathers with intricate abstract designs daubed over his body like some grand deity

50

of the jungle but he looked like any of the others around him. He felt disappointed, even cheated.

Kelly explained to the *tuxuana* why she'd brought Brennan to the *shabono* at such a late hour. He listened silently, occasionally glancing across at him. When he spoke, he addressed Brennan, who although he had no idea of what was being said, focused on him as he spoke, despite the temptation to turn to Kelly for a translation.

She didn't say anything until the Yanomamo had finished speaking. 'He was sorry to hear about what happened to Donald. He'd come to regard him as one of his own brothers – and there's no higher compliment he could have paid him. He said Donald was a good hunter, particularly when hunting monkeys with a bow and arrow. He was better than many of the men in the *shabono*. He was also good with the children, and they'll miss him. He said it's not customary for the Yanomamo to cremate a *naba* in their own *shabono*, but he will make an exception in Donald's case. I'm surprised he's agreed to it, but it shows how highly Donald was thought of here. He has laid down one condition, though. You have to observe all their customs during the ceremony.'

'Which are?' Brennan asked suspiciously.

'As Donald's closest relative, you'll have to light the pyre. Would you have a problem with that?'

'No,' Brennan replied. 'Anything else I should know?'

'It's customary for the bones to be removed from the pyre after the ashes have cooled and crushed into a powder by a member of the family. In this case, you. They use a special pole to grind down the bones.'

'What happens to the powder?' Brennan asked.

'It'll be used as part of a more elaborate ceremony, attended by members of other *shabonos*. I suppose you could say it's their version of a wake. But that needn't concern you. That ceremony will be held long after you've gone. It'll take several weeks just to contact the other *shabonos* to arrange it.'

'And that's all there is to it?'

'Basically, yes,' she replied. 'Sure, there's little idiosyncrasies you'll need to observe, but you'll pick those up as the ceremony unfolds. One member of the *shabono* will be assigned to mourn the deceased for a month after the ceremony. That always involves a lot of crying and wailing. Not a calendar month as we know it, though. They determine time by the phases of the moon.'

'Don't they have a numerical system?' Brennan asked.

'Oh, yes,' she replied, 'but it consists of three numbers – one, two and more than two. That's it. Believe me, it can be a nightmare when it comes to trading.'

'I can believe it,' Brennan agreed.

'It looks like the *tuxuana* wants another word with me. You'd better collect up your things,' she said.

Brennan stuffed them back into the holdall and waited for Kelly to come back. When she did, she said, 'We've been invited into the *shabono*. You'll be expected to trade some of your belongings with the villagers. But the *tuxuana* wants to show you something first.'

Brennan was handed a flambeau and followed the *tuxuana* up the riverbank, through a passage, which had been hacked out of the thick undergrowth, and suddenly emerged into a clearing, in the centre of which was the *shabono*. From the outside it appeared to be a large, oval-shaped house but once inside he realized it was a chain of smaller dwellings, each occupied by a single family.

Each house was marked by four main posts, each about eight feet apart, sunk into the ground. Two were at the back and the other two, about twice the height, at the front. Hammocks were slung between them. Each family was responsible for their own section of the roof, an intricate construction of more poles and saplings bound with thick, sinewy vines into an arc about twenty-five feet high. Long-stemmed densely packed leaves had been used to thatch it. The houses, separated from each other by a few feet of unoccupied space, ran the circumference of the *shabono* leaving an open arena in the centre, which was used for ceremonies and feasts.

The *tuxuana* led Brennan and Kelly to a section of the *shabono* close to the main entrance. It contained a single hammock strung diagonally between two poles and several dog-eared journals, which were stacked up in a corner beside a couple of battered suitcases. Brennan recognized the suitcases – they had belonged to his brother. These must have been Donald's quarters whenever he stayed here. The *tuxuana* whispered something to Kelly as if fearful Brennan might hear.

'The *tuxuana* has invited you to sleep here,' Kelly told him, 'and when you leave, you're to take anything of Donald's you want. Whatever you don't take will be shared out among the villagers. He doesn't know what's in the suitcases. He hasn't allowed anyone to touch them since Donald died.'

Brennan opened the nearest one. A malodorous smell filled his nostrils. 'I guess he didn't get the chance to go to the laundromat last week.' In the second he found clean clothes, a toiletry bag, shaving mirror and a small tape recorder with a microphone. He lifted it out and saw the cassette inside. He spooled it back to the beginning and pressed Play. He heard a single male voice, chanting melodically in a soft, hypnotic tone, then a second voice, more forceful, also male. The first grew steadily louder to compensate for this. It sounded almost as if the two men were chanting in competition with each other.

'*Waiyamou.*'

Brennan looked up at the *tuxuana*, who was standing in the entrance, a wistful smile on his face. 'What did he say?' he asked Kelly.

'It's a chant ritual they have after a feast when they're entertaining a neighbouring *shabono*. One man recites a monologue and the other has to predict what he's going to say next, and counter it with a witty riposte of his own. They continue for twenty, sometimes thirty minutes then they change roles and the second man initiates the chant. When they're finished, one remains in the arena and beckons for another man from the crowd to join him. A *waiyamou* can last for hours.'

'Then I'd better take it back with me,' Brennan said. 'I'll

take his journals as well. My mother will know who to pass them on to at the university.'

'I didn't know Donald was affiliated to a university,' Kelly said in surprise.

'He was a part-time lecturer at Columbia. It's where he graduated. They funded a lot of his research. In return, he prepared papers for them, which they published and sold to other universities around the country. I think he fancied himself as a bit of an Indiana Jones.' Brennan paused to gauge her reaction. It wasn't immediately forthcoming. 'You do know who Indiana Jones is, don't you?'

'I've only been here for ten years, not my entire life,' she retorted. The *tuxuana* spoke to her again and she pointed to the holdall at Brennan's feet. 'You'd better choose some items to trade. Clothes are normally well received here. They'll trade them with the *garimpeiros*. And any novelty items – those always go down well.'

'How about the Walkman?' Brennan asked.

'Donald introduced them to it a few years back. They thought evil spirits had shrunk the musicians and put them inside it as a punishment. But once Donald had demonstrated how it worked, by taping their voices and then playing it back to them, the novelty soon wore off. They've become pretty blasé about recordings since then – that's how Donald was able to collect so much material on tape over the years. But offer the Walkman anyway. It'll be a good trade item for them.'

Brennan set aside a change of clothing from the holdall and the autopsy report, which he slipped into one of the journals, then went after Kelly into the arena where the *tuxuana* and several other tribesmen were seated. Everyone else was gathered in a semi-circle behind them. Brennan was invited to sit down. He sat cross-legged on the ground and laid the rest of his possessions in front of him. He received an intricately hand-painted five-foot bow in exchange for the jeans; a blunt machete and a clay cooking pot for the two T-shirts; and an alligator-tooth necklace for the Walkman. Once the bartering was over the *tuxuana* pointed to the holdall. Brennan gestured for him to look inside and he removed the toiletry bag. He rummaged through the contents then frowned as he lifted out the electric shaver and held it out questioningly towards Brennan, who switched it on. The *tuxuana* flung it to the ground and scrambled backwards a safe distance. Then, grabbing a spear from one of the men, he began to prod it as it hummed softly.

'Have they never seen an electric shaver before?' Brennan asked, looking up at Kelly who was standing behind him.

'Obviously not,' she replied, then stepped forward and switched it off. There was a general murmur of approval from those around her. She explained to the *tuxuana* what it was used for, then demonstrated by pretending to shave her cheek. Brennan took it from her and shaved a small patch of hair on his wrist. The *tuxuana* gasped in amazement then grinned at Brennan, pointed excitedly to the shaver and eagerly held out his hand for it. Brennan gave it to him. The *tuxuana* spoke to a woman behind him, who hurried away. She returned a short time later with small object wrapped in a piece of cloth. The *tuxuana* placed it carefully on the ground in front of Brennan and gesticulated at it. Brennan unwrapped it. Inside was a gold-plated cigarette lighter. The initials inscribed on it were DB. He said to Kelly, 'I can't take this. It's an expensive lighter. That shaver only cost me a few dollars in a sale at Macy's last year.'

'The Yanomamo don't place a monetary value on things, as we do. They're only interested in whether it will be useful to them in their everyday lives, or whether it could be exchanged for something they want. The shaver will probably be a novelty for a couple of days. Then when everybody has tried it, it'll be put aside to be traded.' Kelly took the lighter from him and turned it around in her hand. 'I'm surprised the *tuxuana* gave you this. I remember him telling me he'd traded it with Donald last year. Since then he's been using it to light his house fire every night. He's grown quite attached to it. You must take it,' she insisted, and handed it back to him. 'You'd only insult him if you refused. He wants you to have it.'

Brennan nodded in gratitude to the *tuxuana*, then gathered

together his remaining belongings, which were scattered across the ground, and stuffed them back into the holdall. The *tuxuana* waited until the crowd had dispersed then spoke briefly to Kelly before getting to his feet and walking off, the shaver clutched tightly in his hand.

'There's a dispute between two men in the *shabono*,' Kelly told Brennan. 'One's accused the other of sleeping with his wife. It's not uncommon for the unmarried men to have affairs with wives whose husbands are out hunting for much of the day but the husband's challenged his rival to a duel. They'll be using clubs. The object's to try and force your opponent into submission. Only the Yanomamo are a proud tribe. They'd rather suffer physical pain than the humiliation that comes with defeat. That's why most of them have so many duelling scars on their heads. They just don't know when to stop.'

The two protagonists entered the arena from different houses, both surrounded by their supporters, like two boxers approaching a ring. Each carried a club, which Brennan estimated at about eight feet long, and which resembled a pool cue, but with the thin end sharpened to a point. The older man, whom Brennan assumed to be the husband, had a shaved head which had been anointed with a red pigment to highlight the deep scars interlaced across his scalp. The other was considerably younger, and with a full head of hair. He looked uneasy as he approached the *tuxuana*, now standing in the centre of the arena. Brennan almost expected him to start talking to the pair, like a referee giving final instructions before the fight but he said nothing and withdrew to his own house. Unlike the rest of the *shabono*, he didn't take sides in domestic disputes.

The husband shouted a challenge to his opponent then stabbed his club into the ground and used it as an anchor before lowering his head to receive the first hit. The younger man brought a savage blow down on the exposed scalp. A cheer went up from his supporters when his adversary's legs buckled momentarily but the husband quickly regained his footing, grabbed his own club by the thin end and cracked it

56

down on to the other's head. A second bout of blows followed in quick succession, but neither man showed any signs of giving way.

What Brennan came to realize was that amid this apparent brutality lay a morality he doubted would have been found anywhere else. There was no ill-temper, no striking out of turn, no apparent animosity towards the other man. It was a duel of honour. A third blow from the husband opened a gash on the young man's head and the blood seeped from under his hairline down the side of his face. The sight of blood delighted the older man's supporters, but incensed the others. Scuffles broke out between the two sets of onlookers, which escalated rapidly into a free-for-all when more clubs were introduced into the fray. One villager wrenched one of the *shabono* support poles out of the ground and waded into the fight, swinging it wildly as he went. A second pole was torn up and Brennan had to scramble to safety as a section of the roof gave way and crashed down. The fighting spilled over into the houses and he suddenly found himself trapped in a corner of a room as, only a few feet away, half a dozen men fought ferociously, oblivious of him. He had to move. Then he spotted Kelly at the front of the house and watched in amazement as she darted nimbly between the flailing clubs to where he was crouched. She grabbed his hand, gestured for him to stay low, then led him back through the scrimmage to the comparative safety of the entrance to the *shabono*.

'I forgot to mention that these duels can sometimes lead to a bit of a shindy,' she said, with a mischievous grin.

'Is that what you call it?' Brennan replied, looking around in disbelief as the fighting continued unabated. 'This would be regarded as a full-blown riot in New York. SWAT teams would have been called out to quell it.'

'It's all pretty harmless, really,' she said. 'A few headaches and some bruises in the morning. It's very rare that anyone gets seriously injured during a club fight. It's just a way of letting off steam.' Brennan pulled her back as a couple of club-wielding villagers, locked in combat, strayed uncomfortably close. 'Come on, let's leave them to it. I've got some *cachaca* on board the *Gal*,' she said.

Brennan followed her through the clearing and down the riverbank to the boat, remembering what Caldwell had told him at Boa Vista harbour earlier that day. 'I believe you can knock that stuff back without any apparent side effects.'

'Who told you that?' She paused at the foot of the boarding ramp, then nodded slowly to herself. 'Tom Caldwell, right? Wait till I see him again,' she muttered angrily. 'He makes me sound like a hopeless lush. But . . . I do drink competitively with some of the other traders sometimes. It's an easy way to pick up a bit of extra money. And it's not that difficult to outdrink them. Half of them are certified drunks anyway. They don't last long, not if you pace them. And I can't really drink much of it. If you can remember the worst hangover you've ever had, multiply it by ten and you'll have some idea what it's like to go overboard on *cachaca*. I'll only drink a lot of it if I'm really strapped.'

Brennan watched her clamber effortlessly up on to the deck, and taking a deep breath, mounted the boarding ramp. In five steps he had reached the top.

'We'll go down to my cabin,' she said.

Brennan followed her below and hovered uncertainly in the cabin doorway. There were only two possible places for him to sit: the single bed or a rocking chair in the corner.

Kelly gestured to the bed. 'Sit down,' she said, then eased herself into the padded seat of the rocking chair. She patted its arms affectionately. 'I've had this for . . . oh, it must be four years now. Since Reuben died. He was a river trader – worked this area all his life. Whenever I visited his boat he always let me sit in this chair and when he died, he left it to me in his will. Not that he had much to leave after his creditors had taken their share. Including the boat. But, then, it's not a very profitable way of life, as I've found out over the years.'

'So why do it?' he asked.

She opened a cabinet and removed a bottle and two glasses. 'Show me a more independent way of life, and in more exotic surroundings,' she said, then uncorked the bottle and poured out two small measures of colourless liquid. She handed him a glass. 'Money isn't that important out here. As long as you can make enough to keep your boat on the water and a little on the side for yourself, that's all that really matters. This is all about a quality of life you won't get anywhere else.' She raised her glass towards him. '*Slainte.*'

'What's that?' he asked.

'Gaelic. It means good health,' she told him.

'Cheers,' he said with a wry grin and held up his glass. The grin vanished when he took a sip of the *cachaca*. He inhaled sharply and gritted his teeth as it spilled down his throat like a cascade of liquid fire. It took him a few seconds to find his voice again and he held up the glass. 'What the hell's in here? Toxic waste?'

'You're probably not far off,' she replied, smiling at his agonized expression.

'And you drink this for pleasure?' he said, then put down the glass on the bedside table. 'I think I'll pass on the refreshments, if you don't mind.'

'I've got some bourbon,' she said. 'Jack Daniel's. Donald brought out a couple of bottles for me last year. I thought you'd want to try the local brew, though.'

'I've tried it, let's leave it at that,' he said, taking the Jack Daniel's and a clean glass from her.

'I suppose it is an acquired taste,' she said thoughtfully, as she turned her glass around in her fingers. Then she put it to her lips and drank the *cachaca* in one gulp.

'Will you go back to Ireland some day?' he asked, after pouring himself a shot.

'No,' she replied tersely, then banged down her glass on top of the cabinet.

He'd spoken without thinking. Just when she seemed at ease with him, she'd abruptly slammed the barriers shut again. He cursed himself silently. Caldwell had told him she'd never spoken about her past. So what makes you so bloody special? he reproached himself. Just for once, stop acting like a cop. She's not a suspect, and this isn't an interrogation. If she wants to talk about herself, then let her do it on her own terms . . .

'Do you smoke?' she asked, breaking the uneasy silence, and proffered an open pack of Marlboro.

'No, thanks,' he replied.

'I only have a couple a day,' she said, and took out a cigarette. 'I have one in the morning with my coffee. And one in the evening. Usually up on deck, when the *Gal*'s at anchor for the night. It makes for a perfect end to the day.'

'I used to get through sixty a day,' Brennan said, 'but I kicked the habit ten years ago. Stopped overnight.'

'Do you mind if I smoke?' she asked.

'Not in the slightest,' he replied, then took out the lighter the *tuxuana* had given him and lit the cigarette for her.

'What made you stop so suddenly?' she asked.

'A woman, can you believe?' he said, his voice suddenly hostile, despite the rueful smile that accompanied his words. 'Her name was Gillian,' he added, more equably.

'Not the same . . .' She trailed off as Brennan nodded.

'One and the same,' he said.

'I had no idea.'

'It wasn't something Donald was proud of. I knew that from the way he kept trying to make peace with me after Gillian died. But I wasn't interested, not after what he and my mother had done to me. I guess you could say I got a certain perverse pleasure from watching him suffer. I've been roundly condemned by all my relatives for it, but then it's always easy to judge someone without knowing all the facts. And they didn't. Then, again, their opinions never meant much to me anyway, except for my aunt Gloria's. She's been my only ally through all of this. I'm a lot closer to her than I am to my mother.'

'What made you so bitter towards your mother?' Kelly asked, without taking her eyes off his face as she handed him the bottle of Jack Daniel's again so that he could refill his glass.

Brennan poured a stiff shot. He knew he didn't have to tell her about Gillian but he felt at ease with Kelly. Normally he

60

wouldn't have let a woman past his first name in the time he'd known her, yet he was prepared to bare his soul to her. And without knowing anything about her either. It was a strange feeling. It was unlike him to confide in anyone – with the exception of his partner, Lou Monks. He couldn't explain it, but he wanted to tell her.

'My mother was the catalyst in breaking us up,' he said. 'But what made it so much harder to take was that she'd planned it from start to finish. And she didn't give a damn about me. All she cared about was pleasing Donald. She did everything in her power to bring him and Gillian together, and push me out of the picture.' He studied his glass. 'Did Donald ever show you any pictures of Gillian?'

Kelly nodded. 'She was gorgeous. She looked like she'd just stepped off a catwalk.'

'We were complete opposites. But, then, they say love is blind, don't they? It was a very physical relationship, which must have made up for our incompatibility. I tried to bridge the intellectual gulf between us by reading up on art but I guess, with hindsight, I was trying to be the person I thought Gillian wanted me to be. I certainly wasn't being myself.

'Donald had a lot more in common with her than I ever did. He was an Ivy Leaguer. Well read. Highly intelligent. Exactly the right sort of mind to attract a woman like Gillian. And that's obviously what happened.' Brennan sank half the contents of his glass in one gulp. 'We'd only been engaged—'

'You two were engaged?' Kelly blurted out in disbelief.

'We got engaged three months after we met. Another impulsive move on my part. But I was a lot younger then. At least, that's my excuse.' Brennan smiled fleetingly before continuing. 'We'd been engaged about six weeks when I first noticed she was becoming increasingly distant towards me. She kept telling me nothing was wrong. And, like a gullible fool, I believed her. Three weeks later the two of them turned up on my doorstep. That's when she dropped the bombshell. Sorry, Ray, but I've fallen in love with Donald. We didn't plan it this way, it just sort of happened. Oh, and by the way,

61

here's your engagement ring back. I won't be needing it any more.

'Six months later they got married. Donald even asked me to be his best man. I couldn't believe him. I didn't go to the wedding. Instead, I went on a bender and nearly got into a fight with a guy who was out on his stag night with a few of his buddies. If my partner hadn't turned up when he did and hauled my drunken ass out of the bar, I'd have got a serious beating. And I'd have deserved it, the way I was behaving.'

'It's only natural you'd be upset.'

'It wasn't a one-off. I'd been drinking heavily ever since Gillian left me. Out of self-pity. That's what made it inexcusable. I should have been above that. But I didn't see it that way. I know now it was just a way of avoiding the truth – that I wasn't good enough for her.' He raised his hand to stop her interrupting him. 'I know what you're going to say but I'm not selling myself short. I didn't match up to her expectations. She thought she deserved better. Only she didn't get that with Donald. I guess in a way that's the final irony. I had little contact with her after we split up, but I do know she was desperately unhappy in that marriage. But, then, that's hardly surprising, considering he'd spend six months of every year over here. His only real interest was his work. The only reason she stayed with him was because of their son.'

'You're still in love with her, aren't you?' Kelly asked, after a thoughtful silence.

'I still love her, but I'm not still *in* love with her. There's a difference. I don't think I could ever block it out altogether, even if I wanted to. Her death affected me deeply. Probably more than it did Donald. I didn't go to the funeral, which gave my family even more ammunition to use against me. I was accused of being selfish and uncaring in not being there for Donald when he needed my support. But as I said earlier, it's easy to criticize when you don't know all the facts. Had they known the truth, perhaps they wouldn't have been so critical. I don't know. And, frankly, I don't care.'

Kelly stubbed out her cigarette then sat back in the rocking chair and begun to tug at her gold bracelet as she slowly looked around the cabin, purposely avoiding eye contact with him.

'Something's bothering you, isn't it?' he said.

'No, why?' Kelly replied, defensively.

'You've got a habit of fiddling with that bracelet whenever there's something on your mind. I noticed you doing it after that goon attacked you.'

'My, but aren't we the observant one?' she said sarcastically.

'It goes with the job,' he replied dispassionately, refusing to rise to the bait.

She sighed, then reached for the glass of *cachaca* he'd abandoned on the bedside table. She was about to sip it, but changed her mind and placed it beside her empty glass on the cabinet. 'You've been straight with me about Donald and there's something I feel you should know. You said his only real interest was his work. That's not . . . entirely true.'

'What are you trying to say?' he asked, when she fell silent. 'That there was something between you and Donald?'

'No!' she shot back indignantly. 'There was never anything between us. The very thought of Donald and me. It wasn't even as if . . .'

'It wasn't even as if *what*?' he asked.

She started to fiddle with the bracelet again but, realizing what she was doing, clasped both hands in her lap. 'The truth is, I never really liked Donald. I know that's a dreadful thing to say, now that he's dead.'

'Not if it's the truth,' he replied.

'Whenever I gave him a lift on the *Gal*, he would always hover outside the wheelhouse. I could feel him watching me. It was unnerving.'

'Did he ever come on to you?' Brennan asked. When she lowered her eyes he had his answer. 'I hope you told him exactly where to go.'

'I always made it clear I wasn't interested, not that it ever seemed to put him off,' she replied. 'But what made it worse was that he was married. His wife and I are friends. There were times I wanted to tell her what a slimeball he was, but

63

she would never have believed me. Donald could do no wrong in her eyes. If I'd said anything, it would only have damaged our friendship.'

'Back up there a moment,' Brennan insisted. 'You and his *wife* are friends? What are you saying here? That he got married again?'

Kelly nodded. 'That's what I was trying to tell you. Her name is Louise Carneiro. She's from São Paulo. Her father works for one of the big Brazilian logging companies. She came out to visit him some years back. That's when I first met her. She was so horrified by what was being done to the forest she gave up her job in São Paulo to fight for the rights of the Yanomamo and their lands. She lived in Boa Vista to begin with but after a few months she moved to one of the *shabonos*. That's when she first met Donald. She was smitten with him right from the start. They got married about three years ago in Boa Vista. I was a witness at the ceremony. He insisted the marriage remain a secret. He even swore me to silence. I never did understand why but I went along with it. I've never told anyone about it. Until now.'

'I assume Louise isn't from a wealthy family?' Brennan asked.

'Hardly.'

'There's your reason why he wanted it kept under wraps,' Brennan said. 'In case our dear mother ever found out. It would have sent her into an apoplectic rage if she'd ever learnt her beloved son had married beneath him. But it's certainly put him up a notch in my estimation. He finally did something without her permission. Does Louise know he's dead?'

'I don't know,' Kelly said. 'I haven't seen her since I found Donald's body. I've been stuck in Boa Vista.'

'I'd like to meet her, if that's possible,' Brennan said. 'She's my sister-in-law, after all.'

'It'll take about three hours to reach her *shabono* by boat,' Kelly told him. 'We'll have to leave at first light if we want to be back in time for the cremation tomorrow afternoon. If she's there, and there's no guarantee she will be, we can bring her back with us. I know she'd want to be here for the ceremony.'

Brennan finished his bourbon then looked at his watch. 'I'd better get back to the *shabono* – try and get some sleep if we're out of here at first light.'

'The hammocks are surprisingly comfortable once you're used to them,' Kelly said, getting to her feet. She picked up a torch and followed him out of the cabin. 'You'll probably have some difficulty getting to sleep though,' she added, as they emerged on to the deck, 'but once you get used to the noises, you'll soon drop off.'

'What noises?' he asked suspiciously.

'The usual ones you'd associate with a *shabono*. Dogs barking. Children crying. Couples arguing. And, of course, the sound of the jungle. Insects. Owls. Monkeys. That sort of thing.'

'I wish I hadn't asked now,' he said, with a smile. 'I'm counting on you to get me up in the morning. I've got a feeling I'll be dead to the world by then.'

'The villagers will wake you, don't worry about that,' she replied. 'They're always up at first light.'

'It sounds like the police academy all over again,' Brennan said, then went down the ramp, and made his way back to the *shabono*. The arena was deserted: everyone had retired for the night. He entered the guest-house and applied insect repellent to his face, neck and arms, then hoisted himself into the hammock and wriggled about until he was comfortable.

Then a dog began to bark and another joined in, which started a baby crying. A voice shouted angrily, which was followed by a yelp of pain. One of the dogs was quiet, then the other dog fell silent and the baby settled. Only the mellifluent sounds of the night remained. He stifled a yawn and closed his eyes.

After Brennan had left the boat Kelly remained on deck. She crossed to the wooden bench and sat down, untied her ponytail and shook her hair over her shoulders. She closed her eyes and tilted her head back, allowing the cool night breeze to caress her throat. Brennan, she now knew, was the one she'd been waiting for, to whom she could unburden all the pent-up emotion that had been eating away at her for the past ten years. Even Reuben, who'd been her closest confidant, had never known anything about her life before she arrived in the Amazon. She'd never said anything, and he'd never asked. It was a mutual understanding that had been the cornerstone of their friendship.

She still felt guilty for having snapped at Brennan earlier when he'd asked her whether she'd return to Ireland. It had been an innocent question but she had instinctively clammed up. She had been impressed that he'd dropped the subject, unlike her fellow river traders who'd come to regard her reluctance to say anything about her past as a challenge to inveigle the truth out of her. No one had ever succeeded. She could never go home. Not after what had happened. She would never tell *them* that but she felt she could tell Ray Brennan. A man who'd be gone in a few days. It made no sense whatsoever but it seemed the right thing to do. The thought troubled her, but she quickly pushed it from her mind. Telling him about herself was one thing, but any emotional attachment was out of the question. She knew she was strong enough to resist that.

Her eyes flew open as a lingering doubt permeated that once resolute self-belief. *No, it would never happen.* It *could* never happen. She touched the gold bracelet, unclasped the hook and turned it in her fingers. There were so many memories attached to the bracelet, all part of the life she'd been forced to leave behind in her beloved Ireland.

She looped the bracelet round her wrist again and struggled to do up the clasp. Some years earlier it had been damaged, leaving it slightly loose inside the eyelet. How many times had it fallen off since then? Whenever it did, though, it was always aboard the *Gal*. There had to be an irony in that somewhere. Each time she found it, she swore she'd get the clasp fixed before she lost it for ever but she'd never got round to it.

Hearing footsteps on the ramp she looked up and was disappointed to see one of the crew. 'I thought you'd be

66

asleep by now?' she said sharply, but her anger was directed at herself.

'Are you cross with me, Rasha?' he asked uncertainly.

'No, of course not,' she replied, with a disarming smile. 'I'm just a bit tired, that's all. What are you doing back here?'

'I came to get my hammock,' he said. 'The one they gave me, it's no good.' When he returned with his neatly folded hammock hanging loosely over his shoulder, he said, 'I saw the *naba* when I came here. He's sleeping like a child. The spirits will look after him tonight.'

'Good, because we're leaving again at first light.'

'Where are we going?'

'Your *shabono*,' she replied, and a broad smile lit up his face. 'I'm taking the *naba* to see Louise. If she's there.'

'I can see Rasha likes the *naba*,' he said. 'I also like him. He's strong. A good man for Rasha.'

'I think I can take care of myself, don't you?'

'His strength lies in here,' the Yanomamo replied, placing his hand to his chest. 'Like Rasha. That's why he's good man for you.'

'Well, he'll be gone in a few days, so I guess we'll never know,' she said.

'The spirits know. They have already spoken to the *hekura*,' he said pointing in the direction of the *shabono*.

'Oh, they have, have they?' she said. 'And just *what* did they have to say?'

'They said you will find harmony with the *naba*.'

'I think the *hekura*'s had a bit too much *ebene* tonight,' she retorted, referring to the hallucinogenic drug taken each night by the men of the village.

'The spirits never lie, Rasha,' he reprimanded her.

'I'd say that was a matter of opinion,' she muttered in English. She didn't want to offend him, knowing, as she did, how revered the spirits were in Yanomamo culture.

'The *hekura* didn't speak to the spirits tonight, Rasha,' the Yanomamo called after her as she walked towards the hatch. 'He's away.'

Kelly froze at the top of the stairs. 'So when exactly did they tell him about the *naba*?'

'More than two nights ago,' came the reply.

'But how could the *hekura* have known the *naba* was coming?' she asked in disbelief. 'He only arrived today.'

'The spirits can foretell everything,' he said solemnly, and arced his hand reverently across the night sky. 'I'll see you at first light. Good night, Rasha.'

Kelly shuddered. She could feel goose-bumps prickling her flesh. She'd always regarded the spirits at best with scepticism and at worst with contempt, having seen children die because the spirits had told the *hekura*, in a drug-induced stupor, that they would heal them. No amount of pleading on her part had ever made any difference. The *hekura* would never defy the spirits. Now she didn't know what to think. How could he have known Brennan would be coming? It made no sense to her. Unless . . .

She dismissed the idea even before it could take shape in her mind. There were no such things as spirits. And they certainly couldn't make prophecies about the future. It was all just superstition passed down through the generations. So why was she finding it so hard to believe at that particular moment? When she went below to her cabin she'd already resigned herself to a troubled night's sleep.

5

Kelly awoke with a start. Shouting was coming from the *shabono*. Then she heard Ray Brennan's voice above the commotion. She leapt out of bed, pulled on a T-shirt and a pair of shorts, slipped her feet into the scuffed plimsolls by the door and ran to the foot of the stairs where she almost collided with one of the crew who was on his way to wake her.

'Come quickly, Rasha,' he urged her. 'The *naba* has gone crazy.'

'What happened?' she asked, hurrying up the stairs after him.

'I didn't see,' he said as he ran down the ramp and jumped the last few feet to the bank. 'I don't understand what he's saying, but he's very angry.'

She followed him into the *shabono*. A dozen Yanomamo tribesmen had Brennan trapped in a circle in the centre of the arena. Most were armed with spears, the others with bows and arrows. It was then she saw the man lying motionless on the ground, his spear beside him. Several Yanomamo, including the *tuxuana*, were crouched beside him. For a horrifying moment Kelly thought he was dead – and that Brennan was somehow responsible for his death. Then, to her relief, the man moved.

'Have you seen what they've done to Donald? *Have you?*' Brennan roared as she shoved her way through the mêlée towards him. 'They've got him hanging in a tree back there,' he said, stabbing his thumb towards the rear of the *shabono*. 'Jesus, what is he? Some carcass in an abattoir?'

'It's their—' She stopped abruptly as a spear prodded her in the back. She swung round and yelled at the man to give her some room. He was about to shout back at her when the *tuxuana* appeared. The circle parted to allow him through. He told Kelly what had happened and she turned back to Brennan. 'You laid out the guard when he tried to stop you cutting down Donald's body.'

'Damn right,' Brennan replied indignantly, then levelled a finger at the *tuxuana*. 'Now tell your friend here I want the body cut down now!'

'No, you listen to me,' she snapped, her eyes blazing. 'You agreed to respect their customs, remember? And hanging the body in a tree prior to cremation is an important part of the funeral rites.'

'You never said anything about this before,' Brennan said.

'Because I knew it would upset you. That's why I asked the *tuxuana* to hang it out of sight of the *shabono*,' she said.

'And that makes it all right?' Brennan retorted.

'This is what Donald wanted. He knew what the customs entailed. It was his choice, not yours. You have to respect that.'

'It just seems so . . .'

'Barbaric?' She finished the sentence for him. 'Granted it may seem like desecration to us, but the Yanomamo don't see it like that. Death is sacred to them. Why else do you think they had a guard watching the body last night? He was protecting it from the evil spirits.'

'You don't believe all that, do you?' Brennan asked, contemptuously.

'*They* do, and that's all that matters,' she replied. She wasn't sure what she believed any more, not after last night.

Brennan gazed at the circle of faces staring intently at him. 'Perhaps I did jump in without thinking,' he conceded. 'It's just that it was a hell of a shock to see Donald strung up like a piece of meat. We may not have been close, but he was still my brother. It just seemed so undignified, that's all. But, as you said, it's what he wanted. And I have to accept that.'

'I take it that's an apology of sorts,' she said.

70

'Yeah, I guess it is,' he replied. 'Question is: will they accept it?'

'I'm sure they will, once they realize it was all a misunderstanding,' she said, then spoke to the *tuxuana*. A chorus of 'aahs' went up from the tribesmen and the weapons were lowered. Several patted Brennan on the back and spoke to him. One pointed to the unfortunate guard who was still lying on the ground, a dark bruise now visible on his cheek where Brennan had struck him.

'What did you tell them?' Brennan asked, as the circle disbanded.

'That it was simply a misunderstanding on your part,' she replied.

'Kelly?' he said, and grabbed her arm. 'I don't believe it was that simple. What did you say? One minute they're ready to use me for target practice, and the next they're patting me on the back like I'm one of the family.'

'I told them you thought you saw a *naiki* enter the guard. That's why you hit him.'

'And that is?'

'A cannibalistic spirit. The Yanomamo hold them in great esteem, but they also fear them. So by knocking out the guard you prevented the *naiki* from using the guard as a means of entering Donald's body. If it had managed to get inside Donald, it could have stolen his *moamo* – a part of his soul contained inside the liver. That would have left his soul vulnerable to an attack by supernatural forces once it drifted free of the body. And if the soul is lost, it's sent to the *shobari waka* – our equivalent of hell.'

'But surely they don't think I believe in any of that stuff?' Brennan said in amazement.

'Why?' she replied. 'They believe their cosmos is the centre of all existence. And why shouldn't they? They don't know any different. They know there are non-believers, particularly among the river traders. But they regard you now as a believer. And that's important to them.'

'Are you a believer?' he asked.

'I'm a sceptic . . . who always keep an open mind,' she

replied, then looked at her watch. 'It's five thirty. I think we should be making tracks. It'll take us three hours to get to Louise's *shabono* and we must be back by the early afternoon, in time for the ceremony.'

'Would they wait if we were late?' he asked.

'I don't intend to be late. It would be an insult to them. The sooner we leave, the sooner we can be back.'

'Louise isn't here.'

They were seated cross-legged with the elderly *tuxuana* in the centre of the *shabono*. It was considerably larger than the other one and the villagers were less traditional in their clothing. Most wore loincloths, but Brennan saw several men in shorts and a couple wearing grubby T-shirts as well. Once again, he found he needed to offer gifts before business could be discussed and Kelly had suggested giving the *tuxuana* the *pistoleiro*'s revolver. It had been gratefully accepted, but Brennan couldn't help wondering how long it would be before it ended up in the hands of some *garimpeiro*. And who was to say it wouldn't be used against Yanomamo in the on-going feud between the two factions?

'Does he know where she is?' Brennan asked, his eyes flitting between Kelly and the *tuxuana* as they spoke together.

A look of apprehension crossed her face and she glanced at him but turned back to the *tuxuana*. It was some time before the conversation ended.

'What did he say?' he queried.

'She's "disappeared", that's the word he used,' Kelly told him. 'She left shortly after the news of Donald's death reached the *shabono*. But nobody saw her go. And she hasn't been seen since. What's odd is that she hasn't taken anything with her. It seems as if she just walked off into the jungle.'

'She could have been suicidal,' Brennan said.

'I don't buy it,' Kelly replied. 'Not Louise. She may have been smitten with Donald, but she was also obsessed with helping the Yanomamo. She gave up everything in São Paulo to come out here to fight for their rights. It had become her whole life. These were her people. She wouldn't abandon them. I don't believe for a moment that she went off to kill herself.'

'Then where is she?' Brennan said.

'I don't think she killed herself, but she might be dead anyway, and it's also possible she may have met up with a hunting party from another tribe and gone back to their *shabono*, just to get away from here.' The *tuxuana* placed a gnarled hand gently on Kelly's arm to get her attention. When they'd spoken she said to Brennan, 'He thinks she's been stolen by evil spirits, like the other eleven villagers who've also gone missing over the last year. Not that it's uncommon for villagers to vanish like that – there's still a lot of inter-tribal fighting between the *shabonos*. If the villagers were ambushed and killed in some isolated area of the forest, and left where they fell, their bodies would quickly be eaten by wild animals.'

'I could imagine two or three disappearing without trace,' Brennan said, 'but eleven, in the space of a year? That seems a lot.'

'Ah, the investigative instincts coming out again!' she said, then shook her head. 'There isn't some great conspiracy going on out here, Ray. Believe me, they were either killed by another tribe or by animals. It's nothing more sinister than that.'

'Ask him whether they were last seen in any particular area?'

'Look, I told you—'

'Humour me,' he cut in, his hands extended towards her in a placatory gesture.

She passed on his question to the *tuxuana*. 'He says several were last seen near the Silva ranch,' she told Brennan.

'That's where Tom Caldwell works,' Brennan added.

'It might have been suspicious before Caldwell took over there as head of security,' Kelly said.

'Why do you say that?'

'At one time there was a lot of trouble between the Yanomamo and the *vaqueiros*, the cowboys who work the ranchland, because the Yanomamo were thought to be rustling cattle. The previous head of security organized several

73

raiding parties but never found anything to incriminate the villagers. But he was certain they were responsible – with good reason – so he banned the Yanomamo from using the footpaths which crossed the ranchland. The Yanomamo used them as shortcuts to neighbouring *shabonos* and at first they defied him and continued to use them. That's when he ordered the *vaqueiros* to shoot on sight any Yanomamo found trespassing. Dozens were killed in the first couple of months. There was even talk that the *vaqueiros* were shooting them in the jungle then dumping the bodies on ranchland, to make it look as if they'd been trespassing. They were in a no-win situation. Louise went with several of the local *tuxuanas* to the authorities in Boa Vista but they didn't receive a sympathetic hearing. Eduardo Silva has a lot of clout there. So they left without resolving anything and for the next six months the Yanomamo were forced to steer clear of ranchland.

'Then Silva brought in Tom Caldwell, who called a meeting of all the local *tuxuanas* to negotiate a peaceful settlement to the dispute. Not only did he offer to open the footpaths again but also to let them hunt in certain areas of ranchland. In return, he asked that all rustling stopped. If it didn't, he'd withdraw the concessions. The *tuxuanas* agreed and since then there's been no trouble. He'd have nothing to gain, and everything to lose, by jeopardizing the special relationship he's built up with them.'

'You certainly put a good case for the defence,' Brennan replied.

'But you're not convinced?' she said.

'Did I say that?' he asked.

'You didn't have to. I can hear the doubt in your voice. Only this time you're wrong.' She got up. 'There's no point in us hanging around here any more. We may as well return to the *shabono*. At least we'll get back in plenty of time.'

They were walking up the ramp of the *Shamrock Gal* when Brennan asked, 'How well do you know Caldwell and Dixon?'

She looked round slowly at him, with a pained expression. 'You're not still looking for some conspiracy, are you?'

'It was an innocent question, that's all,' he replied.

74

'Since when do cops ever ask innocent questions?' she retorted, then barked a string of orders to her crew. They exchanged uneasy glances, not knowing what had triggered off her anger, before they scurried away.

'What the hell's got into you all of a sudden?' he asked.

'Nothing,' she replied sharply. 'I just think you're wasting your time, that's all.'

'It's my time.'

'And mine,' she reminded him, then went off towards the wheelhouse.

'Surely seven hundred and fifty dollars should buy me a little of yours?' he called after her.

She took a deep breath then turned to face him. 'I don't know either of them well but when we do bump into each other, usually in Boa Vista, Tom Caldwell's always been very friendly and courteous towards me. I've hardly spoken to Bobby Dixon. He doesn't say much at the best of times.'

'Has Caldwell ever talked about what he did before he came here?'

'No, and I've never asked him either,' she replied. 'He doesn't pry into my past and I don't pry into his. I've heard the *vaqueiros* call him Colonel a few times, which could mean he was once in the military.'

'I'd guessed as much,' Brennan said. 'What were Caldwell and Dixon doing at the harbour when I arrived there?'

'I've no idea. They'd only been there a few minutes. We didn't say much. Now, if that's all . . .' A frown creased her forehead.

'What is it?' Brennan asked.

'Probably nothing,' she replied, dismissively.

'Kelly?' Brennan said, exasperated.

'Caldwell did ask whether I'd seen Louise in the last couple of days. I told him I hadn't and he left it at that. I didn't think any more of it until now.'

'Were they friends?' he asked.

'She doesn't like him,' Kelly said, as she started up the engine. 'But then that's hardly surprising, since Donald didn't like him either.'

'Caldwell certainly didn't give that impression when I met him at the harbour,' Brennan said, approaching the open wheelhouse door. 'He was oozing sympathy.'

'What do you expect?' she replied. 'He was hardly going to criticize Donald at a time like that, was he?'

'Why didn't they get on?' he asked.

She stared out over the river for a few moments before answering. 'Donald also thought there was something suspicious about the number of Yanomamo who were disappearing near Silva's ranch. He reckoned the *vaqueiros* were still killing them and hiding the bodies.'

'Why didn't you tell me this before?' Brennan demanded.

'Because he had no evidence, yet he still went ahead and confronted Caldwell with it. Not at the ranch, but publicly in Boa Vista. Caldwell denied it and welcomed any investigation. It backfired badly on Donald because several *tuxuanas* denounced him as a troublemaker, trying to sabotage the new agreement they'd made with Caldwell. He wasn't welcome at their *shabonos* after that.'

'Donald wouldn't have jumped in feet first without a good reason. There had to be something to those allegations,' Brennan said.

'If he had something on Caldwell, then why didn't he produce it when he had the chance in Boa Vista?' she asked.

'I don't know,' Brennan said, then walked over to the stern railing and sat down on the bench.

Brennan felt uneasy in his stomach. It was a sensation he knew only too well. It told him something didn't add up. Just a hunch. But his hunches had always been important to him. Just as they had to Donald. It was the one characteristic they'd both inherited from their father. If Donald had a hunch that Caldwell was linked in some way to the disappearance of the Yanomamo in the area, there was probably some basis to it. Brennan had often thought his brother would have made an excellent cop, such was his natural instinct to pick up on any fragment of evidence that would have been overlooked by anyone else.

He'd been nurturing his own hunch about Donald's death

ever since he first saw the body in the morgue. There was no doubt that Donald had drowned. But what about all those scratches on his hands and forearms? The pathologist said they could have been caused by Donald grabbing at bushes as he fell down an embankment into the water. But there were too many, particularly on his forearms. How many bushes could he have grabbed at if he had fallen down an embankment? Enough to leave that many scratches? He had his doubts. What if Donald had been pushing his way through undergrowth as he ran through the jungle? But why would he run? Was he being chased? And if so, by whom? Had he lost his balance at a crucial moment and plunged into the water? He knew that Donald must have received the head wound once he was already in the water – if he'd been chased by Caldwell's men, they would have been armed and wouldn't have had to hit him with a piece of wood.

But he had no evidence to support any of this. Only a hunch. He couldn't go to the authorities with a hunch. And, even if he had more tangible evidence, who's to say they'd take any more notice of him than they had of Louise Carneiro? He thought about postponing the cremation, but dismissed the idea. All the evidence pointed to it having been nothing more than a tragic accident and putting off the ceremony wouldn't achieve anything. Yet he still believed there was more to Donald's death then met the eye.

'A penny for them,' Kelly said, as she sat down beside him.

Brennan saw that one of the crew had taken the helm. 'It's all pretty scrambled up here right now,' he said, tapping the side of his head.

'You do think Caldwell had something to do with Donald's death, don't you?' she said.

'It's a hunch, that's all,' he replied despondently. 'And hunches don't count. I should know. I've seen enough scumbags slip through the net over the years through lack of evidence, even though you know they're as guilty as sin. There's nothing you can do about it. That's what makes it so frustrating.'

'I'm sorry I didn't tell you earlier about Donald and Caldwell. I didn't think it was important. Not now.'

'It shouldn't be, should it?'

'Do you want to see the ranch?' she asked. 'I can show you, if you're interested. There's a hill overlooking it with a view of the whole spread – or so I've been told by the other traders. I've never seen it myself. We'll have to branch off on to one of the tributaries further downstream. As far as I know, that's the only accessible route to the hill. It shouldn't take us any more than forty minutes to get there. There's supposed to be a jetty close to it. It was used by a mission many years ago.'

'I'd like to see it. Thanks.'

Forty minutes became an hour and a quarter. Kelly had already decided to give it another ten minutes before turning back – five of which were already up – when one of the Yanomamo shouted from the bow and pointed to the skeletal remains of a jetty on the riverbank a few hundred yards ahead. 'At last,' she muttered irritably – to herself, she thought, but Brennan had overheard.

'You did say you've never been up here before,' he said, gently. 'You couldn't have known it was going to take so long.'

'Then I should have kept my mouth shut, shouldn't I?'

'It's all right to make mistakes, you know,' he said.

'And just what's that supposed to mean?' she snapped.

'I wouldn't insult you by saying I could even begin to imagine what it must have been like for you here in the last ten years. There must have been so much prejudice towards you as a woman when you first started trading on the river, and I bet there's still some of it around to this day. You chose to deal with it by building barriers around yourself to deflect the criticism. You've had to become hard to survive. Particularly on yourself. And it shows. It's as if you plan your every move in advance in case you make the slightest mistake those Neanderthals could use against you. Well, I'm not one of them, Kelly. I'm on your side. I have been ever since I first met you. You've got nothing to prove to me.'

'I don't need you, or anyone else, on my side,' she said, as she manoeuvred the *Shamrock Gal* towards the riverbank. 'I don't need any allies. And I sure as hell don't need to prove myself to anyone. Least of all to the other traders. I don't give a damn what they think about me. I'm not out to impress them – or anyone else for that matter.'

Brennan could almost hear the sound of bolts being flung into place as the barriers clanged shut. But he didn't regret what he'd said. He knew it had touched a nerve or she wouldn't have become so defensive. He found that comforting.

'You'll need these,' she said, pushing a pair of binoculars into his hand.

'Zeiss?' he said. 'These must have set you back a bit.'

'Twenty-four second-hand T-shirts,' she replied. 'That's the beauty of bartering in the Amazon. It's not the price that matters, it's what you can offer in exchange.'

She shouted to one of the Yanomamo to drop anchor then helped the other to lower the ramp over the side of the boat. Brennan followed her down to the riverbank where he paused to look around him as every sound emanating from the surrounding jungle suddenly became a potential threat. He wished he hadn't traded the revolver at the *shabono*.

'If you're worried about being attacked by a predator, then don't be,' she told him, as if reading his thoughts. 'The only one is the jaguar, and it's already an endangered species here. The chances of there being one within a five-hundred-mile radius of us is remote. But keep your eyes on the ground for snakes. The bushmaster and the pit viper are the two deadliest found in these parts.'

'Now I know we shouldn't have traded the gun back at the village,' he said.

'It wouldn't have done you any good. You won't see the snake until you've already been bitten. And unless you have the antidote on you, you'll die.' She noticed the unease on his face. 'Don't worry, I always keep anti-venom serum on the *Gal*. You never know when you might need it.'

'Let's hope not today.'

'I'll lead the way,' she told him. 'Follow in my footsteps and you'll be fine.'

They set off on the old path that had once been used by the missionaries to travel to and from the jetty. The hill was a couple of hundred yards beyond the overgrown ruins of the mission buildings. Once they reached the top Kelly held out her arms as she marvelled at the spectacular view around her. 'This is incredible, isn't it?' she said in awe.

'Yeah, it's something else,' he said, the binoculars already to his eyes. But he wasn't interested in the canopy of forest, which stretched out into the distance until it merged with the shimmering blue horizon. He was concentrating on the ranch-land below, a lush plateau of green as far as the eye could see. He panned the binoculars across it until he saw a couple of men on horseback riding across the plain. Both were dressed in scruffy jeans and plaid shirts. What caught his eye, how-ever, were the submachine-guns slung over their backs. He recognized them as 9mm Madsen CELs – he'd confiscated several from Hispanic youths in the South Bronx over the years.

'See anything?' Kelly asked, crouching beside him and resting an arm on his shoulder.

'Just a couple of *vaqueiros*.'

She put her hand lightly on the binoculars and directed his gaze away from the riders. 'That's the *fazenda* – the farmhouse.'

'It's massive,' he said, as he took in the double-storey building and the staff quarters annexed to it. The stables, which were as big as the two buildings put together, were some distance away. Then he focused on the private runway. He counted five light aircraft parked in the spacious hangars. He continued to pan the binoculars and stopped when he spotted a white Mercedes parked at the far end of the runway. Bobby Dixon was leaning against the driver's door, his arms folded across his chest. Tom Caldwell, in a lightweight white suit, stood on the other side of the car. Both men were wearing reflective sunglasses.

'What do you see down there?' Kelly asked.

'Caldwell and Dixon,' he replied, then handed the binoculars to her.

'I'd say they were expecting company,' she said, as she watched both men look skywards.

Caldwall removed a two-way radio from his belt and spoke into it as he continued to scan the sky. Tilting the angle of the binoculars, she followed Caldwell's gaze and saw the shimmering silhouette of an aircraft approaching in the distance. She handed the binoculars to Brennan. 'It could be Silva,' she said, 'or one of his business associates.'

Brennan followed the jet down. After landing it taxied to within a few feet of the Mercedes. The engines were switched off. Brennan kept the binoculars trained on the door but it was another few minutes before it was pulled open, and the stairs lowered to the ground. A lone figure came out, dressed in a sombre grey suit and carrying an attaché case. 'Somehow I don't think it's Silva,' he said, as he watched the man negotiate the stairs and shake hands briefly with Caldwell. 'Fair hair. Blue eyes. Pallid features. Hardly your average Brazilian, is it? See if you recognize him.'

'Can't say I do,' she replied, as the man walked with Caldwell to the Mercedes. Dixon opened the back door and the two men got in. 'Could be from your neck of the woods.'

'Could be,' he agreed. 'But what's he doing out here?'

'As I said before, perhaps he's one of Silva's business associates,' she said as Dixon climbed behind the wheel of the Mercedes and drove off towards the *fazenda*.

'So why meet with Caldwell? He's only the head of security here, not a financial player in Silva's empire.'

'I don't know,' she replied, then looked at her watch. 'Come on, we'd better make a move if we want to get back in time for the ceremony.'

'Yeah, I guess. There's nothing else we can do here,' he said.

Dixon stopped the Mercedes in front of the *fazenda* and switched off the engine. An armed *vaqueiro*, on guard at the foot of the verandah, hurried forward and opened the back door. The grey-suited man got out and looked around the deserted courtyard. His eyes finally settled on the two leashed Alsatians sleeping on the verandah. 'I'd have thought someone with your military background would have been a lot more security-conscious than this,' he said, as Caldwell climbed out of the car after him. 'You don't have any guards posted at the main gates or on the perimeter walls. In fact, all you have is one guard to cover the whole courtyard. It's hardly adequate, is it?'

'We may not be in your league when it comes to security arrangements, Jackson, but I think you'll find it satisfactory.'

'No names,' the man responded tersely.

'And who's going to hear us?' Caldwell retorted, gesturing around him. 'We're in the middle of nowhere.'

'It doesn't matter. We don't use names.'

Caldwell gave an indifferent shrug. 'We have a fully operational control room in an underground bunker which handles all the necessary security requirements. It's manned twenty-four hours a day. Closed-circuit television cameras cover a twenty-mile radius of the farmhouse and are activated by infra-red sensors that automatically lock on to – and track – body heat. Each camera is attached to a laser cannon, which can only be activated from the control room at the discretion of the duty officer. Fortunately it hasn't had to be discharged for anything more dangerous than a stray deer. I'm told it made a very palatable venison stew for the *vaqueiros*. In addition, the top of the perimeter wall around the courtyard is electrified. If someone were to put their hand on the cable, they would be killed instantly. That's why I have the guard out here, in case any bodies need to be cleared away.' Caldwell climbed the steps on the porch where he paused. 'I hope that allays your fears. We're quite impenetrable here.'

Jackson nodded, then followed Caldwell into the house. Dixon remained on the verandah. Caldwell led him into the study and used a remote control device to activate a false wall, which opened on to an area the size of an elevator. He pressed another button and the wooden floor slid back to reveal a flight of stone steps. They went down the steps and Caldwell used the remote control to close the floor after them.

They found themselves in a spacious room with spotlessly clean whitewashed walls. It was empty, apart from a glass partition which divided it into two equal halves. Caldwell removed his radio from his belt and spoke softly into it. A door, camouflaged as part of the wall, slid open behind the glass partition and a woman, dressed in a white coat, led three Indians into the room. All three were naked, apart from the traditional penis sheaths tied around their waists. She spoke briefly to them and they stood obediently in a row against the wall. She disappeared back through the open doorway and returned moments later with a fourth Indian, wearing a suit. It was a strangely disturbing image, almost surreal. She told him to stand in front of the others then withdrew discreetly and the door slid back into place, sealing the four motionless figures inside the room. None of them moved. It was as if they were in a trance. Jackson asked about their apparent compliance.

'Psychotomimetic drugs,' a female voice said behind him.

The woman was standing in a second doorway which had opened silently behind him. She entered the room, followed by a man also wearing a white coat. They both shook hands with Jackson. Although he'd never met either before, he felt as if he already knew them from the progress reports Caldwell had been sending him for the last few months. The man was a cardiologist, the woman a psychiatrist. Husband and wife. Both were key members of the research team at the ranch.

'What exactly do these drugs do?' Jackson asked.

'They induce a state of mind similar to hypnosis. They enhance hypnotic susceptibility, rather than a true hypnotic trance.' Caldwell beckoned the cardiologist forward. 'Would you care to explain to our guest what he's going to witness here today?'

The man removed an electronic device from his coat pocket and held it out on the palm of his hand. It was roughly the size of a cigarette packet and had a thin outer casing of titanium. 'I assume you know what this is?'

83

'It's a pacemaker,' Jackson replied.

'Not quite. It's the same size and weight as a regular pacemaker. Only that's where the similarity ends. This contains a small explosive charge powerful enough to tear through the chest of the host as well as several layers of clothing. The host would die instantly but, then, they're expendable. What is crucial to the whole operation, however, is that the explosion would also shatter a vial of hydrocyanic gas which is also secreted inside the casing. One breath of this gas would be sufficient to kill anyone within ten feet of the host. And, as it would happen so quickly, the target wouldn't have time to take evasive action. The idea comes from a gun developed by the KGB, which fired a glass pellet filled with hydrocyanic gas. It was used a number of times in the late fifties and early sixties to eliminate dissidents outside the Soviet Union. Once fired, the gas would dissipate in the air, leaving no trace. The victim appeared to have died of heart failure. This just takes the process a step further.' He pointed to the Indian in the suit, who was still standing motionless behind the partition. 'I implanted one of these devices in his chest last night. I'm sure you'll be as impressed as we are with the results.'

The cardiologist handed Caldwell a remote control, the size of a cigarette lighter. It had two buttons – one green, one red – underneath a protective plastic cover. Caldwell flicked open the cover with his thumb and pressed first the green button, then the red. There was a muffled bang as the explosion ripped through the host's chest cavity, spraying a jet of blood across the whitewashed wall. Even before he'd collapsed it was apparent that the others had already inhaled the lethal gas. They clawed frantically at their throats, gasping for air as the gas instantly paralysed their hearts. Within seconds they, too, were dead. Jackson took a hesitant step towards the glass partition, his face ashen as he stared at the four bodies lying on the concrete floor.

'The innocent always make the best assassins,' Caldwell said, breaching the silence. 'A lonely woman seduced by the attentions of a handsome lover, then duped into carrying a bomb on to a plane. An explosive device placed inside a child's teddy bear, which is then taken aboard a bus of schoolchildren. Or, in this case, a nondescript Joe Citizen, who'll be made to believe he's suffered a heart attack and has been given a pacemaker. Someone who could get within a few feet of the intended target without alerting suspicion. Someone who always stands in the front row whenever a particular head of state, or a member of royalty, does a walkabout – a journalist at a press conference, a loyal supporter at a party rally. The list is endless. But they all have one thing in common. They don't know they're a potential assassin.' He took a packet of cigarettes from his pocket and lit one. 'It took us ten months to perfect the device. There were times when I despaired that we'd ever get it right. But we did. Very effectively, as I think you'll agree.'

'And you've been using the local Indians for the experiments?'

'They regard me as a friend because I've allowed them access across ranchland as a short cut between their villages. It was a simple task for the *vaqueiros* to bushwhack lone Indians and bring them back here where they'd be kept under sedation until they were needed. After each experiment the bodies were dumped into a river a few miles away. The piranhas destroyed any evidence that could have incriminated us. The Yanomamo believe that they were taken by evil spirits. They're a bunch of gullible savages, but they've served their purpose.'

The door opened behind the partition and four *vaqueiros* entered the room to remove the bodies. 'I was given the necessary authorization before I left Washington either to sanction or veto the next stage of the operation, depending on the effectiveness of today's demonstration,' Jackson said to Caldwell. 'I'm sure they'll be as impressed as I was, once I've briefed them in full. Needless to say, you have the green light to go ahead with the assassination on Independence Day in five days' time.' Jackson removed a file from his attaché case and handed it to Caldwell. 'That contains details of the man we've chosen to carry it out. As you said earlier, just another nondescript Joe Citizen. Destroy the folder and its contents

85

before you leave for New York. And now, if you'll excuse me, I've got to get back to Caracas by nightfall.' He indicated the stone steps. 'I'll let you lead the way.'

Dixon was waiting by the Mercedes when they emerged from the *fazenda*. He opened the back door. 'Contact me once you arrive in New York,' Jackson told Caldwell, who'd remained on the verandah.

'You can count on it,' Caldwell replied brusquely then turned sharply on his heels and went back into the house.

'I'll be leaving for New York in the morning,' Caldwell said to Dixon.

'What do you want me to do?' Dixon asked, pouring himself a measure from the bottle of Jack Daniel's he'd taken from the liquor cabinet in the corner of the lounge.

'I want you to remain here and co-ordinate the search for Louise Carneiro,' Caldwell said. 'Draft in as many men as you want, but it's imperative we intercept her before she can reach the authorities.'

'Assuming she has Donald Brennan's diary with her,' Dixon said.

'We already know the diary wasn't among his possessions,' Caldwell said. 'That means it was either lost in the river when he drowned or, more plausibly, that he gave it to her for safe-keeping before his death. And if she does have it, he'd have told her to get it to the American Embassy in Rio if anything were to happen to him.'

'He could have sent it there himself before he died,' Dixon suggested.

'Then why did she disappear so suddenly?' Caldwell challenged. 'No, she's got to have it with her. I'd stake my life on it. I want it found!'

'I'll get on to it right away,' Dixon said.

'I still think she'll turn to Kelly McBride for help,' Caldwell said thoughtfully. 'She's Carneiro's oldest friend out here. Not only that, Carneiro doesn't speak any English. McBride could be very useful to her when it comes to translating the contents of the diary.'

'I've already got men watching the harbour around the clock,' Dixon told him. 'They'll tail McBride the moment she returns to Boa Vista. So if Carneiro goes to her, they'll know about it.'

'Tell them to be extra vigilant now that she's teamed up with Brennan's brother,' Caldwell said. 'The guy's a cop.'

'You think he suspects anything?' Dixon asked.

'Why should he? There was nothing suspicious about his brother's death. It was an accident. Even he can't argue with the autopsy report.'

'What if Carneiro does make contact with them? As you said, the guy's a cop. If we start killing cops, the local authorities will have to investigate.'

'You've got your orders,' Caldwell said sharply. 'Kill Carneiro and destroy the diary before it can fall into the wrong hands. And if McBride and Brennan get in the way, kill them too.'

'Consider it done,' Dixon said.

6

Brennan stood silently beside the pyre the villagers had built in the centre of the *shabono*: six tiers of interlaced logs covered in a thick carpet of brushwood and topped with a cushion of dry leaves. Bundles of kindling lay nearby, which he assumed would cover Donald's body. He looked around slowly at the villagers, who were watching him from their houses. The *shabono* was shrouded in an eerie silence; even the surrounding jungle seemed subdued. There were no children – it was customary for them, and the sick, to leave the village during a cremation as the fumes given off by a burning corpse were a contaminant which might affect them.

Two young men entered the clearing, bearing Donald's body between them. Their faces were painted with red dye and they wore yellow feathers in their ears, with a single feather inserted through the tiny hole that all Yanomamo men have drilled into the tips of their chins. Donald's body was naked, except for a red loincloth, the face smeared with red and black dye, and more patterns on the chest and abdomen. The men placed the body carefully on the pyre, added the kindling, then nodded sombrely to Brennan before they withdrew. The *tuxuana* then entered the clearing, flanked by his two most experienced warriors. Their heads were shaved and coloured with red pigment. They too wore feathers in each ear and through the chin. Both carried spears upright in their right hands. The *tuxuana*, by contrast, wore no feathers, nor any pigment, and held a flambeau. The party crossed to the pyre and the two spears were laid at either side of the body. The *tuxuana* handed the flambeau to Brennan then fell back with the warriors to the edge of the clearing.

'You can light the pyre now,' Kelly said beside him.

Brennan nodded, but made no move towards it. It was the moment he'd been dreading. All he had to do was touch the flame to the tinder yet he couldn't do it. It was as if his ankles were shackled. He could feel the eyes of the villagers on him. They couldn't understand his torment. When he ignited the kindling, Donald would be gone for ever and there was still so much left unsaid between them. Now it was too late for that. If only he could have had one last chance of reconciliation. But it had taken Donald's death to spark his conscience. He'd have to live with the guilt for the rest of his life.

'Ray,' Kelly said softly to him, 'let him go.'

Brennan glanced at her. Were his feelings that transparent? Or just to her? He took a hesitant step forward. Then, taking a deep breath, he thrust the flambeau deep into the pyre. Within seconds the flames began to spread hungrily through it, and as he walked away he could hear the brushwood crackling.

'I'm going down to the river,' he said to Kelly. 'I'd like to be alone right now.'

'I understand,' she replied.

He left the *shabono* and walked the short distance to where the *Shamrock Gal* wallowed gently in the silty water. One of the Yanomamo crew was on deck. He waved to Brennan, who didn't respond. Instead he thrust his hands into the pockets of his jeans and continued to walk along the bank until it ended in a mass of tangled undergrowth. He decided against trying to go further and sat down on a log, which from its hollowed-out centre, he guessed was being shaped as a canoe.

Removing his sunglasses, he rubbed his eyes with his thumb and forefinger and for the first time in years found himself craving a cigarette. But he knew that if he had one, he'd take only a few puffs before tossing it away – he'd long since lost the taste for them. Gillian had persuaded him to give up

89

smoking when they'd first starting going out. At least something constructive had come out of the relationship.

He could clearly remember the night she had died. A wet and windy January evening eight years ago. He'd been out celebrating a colleague's birthday with a few beers at Pete's Tavern on 18th Street. When he'd got home around midnight, five messages had been waiting for him on his answering-machine, all from Donald. The first had been to tell him that Gillian had been killed in a head-on collision with a drunk driver on her way home from work, the others were desperate pleas for him to call the moment he got home. With their parents on holiday in Europe, Donald had no one else to turn to in his despair. But he hadn't returned Donald's calls that night. Instead he'd unplugged the telephone and retreated into the lounge with a bottle of Jack Daniel's. The bourbon had gone some way to numb the pain, but it couldn't erase it. Next day he'd felt strong enough to ring his brother, but even then the conversation had been strained. He didn't want Donald to intrude on his own grief, and had refused to see him. Their parents had returned to New York later that day. He wouldn't see them either or attend Gillian's funeral.

If only he'd reached out to Donald after Gillian's death, instead of pushing him even further away . . . He wondered if he would eventually have come to his senses if Donald had not died. Death was a powerful catalyst when it came to examining personal feelings – both towards the deceased and towards others. He'd never been close to his mother, even as a child, had always turned to his father. He'd come to realize that his father had had two distinct but opposite personalities: in a courtroom he was strong, determined and unyielding, while at home he was content just to ride with the tide, irrespective of where it took him, the tide being Brennan's mother. It hadn't been apparent until after his father's death, however, just how important his quiet inner strength had been to her. She was lost without him, had withdrawn into herself, and there were times Brennan could almost have believed she'd given up on life. But she found a new passion: her grandson. Jason would live with her now that Donald was dead. Which was just as well, really. He himself couldn't have looked after the boy, not with his work schedule and he hardly knew him. But he'd change all that. He'd visit him, take him places – a ball game, maybe the movies. Only that would mean more contact with his mother. Could he handle that?

The question was still lingering uncomfortably in his mind when he sensed someone behind him. He looked round. The boy was about the same age as Jason, naked, apart from the customary penis sheath, and carrying a fibre-glass fishing-rod, which seemed out of place: he would have expected the locals to fish with a hand-carved rod.

The boy tapped the rod excitedly and said something. Brennan gave him a helpless shrug, which seemed to amuse the child for he laughed, his white teeth contrasting vividly with his honey-brown skin. Then he hurried away into the undergrowth.

Brennan got to his feet and looked in the direction of the *shabono*. Although he couldn't see the village from where he was standing, smoke from the pyre was drifting over the trees. He contemplated returning but dismissed the idea. He glanced at the *Shamrock Gal*. The Yanomamo was no longer on deck and there was no sign of Kelly either. Since those unsettling thoughts the previous night, he'd managed to suppress any feelings he had for her. He would be gone in the next couple of days. Normally that would have suited him perfectly. A one-night stand with no comebacks. But Kelly meant more to him that that. *She meant more to him than what?* Certainly not Gillian. Nobody would ever mean more to him than Gillian. *Did it matter what Kelly meant to him?* No, because once he'd returned to the States he'd never see her again.

A sudden scream from further down the bank interrupted his reverie. The boy with the fishing rod! He sprinted towards where it had come from, crashing through undergrowth until he found himself in another clearing. The boy was twenty yards ahead, his hands clutching the rod, which was bent almost double, his heels dug into the ground. The boy glanced at him, eyes wide with fear as he was dragged ever closer towards the river.

'Let go of the rod!' Brennan shouted, and ran to where the boy was struggling a few feet from the water's edge. There was a sharp jerk on the line and he grabbed the child around the waist to prevent him from pitching headlong into the river. He released one hand from the boy's stomach, clamped it tightly around the rod and immediately felt an incredible pull. He was amazed that the boy had managed to hold on for so long. He was going to have to help him land whatever was lurking beneath the murky water. He spooled out some line and felt the pressure relax. The boy grinned at him excitedly, as if they were playing some game. Brennan gritted his teeth as he tried to reel in the line. At first it wouldn't budge but then the handle turned.

The fish burst out of the water but immediately disappeared again. Brennan estimated it at about five feet long. He could sense the boy's determination not to give up and found himself digging his heels into the mud to get a better footing from which to fight the monster. He could feel the sweat streaming down his face and he blinked it away irritably as it trickled into his eyes.

The struggle went on for several minutes until he could feel the fish beginning to tire, which increased his urge to land it. The monster surfaced again, now only a few yards from the bank, thrashed its head wildly from side to side, then abruptly dived beneath the water again. But Brennan knew now that he had the upper hand. It was only a matter of time before he reeled it in.

The end came quicker than he expected and the exhausted fish was finally hauled into the shallows. He'd never seen anything like it. Around five feet long, with a brown back and silver underbelly, the tail was spherical and there were two large fan-shaped dorsal and anal fins at the base of its back. He knew little about fish, apart from treating himself to the occasional turbot or Atlantic salmon whenever he and Lou Monks were near the Fulton fish market on South Street during one of their graveyard shifts.

Out of the corner of his eye, he saw a Yanomamo, armed with a cudgel, hurry into the shallows and rain several blows on the beast until it was still. Then he grabbed it by the gills and dragged it ashore. Only then did Brennan realize that several onlookers were standing behind him, Kelly among them. He'd been too preoccupied with landing the fish to notice her. The boy tugged at his sleeve but his grin of triumph was instantly replaced by a look of fear and he ran off towards the undergrowth. A man had thrust his way through the onlookers, was chasing him and caught him quickly. He slapped the child across the back of his head, knocked him to the ground and continued to hit him. Brennan darted over, grabbed the man's arm and shoved him away. The Yanomamo jabbed a finger angrily at him and shouted something, but when he tried to get at the boy again, Brennan blocked his path and shook his head.

'That's Maowa, his father,' Kelly said. Maowa turned his anger on Kelly and pointed at the boy, who was now hovering uncertainly behind Brennan. 'His son was supposed to have left the *shabono* with the other children before the cremation,' she told Brennan. 'Instead he doubled back and took the fishing rod from his father's house without permission and came down here.'

'That still doesn't give him the right to beat the kid like that,' Brennan said angrily.

'Yes, it does,' she replied. 'He can hit the boy as much as he wants, just as he can hit his wife if she upsets him. And by preventing him from punishing his son, you're disgracing him in front of his peers.' She put her hand lightly on Brennan's arm. 'If this was New York, you'd have every right to protect the boy from an abusive father. But it isn't, and you have to respect Yanomamo customs, however they seem to you.'

Brennan looked from Maowa to the boy, who was still standing behind him. Reluctantly he stepped aside to allow the boy's father past him. Maowa spoke tersely to the boy, who scampered away. The fishing rod was handed to him, then he spoke to Brennan and pointed to the fish.

'He wants to know what you want to do with the pirarucu,' Kelly translated. 'You caught it, so that makes it yours.'

'The kid caught it, I just helped him reel it in,' Brennan said.

'As far as he's concerned, you caught it,' she told him. 'Now, what do you want to do with it?'

'What do you suggest?' Brennan replied.

'You could donate it to the *shabono*. That would go down well.'

'With pleasure,' Brennan replied.

There was a general murmur of approval from the onlookers when she passed on what Brennan had said. But Maowa glowered at him then pushed his way through the crowd before vanishing after his son. Several women picked up the fish between them and carried it off. 'What did you say it was?' he asked Kelly once they were alone.

'A pirarucu. It's said to be the largest freshwater fish in the world and a couple of years ago an eleven footer was caught on the Rio Amazonas. It weighed almost four hundred pounds.'

Brennan whistled softly to himself. 'And I thought this was one big sonofabitch.'

She watched him pick up a flat stone and skim it across the water. His eyes lingered on the ripples it left in its wake. 'Do you want to come back to the *Gal*?' she asked. 'You look like you could use a drink.'

'No,' he replied. 'I'd like to hang out here for a while. But thanks anyway.'

'Sure. You know where to find me if you change your mind.' With that she was gone.

Kelly went below to get her cigarettes. When she returned topside she looked across at the riverbank but couldn't see Brennan behind the thick undergrowth. She sat on the bow deck, her legs dangling over the side, pulled out a cigarette and lit it, dropping the spent match into the turbid water. She sucked deeply on it as she gazed across the river. A couple of

94

children were playing on the opposite bank, while an elderly woman sat nearby, watching them.

Kelly found herself thinking about what Brennan had said earlier. He'd been right: she would never be accepted in the river trader's world and their resentment still hurt after eight years on the river, although she knew the hostility stemmed from fear that she was better than them at their own game. And there were some exceptions who had welcomed her – like Reuben. She'd loved to sit with him at night, either on the *Gal* or on his boat, while he reminisced about his forty years on the river. She'd never tired of his stories, even when he'd repeated them endlessly but changed the details each time to make them that bit more exciting. She'd often wondered how many were true. Not that it had ever mattered.

How often had Reuben told her she should find herself a good man to settle down with and give her the kind of life she deserved? It had been almost a paternal plea. He'd set her up on several dates with some of the more affluent businessmen in Boa Vista, and she'd gone along with it to please him but had made sure nothing had ever come of it.

She knew where her thoughts were leading and was quick to dismiss them. She liked Ray Brennan but that was as far as it went. Or did she just *want* to believe that, knowing he'd be gone in a couple of days? She couldn't get over how relaxed she felt in his company. She hadn't felt that way since . . . well, since Reuben died. But with Reuben it had been completely platonic. *It's the same with Ray,* she was quick to remind herself.

'That drink still on offer?'

She jumped, startled by his voice. 'Ray . . . I wasn't expecting you,' she stammered, then scrambled up.

'You OK?' he asked. 'You look a bit flushed.'

'It's the sun,' she replied quickly, knowing how lame it sounded, then tossed the cigarette over the side of the boat. 'I thought you wanted to be on your own.'

'I did, but it was beginning to get me down.'

'Where do you want to have that drink? Up here or in the cabin?'

'It's such a beautiful day, let's have it up here,' he said. 'If you can handle the sun, that is.'

His gentle teasing wasn't lost on her. 'I'm sure I can find a bit of shade,' she said, with a fleeting smile then disappeared below deck to fetch the bottle of Jack Daniel's from her cabin.

'I guess if you want a bath around here, you just jump in the river,' he said, as she tipped a generous amount of bourbon into a glass and handed it to him.

'I wouldn't advise it,' she replied, pouring a shot for herself. 'You're likely to come out dirtier than you went in.'

'So where d'you go?'

'There's a cascade pool not far from here. It's clean, and also pretty cold – but refreshing.'

'I'm going to take a dip after I've had this,' Brennan announced. 'You'll have to point me in the right direction.'

'I'll come with you.'

'In . . . the water?' he said uncertainly.

'Don't worry, I won't corrupt you,' she said. 'I'll be sure to keep on my T-shirt and knickers. And I'd advise you to keep your pants on as well. As a precaution against the candiru.'

'What's that?' Brennan asked suspiciously.

'A parasitic fish which penetrates the gills of larger fish then extends the barbs on its own gill covers to hold it in place while it sucks the host's blood. It also has a nasty habit of entering human, or animal, orifices. As you can imagine, it's excruciatingly painful once the barbs have been extended. Normally it would have to be surgicially removed.'

Brennan shifted uncomfortably on the bench. 'On second thoughts, I think I'll skip it.'

'You'll be perfectly safe as long as you stay covered up,' she assured him. She swallowed the bourbon. 'I'll get us a couple of towels from my cabin.' With that she skipped down the stairs.

Moments later one of the Yanomamo emerged from the hatch, hurried across the deck, down the ramp and ran towards the *shabono*. 'He's gone to fetch your holdall,' she said, following Brennan's stare. She was carrying two towels with a clean T-shirt and her dungarees. She handed one of

96

the towels to Brennan, who took a mouthful of bourbon before pushing the glass under the bench to finish when they got back. When the Yanomamo returned with his holdall he took out the only T-shirt he had left, having traded the others with the Yanomamo the day before.

'Are you coming?' Kelly called from the bank.

The thought of stripping down to his underpants in front of her was making him feel awkward, but he went down the ramp and followed her along the riverbank, in the opposite direction to where he'd helped the boy land the pirarucu. A trail had been hacked out of the undergrowth and she led the way down the narrow path until they came to the edge of the cascade pool. It was like a tranquil millpond, surrounded by a rainbow of multicoloured flowers, with a gentle chute of shimmering water tumbling down from an overhanging ledge. He couldn't believe the crystal clarity of the water, with the heavy silt-laden river only a few hundred yards away.

'It's beautiful, isn't it?' Kelly said.

'It's incredible,' he agreed, putting the T-shirt and towel on a rock behind him. He watched her strip off her jeans, then fold them up neatly, and put them on the ground. Without thinking, he was running his eyes the length of her bronzed legs and had to admit that he liked what he saw. Then he realized she'd seen him and he immediately looked away like a naughty schoolboy. She dived into the water and swam towards the waterfall. He removed his jeans and T-shirt then crouched down and traced his fingertips in the water. It was ice cold. Best just to take the plunge. He threw himself off the rock, wrapped his arms around his knees in mid-air and hit the water with a great splash. For those first few seconds he doubted whether the water could have been any colder had he jumped off a glacier into the Antarctic. But his body quickly adjusted to the temperature and he swam over to where Kelly was already shampooing her hair beside the waterfall. Eyes closed, she put out a hand until she could feel the cascading water, then edged forward under it, tilted her head back and let it rinse her hair. Then she ducked under the water, emerging seconds later with a wide grin.

97

'You show me any five-star hotel in the world with a better shower than this!' she said, pushing her wet hair back over her head.

'You've got me there,' he replied.

It was then that she noticed the tattoo on his arm: a graceful white dove in full flight with an olive branch in its beak and the words *Freebird Flies Forever* in red italics underneath it. 'I take it there's a story behind this?'

'"Freebird". Lynyrd Skynyrd.' He waited for a response. There was none. 'One of the greatest R&B bands to ever come out of the States,' he said. She stared blankly at him. 'Several members of the band were killed in a plane crash in seventy-seven, including their lead singer. I had this done as a tribute to the guy.'

'They obviously meant a lot to you,' she said, after a moment.

They were so close that he could smell the scent of her newly washed hair. Her head was tilted fractionally as she looked into his eyes. He knew what would happen if he reached out a hand to touch her. It was all he had to do. But he couldn't. Something was holding him back.

'Ray!'

Her anxious voice shattered the silence and her eyes flicked past him. He turned: four Indians were standing in the clearing close to the pool. He recognized only one. Maowa. Their heads were shaved and anointed with red dye, and there were red streaks on their faces and chests. All were armed with spears. Maowa stepped forward and stabbed his into the ground. He spoke angrily, his finger constantly jabbing in Brennan's direction. Then he jerked the spear from the ground and the men disappeared back into the undergrowth.

'What did he say?' Brennan asked.

'That you've dishonoured him in the eyes of the villagers by stopping him disciplining his son. Until he can get even with you the other men will carry on humiliating him. That's why he's challenged you.'

'To a club fight?' Brennan asked, in trepidation.

'It's possible,' she replied grimly then added, 'but unlikely.

It's my guess it'll be a chest-pounding duel. Any contest of this sort has to be approved by the *tuxuana* – and he likes you. He told me that himself, and I don't think he'd agree to a club fight if you were involved. Donald got himself into a few scrapes over the years, but they were always sorted out with chest-pounding.'

'And what does it involve?' he asked.

'You take turns in punching each other on the chest. The winner is the one who stays on his feet. You're far stronger than Maowa, so you shouldn't have any trouble winning.'

'Except he's got experience behind him,' Brennan pointed out.

'I'm sure you've thrown a few punches in your time,' she said, with a half-smile, then swam across the pool and pulled herself out on to the ledge where she'd left her clothes.

He swam after her. 'Am I expected to lose?'

She looked puzzled. 'What do you mean?'

'Do I let him save face and knock me down, or do I try and win?'

'You take a dive and you can walk back to Boa Vista,' she said. 'You saw the way he laid into his son this afternoon. I've seen him hit his wife with a piece of burning firewood. He's a bully, and it's time he was put in his place.'

Brennan didn't say anything. There was no need. He swam over to where he'd left his clothes and ducked into the trees to get dressed. He dropped his jeans and T-shirt on the ground and began to towel himself down. He was about to reach for his T-shirt when a movement caught his eye and he stumbled backwards in horror as a spear lanced the ground inches away from where his clothes lay. An Indian came silently from the thicket in front of him.

Then Brennan saw the snake. It had been concealed underneath his jeans and the tip of the spear was embedded just behind its head. It was writhing from side to side, trying desperately to free itself. As the man eased the spear carefully from the ground, the thrashing snake still skewered to it, Brennan noticed the distinctive scar on the back of his hand. The man turned away and melted back into the undergrowth.

Brennan was still staring at the spot where the man had vanished when he heard Kelly calling him. He retrieved his jeans gingerly, pulled them on, then slipped into his clean T-shirt. He only tugged on his boots after he'd turned them upside down and shaken them vigorously.

'My God, you look like you've just seen a ghost,' she said anxiously, when he appeared. 'What happened?'

He told her.

'And you're sure it wasn't one of the Yanomamo with Maowa?' she asked, when he'd finished.

'This guy had more red pigment on his face. And he had hair. No, it wasn't one of them, I'm sure of that.'

'What colour was the snake?' she asked.

'Kind of greenish-brown with white markings on its back,' he said.

'It sounds like a fer-de-lance. You probably disturbed it when you threw your clothes on the ground. There's every chance it would have bitten you.'

'The guy saved my life,' Brennan said.

'He did, considering I don't have any fer-de-lance anti-venom on the *Gal*. I thought I did, until I checked the medical kit. I'd guess one of the crew traded it with the *garimpeiros* – probably for a bottle of *cachaca*. And I've got a pretty good idea which one it was.' She gestured to the pathway leading back to the riverbank. 'Are you up to the return journey?'

'Yeah, let's go,' he replied, then looked across at the trees one last time. No one was there. He followed closely in Kelly's footsteps, his eyes fixed on the ground.

'Oh, that's all we need,' she exclaimed despairingly as they got to the riverbank. 'What's *he* doing here?'

Brennan saw a second boat moored close to the *Shamrock Gal*. It was roughly the same size, but in a considerably worse state of repair. The sun had taken its toll on the faded blue hull and there were patches where the paint had flaked off, revealing the bare wood beneath. The railing was rusted and a section of the bow was missing altogether. Several wooden crates were stacked on top of each other on the aft deck and the vessel was listing noticeably in the water. 'Do I detect that he's not exactly a friend of yours?'

'No, he's not,' she retorted. 'His name's Cesar. He's been doing this run for over thirty years and he cut me a bit of slack when I first started out – he was one of the few who did.'

'So you owe him for letting you share his route?'

'I've paid my dues,' she said vehemently. 'We made a deal that he'd take twenty per cent of my takings for the first two years then we'd be quits. And now we are. I don't owe him a thing.'

'OK, OK,' he said, anxious to dispel the sudden tension.

'I'm sorry, I didn't mean to fly off the handle like that,' she said. 'I'm just so used to sticking up for myself out here.'

'Kelly!' a voice boomed from the entrance of the *shabono*. A corpulent man in his mid-sixties, with a sparse white beard and a sweat-stained Panama hat approached them, his arms held out towards her. Brennan saw the look of disgust on Kelly's face when he embraced her. She pointed towards him and told Cesar who he was. The smile faltered on the other man's face and he shook Brennan's hand solemnly. He spoke in Portuguese and touched the tattered rim of his hat.

'He's offering his condolences for your loss,' Kelly said.

Cesar said something to which Kelly responded with a forced smile. 'We've been invited aboard his boat for a drink,' she told Brennan. 'And knowing how much he can knock back, we might be there for a while.'

'I'm not drinking that damn *cachaca*,' Brennan said forcefully.

'I'll get the Jack Daniel's for you. You go with Cesar. I'll be back.' She hurried off in the direction of the *Shamrock Gal* before he could argue.

Cesar paused at the foot of the rickety ramp leading on to his boat and beckoned to Brennan. '*Vem comigo. Vem comigo.*'

Brennan cast a despairing look at the *Shamrock Gal* but there was no sign of Kelly. He crossed to where Cesar was waiting to take him aboard.

★

They spent the next three hours on Cesar's boat. At first Kelly had translated everything into English for Brennan's benefit, but then her enthusiasm had waned and after an hour she'd all but given up the struggle to keep him in the conversation. Not that it had bothered him. He hadn't been remotely interested in the gossip about the other traders that seemed to be Cesar's speciality. He wasn't even sure Kelly had been either, but she'd listened dutifully while constantly plying the man with *cachaca*.

Then, when she'd got Cesar canned, it dawned on Brennan that she'd taken over the talking, often leaning forward to catch the man's mumbled reply. She was up to something but it was pointless trying to work out what as he didn't understand the lingo. Instead he concentrated on the cockroaches, stamping on any that came within striking distance of his chair as they scurried across the moonlit deck. But as the level of bourbon steadily decreased in the bottle he was nursing, his success rate became ever more erratic.

By the time Kelly announced it was time to leave, Cesar was muttering incoherently to himself as he lay in an inebriated heap on the deck and Brennan had long since given up his one-man crusade.

He felt unsteady on his feet as he made his way across the deck to where Kelly was waiting to help him down the ramp.

'Another guy who can't hold his liquor,' she said, with a mischievous smile, once they were safely on dry land.

'What do you expect? I polished off most of the bottle on an empty stomach,' he replied. 'How much *cachaca* did you put away tonight?'

'Enough to know I'm going to be sorry in the morning,' she said, touching her head. 'I set out to get Cesar drunk tonight.'

'Yeah, I guessed you were up to something.'

'I needed to find out when he'd next be visiting the various *shabonos* in the area,' she said. 'Now I can reschedule my own plans, and make sure I get to each at least a day ahead of him.'

'That's despicable,' Brennan said, but he was smiling.

'That's the way it works out here.'

'Of course,' he replied, then looked across at the entrance to the *shabono*. 'Am I going to be safe sleeping in there tonight? Maowa isn't going to slit my throat while I'm asleep?'

'You'll be quite safe,' she said. 'In fact, he'll probably have somebody watch over you tonight. It's in his interests to make sure nothing happens to you before he can take up his challenge.'

'Perhaps that guy at the pool was working for him, after all,' Brennan mused thoughtfully.

'Perhaps,' Kelly agreed, then put her hand to her mouth to stifle a yawn. 'Well, I'm going to turn in. Will you be able to find your hammock OK?'

'I'll manage.'

'Good night, then.' For a moment she wanted to kiss him. Then, as quickly as the thought had entered her mind, she crossed to where the *Shamrock Gal* was rocking gently in the dark water.

7

It was a strange dream. He was back in the Manhattan art gallery where he'd first met Gillian, which specialized in abstract expressionism. Instead, though, the walls were lined with paintings of Yanomamo warriors with red pigment smeared over their faces. They were all carrying spears. One was the man who'd saved his life at the cascade pool. Only he did not know which he was.

Then he heard the rhythmic clicking of stiletto heels, just as he had the day he and Lou Monks had gone to investigate the break-in. And, also like that day, all he could see were her legs as she walked slowly down the wooden stairs, exquisite legs, sheathed in black stockings, and as more of her slender figure came into view he waited breathlessly to catch the first glimpse of her face. Finally he saw it. Only it wasn't Gillian. It was Kelly. She crouched at the foot of the stairs and a fer-de-lance emerged from the sleeve of her jacket. It slithered across the floor towards a painting, wriggled effortlessly up the wall, and as it slid over the the canvas it became part of the picture. Yet even though it was now only a painted snake, it continued to move closer to the man. Brennan wanted to call out to him, to warn him, but he couldn't speak. The snake bit the man's leg, then faded from the painting. The red pigment began to trickle down the canvas but before he could see the man's face, Kelly put her hand lightly on his cheek and turned his face towards her. As she was about to kiss him, he felt a sharp tug on his hair. Then another tug, this time more painful. And somewhere in the distance, the sound of laughter.

With great reluctance he forced himself to drift out of his dream and as his eyelids flickered open he found himself staring into two dark eyes, which were peering back at him from beneath a golden mane of shoulder-length hair. They weren't human eyes.

Panic took hold and, forgetting where he was, he twisted away violently from the creature, overbalanced in the hammock, and ended up on the ground. There was more laughter and when he sat up slowly he saw several Yanomamo children standing around him. Then he discovered what he'd seen when he'd opened his eyes: it was a Golden Lion tamarin, attached to a chain which one of the youths was holding. The tiny monkey was clearly agitated and every few seconds it let out a piercing shriek, which drilled through Brennan's aching head.

'Shut that monkey up!' he yelled furiously, then winced as a bolt of pain shot through his head. A woman from one of the neighbouring houses, alerted by the sound of his raised voice, shouted at the giggling youths who ran away. She stared at Brennan for a moment, then shook her head and went back to the food she was preparing.

Brennan could understand her reaction. If he looked anything like he smelt, she'd every reason to be disgusted. He glanced at his watch and groaned at the time: 6.08 a.m. He got to his feet and set off for the river.

When he came out of the undergrowth, he was surprised to see that Cesar's boat had gone. The guy had been totally skulled the previous night. How could he have recovered so quickly?

'It looks like you had a pretty good time last night.'

Kelly was leaning on the bow rail of the *Shamrock Gal*, a faint smile on her lips.

'What are you doing up this early?' he asked. 'And why are you so goddamn cheerful?'

'I always get up around now,' she replied, 'and I'm cheerful because it looks like it's going to be another beautiful day.'

'What about the hangover you were predicting last night?'

'I must have tossed more *cachaca* overboard than I'd originally thought.'

'So that's the secret,' he said.

'You have to look out for yourself here. I'm not going to let my guard down by getting pissed in front of these bastards. I have enough trouble with them when I'm sober.'

'What happened to your pal Cesar?'

'He's got a couple of crewmen who handle the boat and any business whenever he's had a skinful and needs to sleep it off the next day,' she said. 'I doubt he'll surface before midday, not after the amount he got through last night.'

'Do they all drink like him?' he asked.

'I know some traders who'd regard that as a night of abstinence,' she said. 'Come on, breakfast's about to be served.'

'Breakfast?' he said. 'You must be joking.'

'You haven't eaten anything since yesterday afternoon,' she reminded him. 'It'll do you a power of good to get some solid food into you.'

Once aboard the *Shamrock Gal* he forgot his queasiness. There was a rich vegetable stew, made with carrots, cabbage, black beans and sweet potatoes, then coffee and fresh fruit. He felt considerably better once he'd consumed a generous helping of the stew, two mugs of coffee and a thick wedge of watermelon. Afterwards, he stood up. 'I'm going to have to take off this T-shirt. It stinks of bourbon.'

'I had noticed,' she said. 'Go and take another dip in the cascade pool. I was up there earlier. It's beautiful at this time of morning.'

'After what happened there yesterday, I think I'll settle for a wash in the river. See you later.'

He returned to the *shabono* to collect his other dirty T-shirt and was about to make for the river when he glanced at where the funeral pyre had been the previous afternoon. All that remained was a rectangular pile of smouldering ashes. He was about to take a closer look, then thought better of it and walked back to the river, where he pulled off his T-shirt and washed first himself, and then the T-shirts. As he was wringing them out he noticed the young Yanomamo woman

106

standing silently behind him. She was staring at the tattoo on his arm. She said something to him.

'She's asking you whether the dove's spirit is inside your arm,' Kelly called down from the *Shamrock Gal*.

'I'll leave you to explain it to her,' he replied, then nodded genially to the young woman before returning to the *shabono*, where he hung his wet T-shirts over the edge of the hammock. The couple in the adjoining house also noticed the tattoo, which quickly became a talking point as word spread through the *shabono*. A small group of villagers congregated outside the guest house and talked excitedly among themselves. An old man stepped forward, tapped his own arm and pointed to the tattoo.

'It's a dove. A bird.' Brennan made flapping gestures with his arms, and the onlookers burst into fits of laughter. Then he saw Kelly watching from the entrance of the *shabono*, a lop-sided grin on her face. 'Help me out here, will you?' he pleaded.

'And spoil the show?' she replied.

The *tuxuana*, who'd been watching from his hammock, waited until the onlookers had dispersed before walking over to Brennan. He, too, was intrigued by the tattoo but wanted to know why Brennan had put a dove on his arm rather than a jaguar, which would have frightened away his enemy.

'Tell him about the snake,' Brennan said to Kelly. 'He might know who the guy was. I'd sure like to thank him for saving my life.'

She was recounting the episode to the *tuxuana* when Brennan interrupted, 'Don't forget to mention the scar across the back of his hand,' and ran his finger from knuckle to wrist across the back of his own hand. The *tuxuana* let out a gasp and Kelly had to listen carefully as the words tumbled from his mouth.

'What was that all about?' Brennan asked after the *tuxuana* had gone.

'You're not going to like it,' she said. 'He knows the man you saw at the pool yesterday. But you won't be able to thank him for saving your life. He's dead.'

107

'What?' Brennan asked in horror.

'He was bitten by a snake near that pool . . . four years ago.'

'Four years ago?' Brennan repeated disbelievingly. 'So what you're saying is a ghost saved my life yesterday.'

'I told you you weren't going to like it,' she replied.

'Oh, come on, Kelly,' Brennan said. 'I'm as open-minded as the next guy, but I sure as hell don't buy any of this hogwash about the spirit of some dead Indian watching over the pool.'

'I'm just telling you what the *tuxuana* told me. I'm not asking you to believe it.'

'Well, I don't,' came the firm reply. 'The guy was as much flesh and blood as either of us. I should know, I was standing as close to him as I am to you. OK, so maybe he's not from this village. He could be from one of the neighbouring villages. Perhaps he was on his way back home, or perhaps he was going to another village for some feast or something. I don't know. You said that kind of thing happens a lot out here.'

'It's OK, Ray, you don't have to convince me he was real. But, then, perhaps you're not trying to convince *me*. Perhaps you're trying to convince yourself.'

'I know what I saw, Kelly,' he said tersely. 'And it wasn't any damn ghost.'

'I believe you. Now let's drop it, all right?'

He raked his fingers through his hair then exhaled deeply. 'I'm sorry. I guess I'm just a bit tetchy right now. I'm not exactly at my best when I'm nursing a hangover this early in the morning.'

'I'd never have guessed,' she replied, with a good-humoured smile. 'Why don't you put your head down for a few hours? There's not much else to do right now.'

'I won't get any sleep here,' he said, jerking his thumb at the hammock. 'There's too much noise.'

'I meant on the *Gal*. You can use my bed. Nobody's going to disturb you down there. I'll wake you in good time for the feast this afternoon.'

'Sounds good,' he replied. 'What about you?'

108

'I've got a few things planned. The first being a little chat with the *tuxuana* about his meeting with Cesar yesterday. I want to know what he was selling, and at what price. That way I can undercut him and get the business instead.'

'You ever thought about a career on Wall Street?' Brennan asked.

'Wall Street would be too tame for me,' she said, then pointed to the two T-shirts hanging over the side of the hammock. 'There a washing line on the *Gal*. It's at the side of the wheelhouse. In this weather, they'll be dry in a couple of hours. I'll see you later,' she said, heading for the *tuxuana*'s house.

'Kelly?' he called after her. She paused to look back at him. 'Thanks for everything. I couldn't have done any of it without you. I appreciate it.'

'I should hope so,' she replied with a grin, then walked off.

'Ray?'

Brennan shrugged off Kelly's hand as she shook his shoulder.

'Ray, it's time to wake up.'

He rolled over slowly on to his back and squinted up at her. 'What time is it?'

'One o'clock.'

'Jesus, I've been out cold for hours,' he said, rubbing his eyes.

'Well, now it's time to get up,' she said, dropping one of his dry T-shirts over his face. 'I'll see you up on deck. And don't go back to sleep.'

'The idea never crossed my mind,' he muttered, but when he brushed the T-shirt away from his face Kelly had already gone. Swinging his legs off the bed, he was about to get up when he spotted the bowl and jug of water on the bedside table. He splashed some water over his face, then reached for the towel draped over the arm of the rocking chair. He pulled on his T-shirt and boots then slipped on his sunglasses and made his way up on deck. Kelly was standing at the bow, her hands resting lightly on the railing as she gazed out over the river.

She looked round when she heard his footsteps behind her. 'Back in the land of the living, I see?'

'Yeah, just about,' he replied, his eyes following the smoke that spiralled up from the *shabono* into the clear blue sky. 'How long before this feast gets under way?'

'About an hour,' she replied, as she tugged absently at the bracelet on her wrist.

'Something's bugging you.'

'How do you . . .' She trailed off when she realized what she'd been doing. 'It's Maowa. He went to see the *tuxuana* this morning to get permission to challenge you to a duel. The *tuxuana* summoned me to his house to tell me he's agreed to it. He had no choice. He asked me to tell you that, because when you accept the challenge he can't be seen to be taking sides. As the headman, he has to remain impartial.'

'He's sanctioned a club fight, hasn't he?' Brennan said, already fearing the worst.

'Maowa did request a duel with clubs, but the *tuxuana* wouldn't agree to it. That caused a lot of resentment among Maowa's supporters, who felt he'd been further humiliated, but the *tuxuana*'s decision can't be questioned. So Maowa had to swallow his pride and approach the *tuxuana* again, this time for permission to challenge you to a chest-pounding duel. He agreed to that.'

'It's what you figured would happen,' Brennan said.

'Except I didn't know that Maowa has never been defeated in a chest-pounding contest. And I get the impression he's been in quite a few. They already regard the outcome as a foregone conclusion. It's up to you to prove them wrong.'

'Easier said than done,' Brennan said. 'So when is it supposed to take place?'

'Within the next half-hour. I would have woken you earlier, but the *tuxuana* only told me a few minutes ago. Normally these kinds of duels are held after the feast, but because the feast's being held in Donald's honour – and you're his brother – the *tuxuana* wants it out of the way first. A messenger will come to summon you to the *shabono* shortly before the contest's due to begin.'

'You're coming as well, aren't you?'

'We all are,' she said, indicating her two crewmen, who were standing beside the wheelhouse. She gestured one forward. 'The *tuxuana* asked me to explain the basics to you. Kanibawa here is an experienced fighter. He'll show you how to stand to receive a punch, and the best way to throw one of your own. It's really quite straightforward.' She spoke to the Yanomamo who stepped forward, his legs apart to gain the best possible footing, and his hands clamped tightly behind his back. 'That's how you stand. You're baring your chest to your opponent, daring him to hit you. The position of the legs is important. If you haven't braced yourself properly for the impact of the punch – both mentally and physically – you'll go down straight away. Don't forget, the Yanomamo are raised on these duels. They know how to deliver a punch. So be prepared for it.' She spoke to the Yanomamo again and he moved forward, placing his clenched fist lightly against Brennan's chest. 'Now he'll demonstrate how to line up the punch, but he won't hit you.' The Yanomamo turned Brennan slightly to the left then placed his fist against his chest again. Then he carefully measured an arm's length distance between himself and Brennan and made several dummy runs by shooting his arm forward, each time stopping short of Brennan's chest. 'Not only do the dummy runs allow you to line up the best possible punch, but it's also an important psychological move. Your opponent has no idea which punch will hit him. It can be unnerving to an inexperienced fighter.'

'Except Maowa doesn't fit into that category, does he?' Brennan said.

'You can beat him, Ray,' she said resolutely. 'You've got a weight advantage over him and that'll certainly work in your favour.'

'And you can be sure he knows every little trick there is to know about outsmarting an opponent,' Brennan countered. 'That's what I call a real advantage. But you're right. I have

111

to draw on my own strengths. It's my only realistic chance of beating him.'

'It looks like you're on,' she said, as a Yanomamo approached the boat. He called up to them from the river-bank. Kelly shouted back and he returned to the *shabono*. 'Are you ready?' she asked Brennan.

'As I'll ever be,' he said.

'Once you reach the *shabono*, go to the guest house. That's where you'll wait for the official challenge to be thrown down, either by Maowa or by one of his supporters.'

Kelly led the way across the deck and down the ramp. Her crew brought up the rear and as they walked towards the *shabono* Brennan had a feeling that this would be his full complement of supporters once the contest began. Assuming, of course, that the two Yanomamo weren't going to defect to the swelled ranks of Maowa's followers once they'd entered the *shabono*. Yet something told him they'd remain in his corner, if only to show their solidarity with Kelly.

She had dropped back behind him before they reached the *shabono* – it would have reflected badly on him in the eyes of the villagers if he'd allowed a woman to walk in ahead of him. Her gesture wasn't lost on him, but Brennan said nothing.

He became aware of the smell of food cooking as he entered the *shabono*. It was a momentary distraction. Nothing more. His mind was elsewhere. Although there was little noise, he could feel the eyes of the whole village on him as he walked purposefully towards the guest house. Once there he stripped off his T-shirt and wiped his sweating face. The waiting was unbearable and he began to understand what it must be like for a boxer in those final minutes in his dressing room before making that walk to the ring – the desire, above all else, to win. He knew there was no real reason for him to be feeling like this. It wasn't as if he would forfeit anything if he lost. He had nothing to prove to these people. Then his eyes went to Kelly. Surely he didn't believe he had something to prove to her? But he couldn't help wondering whether if he lost, she would think less of him.

There was a loud cheer as a figure came out of one of the

houses on the opposite side of the arena. The face was concealed beneath a thick application of red pigment, which was also smeared over the bald head and much of the torso. The man wore a bright yellow feather in his chin and had a multi-coloured armband made of feathers and caiman teeth. He strode across the empty arena and stopped outside the guest house. Brennan couldn't tell whether or not it was Maowa under the paint. The man shouted at him, then turned away and strutted confidently into the centre of the arena where he was surrounded by half a dozen of his closest supporters.

'Was that him?' Brennan asked Kelly.

'Yes. He's just thrown down a challenge to you. It's now up to you to respond by joining him in the arena.'

Brennan wiped his face again with the T-shirt then tossed it on to the hammock and walked over to where Maowa was waiting. The noise around him was deafening as the men of the village shouted excitedly and clattered machetes, spears, or any other implement they could get their hands on. The *tuxuana* appeared and nodded to both men. His face displayed no emotion. He raised his hands and a silence fell over the arena. Then he spoke, and although Brennan didn't understand what was being said, he could see it had annoyed Maowa.

Kelly called to him, 'Normally in these kind of contests, the challenger – if he wants – can deliver several punches in succession to his opponent, as long as his opponent is allowed to reciprocate with the same number of blows. But the *tuxuana* has insisted you take turns in throwing one punch at a time. Maowa and his supporters aren't happy about that. He obviously felt he had a better chance against you if he could deliver several blows at once.'

'Who gets to throw the first punch?' Brennan asked.

'Usually the challenger, but there's no hard and fast rule about that. If you want to go first, I'll ask Maowa if he has any objection. Do you?'

'It makes no difference,' Brennan said, his eyes now fixed on Maowa.

'Good luck,' she said, but he didn't hear her as he stepped forward and stood directly in front of Maowa who indicated to Brennan that he would take the first punch.

Brennan clasped his hands behind his back and watched as Maowa carefully measured out an arm's length distance between them. He tensed his body as Maowa swung his arm towards his chest, but pulled back at the last moment. He did this twice more. The fourth punch slammed into Brennan's chest. He stumbled backwards as a sharp pain shot through him. It had been a hard punch, but Brennan knew that if that was the best Maowa could muster, he had the beating of him. And, judging by the look of unease in Maowa's eyes, he sensed it had indeed been the Indian's best shot. It dawned on him that had Maowa been allowed three or four punches like that straight off, the result could have been different. No wonder the man had been annoyed when the *tuxuana* had amended the rules.

Maowa clamped his hands behind his back, exposing his chest for a return punch. Brennan lined up the Yanomamo's chest, wound up his arm as if he were about to deliver the first ball at the Yankee Stadium and followed through. Unlike his opponent, he didn't bother with dummy blows. His fist hammered into Maowa's chest with such force that the Indian was knocked backwards and almost lost his balance. He managed to regain his footing but the pain was etched on his face as he put his hands on his knees in an attempt to catch his breath.

The cheering had subsided. It was almost as if the crowd anticipated the outcome. One of Maowa's supporters broke free from the circle of onlookers and, as he patted Maowa on the back, as if to give him encouragement, Brennan noticed him transfer something surreptitiously into his opponent's hand. Then the man withdrew and was swallowed up again in the crowd. Brennan's eyes went to Maowa's right hand but it was clenched in a tight fist. He couldn't see what he was holding. He guessed it was probably a palm-sized stone, or perhaps even a spear head, to give added impetus to his punch. It was a desperate tactic, but it didn't unduly surprise him. He found himself wondering how many of Maowa's other chest-pounding contests had been won dishonestly. He doubted that Kelly had seen what had happened – if she had, she'd already have been kicking up a fuss. He thought about telling her, then dismissed the idea. He'd fight his own battles, in his own way. But first he had to prepare himself for Maowa's next punch . . .

Brennan noticed the faint smile on the man's face as he stepped towards him. He lined up his fist with the red bruise on Brennan's chest where the first blow had landed. Brennan sucked in several mouthfuls of air as he tensed his body. When the blow struck, a great cheer went up when he rocked backwards. For a horrifying moment he thought he'd lost his balance but he stamped one foot down on to the ground to prevent himself landing on his backside.

The punch had winded him and he felt nauseous and light-headed as he struggled for breath. He was vaguely aware of a voice shouting above the cheering of the onlookers and when he looked up slowly he saw Maowa gesturing for him to approach and throw another punch. Brennan knew he wanted him to throw his second punch while he was still disorientated – it would be weaker.

'Ray, that's enough,' Kelly said beside him. 'You can back out now without losing face. Kanibawa has offered to take your place.'

'Like hell he will,' Brennan hissed, through clenched teeth, as he slowly straightened up. 'Keep an eye on Maowa's right hand when he goes down.'

'What are you talking about?'

'Just do it.'

Maowa motioned Brennan towards him then patted his chest and said something which was met with a derisive cheer from the villagers. Brennan was still unsteady on his feet and he shook his head, trying to clear his mind. He knew he couldn't take another blow from Maowa so this punch had to count. He already knew what he wanted to do, only he wasn't sure whether his co-ordination would be up to it. But there was only one way to find out. He punched his fist several times into his other hand and stared coldly at Maowa, who was standing with his hands behind his back, his chest extended in an almost comical attitude of contempt. But Brennan found nothing amusing in Maowa's conceit. He lowered his eyes until they were focused on the man's torso. He wasn't interested in the left pectoral muscle, where he'd delivered his last punch. He was aiming for the soft tissue at the base of the breastbone. If he could deliver a punch there, with enough force, it would almost certainly put Maowa out of the fight. He knew it would be considered a foul blow, but under the circumstances he doubted whether Maowa would argue. And it would be worth it just to wipe that smug grin off his face. He placed his fist lightly against Maowa's left pectoral muscle, but his eyes were already focused on the spot he was aiming for. He drew back his arm and powered his fist into Maowa's chest. Maowa howled in agony and stumbled backwards before sinking down on to one knee. As he clamped both hands over his chest the cylindrical stone tumbled from his grasp.

The man who'd slipped the stone to him tried to retrieve it but Kanibawa was quick to block his path. Kelly pointed at it, accusing Maowa loudly of cheating, which outraged the villagers, who were already resentful that a *naba* had defeated one of their own in a traditional Yanomamo duel. They were both jostled by the increasingly volatile crowd, before the *tuxuana* picked up the stone and held it out in the palm of his hand to show that she was speaking the truth. The villagers turned their fury on Maowa, who cowered on the ground, his arms wrapped around his head, as blows rained down on him. The *tuxuana* waded into the mêlée, hauled Maowa roughly to his feet and pointed to the accomplice. The man was shoved forward with such venom that he stumbled off-balance and fell heavily. An over-zealous villager stepped forward and hit him hard on the back with the flat side of his machete blade. The *tuxuana* waved him away angrily and ordered the two men to leave the arena. He crossed to where Brennan and Kelly had discreetly withdrawn from the crowd. His face was earnest when he spoke to Brennan.

'He offered you his apologies for Maowa's dishonesty, which has brought shame on the whole *shabono*, and promised that both men will be punished for what they did,' Kelly translated. 'He's concerned, however, that you now think all Yanomamo are as deceitful as them and that you won't allow Donald's soul to join the other souls in the afterlife above the *shabono*.'

'Tell him I know the Yanomamo to be an honourable people, as they've shown with their generous hospitality and overwhelming kindness towards me since I first arrived here, and that I have every intention of going through with the ceremony.'

The *tuxuana*'s face remained expressionless when Kelly translated Brennan's words, then he pointed to the red welt on Brennan's chest. 'He asked if you knew that Maowa had the stone before he punched you the second time,' Kelly said to Brennan. 'I told him you did. He wants to know why you didn't call a stop to the fight when you saw the stone being passed to him. Why did you risk injury by carrying on?'

'It was a risk I was willing to take to beat him at his own game,' Brennan replied. 'My second punch looked innocuous enough, but it was just as illegal as his. And a hell of a lot more painful. It was the only way I was going to put him down, and hurt him at the same time.'

'What did you do?' Kelly asked. Brennan told her. She spoke at length to the *tuxuana*, who nodded in Brennan's direction, as if condoning what he'd just said, before heading off to deal with Maowa and his helpmate.

'He seemed to take that calmly, considering how angry he was with Maowa for cheating,' Brennan said. 'Or is it all right for an outsider to bend the rules?'

'You don't think I told him all that, do you?' she said. 'I told him that, like all great warriors from over the seas, you believe in the honour of defeating your opponent in battle and not by default.'

'It's a bit corny, isn't it?'

'Maybe it is to you, but not to the Yanomamo,' she replied. 'The more courageous a tribe is in battle, the more the

117

Yanomamo will respect them for their valour. And that includes some of their bitterest enemies.'

'So what you're saying is, if you'd told him the truth, I'd be in the same boat as Maowa right now?'

'You're a *naba*. The *tuxuana* has no authority over you. The worst that could have happened to you would have been your expulsion from the *shabono*.'

'What's going to happen to them?' Brennan asked, looking across to where the two men were standing, their heads bowed in shame, before the *tuxuana*. Apart from a few children play-fighting in the centre of the clearing, and several women tending the clay pots that simmered over glowing embers, the whole village was gathered outside the *tuxuana* house to listen to what was being said.

'They'll probably be banished from the *shabono*,' she replied. 'Maybe permanently, but more likely for a month. Two at the most.'

Brennan went slowly to the guest house where he pulled on his T-shirt, then leaned against one of the front posts, his arms folded across his chest, and watched the proceedings. The *tuxuana*'s anger was evident as he berated the two men. A sudden cheer erupted from the onlookers but when Maowa tried to speak the *tuxuana* chopped his hand down sharply. There would be no further discussion. The crowd began to disperse and the two men walked back despondently to their neighbouring houses. Neither spoke.

Kelly broke away from the few remaining villagers still congregated outside the *tuxuana*'s house and crossed to the guest house.

'Well, what happened?' Brennan asked.

'They've been banished for a month,' she replied, 'but some of the older ones think they've got off lightly. But the matter's now closed.'

'When do they have to leave?'

'Before the feast,' she said.

'Are their families going with them?'

'It looks that way,' she said, as Maowa emerged from his house with his wife and children at his side. The other family

118

followed closely behind them. 'The wives would have known their husbands were going to be punished for what they did.'

Neither man looked at Brennan as they passed the guest house, but Maowa's son did. As the boy turned his head Brennan saw the dark, discoloured bruise on his cheek. He said something to Brennan, but Maowa grabbed him roughly by the arm and led him away.

'What did he say?' Brennan asked Kelly, once the two families had gone.

'Nothing,' she replied.

'Kelly, what did he say?' he demanded.

'That he hates you for the shame you've brought on his family.'

'I was only trying to save him from getting a beating. If I hadn't stopped his father when I did—'

'You did what you thought was right at the time, and that's all that matters,' she cut in.

'But it was still wrong. That's what you're really saying, isn't it?'

'I'm saying that in the eyes of the Yanomamo you were wrong to interfere. But you weren't to know that, were you? You have different values. In New York you'd have been in the right, but not out here.'

'And where exactly do your values lie?' he asked, holding her stare.

'I'd say that all depended on where I was,' she replied, then gestured to an approaching Yanomamo resplendent in red dye and brightly coloured feathers. 'It looks like the feast's about to begin. But first you've got to complete the ceremonial rites. That's why the *hekura*'s here.'

'The medicine man?'

She nodded. The *hekura* spoke at length, then clapped his hands together and beckoned Brennan to follow him.

'What did he say?' Brennan whispered to Kelly as they followed him to a hollowed-out log, which had already been placed in the clearing.

'He was explaining what you have to do. The remaining fragments of bone have been retrieved from the ashes and

119

placed in the log. They hollow out a new log for each cremation, which is then burnt after the ceremony. As Donald's next-of-kin, it's your responsibility to grind the bones down into a powder, which will then be transferred to several gourds and stored away to be consumed at a more elaborate feast in a few weeks' time. Normally the gourds are stored in the roof of the deceased's house, but as Donald had no permanent house here, the *tuxuana* has agreed to store them in his roof. It's a great honour he's bestowing on you.'

'Can we just back up there a minute?' Brennan said. 'You did say the powdered bones will be *consumed* at another feast?'

'The Yanomamo are endo-cannibalists, which means they consume portions of their own dead. They mix the ashes with boiled plantain soup, which is drunk by the friends and relatives of the deceased.'

'They've got some real weird customs out here. I'm glad I won't be around for that,' Brennan said, with evident relief.

'Except there is still the small matter of the ashes that will be left in the log after the powder's been transferred to the gourds . . .'

He looked slowly at her. 'And what happens to them?'

'The log's rinsed out with boiled plantain soup, which is poured into gourds and consumed by the villagers – after the next-of-kin has drunk a mouthful from the first gourd.'

'Forget it!'

'The plantain soup's got a very strong flavour. I guarantee you won't taste the ashes,' she assured him.

'But I'll still know they're there, won't I? I can't believe you never mentioned this to me earlier.'

'That's because I knew you wouldn't have gone through with it,' she replied.

'Damn right. I'm not doing it, Kelly. No way.'

'Fine, then don't,' she replied, throwing up her hands in frustration. 'I've done everything I can to make this as easy for you as possible! I've worked this stretch of river for eight years now, and as far as I know no other *naba* has ever been cremated in any of the *shabonos* in this area. And you can bet there will have been a lot of opposition here to the *tuxuana*'s decision to allow it. By refusing to uphold their traditions, not only will you be dishonouring Donald's memory but you'll also have humiliated the *tuxuana* in front of his own people. But then that probably doesn't bother you anyway. You do what you want, Ray. I've had enough. I'm going back to the *Gal.*'

Brennan knew that every eye in the *shabono* was on him as she walked away. They may not have understood what had been said, but the anger in her voice wouldn't have been lost on them. And in their culture, no woman ever spoke to a man in that tone of voice. He could let her go. Or he could swallow his pride, call her back and see this ceremony through to its natural conclusion. Not for him. Or for her. But for Donald. This was his last chance to make his peace with his brother. He'd never be able to live with himself if he screwed this up as well.

'Kelly, wait!' he called after her. The heads turned as one towards her, awaiting her reaction. She stopped, then looked round slowly at him. 'Look, perhaps I did . . . overreact a bit . . . just now . . .' he stammered penitently.

She spoke to the *hekura* then withdrew to the edge of the clearing. The *hekura* used the tips of his fingers to smooth out the bone fragments in the log then gripped the pole in both hands and brought it down with a thump into the crudely shaped cavity. He did this several times, each blow accompanied by a whooshing sound, which escaped from his lips, then leaned forward and carefully poked through the bones with his finger. He offered the pole to Brennan, who took it, peered tentatively into the log and screwed up his face at the sight. Then, clamping both hands around the pole, he began to pound the end repeatedly into the aperture. Soon the sweat was running down his face but he didn't stop to wipe it away. He just wanted to get this unpleasant episode over with.

The *hekura* hovered close by, tapping his foot on the hard ground to the rhythm of the striking pole. After several minutes, Brennan paused to catch his breath. His T-shirt clung damply to his body and he stripped it off while the *hekura* examined the cavity. He said something to Brennan then pointed into the log. Brennan took a closer look. Some of the bones had already been crushed into powder, but it would take another concerted effort to finish the job.

He didn't know how long he'd been pounding when the *hekura* put a restraining hand on his arm before inspecting the cavity again. Brennan picked up his T-shirt and wiped it over his face. When he peered into the hole, he saw that the bones had been reduced to a film of white powder covering the bottom. The *hekura* summoned a young acolyte to him. A long flat leaf was used to transfer the powder into several gourds which were then sealed with feathers and taken to the *tuxuana*'s house. A clay bowl, containing freshly boiled plantain soup, was brought to them by a girl, her eyes lowered modestly. She placed the pot carefully beside the log before returning to her parents' house.

The *hekura* indicated the pot. Brennan picked it up and began to pour the soup slowly into the log. He was given a stick to stir it and then the acolyte returned with more gourds, which were filled with the liquid and placed outside the *tuxuana*'s house.

The *hekura* led Brennan to where the gourds had been left, then stepped back when the *tuxuana* emerged from his house and crouched down beside the gourds. He indicated for Brennan to do the same. He got down on his haunches opposite the *tuxuana*, who picked up one of the gourds and extended it towards him. Brennan stared at it. He was still loath to drink from it. He wetted his dry lips and took the gourd. Then, with a deep breath, he tilted the opening to his mouth and allowed some of the warm soup to spill on to his tongue. He swallowed it. Kelly had been right: the soup did have a strong banana taste. But it contained the powdered remains of Donald's bones. He felt nauseous and fought back the bile that threatened to rise into his throat. He could imagine how insulted his host would be if he threw up at his feet. That thought helped him to regain his composure.

The *tuxuana* picked up the same gourd and took a generous mouthful of soup.

'You can get up now,' Kelly said behind him, after the

tuxuana had returned to his house and clambered back into his hammock.

Brennan was relieved his ordeal was over. 'What happens next?' he asked.

'We eat,' she replied.

They walked over to three wooden troughs that had been placed in the clearing: the first contained the familiar yellow plantain soup, the second a thick unappetizing-looking peach-palm gruel, and the third a cheap draught beer that Cesar had delivered the previous evening. Brennan dipped his finger into the beer. It was warm, watery and decidedly unpalatable. The food cooking over numerous small fires smelt a lot better.

Kelly told him that animal meat was never consumed during a ceremonial feast, although fish was permitted. The pirarucu, which Brennan had helped to catch, had been cut into pieces, wrapped in leaves, and roasted over the hot coals, with several turtles, which had been cooked in their shells, a miscellany of other fish and a medium-sized caiman, caught by two hunters earlier that day. There were fruit and vegetables, too, most of which had been cultivated in the communal garden: thick bunches of bananas, segments of papaya, avocado pears, palm fruits, with a leathery skin covering the sweet-tasting flesh, and tropical nuts collected from deep within the forest. Wild mushrooms, red peppers, sweet potatoes, palm hearts and pulped manioc tubers would accompany the fish, with baked cassava bread – standard fare at every meal.

They were each handed a palm leaf to use as a plate. Brennan had to balance it carefully in his upturned hands as the food steadily piled up until he could feel the middle sag under its weight. He followed Kelly back to the guest house where she sat down cross-legged on the hard ground and placed the leaf in front of her. He did the same. She used her fingers to scoop the food off the leaf and push it into her mouth.

Brennan picked up a piece of fish but dropped it as soon as he touched it.

'It's just come off the fire,' she said, shaking her head in mock despair. 'Of course it's going to be hot.'

'So how come you can pick it up without it burning your fingers?' he demanded.

'Because I've been eating like this for the last ten years,' she replied. 'If you want a knife and fork, I can ask one of the villagers to fetch you a set from the *Gal*.'

'I'm OK,' he bristled. 'You were the one who told me I had to accept their way of life, remember?'

'I did, didn't I?' she mused, staring at the food in front of her. 'Close your eyes.'

'What?' he said in bewilderment.

'Close your eyes. I've got something I want you to taste.'

'Oh no,' he said.

'It's nothing unpleasant, believe me. In fact, it's rather tasty.'

'OK, OK,' he said, with an air of resignation, then closed his eyes and opened his mouth hesitantly. He felt her fingers brush against his lips as she placed something on his tongue. It felt no bigger than a cigarette butt and had a greasy texture. He chewed the morsel quickly then swallowed it.

'Well?' she asked.

He opened his eyes. 'It tasted a bit like fatty bacon. What was it?'

'A roasted white grub,' she said, with a cheeky grin.

'*What?*'

'It's considered a delicacy out here,' she said.

'So are chocolate ants in Mexico. That doesn't mean I'd want to eat them. First I have to drink my own brother's ashes and then . . .' He grimaced in disgust when she popped a shrivelled grub into her mouth. 'How can you eat those things like that?'

'Because I happen to like them,' she replied, licking her fingertips. 'They may be revolting to you, but the Yanomamo would probably feel the same way about a chilli dog or a cheeseburger.'

Brennan turned his attention back to his food, which had now cooled enough for him to be able to pick it up. He

124

declined her offer to get him some fruit once he'd finished and she disposed of the two palm leaves on the fire in one of the neighbouring houses. 'I don't know about you, but I'm going to put my feet up for a few hours,' she announced on her return, and began to unravel a spare hammock that was lying on top of a pile of Donald's journals.

'Let me do that,' Brennan said. 'You take the one that's already up.'

'I can manage,' she said sharply, and pulled the hammock back when he tried to take it from her. 'A woman always puts up her own hammock in the *shabono*. And she would never lie in her partner's . . . that's to say, a man's hammock. She'd probably be beaten if she did.' She strung the hammock underneath Brennan's – it was Yanomamo custom for the women to sleep beneath the men – got in and shifted about until she was comfortable. 'What are you going to do?' she asked.

He noticed that most of the villagers were also in their hammocks. Some were eating; some playing with their children, bouncing them up and down on their chests; some had their eyes closed, arms dangling loosely over the sides. 'I guess I'll just stretch out as well,' he said, easing himself into the top hammock. 'Not that I'm tired after sleeping for most of the morning.'

'Well, I am,' she said, then put a hand to her mouth to stifle a yawn. 'If I'm not up in a couple of hours, wake me, will you?' With that she removed her black peaked cap, placed it over her face, and within minutes was asleep.

8

Maowa stood over the bodies of his wife and children, the short stabbing spear in his hand covered in blood. Only in death could they be delivered from the shame and humiliation of being expelled from the *shabono*. His own life meant nothing to him any more, but he would have to take his revenge on the *naba* who'd brought about his dishonour.

He paused at the mouth of the *shabono*. Some children were playing a few feet away but didn't notice him. He was about to cross to the guest house when he saw the *hekura* standing in the middle of the clearing. It was as if he'd appeared from nowhere. He was holding Rasha's black peaked cap in his hand. He tossed it to the ground at his feet and began to chant a high-pitched incantation as he danced slowly around it. Maowa knew the curse – one the Yanomamo regularly used to despatch evil spirits to attack rival *shabonos*, inflicting sickness and death among their enemies. But this curse was summoning the spirits to attack the *naba* as he slept. Maowa walked the short distance to the guest house. Rasha and the *naba* were both asleep in their hammocks. Maowa raised the spear above his head, ready to strike the *naba*.

'Ray, watch out!' Rasha screamed in horror.

The *naba* opened his eyes but couldn't move. The *hekura*'s spell had immobilized his limbs. Maowa smiled coldly at her as she struggled to get out of her hammock. She couldn't move either.

'No-o-o—' she cried out in anguish as Maowa brought

126

down the spear savagely into the centre of Brennan's chest
. . .

'Kelly! Kelly!'

Her eyes opened. Brennan was standing over her, shaking her shoulders.

'You're alive,' she blurted out, disorientated.

'I was the last time I checked,' he said, gently. 'You OK? That must have been some nightmare you were having.'

'A nightmare?' she said, with a relieved chuckle. 'God, it seemed so real.'

'Thanks for your concern, all the same.'

'What are you talking about?' She was puzzled.

'You shouted out a warning to me in your sleep. It gave me a hell of a fright. I thought somebody was creeping up on me. It took me a few moments to realize you were asleep. That's when I woke you.'

'And why didn't you wake me up before?' she demanded, trying to mask her discomfort. 'I only wanted a couple of hours' sleep. It's almost dark now.'

'I've been looking through Donald's journals. I was hoping there might be something about Caldwell or Dixon. I guess I must have lost track of time.'

'Did you find anything?' she asked.

'No. It's all anthropological notes. Not that I could decipher much of it anyway. He should have been a doctor with that handwriting. I only hope his colleagues back home can make some sense of it.' It was then Brennan noticed a group of men crossing the clearing towards them. Their bodies were decorated with red and black pigment and several wore colourful armbands of macaw and toucan feathers.

Kelly saw the uncertainty on his face. 'They're not coming here,' she said, and indicated the man in the adjoining house, who was equally resplendent in similar attire. 'He made a batch of *ebene* today.'

'That's the drug they use, right?'

The visitors sat outside the adjoining house and the *ebene* was brought out in a small clay bowl, with a hollow tube to

127

blow it into their nostrils. One of the men approached the host, who was squatting with the bowl and tube at his feet. He pushed a small amount of the drug into one end of the tube with his finger then carefully placed the other end in the man's nostril and blew. This was repeated in the other nostril. The man began to cough and gasp for breath as he stumbled backwards into the clearing, clutching his head. Then he doubled over, hugging his stomach. When he straightened up, his pupils were enlarged and strands of green mucus were dripping from his nostrils and running down his painted chest. Several times his legs seemed about to buckle but he kept his balance. Then, raising his hands towards the night sky, he began to beckon the spirits. He sang, softly at first, but as the *ebene* took hold of his subconscious his voice grew louder and more melodious. He held out his arms wide and threw back his head as the spirits streamed into his body. Once they were inside him he could direct them as he saw fit – some were despatched to attack his enemies in the neighbouring *shabonos* while others would enter the bodies of sick villagers and cure them.

A second man went through the same ritual and within moments he, too, was singing mellifluously.

Brennan was fascinated as he watched them, lost in themselves. He found himself drawn into this fanciful world where enemies could be struck down by an invisible force or where sick kinsfolk could be healed by a benevolent geist.

Kelly put a hand lightly on his arm. 'He's asking if you want to try it,' she said, gesturing to the host, who was looking directly at him, the tube extended towards him.

'Why not?'

'You're joking, right?' she said anxiously. 'That stuff's really potent, Ray. They get high for two or three hours at a time, and it takes them just as long to come down again.'

'I know a bit about drugs, and not just from processing the junkies who pass through the system every day. It's been a good twenty years since I last tripped, but you don't forget what it's like. And, as you like to keep reminding me, I should be making a greater effort to understand the Yanomamo

128

culture.' He smiled to himself. 'Who knows, perhaps I'll even get to see some of their spirits dancing in the sky.'

'You know very well you won't,' she said. 'You're not interested in their culture, or in their spirits, are you? You want to see Donald.'

'What are you talking about?'

'This is me, Ray. I know what you're going through right now. All that guilt about not sorting things out with Donald. And you think if you can somehow communicate with him, even if it's only through some hallucinogenic haze, he'll forgive you.' She could see by his face that she'd hit the mark.

'I didn't realize I was that transparent,' he said bitterly.

'You're not. Only I know what you're going through right now. I've been there myself,' she said, and instinctively touched her gold bracelet. 'But you won't achieve anything by tripping out on *ebene*.'

'Tell him to load up the pipe,' Brennan said, in a soft, but firm, voice.

'Ray, listen to me,' she pleaded. 'This may seem like a good way to get rid of the guilt you're feeling right now. But it'll only come back. Don't you see that?'

'Are you going to ask him to load up the pipe, or not?'

She passed on his request then grabbed her peaked cap off the hammock and tugged it firmly over her head. 'I thought you were stronger than that. I guess I was wrong. I'm going back to the *Gal*. See you tomorrow. Enjoy your *trip*.' And with that she disappeared into the night.

Brennan knew she was right. That's what made it so damn infuriating. But if he could just see Donald one last time . . . talk to him.

The Yanomamo had placed a small amount of *ebene* into the *mokohiro* and was now crouched in front of the guest house. Brennan knelt down in front of him then looked across at the entrance to the *shabono*. *I honestly thought you were stronger than that.* Much as he hated to admit it, her opinion meant something to him. Particularly her opinion of *him* . . .

He batted the *mokohiro* away with such venom that the tube was knocked out of the man's hand, spilling its precious load.

The man leapt angrily to his feet, berating Brennan, who raised his hands apologetically. He knew that what he had done had been inexcusable, but he had no way of communicating his remorse.

Then the man took a step forward and pushed him in the chest. Brennan didn't rise to the bait. He did it again and once more Brennan didn't react. He'd spent months as a uniformed officer with the riot control unit. He'd been sworn at, spat on, pushed, punched and kicked on the streets of New York, and he knew it would take a lot more than a couple of prods in the chest to get him to retaliate. He got up and walked away. He could hear the derisive cheers behind him, but he didn't look back.

The moon was concealed behind a passing cloud, and the *Shamrock Gal* was shrouded in darkness. He sprang up the boarding ramp to find the deck deserted. He moved to the hatchway and saw a faint trail of light in the corridor below. 'Kelly, are you down there?' he called.

There was no answer but moments later he heard footsteps in the corridor and Kelly appeared. She glared up at him. 'I don't want you tripping out on my boat. Go on back to the *shabono*.'

'I never took the stuff, OK?'

'You didn't?' she said. 'But I thought . . .'

'Yeah, well, you thought wrong,' he said. 'And to make matters worse, I spilt the powder on the ground. That didn't go down too well.'

'So that's what the shouting was about. I wondered what was going on.'

'I could sure do with a drink, unless I'm still considered *persona non grata* around here,' he said.

Her face softened. 'Come down. I'm sure I've got another bottle of Jack Daniel's tucked away somewhere.'

He went below and found her bent over the wooden cabinet beside the rocking chair. 'Knock, knock,' he said, pushing aside the netting.

'Come in,' she said, without looking up. 'I could have sworn I had another bottle of Jack Daniel's in here.'

'It doesn't matter,' he said, perching on the edge of the bed.

'Sure it matters,' she replied, then closed the doors and peered under the bed. 'Not there either. What's the betting one of the crew's traded it for some *cachaca*?'

'Like the anti-venom?'

'Exactly,' she replied, getting to her feet.

'Have you talked to them about it?'

'Yes, but I always get the same reply. It's not us, Rasha. You are our friend. We would never do that to you.' She shrugged. 'It's not that bad, really. They only take what they think I won't miss – or need. They've never taken any of the supplies.' The finality in her voice signalled an end to the subject. She sat down in her rocking chair and held up a bottle of *cachaca*. 'This is all I've got. Are you sure I can't tempt you?'

'Very sure,' he said.

She poured a measure into a tumbler and drank it in one gulp. 'So what made you change your mind about the *ebene*?'

'Like you said, it would have only been a short-term answer. I have to beat this on my own.'

'I know,' she said, barely audibly. She began to rock gently in her chair as she fiddled absently with the gold bracelet on her wrist.

'You must have loved him very much,' he said, as his eyes settled on the bracelet.

'Yes, I did,' she replied softly, then unhooked the clasp and turned it slowly in her fingers. Engraved on the back was something she'd never shown to anyone. Part of her wanted it to remain that way. Another part wanted to break the taboo. She'd never felt like this before. But, then, in the ten years since she'd left Ireland, she'd never met anyone she felt she could talk to about the event that had changed her life for ever. Nobody, that is, until now.

She held out the bracelet towards Brennan. He took it from her and read the inscription: *Kelly – my special Shamrock Gal – never change from the beautiful person I've come to love so much. Yours for ever, Brian.*

'Two days after he gave me that he was dead,' she said, taking it back.

'I'm sorry,' Brennan said.

'He was murdered because he was a Protestant.'

'Were his killers ever caught?'

'Oh, yes,' she said, with a satisfied smile, then reached for the bottle of *cachaca* and poured herself some more. 'I'm from a working-class family. My father worked on the shipyards. My mother was too sick to hold down a steady job. She suffered from chronic bronchitis for most of her adult life, but that never stopped her getting through forty cigarettes a day. Sometimes sixty, depending on how sorry for herself she was feeling that day. I had no sympathy for her. She always reckoned she was too sick to do the housework so every day after I got back from school I had to clean the house, do the laundry, and get a meal for the family. I was doing that before I was ten.' She took a sip from the tumbler then cradled it in her hands as she continued. 'I have two brothers. Feargal, who's four years older than me – he worked at the shipyard as well – and Patrick's the eldest. He's seven years older than me. He was a taxi driver. I was never close to Feargal. He was a bully, very much like my father. Patrick was the quiet one. I thought the world of him – until I discovered that, like Feargal, he was in the IRA. I was devastated. Around that time one of my classmates had been killed by an IRA bomb. I couldn't help but wonder whether Patrick had been involved.

'My father took me to a Sinn Fein rally when I was sixteen and introduced me to a recruitment officer for the IRA. It was obvious what he had in mind. Only I wasn't having any of it – and I told the man exactly what I thought of him and the IRA. I'd never seen my father so angry. But he didn't hit me. He didn't even scold me. He just told me that, as far as he was concerned, I was no longer his daughter. So you can imagine the hostility towards me in the house for the next couple of years while I finished my schooling. I couldn't wait to get away.

'I moved out into a flat and worked at a book store for the

next three years. That's when I first met Brian – Brian Langan. We'd been going out for a couple of months when Patrick turned up one night at my flat and told me the family knew about Brian and that he'd been sent to tell me to finish with him. I wasn't interested, and nothing he said made the slightest difference. I told him I was going to marry Brian, and that was an end to it. The last thing he said before he left the flat was that I was going to regret defying the family's wishes. Those words have haunted me ever since.

'The next day the police found Brian's body. He'd been beaten then shot through the back of the head. I never saw the body, but I was told that he could only be identified by his dental records. The RUC carried out a murder investigation, much of it centring around Patrick and Feargal, but they didn't have enough evidence to bring any charges.

'I knew that even if they hadn't murdered Brian themselves, they were certainly involved in it. I hired a private detective but he didn't come up with anything new and I was beginning to despair that I would never get to the truth. Then I was approached by a tout – that's what we call an informer back home – who said that the gun used to kill Brian had been thrown into the harbour. He even drew a diagram showing exactly where it was. I took it to the police, who sent divers down, and within a couple of hours it was recovered. Prints lifted from the stock matched Feargal's, which the police already had on file. They also found his prints on two of the bullets still in the chamber.

'He was arrested with Patrick, and they were both tried for Brian's murder. There were rumours that my father had ordered the killing, without the consent of the IRA's Army Council, but nothing could be proved against him. The case against Feargal was overwhelming, but there was nothing to link Patrick to Brian's murder. He would almost certainly have got off, had he not invented an elaborate alibi to try to save Feargal, which the prosecution tore to pieces. They were both found guilty of murder and sentenced to life at The Maze. My father was inconsolable when the sentence was passed. Patrick and Feargal were his whole life. He began

133

screaming at me from the public gallery and I had to be escorted from the courthouse by armed police.

'The next day the police got word there was a contract out on me. Officially, they didn't know who was behind it. Unofficially, they knew as well as I did that it was my father. I was advised to go into hiding while they carried out an investigation, but I decided to go abroad. I went to Rio to stay with a girl who'd worked for a short time at the bookshop. It was a nightmare – she was living with a junkie. The flat looked – and smelt – as if it hadn't been cleaned in months. I managed to stick it out for a couple of days, but only because I had nowhere else to go. That's when I met Father Donnelly. I'd spent the morning walking along Botofogo Bay, just to get out of the flat, and stopped at a bar for a drink. He was in there and when he heard my Belfast accent he struck up a conversation with me. He was a missionary who'd been working with the Yanomamo for twenty years and he was due to fly back to Boa Vista the next day. In a moment of sheer desperation I asked if I could go with him. He told me he couldn't pay me but that I would be fed and have a roof over my head. I agreed – anything was better than having to stay a minute longer in that flat.'

'How did you come by the *Shamrock Gal?*' he asked.

'I discovered her in a shallow inlet a few miles from the mission. Not that she was called the *Gal* then. She'd been holed beneath the waterline. I found out later from the other traders that the previous owner had been killed by the Yanomamo some years earlier.

'I bought a second-hand diesel engine in Boa Vista with what little money I had left and one of the traders installed it for me. Several others taught me how to pilot her. They didn't take me seriously at the time. They thought it was just a whim. I played along with that because I knew that if I told them I was going to be competing for business they wouldn't be so quick to offer help. I started out by making runs to Boa Vista to collect supplies for the mission, but within a few months I'd started to trade with some of the villages along the river. A few months later Father Donnelly died and the

134

mission was closed down. Suddenly I had nowhere to use as a base any more. So I converted this into my living quarters.' She gestured around her with a sweep of her arm. 'This is my life now. But the greatest irony of it all is that if Brian hadn't died I'd never have discovered this whole new way of life. There are times when I almost think it was predestined to turn out like this.'

'What about the contract your father put out on you?' Brennan asked, as she took the Marlboro pack from the bedside table.

'I don't know. And I don't care either.' She lit a cigarette. 'I've had no contact with anyone back home since I came here. I don't know whether the police ever proved anything against my father but even if they had, it wouldn't have changed anything. He'll never lift the contract. Which is why I can't go back. And that's what hurts the most.' She took a long drag on the cigarette and blew out the smoke through the porthole. 'Don't get me wrong, though. I've never regretted blowing the whistle on my brothers. I hate them so much.'

'Do you still think about Brian a lot?'

'Not as much as I used to,' she replied, taking another drag on her cigarette. 'But when I do, I tend to remember the good times we had together. I got all the sorrow out of my system a long time ago. The guilt came later. *If* I'd listened to Patrick when he tried to persuade me to stop seeing Brian. *If* I'd told Brian about Patrick's visit. *If* I'd done one – or more – of these things, then maybe Brian would still be alive today. But I came to realize that wasn't the answer. Why should I have been forced to sacrifice my own happiness just to appease these narrow-minded bigots? The more people who take a stand against that kind of injustice, the more powerful their unity in the face of adversity.' She looped the bracelet around her wrist but found that her fingers were trembling when she tried to do it up. 'Damn thing's loose,' she muttered. 'I'm always meaning to get it fixed, but I never seem to get round to it.'

'You'd never forgive yourself if you were to lose it,' Brennan said.

'I know, but it only ever seems to come loose on the boat.

It's almost as if Brian's up there, watching over me to make sure I don't lose it.' She got out of the rocking chair then sat down on the bed and held out the bracelet. 'Would you mind putting it back on for me?' He took it from her and slipped it round her wrist. 'Do you ever think that Gillian might be watching over you?' she asked.

'If Gillian's watching over anybody, it'll be Jason. She never got to see him grow up.' He finally succeeded in easing the clasp back into the eyelet then pulled gently on the bracelet to make sure that it held firm. 'There you go.'

'Thanks,' she said softly, but made no move to return to her chair.

She looked breathtaking in the reflection of the dimmed lamp beside them. God, how he wanted to kiss her. Yet he hesitated. He didn't want it to be like this. She wasn't like the others who could be instantly forgotten after some dispassionate one-night stand. It was all about trust. And he couldn't trust himself to walk away from her if he were to succumb to his own desires. And he had to walk away . . .

She reached out a hand to touch his cheek but he jerked his head away sharply and got up. 'I'm kind of tired,' he said gruffly. 'I'll see you in the morning. Good night.'

With that he pushed aside the sheet across the doorway and was gone.

Kelly continued to stare at the sheet after Brennan's footsteps had faded away. He'd gone and she was baffled. A one-night stand – with no strings attached. Isn't that what he would have wanted? Or were his feelings for her deeper than that? Like the feelings she had for him. Feelings which had no future. That's what made it all the more difficult to accept.

She drank the *cachaca* in one gulp and checked her frustration as she was about to hurl the tumbler against the wall. It wasn't like her to let her emotions get the better of her. She put it down carefully on the bedside table then lit another cigarette. Like it or not, he'd be gone the next day. And that would be an end to it. Then she could get back to her own life.

It's for the best, she told herself. So why did her words sound so hollow?

The fires had been lit and most of the villagers were in their hammocks when Brennan got back to the *shabono*. A handful of shadowy figures were in the clearing, their bodies swaying rhythmically to the sound of their own voices as they stretched their arms heavenwards to the spirits. The top hammock in the adjoining house was empty and he assumed the man he'd offended earlier was now one of those in the clearing. That suited him perfectly: the guy would be preoccupied for the next few hours and by the time he'd come down from his trip, all he'd want to do was flop into his hammock and get some sleep.

Brennan climbed into his own hammock and put his hands behind his head as he stared thoughtfully at the support beam directly above him. It had taken all his willpower to walk away from Kelly. Another few seconds and his resolve would have crumbled. Not that he regretted leaving her. It would only have complicated matters, had he allowed things to go any further. And he didn't need to add to his already guilt-ridden conscience. It was just as well he was leaving in the morning. Then he could put her out of his mind – or at least try to – and get on with his own life back in New York.

He'd begin by digging deeper into the circumstances surrounding Donald's death. And that meant finding out all he could on Tom Caldwell and Bobby Dixon . . .

Caldwell's flight touched down at New York's John F. Kennedy Airport shortly before eight o'clock that evening. After clearing customs and passport control he picked up an envelope at the passenger information desk. Inside were two keys – one for a car, which was already parked outside the terminal building, the other for an apartment on the East Side, which would be his base for the next few days.

It took just over an hour to drive to the apartment and, after parking the car in the underground bay, he rode the elevator to the third floor. The apartment was sparsely furnished, but adequate for his needs. After dumping his suitcase on the double bed he went through to the kitchen and found several ice-cold Millers in the well-stocked refrigerator. He helped himself to one and took a long quaff. That was something he'd missed while he'd been away. Quality American beer. He went through to the lounge where he opened the wall safe. Inside were several bundles of used five-, ten-, and twenty-dollar bills. It also contained a sealed brown envelope, which he removed before re-locking the safe.

He sat down in the armchair nearest the telephone then slit open the envelope with his finger: inside were the home and work numbers of the man who'd been selected to carry out the assassination, together with a copy of his shift roster for the next week. Caldwell looked at his watch. The man wasn't at work. Picking up the handset, he dialled the home number. It rang half a dozen times before being answered.

'Clive Noonan?' Caldwell asked.

'Who is this?'

'I'm sorry to be calling you so late in the evening but I just got into New York a couple of hours ago. My name's Bill Moreno. Officially, I'm an adviser to the President. I'm also one of the co-ordinators of the Independence Day dinner which the Vice-President will be hosting here in New York in three days' time. A dinner I believe you'll be attending.'

'Well, yes,' came the startled reply. 'I received my invitation from the White House last month. But I wasn't expecting to get a personal call from one of the organizers.' There was a pause. 'It hasn't been cancelled, has it?'

'Not unless you know something I don't,' Caldwell said, with a quick laugh. 'No, the reason I'm calling is to arrange a meeting with you as soon as possible. Ideally, tomorrow, if that would suit you?'

'Yes, of . . . course,' Noonan stammered. 'I don't understand, though. Why would you want to meet with me? I'm just a supervisor at a municipal refuse dump over on Long Island.'

'I'd rather not say over the phone,' Caldwell told him and tried to picture the uncertain look on Noonan's face. 'But it's really nothing to worry about. In fact, you could end up playing an important part in the proceedings. That's what I wanted to talk to you about. When would it be convenient for me to visit with you? If you don't mind me coming to your house, that is.'

'No ... no, of course not,' Noonan assured him. 'I'm working later tonight. I should get home around two o'clock tomorrow afternoon. How would four suit you?'

'Surely you'll be tired after your shift?' Caldwell said, injecting some concern into his voice. 'Won't you want to get in a few hours' sleep? I don't want to put you out.'

'I don't usually sleep straight after a shift. I like to unwind a bit first.'

'Four o'clock will be fine for me. Let me just make a note of it in my diary.'

'Just wait until I tell my colleagues at work about this. A Presidential aide coming to my house.'

'No,' Caldwell said tersely, as he sat forward in his chair. He softened his tone. 'I'm afraid you won't be able to tell anyone about my visit – at least not until after the dinner. For security reasons. I hope I can trust your discretion on this.'

'You sure can rely on me, Mr Moreno.'

'Excellent. I look forward to meeting you tomorrow afternoon, Mr Noonan. Four o'clock.'

'Yes, me too. Good night.'

Caldwell waited until the line went dead then replaced the handset and allowed himself a faint smile of satisfaction as he reached for his beer. The trap had been set . . .

9

Brennan woke at dawn, roused by the sounds of the *shabono* as it prepared for another day. Only the men who had participated in the *ebene* ritual remained in their hammocks. He doubted whether they would wake before midday. His eyes went to the slumbering figure in the adjoining house. He'd be gone by the time the man finally surfaced, thank God.

His stomach growled and he realized just how hungry he was. Time to find out whether they were making breakfast aboard the *Shamrock Gal*. But first he needed to make himself presentable. Armed with his toiletry bag, he went down to the river where he scooped his hands into the murky water and splashed it over his face. He dug out a small mirror and winced at his unappealing reflection. Chapped lips, four-day-old stubble and dark bags under his bloodshot eyes. He had a feeling that his jaded body would be glad to get back to the cocktail of air pollutants and the incessant noise that was New York City. The familiarity of home.

With that upbeat thought lingering in his mind, he boarded the *Shamrock Gal* and made his way to the bow where the two Yanomamo were sitting beside a battered butane gas cylinder, preparing what appeared to be a stew in a clay pot. There was no sign of Kelly. One of the Yanomamo pointed to the pot, then to Brennan, then touched his fingers to his lips. Brennan nodded eagerly. A generous quantity of stew was deposited on a plate and a thick piece of cassava bread dumped on top. Coffee was poured and both plate and mug were handed to him.

140

He retired to the wooden bench at the stern of the boat to eat. When he'd finished he got to his feet again and moved to the hatch. 'Kelly, are you down there?' he called. No response.

He went to the bow where the two Yanomamo were eating. 'Rasha?' he said. One pointed to the forest in the direction of the cascade pool.

Brennan returned to the *shabono* where he gathered together Donald's journals and put them into his holdall. He paused to take a final look around him. He'd always be grateful to these people. But words counted for little in their world. With that in mind, he took Donald's lighter from his pocket and placed it on the ground where the journals had lain.

When he returned to the boat Kelly was standing on deck, a mug of coffee in her hand. She gave him a fleeting glance and he could see that either she was annoyed with him about his abrupt departure the previous evening, or she was feeling as uncomfortable as he was.

'Morning,' he said, with a note of geniality, hoping it would hide the uncertainty in the pit of his stomach.

'Morning.'

'When will we be leaving?' he asked.

'What time do you have to be at the airport?' she replied.

'I have to meet the pilot at ten.'

'Then we may as well leave now,' she said, tossing the remainder of the coffee into the water. 'We wouldn't want you to miss your flight, would we?'

'Kelly, wait up,' he said, as she was about to walk off. 'I know we're both a bit uncomfortable about last night.'

'I don't know what you're talking about,' she replied shortly. 'Now, if you'll excuse me, I've got to speak to the crew.'

'I still believe we were right not to let it go any further,' he called after her.

There was a hesitation in her step, as if she were about to turn and say something, then the moment was gone and she disappeared from view around the side of the wheelhouse.

Leaning his arms on the railing, he gazed out over the magnificent river and felt a genuine sadness. He'd certainly never forget the last three days. He straightened up but as he was about to turn away he noticed a figure standing at the entrance to the narrow path leading to the cascade pool. An Indian, armed with a spear, his face concealed beneath a mask of red dye. Brennan didn't know where he'd come from or how long he'd been standing there but he saw again the distinctive scar on the back of the hand gripping the upright spear. It was the man who'd saved his life at the cascade pool. He turned towards the wheelhouse. 'Kelly, come here. Quickly!' he shouted.

'What is it?' she asked, crossing to where he was standing.

'Look, it's the . . .' He trailed off as he turned back to point out the Indian. No one was there.

'Look at what?' she demanded.

'It doesn't matter,' he said, lowering his arm. 'I thought I saw something. I guess I must have been wrong.'

'We'll be leaving in ten minutes,' she said brusquely, then went back to the wheelhouse.

He continued to stare at the spot where the Indian had been standing. The *tuxuana* had said that a villager with a similar scar on the back of his hand had died after being bitten by a snake at the pool and Brennan had dismissed the ghost theory as superstition. He still did. Only now his conviction wasn't as strong. There *had* to be a logical explanation. *Didn't there?* He shuddered, then left the bow to monitor the preparations which were already under way to leave the *shabono*.

Too abrupt. Too cold. Too distant. Kelly knew she could have handled it a lot better. But, then, she had been on the defensive. Ray Brennan was the first man she'd been attracted to since she lost Brian. And that unsettled her. She didn't want to feel that way. But if she'd been so keen to keep her distance, why had she come on to him yesterday evening? She'd already tried to appease her conscience by arguing that it had been a mistake made on the spur of the moment. Only it wasn't in her nature to make rash decisions. She'd known exactly what she was doing, which added to her guilt. And

142

the only way she had of hiding that guilt was to raise the barriers around her. She knew it was only a short-term solution. She would still have to overcome her feelings once he was gone . . .

Kelly remained at the helm throughout the journey back to Boa Vista. Many times she'd wanted to turn the wheel over to her crew and go and talk to Brennan. But each time she'd resisted the temptation. It wouldn't have achieved anything. It would only have complicated matters – or so she tried to convince herself.

The *Shamrock Gal* finally reached Boa Vista shortly after nine o'clock and she waited until the boat had been moored securely to the quay before switching off the engine. It was the moment she'd been dreading. Taking a deep breath, she left the wheelhouse and crossed to where Brennan was standing by the port railing.

'You made good time,' he said, forcing a quick smile.

'There isn't any cargo in the hold,' she replied. 'That made the boat a lot lighter.'

'And quicker,' Brennan added.

'And quicker,' she agreed, nodding.

'Is there anywhere around here I can get a cab?' he asked, breaking the uneasy silence between them.

She pointed to the two wooden gates at the end of a dirt road leading off from the quay. 'If you turn right, once you reach the street, you'll see a taxi rank a couple of hundred yards further on down the road. You can't miss it. You'll get to the airport well before ten.'

'OK.' Another uncomfortable pause. 'Well, I guess I'd better be going.' He held out a hand towards her. 'Thanks for your help.'

'That's what you'd paid me for,' she said, shaking his hand politely. *You could have come up with something better than that,* she said crossly to herself.

He handed her a sheet of paper he'd torn out of the back of one of Donald's journals. 'I've written down my address in

143

Brooklyn, with my home and work numbers. If you ever find yourself in New York, be sure to look me up.'

'I've never been further than Rio since I came out here, and that's only been twice in the last ten years. But thanks anyway.'

'Yeah, sure – whatever,' he replied, with an awkward shrug. 'You take care of yourself now, you hear?'

Suddenly she flung herself at him and hugged him tightly. 'You, too,' she said, in a soft, emotional voice, then hurried across to the hatch and down the stairs.

He jumped the short distance to the quay and didn't look back at the boat until he reached the gates. Then he went out into the street, turned right and made his way to the taxis he could see parked at the side of the road.

The driver of the first scrambled out from behind the wheel and shouted something to him in Portuguese.

'Airport,' Brennan said.

'*Sim, aeroporto.*' The man nodded then took the holdall from Brennan's hand.

'American!' a voice shouted, and a man hurried towards him, his yellow teeth bared in a broad smile of greeting. It was the driver who'd brought him to the harbour four days earlier. A vociferous argument ensued but the English-speaker finally tugged Brennan's holdall from his colleague's hand. The first man glared at Brennan then returned to his taxi. 'I tell him . . . he . . . not good for you,' his driver told Brennan. 'He . . . no speak English. Where you want go, American?'

'Airport,' Brennan said, as he followed the man to where his taxi was parked.

'You . . . go back . . . to home now?' the driver asked, after he'd put the holdall in the trunk.

'Yeah,' Brennan said, then climbed into the back of the taxi.

'You like Amazonas?' the driver asked, after he'd got behind the wheel.

'You could say that,' Brennan replied, with a thoughtful smile. Then, removing his sunglasses, he leaned his head back on the padded seat and closed his eyes. 'There's an extra ten dollars in it for you if you don't say another word until we get to the airport.' No reply. He opened one eye, unsure whether the man had understood him.

He was acknowledged with a wide grin in the rear-view mirror, then the driver started the engine and swung the taxi out into the road.

Kelly spent the rest of the morning in Boa Vista settling her outstanding debts with the money Brennan had paid her, while negotiating further credit from the unscrupulous back-street dealers. Nobody else would give her credit any more. But all in all, it was a good day's business. And it helped to take her mind off Ray Brennan . . .

When she returned to the *Shamrock Gal* to await the first of the fresh supplies, the two Yanomamo were waiting for her on the quayside. Their eyes went to the carrier bag she had with her.

'What makes you think I've brought you anything?' she asked, a playful innocence in her voice. 'And, more to the point, what makes you think you deserve anything?'

'We are Rasha's friends,' one replied. 'Friends always bring gifts for each other.'

'So what did you get for me?' she asked.

'We have no money, Rasha.'

'Snap,' she said in English. 'I had to pay off my creditors,' she continued in Yanomami. 'All the money the *naba* gave me has gone.'

'So Rasha didn't buy us anything,' the other said, as a crestfallen expression crept slowly across his face.

'That's pathetic,' she said good-humouredly, then dipped her hand into the carrier bag and produced two bottles of *cachaca.*

'Hooch!' they chorused together, but pronounced it 'how-ch'. It was one of the few English words they'd picked up from her.

She pulled back her hand when they reached for the bottles. 'You can have them tonight, *after* the supplies have been loaded on board.'

145

'Rasha!' one blurted out and pointed behind her. The other Yanomamo ran past her and she turned to see a dishevelled figure stumbling towards them on unsteady legs.

It was Donald's wife – Louise Carneiro. Her clothes were torn, her face and arms covered in cuts and bruises. The Yanomamo grabbed her arm to steady her as she almost lost her footing.

Kelly hurried forward to help. 'Louise, what happened?' she asked in horror.

'It's not . . . important,' Louise whispered. She took a battered notebook from the back pocket of her torn jeans and pressed it into Kelly's hands. 'You must take this to . . . to the American ambassador in Rio.'

'Get her on board,' Kelly ordered.

'No, leave me!' she gasped. 'You're in danger with me here. But I – I had to get the book to you. Now you must let me go.'

'You're not going anywhere,' Kelly told her. 'Look at you. You can hardly walk. You need to get to a hospital.'

'No,' Louise said sharply. 'If they were to see me with you, they'd kill you as well.'

'Rasha,' a Yanomamo shouted, and indicated a car that had skidded through the wooden gates and was now speeding towards them.

'Get her on board and prepare to cast off!' Kelly yelled and tore towards the boat.

The two Yanomamo grabbed Louise between them and, despite her protestations, carried her on to the boat where Kelly had already started up the engine. One of the Indians returned to the quay to untie the mooring ropes. The car screeched to a halt and two scruffily dressed *pistoleiros* jumped out and ran towards the boat. One was armed with a handgun. Kelly shouted a warning to the Yanomamo as the thug raised the weapon to fire at him. The bullet slammed into the side of the boat, missing the Indian by inches. He leapt back on to the boat, which was already beginning to drift away slowly from the quay. Too slowly. She knew the men would be able

146

to jump aboard before she could put enough distance between the boat and the quayside.

Her worst fears were realized when she heard a loud thud behind her as the armed *pistoleiro* landed on the deck. The other man followed quickly and she saw to her dismay that he was also armed with a revolver, which he waved menacingly at the two Indians when they tried to prevent him from reaching Louise. Kelly pushed the notebook into the front of her jeans then unhooked the shotgun from the wall brackets beside the wheel and held it tightly against her stomach as one of the *pistoleiros* approached the wheelhouse. She monitored his progress carefully in the reflection of the window, knowing she'd have to time her move perfectly. She would only have one chance to get it right. She had to make it count.

'Switch off the engine!' the *pistoleiro* commanded.

He was still out of range. She had to lure him closer.

'I said, switch off the engine!'

She tightened her grip on the barrel then took her hand off the wheel and slipped it around the stock as he came in. She swung round, slamming the butt into his midriff. As he doubled over she lashed out again, catching him on the side of the head. He was unconscious before he hit the deck. She swung the shotgun on his accomplice, but saw the crew had already disarmed him. One of the Yanomamo took the wheel and she crossed to where the other had the automatic trained on the nervous *pistoleiro*.

She took the weapon from him – neither of the Indians knew how to use a gun – and handed him the defective shotgun in return. 'Were you sent to get this?' she asked, producing the notebook. No reply. 'Who are you working for?' Again silence. 'Are you working for Tom Caldwell?'

There was a momentary flicker of surprise in the man's eyes, then it was gone. She had her answer. But she knew she wasn't going to get anything else out of him. This pair were just the hired muscle sent for the notebook.

'What are we going to do with him, Rasha?' the Yanomamo asked, and jabbed the barrel of the shotgun menacingly at the

147

pistoleiro, who stepped back fearfully until he was pressed against the railing.

'I think we should see if he can swim,' she replied. The Indian nodded in agreement. '*Salto!*' she snapped. The man hesitated as he looked down at the murky water. 'You're going to find it a lot harder to swim with a shattered kneecap,' she said, and lowered the gun until it was trained on his leg. He clambered over the railing and jumped into the water. 'And you can throw that in as well,' she told the Yanomamo, gesturing to the unconscious figure outside the wheelhouse. She tucked the handgun into her belt, then crossed to where Louise was slumped against the railing. 'We can't go back to Boa Vista,' she told her. 'I'll get you to the nearest mission. It should take us about an hour to get there. They'll be able to patch you up until we can get proper medical attention.'

'It doesn't matter about me. They're going to kill me anyway,' she said, then pointed to the notebook tucked into the front of Kelly's jeans. 'That's all that matters now. You have to get it to the authorities. Promise me you will.'

'I promise,' Kelly replied, and glanced round at the splash as the unconscious man was dumped in the river. Then she beckoned the Indian towards her. 'Bring me some clean water and the medicine kit from my cabin.' She waited until he'd gone then pulled the notebook from the front of her jeans. 'So what's in here that's so important?'

'I don't know. It's written in English. It's something Donald was working on shortly before he died. He wouldn't tell me what, though. But he did say that if anything were to happen to him, I was to get the book to you. You were the only other person he felt he could trust to take it to the American Embassy in Rio.' A look of uncertainty crossed Louise's face. 'You will take it to them, won't you?'

'I told you I will,' Kelly said.

'When I heard that Donald was dead, I set out from the *shabono* to find you. I didn't know where you'd be, so I made my way to Boa Vista. I knew you'd come here sooner or later.'

'When did those two bastards first pick up your trail?' Kelly asked.

'Shortly after I got into town. They stopped me in the street and tried to bundle me into their car. I managed to give them the slip and came to the harbour. They must have found out where I was. Thank God you arrived when you did.'

'Have you ever seen them before?' Kelly asked, taking the bottle of mineral water and the medicine kit from the Indian.

'No. They must be working for whoever murdered Donald.'

'Donald drowned,' Kelly corrected her.

'It amounts to the same thing,' Louise said, then grabbed Kelly's wrist as she was about to open the medicine kit. 'I want to know what's in the notebook.'

'I'll take a look once I've put some disinfectant on those cuts,' Kelly replied.

'I want to know now!' Louise snapped, knocking over the medicine kit with a sweep of her arm. 'Please, Kelly. Tell me.'

Kelly righted the medicine kit then picked up the notebook and opened it at the first page. The scrawled handwriting was completely illegible. She couldn't even be sure it was written in English.

'What's so funny?' Louise demanded, when an absent smile touched the corners of Kelly's mouth.

'Oh, nothing,' Kelly said quickly. 'It's just something Donald's brother said about his handwriting.'

'Ray was out here?' Louise said in surprise.

Kelly nodded. 'We went to your *shabono* but you'd already left.'

'I can't say I'm disappointed to have missed him. From what Donald told me about him, he sounded like a selfish, self-centred prick. It was no wonder Donald didn't get on with him.'

Kelly was furious. But yelling at Louise in Ray's defence wouldn't solve anything, and, in any case, they had enough to worry about without squabbling between themselves. 'I think if you'd met Ray, you'd think differently about him.'

'I doubt that,' Louise said tersely.

No, probably not, Kelly thought. Louise had always swallowed anything Donald told her. She turned her attention back to the notebook. Each page was filled with the same scrawled, illegible handwriting. How could she possibly show this to the American ambassador in Rio de Janeiro? He'd take one look at the notebook – if he even agreed to see her – and throw her out.

She'd all but given up hope of finding anything remotely legible when she came to the last page of handwriting. The chilling words had been printed diagonally across the page in capital letters:

VICE PRESIDENT – ASSASSINATION –
INDEPENDENCE DAY

'What is it?' Louise asked. Kelly told her. 'Do you think he meant the American Vice-President?'

'It has to be,' Kelly replied. 'They celebrate their Independence Day in three days' time. That's why he was so desperate to make sure the notebook reached the ambassador. Whatever's written in here must have some bearing on the assassination. If only I could read his damn handwriting, it might have given us a better idea of what we're up against. But you can be sure Caldwell will do everything in his power to prevent the notebook from reaching the authorities.'

'Tom Caldwell?' Louise said. 'What's he got to do with it?'

'There isn't time to explain right now, but there's a good chance he's involved in all of this,' Kelly said.

'I can't say I'm surprised.' Louise's eyes narrowed as another thought struck her. 'Do you think he had Donald murdered to silence him?'

'I don't know, but I'd have thought Donald would have been more use to him alive. He was the one person who could have led them to the notebook. But we won't know the truth until the notebook's been properly analysed at the embassy.'

'How are you going to get to Rio?' Louise asked.

'I'll have to fly there. I've been putting aside a little money over the years in a safe deposit box at my bank in Boa Vista.

Money my creditors know nothing about. There should be enough for a one-way ticket to Rio. I'm sure I'll be able to persuade the ambassador to pay for my return flight.'

'And reimburse you for your outward ticket,' Louise added.

'First I've got to get there,' Kelly reminded her. 'Which means I'll have to return to Boa Vista to get the money. I should be able to hitch a ride back there once we reach the mission. And there won't be a problem getting to Manaus either. Supply planes fly there every few hours from Boa Vista. My only concern right now is how quickly I can get a flight from Manaus to Rio.'

'How long before we reach the mission?' Louise asked.

'Another fifty minutes,' Kelly estimated. Then she stood up. 'I'm going to take the helm again, see if I can shave a few minutes off that time. I know the *Gal* better than anyone. She always responds best to me.'

'Do you think those *pistoleiros* will catch up with us again before we reach the mission?'

'Not if I have anything to do with it,' Kelly replied.

The two drenched *pistoleiros* were helped out of the water by an elderly man who'd been fishing further down the quay. One had a gash above his left eye, where Kelly had caught him with the shotgun butt, and blood was streaming down the side of his face and on to the collar of his floral shirt. The fisherman, concerned about the wound, tried to take a closer look at it but the *pistoleiro* batted aside his hand and ordered him to go away. The old man muttered something under his breath then walked off.

The two men returned to the car. 'You'll have to call Dixon,' the injured man said, dabbing the wound with his wet handkerchief.

'You're the boss here,' replied his colleague. '*You* tell him we screwed up.'

The first man opened the driver's door and retrieved the portable phone from the dashboard. 'He could be anywhere,' he said, staring at the handset.

'Try that hotel he goes to with his whores whenever he's in town.'

'We could say we tried it, but that he wasn't there,' the first *pistoleiro* suggested.

'We're in enough trouble as it is for letting that bitch escape,' his colleague said, leaning his arms on the roof of the car. 'Don't make it any worse by lying to him.'

'We can only die once,' the first man said.

'It's what he'll do to us first that scares the shit out of me,' the other replied, then dropped his forehead on his folded arms.

His colleague swallowed nervously then reluctantly called the hotel.

Dixon opened the door and stood aside for the girl to enter the room. She was in her teens, wearing a black mini-dress and scuffed black leather ankle boots. Her pretty face was plastered with make-up and her greasy hair hung lifelessly on her bare shoulders. She tossed her purse on to the nearest chair then sat on the bed, still chewing methodically on the wad of gum she'd pushed in her mouth shortly after Dixon had picked her up in his car close to the docks.

'How old are you?' Dixon asked.

'I can be any age you want me to be,' she replied, coquettishly.

Dixon caught her a vicious backhand across the face. 'Don't ever try and be smart with me again, sweetheart, because the next time I won't be so gentle with you. You understand me?' She nodded as she fought desperately for breath. 'Good. Let's try again, shall we? How old are you?'

'Fifteen, *senhor*,' she replied, shaking with fright.

'Perfect,' Dixon said, then used his thumb to wipe a smear of blood from the corner of her mouth. He patted her reddening cheek lightly then moved to the window and gazed down at the passing traffic. 'Take your clothes off and get into bed.'

'You said you'd pay me when we got to your room,' she said, and shrank back when he swung round on her.

'I said I'd pay you what I think you're worth – after I've fucked you,' Dixon replied contemptuously.

'I always get paid before,' she said, knowing she was riding her luck now every time she opened her mouth.

'If you don't like my terms, leave,' Dixon said, pointing at the door. She didn't move. 'No, I didn't think so. You whores are all the same. Now either get undressed or get out.'

The telephone rang. Dixon cursed furiously then crossed to the bedside table and snatched up the handset. 'Yes!' he barked, his eyes lingering on the girl as she stripped off her clothes.

'It's Miguel, *senhor.*'

'What do you want?' Dixon snapped.

'It's . . . about the Carneiro woman, *senhor.*'

'You've got her?' Dixon asked.

There was a pause. 'We followed her to the harbour. She met McBride. I think she gave her the book.'

'You think?' Dixon replied in disbelief. 'You mean you haven't already taken them?'

'We tried, *senhor,* but they . . . escaped.'

'You let *two women* get the better of you?'

'They caught us by surprise—'

'I don't want to hear any fucking excuses!' Dixon bellowed into the mouthpiece. 'Where did they go?'

'They're on the *Shamrock Gal, senhor.* It's heading up-river, but it won't have got far.'

Dixon remembered the ranch's private boathouse on the waterfront. It housed several speedboats, as well as the luxurious yacht Caldwell used whenever he entertained the region's more affluent families. 'Go to the boathouse,' he said. 'Take one of the speedboats and follow the *Shamrock Gal.* But keep your distance and await my instructions. I'm on my way. I'll follow in another speedboat. Do you think you can manage that?'

'*Sim, senhor.*'

'I hope so, for your sake. You really don't want to make it any worse for yourself than it already is.' Dixon slammed down the handset then looked at the girl, who'd already slipped under the sheets. 'Put on your clothes and get out.'

She jumped out of the bed as he pulled on his camouflage jacket. 'I will wait for you here until you get back,' she said, putting a hand on his arm.

'Get dressed!' he snapped, shrugging it off.

'You'll pay me now?' she asked, hovering at his side.

'For what?' Dixon replied. 'I told you I'd pay on your performance. You haven't done anything, so you don't get paid. It's that simple.'

'I have no money, *senhor*. I am hungry. I haven't eaten for two days.'

Dixon grabbed her clothes, opened the door and tossed them into the corridor. 'Get out!'

'Please, *senhor*,' she begged. 'Just a few *reais* to buy some food.'

Dixon's fist struck her full in the face. She screamed in agony as her nose shattered under the blow, lost her balance and fell heavily to the floor. Then he grabbed her hair and half pulled, half dragged her out into the corridor and flung her contemptuously against the wall as if she were little more than a doll. She slid slowly to the floor and crouched in abject terror against the wall, sobbing uncontrollably as she cradled her broken nose in her hands.

Dixon took a handful of coins from his pocket, tossed them at her, then walked to the elevator. He cast a last, disparaging look in her direction then stepped inside and pushed the button for the lobby.

Kelly had never believed they had a realistic chance of reaching the mission ahead of the *pistoleiros*, so it came as no surprise when she heard the sound of the speedboat. She despatched the two Indians below deck to fetch their bows and arrows.

The speedboat had already come into view by the time the two Indians were back on deck. They each had a four-foot bow and the cane arrowheads had been dipped in curare then wrapped in leaves. They knelt at either end of the stern railing and notched up an arrow against the bowstring.

'Why don't they shoot?' Louise asked Kelly.

'They'll only shoot if, and when, I give them the order,' Kelly replied, wiping her forearm across her sweating face.

'So give them the order!' Louise screeched.

'The speedboat's out of range,' Kelly said.

'If that notebook falls—'

'I've got enough to worry about right now without you distracting me.' Kelly cut angrily across her. 'So unless you've got something constructive to say, I'd suggest you sit down and shut up!'

Louise opened her mouth to respond, thought better of it, then left the wheelhouse. Immediately Kelly felt guilty about her outburst, after the hell Louise had gone through to get the notebook to her, but she needed to concentrate on getting them out of this alive. She found herself wishing Ray Brennan was there. He'd have found a way, she was sure. But he wasn't there, and she'd have to come up with something herself. Only she had no idea what . . .

The speedboat tailed them for the next ten minutes. Kelly had already considered running the boat aground and fleeing into the jungle, but she didn't know how close she could get the boat to shore before snagging the hull on the riverbed – and this stretch of water was a known breeding ground for the black caiman . . .

'Rasha!'

The voice startled her. One of the crew was pointing towards a second speedboat approaching in the distance. It was closing in fast. The Yanomamo hurried across to the wheelhouse. 'We can't outrun them, Rasha. Either we stay on board and fight, or swim to the shore and hide in the jungle.'

'I say we go ashore,' Louise said, appearing behind him.

'Then go,' Kelly replied defiantly. 'I'm staying here.'

'Do you want to stay on the boat?' Louise asked the Yanomamo.

'We are warriors. We never run from our enemies.' He put a hand to his chest. 'In my heart I know Rasha is right to stay and fight. We will stay and fight with her.'

'You'd be prepared to die for a *naba*?' Louise said incredulously.

155

'Rasha is not a *naba*. She is one of us. We would die for her.' With that he went back to the stern to resume his position at the railing.

Kelly felt a lump in her throat. After ten years of living among these people, she'd finally been accepted by them. Even Louise was taken aback by what he'd just said.

The moment was over and Kelly returned her attention to the second speedboat. When the vessel drew nearer she recognized Bobby Dixon in the passenger seat. He pulled out a bullhorn from the back seat and put it to his lips. 'Kelly, my quarrel isn't with you or your crew,' he said, speaking in English to exclude the others around them. 'All I want is Louise Carneiro and the notebook she has with her. If you hand her over to me, you have my word that you and your crew will be free to continue on your way. Just shut down your engine and tell your crew to lay down their weapons and back away from the railing. Resist, and you'll leave us with no option but to open fire on your boat. I don't want it to come to that. I want to settle this matter without any unnecessary bloodshed. As I'm sure you do.'

'What did he say?' Louise asked.

'Nothing that's worth repeating,' Kelly said. 'But I've got a feeling we're in for a bumpy ride.'

'He wants me, doesn't he?' Louise said. Kelly didn't reply. 'I thought as much. Let him take me. But he'll have to catch me first. You've been a good friend, Kelly. I know you won't let Donald down.' Louise kissed her lightly then ran towards the railing.

'Louise, no!' Kelly yelled in horror. She went after her friend, but too late to prevent her scrambling over the railing and diving into the water. When she resurfaced, twenty yards from the boat, she began to swim for the shore. Dixon's speedboat veered towards her. Kelly knew Louise was an excellent swimmer, but her movements were lethargic and uncoordinated. She waited until the speedboat was almost abreast of her before diving again. When Louise resurfaced, the currents had dragged her further downstream, behind the two speedboats, and she was disorientated. She was now

156

floundering in the middle of the river. Kelly watched help-lessly as the two speedboats, now out of range of the arrows, turned sharply in the water and moved to where her friend was struggling against the swirling currents. Louise was on her own. In a last act of defiance, she submerged again. Dixon raised a hand and both speedboats slowed as they waited for her to reappear. Seconds later she burst the surface of the water, gasping for breath, only a few yards away from where she'd dived. Dixon's boat drew abreast of her. He reached over the side and grabbed her roughly by the hair. She was so exhausted that she could muster no resistance as she was hauled into the back of the craft and shoved face down on the seat.

Kelly watched fearfully as Dixon frisked her for the note-book. When he didn't find it, he withdrew a 9mm Smith & Wesson from a concealed shoulder holster under his flak jacket. He pressed it against the back of Louise's head and pulled the trigger. A cluster of startled white egrets took flight as the shot echoed across the river and disappeared over the crescent of the green canopy.

Kelly knew there was no escape, but she was determined not to give up the notebook without a fight. She secured it in her belt then removed the gold bracelet from her wrist and slipped it into her pocket. She watched as Dixon's speedboat arced out wide, away from the *Shamrock Gal*, and assumed he was preparing an attack from the starboard side. The other speedboat closed in and she gave her crew the order to fire. They dispatched two arrows. Neither found their mark. The *pistoleiro* in the passenger seat fired off a round from a Beretta submachine-gun, forcing the two Indians to dive for cover as the bullets raked the stern. One notched a second arrow into his bow and fired again at the speedboat. The pilot was still turning the wheel violently to try to evade the arrow when it ripped through his chest. The Indians gave a loud cheer as he slumped forward over the wheel. The second *pistoleiro* tried to pull his colleague off the wheel as the speedboat veered out of control, but the arrow shaft was trapped in the spokes. The boat was still gathering speed when the hull struck something

157

under the water, knocking him off balance, and he fell backwards on to his dead colleague. The speedboat ploughed into a thick, gnarled root and burst into flames, hurling debris hundreds of feet into the air.

A furious Dixon raked the *Shamrock Gal* with a succession of rapid three-round bursts from his M16 semi-automatic rifle. Kelly hurled herself to the deck as the bullets strafed the wheelhouse, taking out the windows and showering her with shards of broken glass. When she raised her head she saw one of the Indians lying motionless on his back, his chest matted with blood. The other was unhurt. She gestured for him to remain face down on the deck then gingerly raised her head. She could see that Dixon still had the M16 trained on the *Shamrock Gal*. For a moment she was baffled as to why he'd stopped firing. Then she saw the attachment fixed underneath the barrel: an M293 grenade launcher.

Dixon trained the sights on the hull and squeezed the trigger. The grenade ripped through the side of the boat and, seconds later, there was a shuddering explosion as it struck a barrel of petrol, destined for a *garimpeiro* settlement further up-river. Such was the force of the explosion that the stern deck, and part of the hull, disintegrated in a searing ball of fire. The second Yanomamo, who'd been lying beside the stern railing, hadn't stood a chance.

The *Shamrock Gal* shuddered helplessly and began to list to starboard as the water poured into the hold through the gaping hole in the side of the hull. Kelly knew it would be only minutes before the doomed vessel sank. Yet she was loath to abandon it. It was *her* boat. They'd had eight years together. It was her home. Her work. Her friend. But common sense had to prevail. There was nothing she could do now to save the *Gal*. Another explosion ripped through the cargo hold as a second barrel of petroleum detonated, sending a searing ball of flame up through the shattered deck. Using the billowing black smoke as cover, she made her way cautiously to the port railing. She hesitated for a moment but she knew that if she didn't jump she'd be dragged into the flames, which were already licking at the deck only feet away from her. She steadied herself on the railing, unable to see anything through the thick, swirling smoke around her, but just as she was about to launch herself into the water the *Shamrock Gal* shuddered violently and the torn stern sank beneath the water. Kelly lost her balance and felt a sharp pain sear through her head as she fell heavily against the side of the wheelhouse. Then everything went black . . .

Dixon watched dispassionately as the *Shamrock Gal* finally sank in a seething cauldron of hissing, bubbling water. It was several minutes before the smoke had cleared sufficiently to search the area. It didn't surprise him that there appeared to be no survivors.

He was about to give the order to return to Boa Vista when something floating among the debris caught his eye. He ordered the pilot to take them closer and as the speedboat drew abreast of the object he reached over the side and fished it out of the water. The wet pages were stuck together, and much of the ink had run, making the handwriting impossible to decipher, but he was in no doubt that he'd recovered Donald Brennan's notebook . . .

'And you're sure it's the notebook?' Caldwell asked.

'It fits the description his informer gave me while he was being interrogated,' Dixon replied. 'And considering the agony the guy was in at the time, he had no reason to lie.'

'And no survivors?'

'The two Indians were killed on the boat. That just leaves McBride. We checked the area thoroughly after the boat sank, but there was no sign of her. She's dead, I'm sure of it. Even if she did manage to bail out before the boat went down, she'd never have survived the currents.'

'I'll believe that when her body's found,' Caldwell said. 'I want the word put out to every informer in Boa Vista that there's five thousand dollars in it for the man who can provide us with conclusive proof that she's dead. But if she's still alive, I'll double the reward for any man who can lead us to her.'

'I'll handle it personally.'

'No, you won't.' Caldwell said. 'I want you on the next flight out to New York. We've got work to do. Be here by tomorrow afternoon – at the latest. Call me as soon as you get in.' He severed the connection. He'd never liked Dixon – or his penchant for jailbait hookers – but he'd always been a consummate professional when it came to carrying out orders. Not that he'd chosen the man as his second-in-command. That had been done before either of them had been recruited to oversee the experiments at the ranch. It had been an uneasy alliance, despite their respect for each other as professional soldiers. But other than that they had nothing in common, never met outside work and only spoke to each other about work. It was an arrangement that suited Caldwell perfectly. It meant Dixon knew nothing about his past. And that was the way he intended it to remain.

He looked at his watch. It was time to leave for the meeting with Clive Noonan. On the hall table was an elegant gold-plated cigarette-lighter. When activated close to the victim's face, the lighter would release a jet of anaesthetic gas from the nozzle, rendering them unconscious within seconds. He slipped it into the inside breast pocket of his dark blue Brioni suit, then left the apartment and took the elevator to the underground car park.

He joined the steady mid-afternoon traffic on FDR Drive, along the East River as far as East Houston Street then drove across town to Broadway and down into SoHo and Broome Street to reach the Holland Tunnel, which brought him out on the other side of the Hudson River. A short drive north brought him to the small working-class town of Hoboken. It wasn't difficult to find Clive Noonan's house – one of a row of small, neatly stacked red-brick houses in a cul-de-sac a couple of minutes' drive from Washington Street, the town's main thoroughfare. He parked in front of the whitewashed gate, retrieved an attaché case from the back seat, and got out. A group of children, watched by several bored-looking adults, were playing a game of touch football in the park on the opposite side of the street. One of the adults looked across at him. Caldwell nodded in greeting. There was no response.

He walked up the narrow pathway, bordered on either side by an overgrown lawn, and rang the bell. The door was opened immediately, as if he'd been monitored ever since he'd first pulled up outside the house. It didn't surprise him.

Caldwell recognized Noonan from the numerous photographs included in the dossier. Mid-fifties, beer belly, bespectacled, unassuming features. The perfect choice. He was one of a hundred and fifty Vietnam vets who'd been selected from the New York area to join the Vice-President on Independence Day for a commemorative dinner to be held at the newly opened Richmond Hotel on Fifth Avenue. No officers, or even NCOs. All had to have been regular 'grunts', the foot soldiers who'd been the embodiment of the American struggle in Vietnam.

'Mr Noonan?' Caldwell asked.

'That's right,' the man replied, between puffs on a cigarette.

'I'm Bill Moreno, we spoke on the phone last night,' Caldwell said, and extended a hand, which Noonan shook limply. He took a wallet from his pocket and showed the forged White House ID card to Noonan. 'You just can't be too careful these days.'

'I guess not,' Noonan replied, then gestured Caldwell into the house.

Caldwell stepped inside and the door was closed behind him. He looked around him slowly: an assortment of musty-smelling anoraks on a coat rack beside the door; a dusty display cabinet containing a collection of insignificant little trinkets; a row of black-and-white pictures lining the walls which, on closer inspection, were of Hoboken at the turn of the century.

'You like the photos, do you?' Noonan asked from behind him.

'Fascinating,' Caldwell replied.

'Come through to the lounge. We can talk in there.'

He followed Noonan into a cold, uninviting room at the rear of the house. The walls were papered in a sickly yellow and the backs of the floral armchairs and couch were draped

161

with dirty antimacassars. An overweight ginger tom was curled up comfortably on the chair in the bay window, while an antiquated black-and-white television stood in a corner, the picture on, the sound off.

'Coffee?' Noonan asked, hovering in the doorway.

Caldwell cast another look around the depressing room then forced a smile. 'Not at the moment, thank you,' he said politely. He waited until Noonan had eased himself into the armchair directly opposite the television set before sitting on the edge of the couch. 'I'm sure you must be wondering why I wanted to see you today.'

'Yeah,' Noonan said, resting his hands on his ample girth. 'It's been bothering me ever since you called last night.'

'Well, let me get right to the point. You served with the Vice-President in 'Nam, didn't you?'

'I served *under* him,' Noonan replied, stubbing out his cigarette. 'He was a lieutenant then – and a damn fine officer. Always led from the front, and that earned him the respect of every man in his unit. It was an honour to have known him.'

'I guess you've got a few stories about him, then,' Caldwell said.

'Sure have!' Noonan replied, with a deep belly laugh. 'And not all of 'em repeatable – at least not in front of the ladies.'

'Excellent,' Caldwell said, clapping his hands together. He got to his feet and moved to the window. 'You're one of the five guests who actually served with the Vice-President in 'Nam. What we want to do is to spring a little surprise on him by having the five of you recount some of those tales after dinner. If you'd feel comfortable doing it, of course.'

'I'd be delighted,' Noonan said, beaming at Caldwell. 'My dear Phyllis – God rest her soul – always used to say I was a frustrated actor. And she was right!'

'It goes without saying, of course, that you can't mention this to anyone. Not even to any of the other guests. It's imperative that it comes as a complete surprise to the Vice-President.'

'You have my word on that,' Noonan assured him. 'But I reckon the Vice-President's wife wouldn't wanna hear some of the stuff he got up to in those days – but, then, that was before he found the Lord.'

'I've brought a dictating machine with me. I'll leave it with you tonight and pick it up again in the morning,' Caldwell said. 'Just record a few of your memories, Mr Noonan, then we can decide which ones to use on the night. The Vice-President has a wonderful sense of humour – and so does his wife, which surprises a lot of people when they first meet her. They always think that because her father's one of the country's leading televangelists, she's going to be some nun who only ever talks in parables.'

Noonan reached for the pack of Marlboro on the table beside him.

'Here, try one of mine,' Caldwell said, a case already open in his hand.

'I shouldn't be smoking,' Noonan said, as he helped himself to a cigarette. 'I had a heart-attack last year. The doctors told me to lay off smoking but I'm damned if they're going to spoil my last real pleasure in life.'

Caldwell smiled and extended the lighter towards Noonan. Then he released the gas directly into the man's face. He caught him as he was about to topple forward on to the floor and eased him back into the chair. Then he removed a mobile phone from the attaché case. He called the ambulance, which was waiting in a lock-up garage a few miles from the house, and then the cardiologist, already installed at a private clinic in Brooklyn Heights, standing by to implant the explosive device in Noonan's chest.

His eyes flickered open. At first everything appeared hazy and distorted but as he slowly focused on his surroundings he found he was lying in bed, staring at an unfamiliar ceiling. He lowered his eyes. A window, concealed behind closed Venetian blinds with peach curtains, harnessed by tie-backs, hung on either side. A wash-basin in the corner. Then he heard the sound of approaching footsteps in the corridor.

The psychiatrist from the ranch appeared at his bedside.

She was dressed as a nurse. She smiled at him then crossed to the bed. 'How are you feeling, Mr Noonan?'

'A little groggy,' he replied, rubbing his face. 'What happened? Where am I? What's going on?'

She pressed the button above his bed. 'I think it would be best if I were to let the doctor explain everything to you. He'll be along shortly. In the meantime, would you like some water?'

'I'd rather have a cigarette,' Noonan replied.

'I'm afraid that's out of the question in your condition,' she said.

'A cigarette?' Noonan mused, as he struggled to recall those last moments in his lounge. 'That's right. I was sitting in my armchair. I was about to have a cigarette. He'd offered me one. What was his name again? The guy from the White House. Marino, was it? No, that's the football player.'

'You mean Bill Moreno?' she said.

'Yes, that's right. You know him?'

'Very well,' she said. 'He was the one who had you brought here. If it hadn't been for his quick thinking, you might not have pulled through.'

'You mean I might have died?' No response. 'For God's sake, will you please tell me what's going on? Am I going to die?'

'No, you're not going to die, Mr Noonan,' the cardiologist announced from the doorway. 'At least, not today.'

'I told Mr Noonan you'd explain the situation to him,' the woman said, then smiled briefly at him and left the room.

'My name's John Edsel,' the cardiologist said. 'I'm the Vice-President's personal physician. Bill Moreno called me as soon as you collapsed at your home. I arranged to have you brought here so that I could attend to you personally.'

'Here being?' Noonan asked.

'You're at a private clinic in Brooklyn Heights.'

'You said I collapsed?'

'From the symptoms Bill Moreno described to me, you suffered a classic blackout,' the cardiologist told him. Noonan stared at him blankly. 'It's a temporary loss of consciousness

164

which occurs when there's an insufficient flow of blood from the heart to the brain. It's caused by an irregularity of the heartbeat. I'm told you came round in the back of the ambulance but moments later suffered a second attack. The paramedics were forced to administer cardiopulmonary resuscitation to restore the circulation of the blood to your brain. You were conscious when you arrived here, but totally disorientated. I thought it best to sedate you, and while you were under I implanted a pacemaker which, as I'm sure you know, supplies electrical impulses to the heart. Not only does it regulate the heartbeat but it'll also prevent any more attacks.'

'A pacemaker?' Noonan gasped, then undid the top button of his pyjama jacket and saw the dressing over the stitches. He looked up slowly at the cardiologist. 'This'll prevent any more attacks?'

'That's right. And having a pacemaker doesn't mean you'll suddenly have to change your lifestyle either. All I'd suggest is that you take it easy for the next couple of weeks – certainly avoid any vigorous exercise. After that, you're back to normal.'

'Avoiding vigorous exercise is normal for me, Doc,' Noonan said, patting his corpulent belly through the sheets. 'What about cigarettes?'

'I'd seriously consider giving up, if I were you,' the cardiologist replied. 'You'll be kept in here overnight and tomorrow morning for observation. I certainly don't foresee any problems. It's a precautionary measure more than anything else. You'll be back home tomorrow afternoon.'

'I'm invited to have dinner with the Vice-President tomorrow. I guess I won't be able to go now?' Noonan said, uncertainly.

'No reason why not,' the cardiologist replied, patting his shoulder.

'Thank God for that,' Noonan said, with relief. 'I've been looking forward to it so much – I was in 'Nam with the Vice-President, one of his grunts.'

'You've got a visitor waiting outside to see you. Bill

165

Moreno. He's been very concerned about you. I'll send him in now. And if you need anything at all, just press the button above your bed. One of the nurses will attend to you. I'll drop by later to see how you're getting on.'

'Doc?' Noonan called as the cardiologist headed for the door. 'Thanks for . . . what you did. I guess you saved my life.'

The cardiologist smiled then left the room. He walked to a swing door further down the corridor, pushed it open and found Caldwell and the psychiatrist waiting for him.

'Well?' Caldwell demanded.

'He believed it all,' the cardiologist replied, 'and he's got no idea that he's the only patient here, or that there aren't any other medical staff.'

'But he wouldn't expect the Vice-President's personal physician to lie to him,' said the psychiatrist with a knowing grin.

'I'm sure *he* wouldn't,' the cardiologist replied, then turned to Caldwell. 'It's your cue. The concerned Bill Moreno.'

Caldwell folded his copy of *USA Today* and tossed it down. He made his way along the corridor and knocked at Noonan's door.

'How you feeling?' he asked.

'Relieved that I'm still alive,' Noonan replied. 'Come in.'

Caldwell pulled up a chair and sat down. 'You gave me a hell of a fright back at your house. One moment you were talking to me, the next you just passed out. At first I thought you were dead. Then I found a pulse. That's when I called John – John Edsel. He arranged everything. The paramedics were at the house within minutes.'

'The doc said I woke up in the back of the ambulance. I don't remember that.'

'I believe you did, but I wasn't there,' Caldwell replied. 'I followed you in my car.'

'He said I was disorientated at the time, that's probably why I don't remember anything,' Noonan said, and was silent for a moment. Then he went on. 'This is a private clinic, right? My health insurance won't cover it.'

'Well, I wouldn't worry about it,' Caldwell told him. 'Let

166

the White House pay. I can clear it with a phone call. Don't give it another thought. You just make sure you're well on for the dinner.'

'I will be, believe me,' Noonan told him. 'You still want me to tell those stories?'

'If you think you're going to feel up to it.'

'I sure will,' Noonan said.

'Good. I'll leave the dictating machine for you at reception before I go. One of the nurses will bring it to you. But if the media were to get one whiff of this, it would be all over the front pages. We've got to keep it under wraps until the dinner.'

'Sure thing,' Noonan said.

'I think you're going to be quite a celebrity once this story breaks,' Caldwell said, then got up. 'You're going to have to excuse me now, Mr Noonan. I've got to get back to the hotel. The Vice-President thinks I spent the day with a consortium of local businessmen. I just hope he doesn't want a report on what we were supposed to have discussed. That might prove a little difficult.' He paused at the door to look back at Noonan. 'I'll have the dictating machine sent over to me later tonight, and I'll let you know in the morning which anecdotes we want you to tell. And remember, this has to remain our secret.'

'You bet,' Noonan said with a broad grin. 'I can't wait to see the Vice-President's face when we spring this on him.'

'Me neither,' Caldwell said before leaving the room.

'Rasha?'

The voice sounded like an echo in the deepest recesses of her mind. Then she heard it again. Louder. Something touched her cheek. She opened her eyes. Several figures were standing around her, sombre-faced, peering intently at her. She recognized one as a *hekura*, but it took her another few seconds to determine where she was. A *shabono*, about a hundred miles north of Boa Vista.

Where had they found her? What about her crew? What about the *Gal*? The *hekura* raised his hand as the questions

167

began to tumble from her lips. A hunting party had found her unconscious on the bank and brought her back to the *shabono*. They'd heard two explosions but by the time they'd reached the river there was only debris floating on the water. They hadn't found any other survivors. That didn't surprise Kelly. The question had been more out of hope than anything else. She struggled to sit up in the hammock and only then realized she was naked apart from a blanket, which had been draped discreetly across her. She secured it around her then eased herself out of the hammock and crossed to where her wet clothes had been laid out on the ground to dry. She felt inside the pockets of her dungarees. Her bracelet was still there, as was the sheet of paper Ray had given her before he'd left. The two telephone numbers were impossible to read now, but that didn't matter. She'd already consigned his home number to memory.

Her main concern now was how she was going to get to Boa Vista. Only then could she call Ray and warn him about what she'd seen in Donald's notebook. Before it was too late . . .

It was midnight when the cab pulled up outside the apartment in Brooklyn's Cobble Hill district. Brennan paid off the driver and used his personal security card to access the plate-glass door that led into the brightly lit foyer. Normally he used the stairs to get to his third-floor apartment, but he was so exhausted that he settled instead for an easy ride in the elevator.

The apartment door opened into a short hallway which led directly into the lounge. He kicked off his boots and tossed the holdall on to the sofa. Then, after drawing the curtains, he switched on his answering machine before going to the kitchen to get himself a cold beer from the refrigerator. He didn't take much notice of the first three messages – colleagues from the precinct who'd called to express their condolences. The fourth was from his aunt.

'Raymond, this is Gloria. Please call me the moment you

168

get back. It's very important. I'm staying at your mother's house.'

The line went dead. Had it been anyone else, he'd have left it and called in the morning. But he knew her arthritis often left her in so much pain that she rarely went to bed before two or three o'clock in the morning. And even then she got little sleep. He punched out the number then sat on the edge of the armchair, unease filtering through him as he waited impatiently for it to be answered.

Finally a familiar voice enquired, 'Hello, who is this?'

'Gloria, it's Ray. Has something happened?'

'It's your mother, Raymond. She suffered a mild stroke a few hours after you'd left for Brazil,' she told him. 'Dr Robson didn't feel she needed to be hospitalized but he advised complete rest for the next couple of weeks. Which leaves us with one problem. Jason. I'd have gladly looked after him but with this damn arthritis I can barely look after myself.'

'Gillian had relatives,' Brennan said, having guessed where the conversation was leading.

'Her parents are dead, as you well know. Her mother's sister lives somewhere in Nebraska. But from what Shirley said the husband drinks. And not only that. New York's Jason's home. How can you uproot a nine-year-old who's just lost his father and pack him off to Nebraska to stay with some great-aunt he doesn't even know?'

'So what you're saying is he should stay with some uncle he doesn't even know,' Brennan concluded.

'Of course he knows you,' she replied.

'As a fleeting visitor at his grandparents' house at Christmas and Thanksgiving. If the kid blinked, he probably missed me.'

'I remember you and Jason watching a ball game on TV one Thanksgiving and you helped him build that car track you bought him a couple of Christmases back. It may not have been much to you, but you can be sure it made an impression on him.'

Brennan stood up and paced the room. 'Gloria, I'm not sure I'm the right person for him right now.'

'Your mother's wrapped Jason in a blanket of sympathy ever since he got here and he can't be mollycoddled for ever. Sooner or later, he'll have to face up to the fact that Donald's gone. And you could play a vital role in helping him to come to terms with his father's death.'

'Why do I get the impression you're manoeuvring me into a corner here?' he asked.

'I'm doing no such thing!' was the indignant reply. 'All I'm saying is that it would help your mother greatly if she didn't have to worry about Jason right now and it would be an ideal opportunity for you two to get to know each other better. I'd understand, though, if you didn't feel comfortable about having him staying with you. It was just an idea, that's all. But I'll find an answer.'

'When do you want me to pick him up?'

'Are you sure you want to do this, Raymond?'

'When?' he repeated.

'Should we say around midday? That way you don't have to be up too early tomorrow morning.'

'Sure thing,' he said.

'Good. Jason's had his bag packed ever since I told him he'd be going to stay with you once you got back to New York.' She paused. 'I'll see you in the morning. Then you can tell me all about your trip to the Amazon. Good night, Raymond.'

'Yeah, good night, Gloria.' He replaced the handset. Suddenly he didn't feel tired any more. And he knew why. But there was no use worrying about how he was going to cope with Jason around. He'd have to wing it and hope for the best. Meanwhile, maybe a hot bath would relax him and help him get some sleep.

10

A familiar sound woke him. He reached out a hand to switch off the alarm clock. Except it wasn't in its regular place, within arm's reach on the bedside table. He reluctantly opened one eye – and remembered that before going to bed he'd put it on the floor out of reach to make sure he'd have to get up to switch it off. He kicked off the duvet, got out of bed and silenced the alarm. He resisted the temptation to flop back into bed as he replaced the clock on the bedside table and went to the bathroom where he splashed himself with cold water. He grabbed a towel and dried his face as he walked through to the kitchen to make himself some coffee. The day couldn't begin until he'd had that.

He took the mug to the lounge and sank into his favourite armchair. He couldn't remember the last time he'd had such a good night's sleep. But perhaps it wasn't so surprising after spending three restless nights squirming around in a hammock, jungle sounds playing havoc with his overactive imagination.

Once he'd finished the coffee, he shaved and changed into a pair of jeans and a white T-shirt. He slipped on his watch. It was 9.27. He called the precinct and was put through to his partner, Lou Monks, in the squad room.

'Hey, buddy, welcome back,' Monks said. 'When did you get in?'

'Last night,' Brennan replied. 'About eleven.'

'You should have called me. I'd have picked you up from the airport.'

'Thanks, but I just wanted to get back to the apartment and drop into bed,' Brennan said.

'How did it go out there?'

'Good, but I'll tell you about it when I see you,' Brennan said. 'Do me a favour, Lou. I've got a couple of names I want you to run through the computer. Chances are they'll turn out to be aliases, but it's worth a try.'

'You're on compassionate leave, for Christ's sake. Forget about work for the next few days. Spend some time with your family.' There was an uncomfortable pause. 'Look, I know you don't get on with your mother, but this would be a good time to put aside your differences—'

'What are you? My shrink?' Brennan cut in angrily.

'Your friend.'

'Just take down the names, will you?' Brennan said, but the anger had evaporated from his voice. 'Tom Caldwell and Bobby Dixon. I'll drop by later and see you. Probably some time this afternoon. Oh, and I'll have the kid in tow.'

'What kid?' Monks asked.

'Donald's boy. Jason. He's been staying with my mother, but she's sick. It's not serious, but she needs to take it easy for the next couple of weeks. So I've got the kid until she's ready to have him back again.'

'I guess you're the closest thing he has to a father now.'

'You just worry about running Caldwell and Dixon through the computer, and let me worry about the kid,' Brennan said snappily, as the truth of Monks's words struck him.

'Suits me. See you later.' The line went dead.

Brennan replaced the handset. There were times when he hated Lou Monks for being so blunt with the truth. Him, a father? That was worrying. But what unnerved him most was that the boy must know about the feud between Donald and himself – which had been going on since before Jason was born. Had Donald told him the real reason why his uncle never visited? If he had, Jason would be on his father's side. He was already regretting his decision to look after the kid for the next couple of weeks. He wanted to ring his aunt and tell her he'd changed his mind. It would be the easy way out. But he'd never been one to back away from a challenge. It was time to face up to his responsibilities. He'd already made a

172

start in acknowledging that he should have patched up his differences with Donald when he'd had the chance. Now it was too late for that, but he wasn't going to make the same sort of mistake with Jason. And if that meant being some kind of a father to him, then that's what he was prepared to be. But that was a long way down the road. First he had to get to know the boy – and earn his trust.

He went to his guest bedroom – or the junk room, as he called it, which was full of books, old clothes, gym equipment, all the stuff he'd got attached to and didn't want to throw out. He peered inside and groaned at the amount of rubbish piled up in the room. The bed was lost under the deluge. Maybe Jason could sleep on the Put-U-Up. It was either that or clear out this garbage . . .

The telephone rang. When he answered it the operator asked if he would accept a collect call from Kelly McBride in Manaus. 'Put her through,' he replied.

There was a pause while the line was connected. Then came the sound of her voice, infused with that alluring Irish brogue. 'Ray? Are you there? Ray?'

'Yeah, I'm here,' he replied, grinning. 'I don't mind collect, but you could have picked the cheap time to ring me.'

'Ray, I'm in trouble. Real trouble. They're looking for me. And if they find me, they'll kill me.'

The grin vanished as he sat on the edge of the chair. 'Who's trying to kill you?' Silence. 'Kelly, are you there?' he almost shouted.

'Yes,' she replied, shakily.

'Who's trying to kill you?' he repeated.

'Caldwell's *pistoleiros*. They're crawling all over Boa Vista. That's why I flew to Manaus. I'm on a pay phone at the airport right now. I've got my passport with me, but no money.'

'I'll get you out. Now tell me what happened. From the beginning.'

She started hesitantly, uncertain of herself, but soon she was pouring out her story. He was silent after she'd finished, stunned by what he'd just heard.

'Ray, are you still there?' she asked.

'I'm here,' he said. 'How did you get to Manaus?'

'I got a lift into Boa Vista from a passing trader. That's when I first heard that they were looking for me. I went to the bank to get my passport and what little money I had in my deposit box. It was just enough to buy myself a ticket to Manaus.'

'I'll make some calls at this end and get you a ticket on the next available flight to New York,' he said.

'Just get me out of here, Ray. I'll pay you back for the ticket as soon as I can.'

'Let's just worry right now about getting you to New York, shall we?' he replied.

'This is a loan, Ray,' she said, a hint of the old fire creeping back into her voice. 'I always settle my debts.'

'OK, it's a loan,' he agreed. 'Now give me your number, and I'll call you back when I've got you on a flight.'

Twenty minutes later he'd discovered that all the airlines were fully booked from Manaus to New York well into the following week. Including those routed via Rio and São Paulo.

'I can't say I'm surprised,' Kelly said, after he'd broken the news to her.

'Don't give up on me yet. I've still got an ace or two up my sleeve. You may not hear from me for the next few hours, but just make sure you stay close to the phone.'

'I'm not going anywhere,' she said.

He rang his mother's house to tell his aunt that something had come up at work which meant he couldn't collect Jason until the afternoon. Then he drove to the precinct in the South Bronx and went to the detectives' squad room on the second floor.

Lou Monks looked up from his paperwork as Brennan approached his desk. He pushed back his chair, got up and shook his partner's hand. 'I'm sorry about Donald. Marilyn asked me to pass on her condolences as well. She says you're welcome to come round for a meal one night next week. If you feel up to it, that is.'

'Tell her I'd like that. Thanks.' Brennan took him by the arm and led him out of earshot of anyone else. 'Anything on Caldwell and Dixon?'

'Nothing yet. Who are these guys?'

'Trouble,' Brennan said. 'I need to speak to d'Arcy. Is he in?'

'As far as I know,' Monks replied. 'What's going on, Ray?'

'Come with me and you'll find out.' Brennan crossed to the captain's office and rapped on the frosted-glass door.

'Come,' d'Arcy boomed. He looked up when Brennan and Monks entered the room. 'Ray, it's good to see you back in one piece. But what are you doing here? You're on paid leave. Take it.'

'The Vice-President's due to host a vets dinner at the Richmond Hotel tomorrow night, isn't he?' Brennan said.

'Yes, that's right,' d'Arcy said. 'But we're not involved with the security arrangements. The downtown boys will be handling that with the Secret Service. It's their problem, not ours.'

'It's just become our problem, sir,' Brennan said. 'I have every reason to believe there's going to be an attempt to assassinate the Vice-President tomorrow, probably at the hotel.'

'Go on,' d'Arcy said, and listened with a growing sense of disquiet as Brennan recounted everything Kelly had told him. An uneasy silence followed, then d'Arcy sat back in his chair without taking his eyes off Brennan's face. 'And you think this . . . Kelly McBride is on the level?'

'Without question,' Brennan replied stiffly.

'Very well,' d'Arcy said, after a thoughtful pause. 'I'll inform the Secret Service and let them take it from here. Obviously they'll want to question you further.'

'It's not me they should be questioning,' Brennan said. 'It's Kelly. She was there.'

'If she *is* on the level, then surely she's already passed on everything to you?' d'Arcy said.

'Right now she's stuck at Manaus airport with Caldwell's goons looking for her. And, after what happened yesterday, you can be sure they'll finish the job if they do find her.'

175

'And what exactly do you suggest we do?' d'Arcy asked.

Brennan rested his arms on d'Arcy's desk. 'I suggest we get her out of there before she winds up a corpse . . . *sir*. And you know as well as I do that the Secret Service can arrange it.'

'And just what makes you think they'll agree to any of this?' d'Arcy demanded.

'I don't think it would do the Vice-President's credibility any good if it were to come out that the woman responsible for helping to thwart an attempt on his life was then left to the mercy of the assassins when the White House had the opportunity to save her.'

'I'll be sure to pass on your comments to the Secret Service,' d'Arcy said. 'In the meantime, I want photofits of Caldwell and Dixon on my desk before the Secret Service get here.'

'You'll have them,' Brennan assured him.

'Have you run any checks on them?' d'Arcy asked Monks.

'I'm still waiting for a reply from the National Database, sir.'

'Then get on the phone and tell them to pull their fingers out!' d'Arcy thundered. 'And I think Brennan's right – they're probably using false names. But until we know otherwise, I want a face put to every Tom Caldwell and Bobby Dixon who've ever passed through the system. And I want them on my desk *now*.'

'I'll get on to it right away,' Monks said and crossed to the door.

'And, Lou,' d'Arcy called after him, 'not a word of this to anyone.' He waited until Monks had left the office before he said, 'You care about this woman, don't you?'

'Yeah, but this isn't about my personal feelings. She risked her life by taking a stand against Dixon and his goons. Now she's lost everything and I think she deserves better than to be left to the wolves after that. A lot better.'

'Then let's hope the Secret Service agree with you,' d'Arcy said, picking up the telephone.

'I'm sure you can persuade them to see it that way, sir,' Brennan replied, then left the office.

'Morning,' Clive Noonan said cheerily when Caldwell entered his room.

'How are you feeling today?' Caldwell asked.

'Good. The doctor said I can go home this afternoon.'

'Great news,' Caldwell said, then took an envelope from his pocket and placed it on the bedside table. 'That's the list of stories we feel would be acceptable to tell at the dinner tomorrow night. There won't be time for them all. I'd say three would be fine.'

Noonan picked up the envelope and opened it. He scanned the page.

'I see the ones you've left out,' he said, chuckling. 'I can't say I'm surprised but I thought I'd tell 'em to you anyway.' He slipped the paper back into the envelope and replaced it on the bedside table.

'That wasn't the only reason why I called by this morning,' Caldwell said. 'I thought I should let you know that I won't be attending the dinner. I have to fly back to Washington this afternoon and I'll be busy for the next few days at the very least. But my colleagues will be there and one of them will spring the surprise on the Vice-President.'

'I'm sorry I won't see you,' Noonan said, with genuine disappointment.

'So am I, believe me. I was looking forward to it. But, then, that's the life of a politician.' Caldwell shook Noonan's hand. 'Good luck. I'm sure it'll be a success. And thanks for your co-operation. We really appreciate it.'

'I'm the one who should be thanking you,' Noonan replied. 'But what do you say to someone who just saved your life?'

'It'll be thanks enough if it all goes well tomorrow night,' Caldwell replied then left him.

The cardiologist was waiting in the empty staff lounge. 'Well?' he said.

'Exactly as I expected,' Caldwell replied contemptuously. 'He thinks himself something of a raconteur – and I guess

177

some of his stories could have been OK, but his punchlines are about as funny as a vasectomy with a blunt knife.'

'Sure, but he means well,' the cardiologist said. Then he took the remote control from his pocket and handed it to Caldwell. 'I've done my bit. The rest's up to you.'

'I'll be in touch once the next client's on line,' Caldwell said, pocketing the device. 'It won't be for a few weeks yet. Take a short vacation. You've earned it.'

'I might just do that,' the cardiologist replied. 'Do you have anyone particular in mind?'

'Maybe,' came the evasive reply.

'I guess it all depends on who's prepared to pay the asking price. After all, a million dollars is a lot of money.'

'In return they get our expertise, complete discretion, guaranteed success as well as the added safeguard of knowing there won't be any evidence to link them to the assassination. I'd say it's a good deal.'

'We've still got a problem, though,' the cardiologist said.

'You let me worry about Bobby Dixon,' Caldwell replied.

'That's what you said at the ranch,' the cardiologist snapped.

'I also said he'd be replaced – after tomorrow night,' Caldwell said, with equal acerbity. 'But until then, he's still a part of this team.'

'Do you have someone to replace him?'

'Perhaps.'

'If you want his death to look like an accident, I'll let you have some hydrocyanic gas,' the cardiologist said. 'All you'll have to do is spray it into his face and he'll be dead within seconds. And as you'll have taken an antidote before releasing the gas, it won't affect you. The gas will disperse within a couple of minutes, leaving no trace. It'll look like he had a heart-attack. Death by natural causes. It won't be questioned.'

'I'll keep it in mind,' Caldwell said, then looked at his watch. 'I've got to go. I'm supposed to be at the airport in an hour.'

'Are you meeting someone?'

Caldwell paused at the door. 'Dixon's due in on a charter flight from Miami. I'll be sure to give him your regards. I know he'll appreciate it.'

'You've got a visitor, sir,' a detective said, from the doorway of d'Arcy's office. 'Secret Service.'

'Good. Show him in, will you?' d'Arcy replied, closing the folder in front of him. 'And tell Monks and Brennan to get in here as well.'

'Will do,' the detective replied, then gestured the man into the room before closing the door behind him.

'I'm Special Agent Chip Garrett, head of the Vice-Presidential Protection Detail,' the man announced. 'We spoke on the phone earlier.'

'That's right,' d'Arcy said, as they shook hands. He estimated Garrett to be in his early forties. Clean-shaven. Short black hair. Well-toned physique. Probably a good sportsman in his younger days. He certainly had the build of a running back.

'Right idea, wrong position,' Garrett replied, when d'Arcy voiced his thoughts. 'I was a wide receiver. But that was a long time ago. I haven't played competitive football since I left college.'

'Coffee?' d'Arcy asked.

'Precinct coffee? Are you kidding?' Garrett snorted. 'Unless, of course, you guys make a better brew than your colleagues downtown. I swear they could resurface Fifth Avenue with that stuff.'

'They do, didn't they tell you?' Brennan said, behind them. 'It's all part of the crackdown on public spending introduced by our new Republican governor. And you know, I could have sworn one of his main election pledges was to increase the budget on public spending.'

'That's enough, Brennan!' d'Arcy said testily, then introduced Garrett, who shook Monks's hand before turning to Brennan, who was still hovering in the doorway. He took a sheet of paper from his jacket pocket and said, 'I believe this is what you wanted.'

179

Brennan unfolded it. It was a fax confirming Kelly's seat on the next Miami-bound flight out of Manaus, as well as an interconnecting flight from Miami to New York later that afternoon. Both were first-class seats. 'I rang every damn airline I could find and I couldn't even get her into the baggage hold. You pick up the phone and not only do you get her seats but first-class too. You guys must have some clout at the White House.'

'Being head of the Vice-President's Protection Detail does have its advantages,' Garrett replied, with a knowing smile. 'Normally we wouldn't breach protocol like this, but Captain d'Arcy put across an eloquent case as to why we should get Ms McBride out of Manaus. He did say, however, that he was only quoting what you'd said to him.'

'Yeah, well,' Brennan said, with a shrug. 'I guess you had to bump a couple of passengers to get those seats.' He held up the fax towards d'Arcy. 'I'll need to call Kelly and tell her what's going on.'

'Just hurry up, we've got work to do here,' d'Arcy said gruffly, then handed the pictures of Caldwell and Dixon to Garrett. 'Brennan put those together with one of our police artists. They were wearing shades when he met them. Caldwell kept his on but Dixon didn't and Brennan said he has distinctive blue eyes.'

Garrett studied the two images. 'I take it you've already run them through the system?'

'Nothing,' Monks said. 'The names came up several times, but none of the faces matched.'

'Brennan's maintained all along that he's pretty sure the names are phoney,' d'Arcy said. 'Looks like he was right.'

'Unless they're clean,' Garrett said.

'Or they could have been in the military,' Monks added. 'Ray said that Kelly McBride told him she'd heard Caldwell's men call him Colonel.'

'Have you contacted the military yet?' Garrett asked.

'No, I thought it best to wait till you got here,' d'Arcy said. 'After all, it officially falls under your jurisdiction.'

'Good,' Garrett said. 'Right now, the fewer people who

know about this the better. I'd like to fax these faces through to a contact of mine at our HQ in Washington. If either man has served in the military – and assuming a positive match can be made from these photofits – then at least we'll know who we're up against.'

'Help yourself,' d'Arcy said, indicating the fax machine behind his desk.

'Thanks. I'd better call him first, and let him know what's going on,' Garrett said, picking up the receiver. 'Would you mind?' he added, waving towards the door. He waited until d'Arcy and Monks had gone before punching in an unlisted number at the Pentagon. It was answered after the first ring. He identified himself to the operator then gave his security clearance code. There was a pause while it was cross-checked on the computer. Once it was confirmed, he was asked who he wanted.

'Jim Lovell,' he said, then eased himself into d'Arcy's padded chair as he waited to be connected.

Half a dozen rings later someone answered. 'Yeah?'

'Didn't your mother ever teach you anything about telephone manners?' Garrett said good-humouredly.

'Hey, Chip, how you doing?' came the genial reply.

'Better than you, by the sound of it,' Garrett said.

'Ah, I'm OK. Just too busy.'

'I hate to do this to you, Jim, but I'm going to have to add to your workload. I've got a possible Priority One on my hands,' Garrett said.

'Then that takes preference over all this other shit. What have you got?'

'I'm going to fax a couple of faces through to you. The names on the photos are probably false so you'll have to check that out.'

'Any prints?'

'Unfortunately not,' Garrett replied. 'But they could both be ex-military – one may have been a colonel. See what you can do, Jim, and get back to me as soon as you can, will you?'

'I can't promise anything, Chip, but I'm sure I'll do my best. Where can I get hold of you if I come up with something?'

181

'I'm on a mobile.' Garrett gave Lovell the number then faxed the two images through to him at Secret Service headquarters in Washington. When he opened the door, Brennan, d'Arcy and Monks were talking together in the corner of the squad room.

Brennan got to Garrett first. 'I've spoken to Kelly. She asked me to pass on her thanks.'

'No problem,' Garrett said.

'Do you want to question her tonight?' Brennan asked.

'I don't think there's much point. She's obviously been through one hell of an ordeal. She won't have slept much in the last twenty-four hours and she'll be no use to me like that. She'll forget things that may be important. Shall we say nine o'clock tomorrow morning?'

'Here?'

'Sure, why not?' Garrett agreed.

'I need your help, Lou,' Brennan said to Monks, as they filed back into d'Arcy's office.

'You want me to collect her from the airport,' Monks replied.

'Yeah. How did you know?' Brennan asked in surprise.

'Because you'll have Jason at the apartment tonight, and considering the time of her arrival, you can hardly take him with you to the airport. And you certainly couldn't leave him at the apartment by himself.'

'You know, with that kind of perceptive mind you should have been a detective,' Brennan said with a grin.

'You're right,' Monks replied, and plucked the fax from Brennan's hand.

'Ray, I've got a call for you here,' d'Arcy said, holding the receiver out towards Brennan. 'He says he's a cop. He's phoning from Rio.'

'That was quick,' Brennan said. He listened carefully, occasionally asking a question and noting the answers on a block of paper on d'Arcy's desk.

'What was that all about?' d'Arcy demanded, once Brennan had hung up.

'I put a call through to the Brazilian Federal Police,'

182

Brennan said. 'I asked them to make some discreet enquiries about the ranch in the Amazon. Caldwell claimed it belonged to Eduardo Silva, one of the major cattle barons over there. According to the cop, it *did* belong to Silva but he sold it twelve months ago to a company based in São Paulo. A company owned by the American oil billionaire, Lamar Zander.'

'The *late* American oil billionaire,' d'Arcy corrected him. 'He died earlier this year. Of a heart attack, if I remember correctly.'

'That's right,' Garrett said. 'He'd had heart problems all his life. He even had his own personal cardiologist who travelled with him wherever he went, as well as his own private clinic in Brooklyn Heights. As far as I know, it was never open to the public.'

'You seem to know a lot about him,' Brennan said.

'It was a standard joke on Capitol Hill that the White House was Lamar Zander's *pied-à-terre*,' Garrett replied. 'He was a liberal who was careful to keep one foot in each of the two main political camps so was courted by presidents and senior White House figures. And if he agreed with White House policy, rumour had it he was generous with his cheque book. I met him several times. A charming man. Very witty. And very intelligent.'

'So what's his link to Caldwell and Dixon?' Brennan asked. 'They called themselves "security advisers". Frankly, I don't buy it.'

'The ranch belongs to a company he owned,' Garrett pointed out. 'Who's to say they weren't hired after his death?'

'According to Kelly, they've been at the ranch for the past year,' Brennan said. 'When exactly did Zander die?'

'It can't have been more than six months ago,' d'Arcy said, and Garrett nodded in agreement.

'So what were they doing at the ranch?' Monks said. 'Were they working for Zander at the time of his death?'

'I think you'd better make another call to the Federal Police,' d'Arcy said, holding the handset out towards Brennan.

183

'I've got to get back to the hotel,' Garrett said. 'There's still a lot to do before the Vice-President arrives tomorrow afternoon. I'll be in touch but keep me posted on any new developments.'

'And you'll let us know if your people identify the photo-fits,' d'Arcy countered.

'Of course,' Garrett said, then picked up the pictures. 'I'll take these – they'll be distributed to all security personnel at the hotel. I'll have them sent back to you later this afternoon.'

'I can pick them up when I'm at the hotel,' Brennan said.

'What are you going there for?' d'Arcy wondered.

'I want to be on the team tomorrow night,' Brennan replied.

'Forget it!' d'Arcy barked. 'Let Special Agent Garrett and his men worry about the security arrangements at the hotel. That's what they're here for.'

'I'm the only person who's seen Caldwell and Dixon,' Brennan said. 'What if they change their appearance? Would his men recognize them?'

'Would you?' d'Arcy challenged.

'Maybe not, but at least I've got a better chance,' Brennan replied. 'It's got to be worth a try, surely.'

'I'd like to bring him in on my team,' Garrett said to d'Arcy.

'You want him, he's all yours,' d'Arcy replied.

'I want Lou as well,' Brennan said to Garrett. 'With all due respect to you and your team, Lou's the only person I trust to cover my back.'

'Have you both got tuxes?' Garrett asked.

'What the hell would I be doing with a tux?' Brennan retorted.

'Mine's in mothballs somewhere in the attic,' Monks said. 'The last time I wore it was sometime back in the seventies. And even then it was out of fashion.'

'Then it looks like you're both going to have to hire them,' Garrett said. 'I want you both to report to the hotel at one o'clock this afternoon so you can be shown around the place.'

'We'll be there,' Monks assured him.

'Are you going to tell the Vice-President about what Kelly saw in Donald's notebook?' Brennan asked.

'We treat politicians the same way they treat the voters – we tell them what we think they should know,' Garrett said.

Brennan waited until Garrett had gone, then reached for the handset lying on d'Arcy's paper-strewn desk.

'Making that call to Rio?' d'Arcy enquired.

'First I've got to put off collecting my nephew from my mother's house – for the second time today,' Brennan said, then cast a despairing look in Monks's direction. 'Why do I get this feeling that it's not going to go down too well?'

'Bingo!' Jim Lovell exclaimed, when the computer came up with a possible match for one of Garrett's images. The screen divided in half and the two images appeared side-by-side. His eyes went to the words flashing in the bottom left-hand corner of the screen: *Probability of match – 94%*. 'That's good enough for me, sweetheart,' he said, patting the side of the machine. Then he punched in a code and the corresponding dossier unfurled on the screen. 'You were right, Chip, but then you normally are,' he muttered to himself, as he scanned the information. 'Our friend here is ex-military. And his name isn't Bobby Dixon.' He printed out the dossier and attached it to the relevant picture with a paper-clip, then fed in the second image and sat back in his chair to await developments.

Jim Lovell was a maverick whose whole life revolved around computer technology. All his spare time was taken up with it and when he wasn't devising some revolutionary programme at home for one of his work computers, he would spend hours communicating with like-minded enthusiasts on the Internet. His obsession was well known at Secret Service Headquarters and at their training facility at Laurel, Maryland, where he taught a course on computer programming to every new intake of recruits. Although the information stored in his computer banks had been invaluable in helping to thwart several planned assassinations in the seven years since he'd started working for the Treasury Department – the Secret Service comes under its sway – he'd never been accepted by his peers, who regarded him as an outsider: a desk man with no field experience. There was, however, a handful of operatives he held in high esteem. In particular, Chip Garrett.

'Ouch, freeze out!' Lovell clapped his hands when the screen divided in half again. On one side was the photofit image; on the other a file number with the words *Classified – B2* flashing underneath it. Only two people in the Secret Service had a B2 clearance: the Director and his deputy. Much as he'd tried over the years, he'd never cracked the program that would have gained him access to those high-security files. Not that they would mean anything to him even if he could access them. All he wanted was to prove to himself that he could outsmart the government boffins who'd claimed that the program was foolproof when they'd first installed it. He had every confidence that one day he would succeed. Then he'd move on to another challenge.

He rang the Deputy Director and explained the situation. The man had him read out the file number. There was a pause at the other end of the line while the Deputy Director punched the digits into his keyboard before using his own personal clearance code to access the file. 'And this is the only compatible match to the picture Garrett faxed through to you?'

'It's the most likely match, sir,' Lovell replied. 'The computer will have accessed all possible files before coming up with this one. I could run the programme again, asking the computer to pick out other possible matches, but the probability factor would automatically be decreased. Do you want me to do another run, sir?'

'No. Judging by what Garrett told you, I'd say we've already got our man.'

'How do you want me to proceed, sir?'

'Leave it with me. I'll call Garrett. You'd better give me the number of the Dixon file as well.'

Lovell read it out to him. 'What do you want me to do with the photofits, sir?'

'Considering the sensitive nature of the classified file, I think it would be best if I were to send someone down to

186

collect them from you. Put them in a sealed envelope. The fewer people who know about this the better.'

'Caldwell must be a pretty important *hombre* to warrant this kind of treatment,' Lovell said, whistling softly to himself.

'*Very* important.' The line went dead.

'Come in,' Lovell called in response to the knock on the door. He looked round and smiled at the two figures who entered the room. One man, one woman, both experienced field agents attached to the Presidential Protection Division. The man was tall and muscular with pock-marked cheeks; his nose was noticeably crooked. The woman was gorgeous, and Lovell regarded her as being so far out of his league that he even felt guilty fantasizing about her. He focused on her colleague. 'So how are things topside?' he asked, a reference he always used whenever he referred to the floors above his basement office.

'Kickin',' the man said, with a thumb's-up sign.

'Everything's always "kickin'" to you, isn't it?' Lovell said with a chuckle. 'So, what brings you guys down here.'

'The envelope for Deputy Director Frain,' the woman said.

'It needs two of you to come down here and collect it?' Lovell said in amazement as he handed her the envelope. 'You can tell Deputy Director Frain it's all in there. With my compliments.'

'And this is with my compliments,' she said, then produced a small gas gun from her shoulder bag and fired a capsule into Lovell's face. The glass vial shattered, releasing its load of lethal gas into the air.

Lovell immediately began to gasp for air, his hands clawing frantically at his throat, but within seconds the gas had paralysed his heart. The man grabbed him as he was about to topple sideways off his chair, then leaned his body forward until he was slumped over the desk. The woman went through the motions of checking for a pulse. Nothing.

She eyed the body disdainfully then began to whistle softly to herself as she followed her colleague from the room.

★

187

'Thanks for letting me know,' Caldwell said, then switched off his mobile phone and returned to the lounge where Dixon was sitting on the sofa, watching the latest report on the Vice-President's intended visit to the city the following day.

'Is there a problem?' Dixon asked, and used the remote control to turn down the volume on the television set.

'That was Jackson. Kelly McBride's very much alive,' Caldwell replied.

'I don't believe it.' Dixon took a cigarette from the packet on the table beside him and lit it.

'What's more, she contacted Brennan from Manaus this morning and told him about the notebook,' Caldwell continued. 'I don't know how much *she* knows, but we're not going to get near her now. She's getting VIP treatment all the way through to New York. And, if that wasn't enough, Brennan's put together photofits of us which have already been sent to all the major law enforcement agencies around the country. Including the Secret Service. It's a fucking mess. If you'd followed your orders properly and killed Kelly McBride, none of this would have happened.'

'I could have sworn she died when the boat went down,' Dixon said, then moved to the apartment window and looked down at the late-afternoon traffic below him. 'Are we going to abort the operation?'

'No!' was the sharp riposte. 'You'll check into the hotel tomorrow morning as planned. But you're going to have to change your appearance – and that's what we're going to do tonight. By the time we're finished, even your own mother won't recognize you.'

'What if it doesn't work?' Dixon asked uneasily.

'Then you'll be spending the next twenty-five years in a federal jail,' Caldwell said sharply. 'I'd say that was quite an incentive to get it right, wouldn't you?'

Dixon stubbed out the cigarette. 'When do we start?'

11

The lobby of the Richmond Hotel was dominated by a magnificent tiered waterfall and banks of greenery. Hand-woven tapestries were hung on the surrounding walls – a soothing welcome for harassed guests on their arrival. The corridor leading to the function rooms was lined with an elegant display of silver-and-gold brocade. The commodious room where the Vice-President would be hosting the Independence Day dinner was panelled with rich Brazilian mahogany, and an exquisite crystal chandelier hung from the centre of the sumptuous gold-leaf ceiling.

Monks was caught up in the breathtaking splendour of his luxurious surroundings, but Brennan was unimpressed by what he regarded as little more than a vulgar show of tasteless opulence.

'It's not bad, is it?' Garrett said, from behind them. He nodded to the special agent who'd shown Monks and Brennan around the hotel, and the man left.

'It's incredible,' Monks replied in awe.

'To each his own, I guess,' Brennan said.

'You can be a real Philistine at times, Ray, you know that?' Monks said, shaking his head despairingly.

'We done here?' Brennan asked, looking across at Garrett.

'Sure, let's go through to the lobby,' Garrett replied. 'Your security passes should be ready later tonight. Do you want me to have them sent to the precinct, or will you pick them up here?'

'I can get them in the morning,' Monks said. 'It's on my way to work.'

'When's the Vice-President due to arrive in New York?' Brennan asked.

'His flight's due in at twelve-thirty tomorrow afternoon. He'll be coming straight to the hotel, and won't leave the building again until the next morning. That's a great weight off my shoulders. A few weeks ago he was talking about attending a street parade in Harlem. It took a lot of persuading to get him to drop the idea. He's got more than enough enemies among the country's white population, let alone among the Afro-American community. They regard him as little more than a right-wing bigot with links to the white supremacists.'

'They're probably not far wrong,' Brennan said.

'You don't like him, do you?' Garrett said to Brennan.

'No,' he answered.

'He may have some controversial right-wing views, but he has nothing but contempt for the white supremacists. So don't condemn him out of hand. Not without having met him.' The mobile phone in Garrett's pocket began to ring. When he answered it he was surprised to hear the voice of Deputy Director Frain. He moved away from Brennan and Monks before speaking. 'I was expecting Jim Lovell to call me, sir,' he said.

'Yes, I know,' was the sombre reply. 'Jim Lovell's dead, Chip.'

'Dead?' Garrett replied incredulously. 'But I only spoke to him a couple of hours ago. What happened?'

'It's still too early to know for sure, but the doctor thinks he had a heart-attack. Obviously we'll know more once an autopsy's been carried out. He was only thirty-eight. It's not as if he had any trouble with his heart before. I still can't believe it myself.'

'He did say he was busy when I talked to him,' Garrett said. 'But, then, when wasn't he up to his neck in work? It's what kept him going. Jim wasn't the kind of guy who'd kick back at a club or a ball game. Computers were his whole life.'

'Perhaps that was the problem. Too much work and not enough R and R. I didn't know him very well, but from what

190

I hear he spent all his spare time surfing the Internet. It can't have been healthy being cooped up in his apartment like that.'

'I faxed a couple of faces through to him earlier,' Garrett said.

'Yes, it was logged on his report sheet. He was always meticulous when it came to that. He hadn't come up with a match for either, but I thought it best to double-check.'

'Did you come up with anything, sir?' Garrett asked.

'No, I'm afraid not. I'll contact the Pentagon – the Bureau as well as the various branches of the military – to see if they can come up with anything. But it's a long shot. We already have most of their files in our databanks as it is.' There was a pause. 'Keep me posted on any new developments, Chip. Day or night. It doesn't matter.'

'I will, sir,' Garrett said, then the line went dead. He slipped the phone back in his pocket. 'No joy on the photo-fits,' he told Brennan and Monks.

'I can't say I'm surprised,' Brennan replied.

'Well, if you'll excuse me, I've got work to do.' Garrett snapped his fingers at the two special agents beside the reception desk and the three crossed the lobby to the elevator.

Brennan looked at his watch. 'Jesus, look at the time. I've still got to drive out to the Hamptons and collect Jason, then take him back to the apartment. I'll see you later, Lou.'

'Sure,' Monks replied, but Brennan was already heading for the main doors.

Brennan arrived at his mother's house shortly before five o'clock. The butler showed him into the lounge. Shirley Brennan was seated in her favourite armchair beside the empty fireplace, a plaid rug over her legs. 'Hello, Ray,' she said, then closed the book she'd been reading and placed it on the coffee table beside her.

'How are you feeling?' Brennan asked.

'A little weak, but Doc Robson assured me there won't be any lasting side effects. Just a mild stroke.'

'The main thing is you're OK,' Brennan said, sitting on the sofa opposite her.

'Oh, I feel fine. But you know I've been told to take it easy. That's why your aunt asked you to look after Jason. Not that she told me, mind, until she'd made the arrangements. I still think he should stay here with me.' She gave a sharp tug on the bell pull. Moments later the door opened and the butler entered the room. 'Haskins, will you bring Jason here. And have his suitcase put in Mr Brennan's car.'

'Yes, madam,' the man said formally and withdrew.

'I assume you were able to carry out the instructions Donald left for you in his letter,' his mother asked.

'I had the body taken—'

'I don't wish to know the details,' she cut in sharply. 'I just want your assurance that you did as he asked.'

He nodded.

'Good.'

No gratitude. Just acceptance. It didn't surprise him.

The door opened and Jason came in, his eyes red and puffy from crying. He crossed to where Brennan was standing and held out his hand tentatively. 'Hello, Uncle Ray,' he said.

Brennan took Jason's hand. He knew his mother would have told the child exactly what to do when he met his uncle. Everything always had to be so goddamn formal with her. He could still remember what she'd said to Donald and himself at their father's funeral: *It's imperative to maintain a disciplined stoicism at all times in front of others.* It hadn't mattered that 'others', then, had been family and close friends. Outward appearances had always been of the utmost importance to her.

'What do you say to Uncle Ray?' she asked Jason.

'Thank you for letting me stay with you,' the little voice replied obediently.

'You're welcome,' Brennan said, with a smile. 'I think we'd better make a move. It's going to take us a couple of hours to drive home. Are you ready to go?'

'He's been ready since lunch-time,' Shirley Brennan said indignantly, then turned to Jason. 'Come and give your grandmother a kiss before you leave.'

Brennan noticed the hesitancy in Jason's movements as he crossed to her, and his body stiffened when she hugged him tightly. He gave her a modest peck on the cheek and looked distinctly uncomfortable as she tucked his T-shirt into his jeans.

'Go and wait in the car for your uncle,' she said. Only after Jason had left the room did she address her son. 'I think I've already made it clear that I don't approve of this arrangement—'

'Then that makes two of us,' he interrupted, cutting her off mid-sentence before she could reel off another lecture at his expense. He'd endured enough of them. 'Don't worry, I'll be sure to wrap him in several layers of cotton wool and lock him in the guest room. That way nothing can possibly happen to him. That *is* what you want, isn't it?'

'I may be over-protective but that's only because I care about him. He's all I've got left now. But, then, I wouldn't expect you to understand that.'

'Oh, I understand all right,' Brennan replied coldly. 'It's exactly what you did to Donald when he was a child. And you'd have done it to me as well, given half a chance.'

'Maybe if I had you might have made something of your life. Look what your brother managed to achieve – a world-renowned anthropologist with a loving wife and a son who worshipped him.'

'A loving wife!' Brennan snorted contemptuously. 'Their marriage was over long before Gillian died.'

'That's not true!' she countered angrily. 'They were devoted to each other.'

'You know as well as I do it was all a façade. Then again, it's hardly surprising you won't admit that, considering what you said to me at Dad's funeral.' He saw the uncertainty flash across her face as she struggled to recollect her words and he took a perverse pleasure in her discomfort at suddenly finding herself wrong-footed. *Checkmate*, he thought with satisfaction. He returned to his car and saw that Jason was already sitting in the passenger seat, the safety belt secured across his chest. Brennan got behind the wheel, started up the engine and drove away.

★

In the car his attempts at conversation were rarely met with anything more than a monosyllabic reply. Finally he switched on the radio. It was tuned into his favourite R&B station but assuming that that type of music wouldn't appeal to Jason, he fiddled with the knob until he found a station playing wall-to-wall chart music.

After an hour and a half of it, Brennan was relieved to pull up outside his apartment block. He got out and opened the trunk but as he reached for the suitcase Jason's hand shot forward and grabbed the handle. 'Leave it, I'll take it,' Brennan said, but Jason clung to it as his uncle lifted it out. Brennan shrugged, closed the trunk, and was about to dart across the road between the oncoming cars, as he normally did, when he checked himself. He had to set a good example. With that in mind, he waited until the road was clear before crossing.

They took the elevator to the third floor where he unlocked the door to his apartment and gestured for Jason to enter first. 'It's small, I guess, but it's home,' he said, closing the door behind him, then eased past Jason who was rooted to the spot, the suitcase clutched tightly to the front of his legs. 'Put your case down and come on through to the lounge.'

Brennan cleared several magazines off the sofa and Jason sat down. 'Have you already eaten at your grandmother's house?' A shake of the head. 'Are you hungry?' A pause – then another shake of the head. 'I don't believe that. You've got to be hungry – I am, that's for sure. What kind of food do you like? How about pizza? There's a great pizza place down the road.'

'I like pizza,' Jason said softly, staring at the carpet.

'Me too.' Brennan phoned through an order. 'It'll be about twenty minutes,' he announced. 'Now I'm going to clear out the guest room, otherwise you won't have any place to sleep tonight. Do you want to give me a hand?' A nod. 'Great. Come on then, let's get stuck in.'

Cardboard boxes crammed with dog-eared paperbacks, old clothes stuffed into plastic bags, teetering piles of sports magazines – and stacked against one wall, his LP collection.

They transferred everything to Brennan's bedroom then made up the bed. As he was tucking the bottom sheet under the mattress Brennan's fingers brushed against something under the bed – a football.

'So that's where you went,' he said, smiling to himself as he turned it around slowly in his hands. He delivered a short shovel pass to Jason, who deftly caught it. 'That was given to me by one of the greatest players ever to pull on a Giants' shirt. The legendary LT – Lawrence Taylor – just after they'd won Superbowl Twenty-five. He even signed it for me.'

'Lawrence Taylor gave you this?' Jason said in awe, as he stared at the signature scrawled across the ball in black marker pen.

'I didn't think you'd have heard of him. He's been retired for a few years now.'

'Every Giants' fan knows about LT.'

'You're a Giants' fan?' Brennan said, surprised.

'You were the one who first got me interested in football, Uncle Ray,' Jason said. 'We watched a Giants' game together on TV at Grandma's house a few years ago. You explained the rules and all the different plays to me.'

'Yeah, I remember that,' Brennan said. 'I didn't think you were listening much, though.'

'I didn't understand everything you said, but it got me started. Now I always watch the Giants whenever they're on TV. I've always wanted to go to a game, but I know it's really hard to get tickets for the Giants Stadium. Perhaps I'll get the chance one day, when I'm older.'

'I can probably get us a couple of tickets for a game next season,' Brennan said.

'Oh, Uncle Ray!' Jason said excitedly. 'But where will you get them from?'

'I've got my contacts,' Brennan said, knowingly.

'Does that mean we can go to any game?' Jason asked, barely able to believe his luck.

'I don't see why not, providing I can get the tickets.'

'That's neat,' Jason said, then held out the football to him.

'It's yours.'

195

'You *mean* it?'

'Yeah, you keep it.'

'Gee, thanks, Uncle Ray.'

There was a knock at the door. Pizza delivery. Brennan answered it, paid the courier then went through to the lounge where Jason joined him, the football now held tightly under his arm. Brennan switched on the TV and watched the news while he ate, taking a special interest in the segment about the Vice-President's upcoming visit to New York the following day.

'Grandma likes him,' Jason announced, pointing to the Vice-President when he appeared on screen. 'She says he'll make a good President one day.' He fell silent then and when he'd finished the last piece of pizza he closed the lid and put the empty box carefully on the magazine-strewn table in the middle of the room. 'Thank you for dinner, Uncle Ray.'

'It was good, wasn't it?'

Jason nodded. 'Dad and I often used to eat like this. But Grandma never lets me eat in front of the TV. We always have to sit at the table. And Grandma . . .'

'. . . takes for ever to eat,' Brennan concluded, when Jason's voice trailed off. 'You can count yourself lucky, I had to put up with it for seventeen years. What's more, I had to wear a suit and tie to dinner until I was twelve. By then I had more suits in my wardrobe than I did jeans. The other kids used to tease me all the time about it. That's when I decided enough was enough.'

'What did you do?'

'One day I cut the arms off all the jackets, cut off all the trousers above the knees and cut all the ties in half. So come dinner time, I put on one of my spoiled suits, half a tie but no shirt, a pair of old sneakers and my football socks. Your grandmother threw a fit and sent me straight to my room. But it worked. I never had to wear a suit to dinner again.'

'I could never do that . . . not with Grandma.'

'Are you frightened of her?' Brennan asked.

'No,' Jason said defiantly. But there was a hesitation in his eyes. He shrugged uncomfortably. 'Well . . . sometimes, I

196

guess. When she gets mad at me. She shouts real loud. And her face gets all twisted and angry. It's like it's not Grandma. And I always think she's going to hit me. But she doesn't. She just keeps shouting. It can be real scary.'

'That's how she was when I was a kid,' Brennan said. 'She never hit me either, but I always thought she was going to when she got mad at me. And that happened a lot. Your grandmother thinks that children should be neither seen nor heard, especially when she's entertaining her friends. Then they should be in their rooms, out of sight and out of mind. It's the way she was brought up. You never knew my grandmother – your great-grandmother. Now she was a *really* terrifying woman. When we were children, your father and I were only allowed to speak in her presence when we were asked a question. And if we so much as whispered to each other while she was in the room, off would come one of her slippers and she'd hit us across the shoulder blades with it. That probably doesn't sound too painful to you – except she was built like Hulk Hogan.' Brennan picked up the two empty boxes and got to his feet. 'You want a drink? I bought some Pepsi earlier today. I was told it's your favourite.'

'It is, but I'd rather have some milk – if you have some.'

'One glass of milk coming up,' Brennan said, and disappeared into the kitchen. When he returned he had the milk in one hand and a Budweiser in the other. He handed the glass to Jason then sat down in his favourite armchair by the window and drank a mouthful of the ice-cold beer. He told Jason about Kelly and that she'd be arriving at the apartment later that evening to stay with them for a while, although he was careful to omit any references to the sinking of the *Shamrock Gal*. As far as Jason was concerned, she was coming for a holiday. That was enough for him to know.

'Did she know Daddy?' Jason asked, when Brennan had finished.

'Yeah, she did. You can ask her about that in the morning. She's really nice. I know you'll like her.'

'Is she your girlfriend, Uncle Ray?'

'No, of course not.' The rebuttal sprang from his lips before

197

he could stop it. *Too quick*, he chastised himself. 'I only met her a few days ago. We're friends, that's all.'

'Do you want her to be your girlfriend? Is that why she's coming?'

Brennan chuckled. 'I think you've been watching too much TV. Like I said, we're just friends. And I'm quite happy to keep it that way.' *Just as well you're not wired up to a polygraph,* he thought cynically to himself, *otherwise the needle would be off the page by now.*

But what was he supposed to say? That his body was tingling with excitement, as if he were a teenager anticipating his first big date? He hadn't felt this way since that magical moment when Gillian had agreed to have a drink with him.

Jason finished the milk, wiped the white moustache off his upper lip, then got to his feet. 'I'd like to go to bed, Uncle Ray.'

'You're not at your grandmother's house now. You don't have to ask my permission every time you want to do something. I only have one rule in the apartment – that there aren't any rules. You want a bath or a shower – take it. You want a drink or something to eat – help yourself. You want to watch TV – switch it on. You want to go to bed – off you go. You do what you want here. OK?'

'Thanks, Uncle Ray,' Jason said with a grin.

'And you don't have to call me "Uncle" either, if you don't want to,' Brennan told him. Jason looked uncertain at that. 'But I really don't mind either way,' he added quickly.

'Good night . . . Uncle Ray.' This was followed by a quick smile. He'd had no trouble making his choice.

'Yeah, see you in the morning,' Brennan replied. 'And if you need anything, I'm only a shout away.'

Brennan stretched out lazily in the chair and took another mouthful of beer. He looked down into the street where a group of boisterous teenagers were passing in front of the building. Probably on their way to a club – most of the clubs in Brooklyn only came alive around midnight. There were a couple of late-night ones in his street, but the music was so faint it had never bothered him. Sometimes when he couldn't

198

sleep he'd sit by the open window, listening to a CD while he watched the nocturnal prowlings of the surreal night people in the street below.

He twisted round in his chair and ran his finger along the rack of CDs, selected a Neil Young album, and placed it carefully in the tray. He turned the volume down before pressing Play. He put the bottle on the window sill then leaned his head back and closed his eyes. He wanted to think about Kelly, and her impending arrival, yet his mind turned instead to Jason. The football had been the ice-breaker. What if he hadn't found it under the bed when he did? Had it been fate? He didn't know, but it had been a godsend all the same. He made a mental note to get tickets from his contacts on the black market. He'd already decided to take Jason to see the Cowboys *and* the 49ers when they visited Meadowlands later in the year. The irony wasn't lost on him: here he was, planning his first outing with the boy when only hours earlier he'd been dreading the prospect of having him to stay. Now he was looking forward to the next couple of weeks. He'd finally get to know Jason. It was long overdue. Although he still had so much to learn about his nephew, he'd discovered more about him in the last hour than he had in the previous nine years. And from what he'd already seen, Donald had raised him well. It hadn't been lost on him that, although Jason had mentioned his father several times, his voice hadn't faltered once or his eyes moistened. He knew Shirley Brennan would have had a lot to do with that. If he had the chance, he'd let Jason cry it out of his system, irrespective of how long it took him to get over it. Not that he'd force the issue but, then, neither would he try to stop him letting his grief come out into the open. Best to let him move at his own pace . . .

He yawned generously and put a hand belatedly to his mouth. The tedious journey to and from the Hamptons was beginning to catch up with him. He looked at his watch. Kelly's flight wasn't due for another hour. It would be an hour on top of that before she got to the apartment. Enough time for a quick snooze. He lay back on the sofa, cushioning his head on the soft padding of the arm. So comfortable. So relaxing. Especially with a philosophical Neil Young searching for 'Peace Of Mind' on the stereo.

Brennan was asleep even before the track had finished.

'Wake up!'

Brennan opened his eyes abruptly and was startled to find Lou Monks standing over him. 'Lou, how did you get in here?' he asked, bewildered, and stifled a yawn as he struggled to clear the sleep from his head.

'I've got the spare key you gave me after you'd locked yourself out of the apartment and kicked the door down.'

'Yeah, yeah, I remember,' Brennan muttered, as he rubbed his eyes wearily.

'I didn't want to knock too loudly in case I woke Jason. That's when I used the key. And what do we find when we get in here? You catching some Zs on the sofa. Some welcome for your guest, I must say.'

Brennan slowly followed Monk's eyes to where Kelly was standing. From what she'd told him on the phone, he'd expected her to be wearing the same oversized jeans and plaid shirt she'd been given by the river trader who'd taken her to Boa Vista. Instead, she was dressed in a loose-fitting grey track suit, a pale blue T-shirt and white plimsolls. Her blonde hair was loose on her shoulders.

'Hello, Ray,' she said, faltering a little.

An overwhelming sense of relief and joy swept through him like a warm wind blowing away the fears and doubts he'd been harbouring about her ever since she'd called from Manaus that morning. Then he was moving towards her, oblivious of his surroundings. All he wanted to do was hold her, reassure her, and never let her go. It struck him in the split second before they embraced just how corny that sounded, but at that moment it really didn't matter. All that did was knowing she was safe.

Neither spoke as they held each other tightly, like two statues locked together in an eternal embrace. The intensity of the silence between them was finally shattered when she sniffed back the tears that were threatening to spill down her face. She reluctantly eased herself from his embrace and grinned sheepishly at him.

Monks, who'd been hovering in the background, took a step forward and patted Brennan's arm. 'I gotta go,' he announced, with a quick smile. 'I'll see you both in the morning.'

'What's the rush?' Brennan replied. 'You can stay for coffee. I've even got some bourbon. I'll slip in a shot for you. What do you say?'

'Thanks, buddy, but I promised Marilyn I'd be back before the witching hour. And if I'm not she'll be waiting for me at the door with my night stick. I'll have a word with her about having the two of you over for a barbecue, once Kelly's had a chance to settle in.'

'Yeah, that would be great,' Brennan said.

'And don't forget Garrett wants to see Kelly at nine o'clock tomorrow morning.'

'We'll be there,' Brennan said, as he walked Monks towards the front door.

'Lou, thanks again for collecting me from the airport,' Kelly called after him.

'Don't mention it,' Monks replied. 'See you in the morning.'

'Yeah, thanks, Lou. I appreciate you going to fetch her,' Brennan said, as he opened the door.

Monks put a hand lightly on Brennan's arm, purposely keeping his voice low. 'You know I never liked Gillian. She wasn't right for you.'

'But you think Kelly is, is that it?' Brennan said, with a questioning look.

'I *know* she is. And I think you do too,' Monks said, before heading towards the stairs.

Brennan closed the door and returned to the lounge, where Kelly was perched on the edge of the sofa, the morning edition of *USA Today* spread out on the floor at her feet. She looked up from the article she was reading and smiled at Brennan. 'I like Lou, I really do.'

'Me too,' Brennan said.

'Have you got anything on Caldwell and Dixon?'

201

'No. We drew a blank when we ran them through the system. Neither of them has a criminal record – at least, not under those names. The Secret Service also checked them out. No luck there either.' Brennan took a sip of beer and screwed up his face in disgust. It was warm. 'You want something to drink?' he asked her. 'I'm clean out of *cachaca*, though.'

'Very funny,' she said, straight-faced. 'Coffee, please.' She followed him to the kitchen. 'How's Jason taking Donald's death?'

'He's got to be hurting inside, only he's not showing it. Well, at least not in front of me. But he's a good kid all the same.' He made the coffee and handed the mug to her. 'Where'd you get the clothes? They look new.'

'They are,' Kelly replied, as they returned to the lounge. She sat cross-legged on the sofa beside him, the mug cradled between her hands. 'I went to get the tickets from the Delta Airlines check-in desk and the next thing I know I'm being ushered into a back office. These clothes were on a table, together with some cigarettes and a toiletry bag. All I was told was that they came compliments of the airline. I guessed your contact had something to do with it, but I didn't say anything. I was just glad to get rid of the filthy stuff I had on.' She paused to take a sip from the mug. 'That's also when I found out I'd be travelling first class. I couldn't believe it. One minute I'm being watched by the airport police at Manaus, who must have thought I was a bum, and the next I'm being treated like royalty. The cabin crew couldn't do enough for me.'

'If I'd known you were going to travel in such style, I'd have made an effort to clean up the apartment before you got here,' he said.

'I'm glad you didn't. I've always liked the lived-in look,' she replied, glancing around. 'It gives it . . . character.'

'You mean, like the *Shamrock Gal*?' He immediately regretted what he'd said and cursed himself silently. 'I'm sorry, Kelly.'

'Good,' she said, to his amazement. 'Of course I'm going

to miss the *Gal*. She's been part of my life for eight years. But that doesn't mean you have to tiptoe around the subject. You should know me better than that. Of course it was gut-wrenching to abandon her when she was sinking, but it was also necessary. I did cry when I came round – partly out of relief that I was still alive, but mainly for Kanibawa and Matowa. They were more than just my crew. They were my friends. And I'm going to miss them a lot more than I will the *Gal*.'

'Will you go back again?'

'No,' she replied, without hesitation. 'What would I do if I did? Live in a *shabono*? Not after eight years on the river. That part of my life's over now. It's time to move on.'

'Where will you go?' he asked.

'I haven't even been here an hour and already you're trying to get rid of me.'

'You know you can stay here as long as you want,' he replied defensively, before noticing the teasing smile tugging at the corners of her mouth. 'Well, I hate to be the party-pooper, but it's almost midnight and you've got a nine o'clock appointment with Special Agent Garrett at the Four-O in the morning.'

She finished her coffee then got up. 'Do you mind if I have a shower before I go to bed? The last all-over soaking I had was when the *Gal* went down and I ended up in the river.'

'As I said to Jason earlier, there's only one rule in this apart-ment – there aren't any rules. Treat the place as if it were your own. I'll fix you up a bed while you're in the shower.'

'Any chance of me borrowing a baggy T-shirt and a pair of shorts to wear tonight?' Kelly asked.

'Yeah, sure. I'll go get them for you.' Brennan went to his bedroom, rummaged through his drawers and found a pair of running shorts and Yankees T-shirt that was even baggy on him. When he returned to the lounge Kelly wasn't there but the faint sound of running water was coming from the bathroom. He knocked lightly on the door. No response. He knocked louder. Still nothing. He eased open the door and peered in. Her clothes were folded neatly on a stool beside the plastic shower curtain, which had been drawn across the cubicle. He was still hovering in the doorway, uncertain where to leave the clothes when Kelly's face appeared from behind the curtain.

'I'll just leave them here for you,' he said quickly, and pointed to the floor at his feet.

'Put them on the stool,' she replied.

He was acting like some flustered schoolkid who'd just been caught peeking into the girls' locker-room. What the hell was wrong with him? *Just put the damn things down and get out*, he said to himself. He crossed to the stool and dropped the shorts and T-shirt on top of her tracksuit but as he was turning away her hand sneaked out from behind the curtain and pulled him into the cubicle.

Then she was kissing him, teasing and probing her tongue inside his mouth, and fumbling to unbutton the front of his shirt. She ripped it open then slid her hands down his bare stomach. He pulled her to him, his mouth eagerly exploring the exquisite contours of her honey-skinned body as she struggled to unfasten his jeans. He reached down and loosened them for her then felt them being tugged down over his thighs. He kicked them off. She threw back her head into the deluge of cascading water as he caressed her face before tracing his lips down her arched neck to her nipples. Water streamed into his mouth and up his nose, and he inhaled sharply as he felt her hand between his legs. Not that he needed any help. Her fingers were gentle as she kneaded him with slow, sensual strokes and just when he felt as if he were about to spin deliriously out of control she stopped and guided him into her. The steam inside the cubicle was now so thick that they could barely see each other but it didn't matter. All that did was their insatiable hunger for each other. Everything else was forgotten in the intensity of the moment.

He had no idea how long he'd been thrusting deep inside her before he felt himself coming. Suddenly Gillian's face appeared in his mind's eye, with hurt in her eyes. *You have to forget about Gillian.* The image was gone, as suddenly as it had appeared.

He felt Kelly's fingers dig into his back as his breathing became increasingly ragged and he crushed his mouth down hard on hers to smother her ecstatic cry when his body shuddered as he came. He hissed through gritted teeth as she raked her fingernails agonizingly across his back, then pulled her to him and cocooned her in his arms. She nestled against his chest and wrapped her arms tightly around him. Neither moved. Neither spoke.

It was several minutes later before she reluctantly eased herself gently from his embrace and turned off the water. Then, pulling back the curtain, she stepped out of the cubicle, reached for the nearest bath towel and began to dry herself. 'Didn't your mother ever tell you that you shouldn't stand around dripping wet?' she asked with a cheeky grin.

'Not that I can remember, but if she had I'm sure she'd also have told me never to allow a beautiful woman to pull me into the shower with all my clothes on,' he replied.

Kelly picked up her clothes. 'Do you still want me to sleep alone?'

'I never did.'

'I know,' she said, with a smile, then left the room.

He dropped his sodden clothes into the wicker laundry basket, dried himself and wrapped the bath towel around his waist before going to his bedroom where Kelly was drying her hair in front of the mirror. She was already wearing his T-shirt, but not the shorts.

'I like this,' she said, pulling at the T-shirt as she spoke to his reflection in the mirror.

'It's yours,' he replied, then discarded the towel and pulled on the shorts he always wore in bed. 'We're going to have to get you some clothes. You can't live for ever in that tracksuit.'

'Sounds interesting,' she said. 'I've heard there are some chic boutiques here in New York.'

'There are some equally chic *discount* boutiques here in New York,' he was quick to reply. 'Daffy's. Dollarbills. Loehmann's. Quality stuff all the same. That's where we'll be going.'

'A couple of pairs of jeans, a jacket and a few T-shirts will do me just fine,' she said, running a brush through her hair.

'I think my budget could just about stretch to that,' he said, approaching her from behind and slipping his arms around her waist.

She leaned her head back against his bare chest. 'Only if you agree that it'll be a loan.'

'Whatever you say. But I can tell you now you're not going to find it easy to get legal work here. Not without an H-1 visa.'

'In other words, I'm going to have to kick my heels around here like some kept woman,' she said, pulling out of his embrace.

'I've got a few contacts in the neighbourhood. It may only be waiting tables, or working behind a bar.'

'That's fine. As long as I can put something towards my keep. You've done more than enough for me as it is. I'm not going to be a burden on you while I'm here.'

'Don't be silly—'

'No, I mean it,' she interrupted and pulled away her hands when he tried to reach out for her. 'If we're going to make this work between us, I have to have my own independence. I don't want to be a passenger along for the ride.'

'I hear what you're saying. I'll put out some feelers in the next few days. See what I can do.' He crossed to his favourite side of the bed and set the alarm clock for seven. Then he got in. He waited until Kelly had joined him then switched off the bedside lamp.

She wriggled backwards until she was pressed close to him, then reached behind her for his arm and slipped it around her waist. 'Night, Ray,' she whispered.

'Yeah, night,' he replied then smiled contentedly and closed his eyes.

He awoke thirsty. The kind of dry, uncomfortable thirst he would normally have associated with fear. But fear of what? He hadn't woken from a bad dream. He wasn't sweating. His heart-rate felt normal. He thought of the dinner to be hosted by the Vice-President that evening. That wasn't it, though. So what else could it be? His eyes went to Kelly who was lying on her stomach beside him. He could hear by her breathing that she was asleep. He dismissed the idea that she could be the source of his angst. Or was that just what he wanted to believe? He'd certainly never felt this way about any woman since Gillian.

Was it, then, fear of commitment? Now his throat felt parched. He eased himself out of bed, not wanting to disturb Kelly, then gently pulled the comforter over her body before going through to the kitchen and taking a long drink of cold milk. Replacing the carton in the refrigerator, he wiped the back of his hand across his mouth and was about to return to bed when he heard muffled sobs coming from Jason's room. Should he go in – or turn his back on the boy when he maybe needed him most? He couldn't walk away. He knocked lightly then opened the door a little way and peered in.

Jason was sitting up in bed, the pillow cushioning his back against the wall, the football clutched tightly to his stomach. Brennan could see his face in the sliver of light from the partially open door. The boy's eyes were red and his freckled cheeks glistened with tears. 'I'm sorry, Uncle Ray, I didn't mean to wake you,' he said, brushing his fingertips across his moist eyes.

'You didn't wake me,' Brennan said reassuringly. 'I only heard you when I went to the kitchen to get some milk. You want something to drink?' Jason shook his head. 'Would you like me to stay, or do you want to be on your own?'

'Stay,' Jason pleaded.

Brennan went in and closed the door behind him before switching on the light. He sat down on the bed but didn't say anything. He'd let Jason start it off.

Jason turned the football around in his hands, as if trying to marshal his confused thoughts, before putting it down beside him on the bed. 'Daddy said you never came to the house to see us because you were angry with him for marrying Mommy. He said that Mommy used to be your girlfriend. Is that true, Uncle Ray?'

Just like a child to go straight for the jugular without even realizing it, Brennan thought. A week earlier he'd have tried to wriggle his way out of an answer. Not any more. 'Yeah, it's true,' he admitted. 'But, then, your mother and I had been drifting apart for some time before she met your father. If it hadn't been him, she'd have met someone else. I guess we just weren't meant for each other.' Why had he lied like that? Had it been to save face, or play down Donald's treachery in the eyes of his son? He preferred to think it was the latter, although he wasn't entirely convinced of that. 'Do you remember much about your mother?'

'Not really – but Daddy told me all about her. And I have lots of photographs. She was very pretty.'

'Yeah, she was,' Brennan replied thoughtfully.

Jason prodded the football absently with his finger. 'Grandma said you went to the Amazon to . . . bury Daddy?'

Brennan nodded. For once he found himself agreeing with what lay behind his mother's subterfuge. Burial sounded peaceful, easier than cremation somehow. Jason could be told the truth when he was older.

'I hated it when Daddy went to the Amazon every year,' Jason said, as the tears threatened to spill down his cheeks again. 'He was always gone for so long. Last year he was there for six months. And when he came back he locked himself up in his study for another few weeks, putting all his notes on his computer. Some boys at school used to say he loved his work more than me.' Tears began streaming down his face. 'It's not true, Uncle Ray. It's not true.'

'Of course it's not true,' Brennan said, and squeezed the child's arm gently. 'Your father and I may have had our differences, but when we did get together he always talked about you – usually when I was watching a ball game on TV.' He smiled faintly. 'I'd be concentrating on an important play and he'd be telling me about your grades at school. I remember the time when he had these paintings you'd done. It must have been five, maybe six years ago. I was trying to watch a game but he wouldn't let up until I'd looked at them all. He was real proud of you, kid. And don't you ever forget that.'

Jason chuckled through his sobs. 'Daddy hated football,' he said between sniffs. 'He never watched it on TV. He only watched documentaries and black-and-white movies.'

'Just like your grandmother. She loves those old movies too. You take after your grandfather. He and I were the sports fans in the family.'

'Did Grandma let you play football in the garden?'

Brennan certainly didn't need to think of an answer to that. 'Never,' he said straight away. 'She's always been very proud of her garden. It's won a lot of competitions over the years. So if your grandfather and I wanted to play some ball, which we did most weekends, we had to go off to the park.'

'She doesn't let me play either. And I don't have any friends there. All my friends live near Daddy's house. I once asked Grandma if my best friend, Danny, could stay for the weekend, but she said no and that I was never to ask her again.'

Brennan realized then that there was more to Jason's anguish than the loss of his father. Although he hadn't said it in so many words, he was dreading having to leave where he'd grown up – and where all his friends were – and move in with his grandmother. He wondered if Jason had enjoyed staying with her when his father was away. Brennan knew his mother was only doing what she thought was right for Jason, but the boy was very much like he had been as a nine-year-old. He needed freedom to express himself. But, like her dominant, overpowering mother before her, Shirley Brennan had always felt there was a fine line between independence and rebellious-ness and having been through it himself, Brennan knew that Jason was almost a prisoner within his grandmother's protec-tive cocoon.

'Did Grandma ever let you have friends stay over at the house when you were young?' Jason asked, breaking his uncle's train of thought.

'No. And your father and I weren't allowed to sleep over at friends' houses either. But she loves you. You're all she's got now. She just wants you to be a success, like your father. She was always so proud of him.' Brennan reached over and picked up the football. He stood up. 'It's not going to be as hard as you think, living with her. She'll begin to back off soon and let you do your own thing. That's what she did with your father. And he didn't turn out too bad, did he?' Brennan tossed the football to him. 'You know I'm always just a phone call away if you want me. I'll come and fetch you and you can stay weekends here – or maybe during vacations. And if you want you can always go hang out with our buddies over in Yorkville. What do you say?'

'I'd like that.'

'Me too. You get some sleep now. We've got an early start in the morning. I've got to be at work by nine. Have you ever been in a precinct before?'

'No. I've only seen them on TV.'

'Then I'll see you get the five-star tour,' Brennan said. 'That includes meeting the captain and sitting in his special chair. None of the other detectives have ever sat in his chair. They're going to be real jealous of you. Me included.' He switched off the light. 'Sleep tight, buddy.'

'Uncle Ray,' Jason called in the darkness, 'thanks.'

'Any time,' Brennan replied, then returned to his own bedroom.

Kelly had turned on to her side, her arm now spread out across his pillow. He lay down carefully and was about to lift her hand off his pillow when she rolled over on to her back and smiled up at him in the semi-darkness.

'I didn't mean to wake you,' he said apologetically.

'You didn't,' she said. 'I woke up a few minutes ago. When I realized you weren't in bed I went to look for you and I heard you talking to Jason. So I came back to bed to wait for you.'

'He's obviously got a lot on his mind right now, not least having to move in permanently with his grandmother.'

'When are you going to admit you've got a soft spot for him?' She put a finger lightly to his lips as he was about to reply. 'Don't try to deny it. It won't wash with me. I know you better than that, Ray Brennan.'

'Really?'

'Go on then, look me in the eye and tell me that you don't have a soft spot for Jason,' she said, and moved her face to within a couple of inches of his. 'Go on.'

'This is intimidation,' he complained good-humouredly.

'See, I was right, you can't,' she said, then lowered her mouth to his and slowly moved her hand down his belly towards his groin.

He was quick to intercept it. 'You're insatiable, you know that?' he said breathlessly.

'That comes from all those long nights of frenzied passion in the Amazon,' she said, with a wicked grin. 'There were always foreign scientists passing through the area who were prepared to pay for a passage up-river. Most were old enough to be my grandfather but there were a few young ones too. Good-looking. Intelligent. One thing led to another. Well, you know how it is. Not that I ever saw any of them again once I'd dropped them off. It was ideal, as far as I was concerned.'

'The perfect one-night stand,' Brennan declared.

'That depended on how long it took to get them where they wanted to go,' she replied, the grin widening. Then she rolled on to her back. 'Not that it happened very often,' she added.

'I'm sure we can do something to change that,' Brennan said, as she turned her head on the pillow to look at him.

'I *know* we can,' she purred, sliding her hand back on to his stomach. This time he didn't stop her.

12

The aromatic smell of frying bacon woke him. He squinted sleepily at the alarm clock on the bedside table: 7.15 a.m. He switched off the alarm and turned over. Kelly wasn't there. He got up, slipped on a T-shirt, and went through to the kitchen. She was tending the bacon and a couple of eggs in the frying pan; Jason was buttering toast on the work surface.

'Good morning,' Kelly said cheerily, when she saw Brennan in the doorway. 'Sleep well?'

'Eventually,' he replied, with a wry smile. Then his eyes settled on the frying pan. 'Where'd you get the food from? I didn't have any bacon or eggs in the refrigerator.'

'You didn't have *anything* in the fridge,' Kelly corrected him.

'That's because I haven't had a chance to go to the store since I got back,' Brennan replied, shamefaced.

'I got the bacon and eggs from the deli on the corner, Uncle Ray,' Jason said. 'Kelly paid for it.'

'I thought you were completely cleaned out,' Brennan said, eyeing Kelly suspiciously.

'I . . . ah, took ten dollars from your wallet,' she replied, then scooped one of the eggs and a couple of rashers of bacon out of the pan and put them on a plate, which she handed to Jason. 'You did say I should make myself at home,' she said to Brennan.

'I did, didn't I?' he said ruefully.

'Can I watch TV, Uncle Ray?' Jason asked.

'Go on,' Brennan replied, 'but only while you're having

your breakfast. Then I want you to get dressed. We have to be out of here by eight at the latest if we're going to make it to the Four-O by nine.'

'He's adorable,' Kelly said, after Jason had left the room. 'I still can't believe Donald was his father. They're so different.'

'Whatever else you could say about Donald he sure as hell wasn't a lousy father. And, when it comes down to it, you can't ask any more than that, can you?' Brennan said, then laid three rashers of bacon on a slice of toast, placed a fried egg on top and added a second slice of toast to complete the sandwich.

'It's as if he were two different people,' Kelly said. 'With Jason, he was a loving father who doted on his son. Yet all I ever saw was an odious, foul-mouthed man, who seemed to get some kind of perverse pleasure from demeaning women.'

'Donald was never comfortable around women. I blame my mother for that. In the end she even had to find him a wife. He'd never had a date before she pushed Gillian on to him. Sometimes I wonder whether he married Gillian for himself or just to please my mother.'

'I can't say I'm looking forward to meeting your mother,' Kelly said.

'You can be sure the feeling will be mutual,' Brennan replied, picked up his coffee in his free hand and returned to the bedroom to get ready for the day ahead.

Eddie Morrison was led into the lobby of Precinct 40 by a uniformed officer and taken to one of the wooden benches that lined the wall opposite the main desk. The policeman unlocked the handcuffs, pushed Morrison down on to the bench, and snapped on a second pair which were already attached to the underside of the seat. He had a brief word with the desk sergeant then left the station.

'Hey, how long am I going to be chained up here?' Morrison shouted. 'I ain't done nothing wrong. This is harassment and my lawyer's going to hear about this.'

'Yeah, yeah, Eddie,' the desk sergeant said resignedly, not looking at him.

Morrison cursed angrily to himself, loud enough to be heard by the man at the other end of the bench, a man he'd helped to put away some years earlier. Not that the man had any idea that Morrison's information had led to his arrest and conviction. As far as he was concerned, Morrison was a born loser who'd spent more than half his adult life in jail. Everybody knew Morrison, but nobody took much notice of him. It was the perfect cover for an informer. Even his arrest that morning had been a charade. That way he could meet with a detective in the sanctity of the precinct and pass on information to him. He'd be released by midday, with a hundred dollars in his pocket. Money that would help pay off another week's interest on his gambling debts. Or maybe he'd chance his luck and put it all on one of the afternoon races over at Belmont Park . . .

The front door opened and he saw Detective Ray Brennan enter the lobby. Morrison liked Brennan. They'd done business in the past, and Brennan had always been straight with him. In return, he'd always provided Brennan with reliable information. His eyes went to the woman and the boy who'd come in with him. He was puzzled. As far as he knew, Brennan wasn't married. He allowed his eyes to linger on the woman. *Some guys get all the breaks*, he thought. All he ever got were street-corner skanks, *and* he had to pay for it.

Kelly and Jason paused a few feet from where he was sitting, while Brennan spoke to the desk sergeant. Morrison realized there was something familiar about her face. The more he studied her, the more certain he was he'd seen her somewhere before but she certainly wasn't the type who'd hang out at any of his regular haunts.

'What's your problem?' Kelly snapped.

'Sorry, ma'am. I thought I'd seen you someplace,' Morrison replied.

'I doubt it,' she retorted.

The front door burst open and two uniformed officers bundled a scantily clad transvestite into the lobby. He was met with wolf-whistles from several similarly attired prostitutes, who were being booked at the main desk, and he spat out a string of expletives at them as he continued to struggle furiously with the policemen. Another cop hurried over to help and the desk sergeant shouted at them to take the transvestite to the cells to let him cool off. In a last defiant gesture, the transvestite managed to shove one of the cops away from him before the other two overpowered him. The cop lost his balance, stumbled backwards into Kelly and they both landed on the floor.

The gold bracelet slipped from Kelly's wrist, slithering over to Morrison's scuffed shoe. His first thought was that it would fetch a good price from someone he knew who specialized in stolen jewellery. He picked it up but the chain tethering his wrists wasn't long enough for him to put it into his pocket. He'd just have to wait until the cuffs were removed.

'I'll take that, Eddie.'

Morrison looked up sharply, startled by the voice. 'Mr Brennan, you shouldn't creep up on a man like that,' he said. 'You scared the life out of me.'

'And you shouldn't take what isn't yours,' Brennan said, extending an upturned palm towards Brennan. 'Give me the bracelet, Eddie.'

'Oh, yeah,' Morrison said, with a nervous chuckle, and dropped it into Brennan's outstretched hand. 'I figure it came off the lady's wrist when she fell. I thought I'd better pick it up before some scumbag took off with it. Just look around you, Mr Brennan, they're everywhere.'

'I'm looking,' Brennan replied, without taking his eyes off Morrison.

'I was going to give it back to her, Mr Brennan,' Morrison whined.

'Sure you were, Eddie,' Brennan said, then handed it to Kelly.

Morrison watched her fasten it on her wrist. He still couldn't place her face. But, having seen the inscription on the back of the bracelet, at least he had a name to go on . . .

Brennan waited until the prostitutes had been led away before going up to the desk again, this time with Kelly and Jason.

'Are you all right, ma'am?' the sergeant asked Kelly.

'I'm fine,' she replied.

The sergeant leaned forward, his arms resting on the counter, and looked down at Jason. 'Your uncle says you want to have a look around the station.'

'Uncle Ray said I could have the five-star tour,' Jason replied.

'The *five-star* tour?' the sergeant asked.

'I also get to meet the captain and sit in his special chair,' Jason told him.

'Does Captain d'Arcy know about this?' the sergeant asked Brennan softly.

'Not yet,' Brennan replied, 'but leave it to me. I'll clear it with him.'

'Just be sure you do,' the policeman replied and beckoned to Jason with his finger. 'We'll start the tour right here, young man. Come on, I'll show how we book the bad guys when they're brought in here.'

Brennan got down beside Jason. 'He always keeps a box of jelly doughnuts hidden under his desk. Make sure you get one.'

'Thanks, Uncle Ray,' Jason said, then disappeared with the sergeant.

Brennan led Kelly up the stairs to the squad room. Monks waved and closed the folder he was working on as they crossed to his desk.

'Morning, Lou,' Kelly said. 'Don't get up.'

'Morning,' Monks replied. 'Sleep well last night?'

'Very well,' she replied with a glance in Brennan's direction.

Monks smiled at his friend's pained expression then stood up and pulled on his jacket. 'Garrett's already here. He's in with the captain. We're to go through.'

They filed into d'Arcy's office and Garrett's eyes went to Kelly, who was standing behind the two detectives. 'You must be Ms McBride.' He extended a hand towards her. 'I'm Special Agent Chip Garrett, head of the Vice-President's security team.'

'I believe I have you to thank for getting me out of Manaus

216

yesterday,' she said, snaking an arm between Brennan and Monks to take Garrett's hand.

'It's the least we could do,' Garrett replied.

'Have you had any feedback yet from the other intelligence agencies about Caldwell or Dixon?' Brennan asked.

'No joy. Same with the military. Nobody knows anything about them. It's almost as if these guys didn't exist.'

'Or made to look that way,' Monks suggested.

'It's possible that a senior figure in one of the intelligence agencies is deliberately blocking informaion,' Garrett replied. 'Until we know more, we can't discount any theory.'

'We now know that Caldwell is already here in New York,' d'Arcy told Brennan and Monks. 'He flew into JFK two days ago. Only we don't know where he went after that.'

'What about Dixon?' Brennan asked.

'None of the ground staff at any of the airports recognized his picture,' d'Arcy said. 'And we know from passenger information that if he *is* already here, he didn't travel as Bobby Dixon.'

Garrett picked up the photofits of Caldwell and Dixon from d'Arcy's desk and handed them to Kelly. 'Detective Brennan put those together yesterday. Would you say the pictures were accurate? Is there anything he may have missed out? A scar? A facial blemish? Anything, irrespective of how insignificant it may seem to you. Right now, the faces are all we've got to go on.'

'I never saw the colour of Caldwell's eyes,' Brennan told her.

'Brown,' she said, without hesitation.

'You seem very sure of that,' Garrett said.

'I am,' she replied, and when silence descended over the room she looked up from the photofits and saw that the others were waiting for an explanation. 'I used to have the occasional drink with the guy, OK? When you're sitting directly opposite somebody you notice the colour of their eyes.'

'You used to drink with him?' Garrett queried.

'Occasionally,' she said. 'Sometimes I'd bump into him in one of the bars if I was staying overnight in Boa Vista. We'd have a drink together and a bit of a chat, then we'd go our separate ways. He was the only English-speaking person I came into contact with out there, apart from the odd botanist or anthropologist who'd be passing through the area.'

'What about Dixon?' Monks asked.

'I rarely came into contact with Bobby Dixon. I certainly never had a drink with him. And I wouldn't have even if he'd offered. I never felt comfortable around him – but what woman would, given the talk that used to circulate around Boa Vista about him?'

'What sort of talk?' Garrett asked.

'That he had a bent for the teenage hookers who work the harbour area,' she replied, her disdain evident in her voice.

'Did Caldwell ever tell you anything about his past?' Garrett asked.

'No, and I never asked. Just as he never pried into mine. Come to think of it, all I knew about him was his name and that he was head of security at the Silva ranch. I'm sorry I can't be of more help.' Kelly handed the images back to Garrett. 'The faces are spot on. The only other thing that may be of some use to you is that Caldwell's missing the tip of his index finger on his left hand.'

'I didn't notice that,' Brennan said, embarrassed.

'I'm not surprised,' she replied. 'He has a tendency to clench his left hand by his side when he's talking. I don't know if he does it deliberately, or whether it's subconscious.'

'That could be useful,' Garrett said, as he made a note of it. 'Ms McBride, I'd like to talk to you in more detail about the events leading up to the attack on your boat. I realize it may not throw up anything new, but I'd still like to hear your version of what happened.'

'I'll help in any way I can.'

'I appreciate that,' Garrett said, then turned to d'Arcy. 'Could we use one of your interview rooms?'

'I'll see which one's free,' d'Arcy said, picking up the phone. He spoke briefly then hung up. 'Room two. One of these detectives will show you where it is.'

'Lou, could you do that?' Brennan asked Monks. 'I'd like a word with the captain.'

Monks ushered Kelly and Garrett out of the office before closing the door behind him. 'What's on your mind?' d'Arcy asked.

'I'm looking after my nephew for the next couple of weeks,' Brennan said. 'I had to bring him in with me today. I told him I'd arrange from him to meet you, and . . . well, sit in your chair.'

'You know you have to earn the right to sit in this chair. That's why I won't even let any of you bums sit here,' d'Arcy replied as he patted the padded arms.

'He was really down last night and I said it to cheer him up. I know he'd get a real buzz out of sitting in the boss's chair, especially as no one else is allowed to.'

'Under the circumstances, I'll bend the rules,' d'Arcy said, his granite features cracking into a rare smile. 'Close the door on your way out.'

Brennan left the office and went to the interview rooms in the bleak, featureless corridor next to the squad room. One of the doors was ajar and he saw Kelly sitting at the table in the centre of the room. She was turning the plastic ashtray around in front of her as she smoked a cigarette. Monks and Garrett were talking together in the corridor. Brennan went up to them.

'I was just telling Detective Monks that as soon as I've had the eyes changed in Caldwell's photofit, I'll fax the picture through to the hotel, with the new info about his index finger. It's going to make it that much harder for him to breach the security cordon around the hotel.'

'He could use a prosthetic,' Brennan suggested.

'He could, but from what Ms McBride said, there's every chance he'd still be inclined to clench his hand at his side. An instinctive reaction. Old habits die hard. And that would be a dead giveaway.' Garrett crossed to the open door. 'Six o'clock in the hotel lobby.'

'I just hope we won't be needed,' Monks said philosophically.

219

'So do I,' Garrett agreed, 'but we can't afford to take any chances. Not when we're up against someone like Caldwell. If he thinks he's found a way past the security cordon, he'll try it. You can be sure of that.'

The doorman, resplendent in top hat and black tail-coat, hurried forward to open the back door when the taxi pulled up in front of the Richmond Hotel. Dixon gave him a nod after he'd got out and a porter retrieved his suitcase from the trunk. He slipped a ten-dollar bill into the doorman's gloved hand, then followed the porter up the steps and through the electronic doors into the hotel lobby.

The security presence was as conspicuous as it was impressive. He counted over a dozen black-suited Secret Service agents, as well as several uniformed cops, although nobody moved to intercept him as he followed the porter to the reception desk. He knew that two Special Agents were seated behind the two-way mirror that ran the length of the wall at the back of the reception area, carefully scrutinizing everyone who approached the desk. It reminded him of what Caldwell had said the previous evening about changing his appearance so that even his own mother wouldn't recognize him. Not that that would have been very difficult, considering the amount of booze she waded through every day. But as he stared back at his own reflection in the two-way mirror, he had to admit that Caldwell had done a professional job. His blue eyes were now hidden behind a pair of brown contact lenses and he was wearing a black hairpiece flecked with fine streaks of silver-grey to complement the grey moustache, whitened around the edges to make it more prominent and draw attention away from the rest of his face. A liner stick had enhanced wrinkles. He was wearing two plastic mouth inserts to swell out his cheeks, while a third insert under his palate changed the pitch of his voice. He now looked nothing like the photofit that had been faxed to Caldwell at the apartment.

The receptionist asked him to fill out a reservation card. He knew the Secret Service had already cross-checked the identity of everyone staying at the hotel that night. The address Caldwell had given the reservations officer was of an apartment in Dallas. A colleague, who'd been staying there since the booking had been made, had received a call from the Secret Service. He'd merely confirmed the details Dixon was writing on the card. The apartment was now empty, the man having flown to New York to add further credibility to Dixon's cover. Dixon had met with him briefly at the airport to pass on the $20,000 he'd been promised. Then the man had caught a connecting flight to his native Chicago, reverting back to his own name. Dixon had taken a taxi to the hotel.

The receptionist allocated him a room and wished him a pleasant stay as she handed him a key card. As he made his way to the elevator he saw an airport-style archway metal detector being erected in the corridor leading to the main function room where the Vice-President was due to host the dinner that evening. It brought a faint smile to his lips. As if that would deter him. But, then, they were floundering in the dark anyway. And they'd pay dearly for it . . .

He rode the elevator to the eighteenth floor where he alighted and used the key card to gain access to his room. Once inside he removed the mouth inserts, then placed the suitcase on the nearest of the two double beds, opened it, unpacked his tuxedo, black trousers and white dress shirt, and hung them in the cupboard. The gilt-edged invitation was in the inside pocket of the tux. The name printed on the invitation corresponded to a name on the guest list.

He knew every exit would be sealed off the moment the Vice-President was assassinated. But he already had a way around that. He took a NYPD police uniform from the suitcase, brushed an imaginary fleck of dust off the sleeve, and hung it beside his jacket. A laminated ID card, giving the wearer automatic access to and from the hotel, was secured to the breast pocket. It would only take him a couple of minutes to return to his room and change into the police uniform. Then he'd leave the hotel and make his way to a car parked in an underground parking bay a short distance away.

He switched on the TV set. The Vice-President's motorcade was already on its way and Dixon watched the pictures being beamed live from a CNN helicopter. He helped himself to a miniature of brandy from the mini-bar, unscrewed the top, and raised the bottle towards the screen. 'Your good health, Mr Vice-President,' he said disparagingly, then sank the drink in one gulp. He tossed the empty bottle into the bin and reached for the telephone to call room service.

Eddie Morrison couldn't get Kelly's face out of his mind as he rode the subway to St Lawrence Avenue, then walked to his apartment in a rundown tenement block in the South Bronx.

Not that he was complaining about having her face for company. She was some looker. But his thoughts were centred more on avarice than lechery. He was certain he'd seen her before. Recently. Within the past couple of weeks. And he knew exactly where to look to confirm his suspicions. He was about to enter the block when he heard a woman's piercing scream behind him. He looked round and saw a couple in a doorway on the opposite side of the street. The woman was on her knees, her arms wrapped over her head as the man kicked and punched her. Morrison knew better than to intervene. The woman wouldn't thank him. The man would probably cut him. He'd long since come to realize that life here was all about personal survival. He darted into the building, up a flight of concrete steps, then along a corridor to a door with three heavy padlocks. Not that they would be much protection against an aggressive intruder. The print of a black sole was still visible on the door from the last time the apartment had been vandalized.

He unlocked the padlocks, slipped them into his overcoat pocket, then went in and rammed home the four bolts. The apartment was cold and uninviting. The walls were un-papered, the ceiling mottled with patches of damp. The bare wooden floor creaked with his every step. The only furniture in the lounge was a couple of threadbare armchairs, which he'd found at a nearby tip, and a broken black-and-white TV in the corner – it had been flung against the wall by the last intruder. Considering how fortunate he was to have been out at the time, losing the television was a relatively small price to pay to be alive. He went through to the bedroom. It was empty, apart from a mattress and a couple of filthy blankets on the floor against the far wall. A section of the skirting board had rotted away and the gaping hole had quickly become a favourite entry point for the rats that infested the derelict apartments on either side of his.

He slid back the door of the built-in cupboard and a bloated rat darted out of the semi-darkness, scurrying towards the hole. Morrison lashed out angrily with his foot and caught it with the tip of his boot, launching it across the room. It slammed into the opposite wall, and fell to the floor, its back broken, the only movement the occasional spasmodic jerk of its tiny feet. He felt no remorse as he stamped savagely on its head then kicked it into the hole. One less to worry about.

He returned to the cupboard and removed a cardboard box from the top shelf. Inside were hundreds of 'wanted' posters which he'd been collecting for the past fifteen years. Most had been issued by the NYPD. With his invaluable knowledge of the New York underworld, he'd never had any trouble in procuring them from his contacts at precincts across the city. He would only toss a poster once the felon had been apprehended and the reward money paid out. Then it was of no more use to him. He'd had a major clear-out only a couple of weeks back – and he was certain that's when he'd seen her face. Not that he thought she was wanted by the NYPD: there were other 'wanted' posters in the box that hadn't been distributed by any of the city's law enforcement agencies. He grabbed a handful and began the tedious process of going through them.

He eventually found the one he wanted. An old, scruffy poster, gnawed by rats. But the face in the centre of the page was unblemished. He was right. It hadn't been issued by the NYPD, although he couldn't remember where he'd got it from. He always wrote the date of receipt on the back of the poster. He turned it round, but the corner where it would have been written had been chewed away. He looked more carefully at the face. She was younger. Early twenties, he guessed. The hair was shorter, the skin paler, the eyes lifeless. But it was her. Above the picture the word **WANTED!** was printed theatrically in bold, black letters. Underneath her picture was a name in equally bold lettering: **KELLY McBRIDE**. The script that accompanied the poster offered a cash reward of $15,000 to anyone with information as to her whereabouts. It also carried an overseas telephone numbers. Of course! The poster had been given to him by a contact he'd once had in Noraid. That would date it back to the eighties. Fifteen thousand bucks! It would pay off all his gambling debts. It would get him out of the apartment. It would get him out of the South Bronx. That had to be worth a few bucks for an international call, even if nothing were to come of it . . .

Kelly had been too young to remember where she was when Kennedy had been assassinated, or when Armstrong had set foot on the moon. But as an avid fan of the Beatles from an early age she could still vividly remember the moment in December 1980 when she'd first heard that John Lennon had been murdered. The day had begun like any other. The radio alarm had woken her and 'Just Like Starting Over' had been playing, but when the song finished a sombre-voiced DJ had announced that at 10.50 p.m. the previous evening, Eastern Standard Time, John Lennon had been shot five times with a .38 revolver outside the exclusive Dakota building in New York where he lived with his wife, Yoko Ono. He'd been officially pronounced dead at Manhattan's Roosevelt Hospital at 11.07 p.m. When Elvis had died three years earlier, it had been universally regarded as the passing of a legend. But to her, John Lennon had been more than a legend, and she'd vowed that one day she would make the pilgrimage to New York to pay her own respects to him. That day had finally arrived . . .

After Garrett had finished questioning her at the station, Brennan had driven her and Jason back to the apartment where he'd left the car and the three of them had then taken the subway to 72nd Street. It was only a short walk to the

Dakota building and its magnificent view of Central Park. She'd bought a single red rose and placed it beside the other floral tributes, left daily by his fans outside the main entrance to the tenement block.

Then Brennan took her to Strawberry Fields, a tranquil two-and-a-half-acre peace garden in Central Park, directly opposite the Dakota building; a kaleidoscope of colourful plants from around the world, opened in March 1984, and since maintained by Yoko Ono. Jason was becoming restless and they decided to head for Sheep's Meadow, a fifteen-acre spread of lawn, where they found youngsters playing touch football. One game became a player short after an unsympathetic parent decided to go home.

'Can I play, Uncle Ray?'

'Go on,' Brennan replied, and Jason ran off. 'We might as well sit here,' he said to Kelly. 'Catch some rays while we can.'

'Sure,' she said absently.

He sensed that something was troubling her. She'd hardly said a word since they'd left the precinct. He eased himself down on the grass then reached up and took her hand. They sat quietly for some time, watching Jason. Then, 'You OK?' he asked.

'Sure,' she said again.

'What's bugging you?'

'I've never seen so much despair as I saw when we drove through the South Bronx today. How long have you been working there? I don't know how you can bear it,' Kelly said.

'Ten years. I've been offered transfers to other precincts over the years, all of them regarded as a lot more prestigious than the Four-O, but I've never been tempted to leave.'

'Did you ask to be assigned there?'

'Nobody asks to work in the South Bronx,' he replied. 'You're usually dumped in it, then try to wangle your way out as quick as you can. I certainly felt that way when I first got there. But once I'd got the feel of the place, I began to warm to it. And having Lou as a partner was a hell of a bonus. I couldn't imagine working with anyone else.'

225

He sat up and grinned as Jason hurried towards them. 'Game over?'

The child nodded. 'Mark had to go home. It was his ball,' he replied breathlessly. 'Did you see my two touchdowns, Uncle Ray?'

'Sure I did,' Brennan replied, even though he'd only seen the first. 'We'll make a wide receiver out of you yet – but now let's go and get a soda.'

'Any chance of a bite to eat as well?' Kelly asked, as Brennan helped her up. 'I don't know about you two, but I'm starving. That bacon sandwich didn't go far this morning.'

'Do you like teriyaki?' Brennan asked.

'I don't think I've ever tried it,' she replied.

'Then we'll have to put that right, won't we?' he said. 'And I know just the place to go.'

'You've just convinced me,' Kelly said.

'Can I have a burger, Uncle Ray? With ketchup?' Jason asked hesitantly.

'Sure thing,' Brennan said, and they set off towards the nearest exit.

'What time do you have to be at the hotel?' Kelly asked after they'd returned to the apartment.

'Lou and I are meeting Garrett in the lobby at six,' Brennan said. He glanced at his watch. It had gone three o'clock.

'I like Chip,' she said. 'He really went out of his way to make me feel at ease when he questioned me this morning.'

'Oh, so it's Chip, is it?' Brennan said good-humouredly.

'Only when we're alone,' she replied, teasingly. 'We wouldn't want to start any tongues wagging, now would we?'

'I guess not,' Brennan said, with a wink, then entered the kitchen. 'You want coffee?'

'Please,' she replied from the doorway. 'That chicken teriyaki was delicious but filling. I won't need to eat for another week.'

Brennan opened the refrigerator. 'Great,' he muttered, and closed the door again. 'We're out of milk.'

'That's my fault,' she said apologetically. 'I must have used up the last of it at breakfast. I'll pop out and get some more.'

'Jason can go. He knows where the deli is.'

'I'll go with him,' she said. 'It's time I started to find my way around the neighbourhood.'

'You'll need some money,' he said, reaching for his wallet.

'I've still got the change from the ten dollars I gave Jason this morning,' she told him.

She found the child in the lounge, flicking through the television channels but nothing held his attention for more than a few seconds. When she asked him whether he wanted to go to the shop with her he nodded and dropped the remote control on to the seat beside him.

'We'll be back in a tick,' she said to Brennan, as they passed the kitchen on their way to the front door. He had his back to them and was engrossed in the copy of the *New York Post* he'd bought on the way home. She closed the door and they made their way down the corridor to the elevator.

'You like Uncle Ray, don't you?' Jason asked, after he'd pressed the button to summon the elevator.

'Sure I do,' she replied, surprised at the question.

'A lot?'

She chuckled to herself. 'Where exactly is this going?'

Jason shrugged. 'He likes you, too. But he told me yesterday you're not his girlfriend. He thinks I'm too young to understand about that kind of thing. I'm not, though. You are his girlfriend, aren't you?'

'Maybe,' she replied, with a bemused smile.

'So why are you going back to the Amazon?'

'I'm not,' she replied, as the elevator doors parted in front of them.

'Really?' Jason exclaimed, stepping into the elevator. He pressed the button for the lobby. 'Uncle Ray said you only came here for a holiday. Does he know you're not going back?'

Kelly felt as if she'd just walked into an ambush. Only she didn't know if Jason had manoeuvred her into it or if she'd trapped herself by the way she'd answered his questions. If he

227

was anything like his father, she'd have gone for the former. Except he *wasn't* anything like Donald. 'He knows I'm staying,' she admitted, but was quick to add, 'but I only told him about my change of plans this morning. He didn't know that last night.'

'Are you going to stay in the apartment?' Jason asked, as they emerged from the elevator into the lobby.

'Maybe,' she replied. 'Why all these questions?'

'It's just . . .' Jason started, then trailed off. 'It doesn't matter,' he added, but when he reached for the door she put a hand gently, but firmly, against the glass to prevent him opening it.

'It's just what?' she asked, bending down to him.

'You'll think it's silly,' Jason said awkwardly.

'Perhaps I will, but we won't know that unless you tell me.'

Jason cast his eyes downward. 'I just thought that maybe I could come and live with you and Uncle Ray at the apartment. I really like it here.'

Kelly smiled at him. 'Well, that would be for your uncle Ray to decide, wouldn't it? After all, it's his apartment. And even if he did go along with it, your grandmother would still have to agree. I've never met her, but from what I've heard I reckon she might just have something to say about it.'

'I don't want to live with her,' Jason said defiantly.

'I'll tell you what. We'll talk to Ray about it in the next few days, once we've all had a chance to get to know each other a bit better. Let's face it, we're all still pretty much strangers right now.'

'Do you think he'll let me stay?' Jason asked, the uncertainty in his voice mirrored by the anxiety on his face.

'We'll see.' She'd broach the subject with Ray that night. She didn't know how he'd react but there was no point in raising Jason's hopes only to see them dashed if Ray decided against adopting him. Because that's what it would amount to. Legal adoption. It would be the only way he'd ever get custody of the boy. Shirley Brennan certainly wouldn't give him up without a fight. But would Ray go to those lengths?

228

More to the point, would he be in a position to win custody if he did?

She followed Jason out into the street and immediately noticed the battered red Chevrolet van parked in front of the building. The driver was staring straight at her. His features were partly concealed by a sweat-stained peaked cap and a pair of cracked sunglasses, but she still recognized him. Her attention was suddenly drawn to an approaching jogger, a hood pulled up over his bowed head. He was heading straight for her and she instinctively stepped back to avoid collision. Only when he drew abreast of her did she see the stun gun in his hand, which moved in slow motion towards her.

He jabbed the prongs of the gun into her ribcage, sending a 70,000 volt charge through her body and caught her as her legs buckled. The van's side door slid open and a second man jumped out, his features distorted by a black stocking mask. Jason grabbed at Kelly's arm in a hopeless attempt to pull her away from her attackers but the second man knocked him to the ground. By now several onlookers had gathered on the sidewalk but none went to Kelly's aid as she was dumped into the back of the van, which pulled away in a screech of rubber and disappeared.

Only then did a woman hurry over to Jason. He scrambled to his feet and glared at the adults around him. She'd been kidnapped and nobody had tried to stop it. Tears filled his eyes as he ran back into the building and up the stairs to the third floor. He didn't stop running until he'd reached the apartment. He pounded on it with his fists until Brennan opened it.

'Jesus, what happened?' he almost shouted, seeing the bruise on Jason's cheek.

'They've taken Kelly,' Jason blurted out between sobs. 'I tried to stop them, Uncle Ray, but I couldn't.'

'Who's taken Kelly?' Brennan demanded.

'I don't know. A jogger – he had a gun. Then they put her in – into the back of the van. Then it – drove off. I wanted to help her, Uncle Ray, but I couldn't!'

Brennan ran out and leapt down the stairs two at a time

229

until he reached the lobby. He could see the crowd on the sidewalk. He pulled open one of the glass doors. 'Did anyone see what happened?' he yelled. Several voices answered at once, each trying to shout over the others. 'Shut up!' he bellowed, then stabbed a finger at a man standing at the foot of the steps. 'Did you see what happened?'

'Damn right I did. It happened right in front of me,' the man replied, shaking his head in disbelief. 'It was like something out of the movies. It all happened so quickly. Hell, there wasn't time to do anything.'

'Just tell me what you saw,' Brennan said, through clenched teeth. So many different emotions were writhing around in the pit of his stomach. Anguish. Despair. Frustration. Helplessness. Uncertainty. But right at that moment they were all suppressed by bitter resentment that not one of these people had tried to help Kelly.

'You just make sure you tell the cops what you've told me when they get here,' Brennan said, when the man had finished. 'I guess somebody *has* called the cops?'

'I did.' The voice came from the back of the crowd. 'They're on their way.'

'Tell them I'm in apartment nineteen. Third floor,' he grated, then went back up to his apartment. Jason was sitting in the lounge, his hands covering the bruise on his cheek. Brennan wrapped ice in a dishtowel then knelt beside him and gently pried away his hands. 'Hold this against your cheek. It'll help to keep down the swelling. Here, let me show you.' Jason breathed in sharply when the ice was clamped to his face. He reached up a trembling hand to hold it in place. 'It took a lot of guts to stand up to those kidnappers – I'm real proud of what you did out there, son. And I know Kelly will be as well when she finds out.'

'Why would they want to kidnap her, Uncle Ray?'

'I just don't know,' Brennan replied, then got up and went over to the window. The crowd had thinned but a core of onlookers were still milling around in the street below. There was no sign of the police. 'Did you get a good look at any of the kidnappers?' he asked, turning away from the window.

'I saw the driver,' Jason replied.

'Do you think if you saw him again you might recognize him?'

'I might,' Jason replied hesitantly. 'He was wearing cheaters and a peaked cap.'

'What about the others?'

'The one who hit me had a black stocking on his head. And the jogger had a hood, and a mask over his mouth.'

'It's worth you having a look at some photographs at the precinct anyway.'

'Will you come to the station with me?' Jason asked.

'Yeah. I'll have to put together a photofit of Kelly.' Brennan picked up the portable phone. 'I've got to make a call. I'll be in the bedroom. If there's a knock on the door, open it. It'll be the cops.' He went out and rang the precinct only to be told that Lou Monks had already left. He then rang Monks's home number. Monks answered and Brennan told him what had happened.

'Caldwell?' was all Monks said, once Brennan had finished.

'That was my first thought as well,' Brennan replied. 'But now I'm not so sure. If Caldwell had found out that the Secret Service were on to him, what could he possibly hope to gain by abducting Kelly? Why not just abort the operation? No, it makes no sense, Lou.'

'If not Caldwell, then who?'

'Probably some disgruntled asshole I sent to the cooler and who's now out for revenge,' Brennan replied.

'Kelly's only been in New York a couple of days. How the hell could they have set up a snatch so fast?'

'I've no idea, but you'll be the first to know once I've got my hands on the bastards,' Brennan snarled. He sat down slowly on the bed. 'Goddamn it, I've never felt so helpless in my whole life.'

'I can understand that,' Monks replied. 'What about tonight? Do you still feel up to it?'

'You know me better than that, Lou, We've got a job to do. Six o'clock. In the hotel lobby. Just make sure *you're* not late.'

'What about Jason? Who's going to stay with him while you're at the hotel?'

'Shit. I hadn't thought of that.'

'I'll ask one of the girls to stay with him at your place. He'll probably be happier there.'

'They might have to collect him from the precinct,' Brennan said. 'He's going to have a pile of mugshots to wade through, and there's every chance he won't be finished by the time I have to leave for the hotel. I'll take my tux with me, and change there.' There was a loud knock on the front door. 'I gotta go, Lou. The cops are here.'

13

Kelly's first sensation on regaining consciousness was a dull incessant pounding in her temples. When she tried to move, a lancing pain shot up her side. She remembered the hooded jogger, and the stun gun. She opened her eyes. It took her several seconds to focus clearly on her surroundings. She was lying on the floor of a small room. No furniture. There was a closed door in the opposite corner of the room and a pair of grubby pale blue curtains were drawn across the only window. She could see a chink of light through a jagged tear in one of the curtains. She heard voices, muffled and indistinct, coming from beyond the window – not that she could call for help with the strip of tape over her mouth. Her wrists were handcuffed, and the chain had been looped behind a rusty pipe, which ran parallel to the wall. She winced in pain as she struggled into a sitting position. She had no idea where she was or why she'd been kidnapped. And that frightened her. But if there was one thing she'd learnt above all else in the ten gruelling years she'd spent in the Amazon, it was the importance of being able to rely on your own inner strength. She was damned if she was going to give her abductors the satisfaction of thinking they'd chained her into submission.

She shuffled round on her bottom until she was facing the wall then, gritting her teeth against the acute pain in her head, pushed her feet against the skirting board and began to tug at the handcuffs, trying to dislodge the corroded pipe from its moorings.

The door was flung open. 'What the fuck are you doing?' a voice yelled at her and she was shoved away from the wall.

233

She landed on her side but when she tried to sit up a foot pressed down on her arm, pinning her to the floor. 'Quit it, OK? Just quit it!'

It felt as though rows of unsynchronized jackhammers were drilling into every part of her head, and all she wanted was to be free of the excruciating pain. The foot was removed from her arm then a hand grabbed the collar of her tracksuit and she was hauled back into a sitting position.

The two men were wearing black stockings over their faces. The nearest was dressed in a sleeveless white T-shirt and a pair of torn jeans, and the other, standing in the doorway, wore a khaki T-shirt tucked into a pair of olive green battle-dress trousers.

The nearest man squatted beside her. 'You're real cute, you know that?' he said, stroking her hair. She jerked away her head and lashed out at him with her foot. He laughed when she caught his outer thigh.

'And pretty spunky too,' his colleague added.

'I like them spunky,' the first man replied with an unpleasant grin and tried to force his hand up the front of her tracksuit. Her foot shot forward like an uncoiling spring, and her heel slammed into his groin. He cried out in agony and crumpled to the floor, his hands clutched tightly between his legs.

The other man burst out laughing. 'You're a real fucking asshole, you know that?' he said. He was about to go over to his colleague when there was a knock at the front door. Three knocks. Pause. Two more. Another pause. Two more.

Kelly waited until he'd disappeared into the outer room then again set about tugging at the cuffs, ignoring the pounding in her head. Suddenly someone grabbed her hair, dragging her head back. She froze in terror when she felt the cold prongs of the stun gun touch her exposed neck.

'You rattle those fucking cuffs once more, bitch, and you're going to know what real pain is,' the voice hissed menacingly in her ear.

'Leave her!' a new voice ordered. The stun gun was

removed from her neck and the man let go of her hair. 'Get the spike,' the voice said, in a softer tone.

Kelly looked round at the third figure standing by the door. He had on the same disguise he'd been wearing when she'd seen him at the wheel of the van. Not that the cracked sunglasses and peaked cap fooled her. She knew who he was. Only she didn't know why he'd kidnapped her. It made no sense. The second man returned to the room with a hypodermic and she lashed out frantically with her feet when he tried to grab her arm.

'It's only a sedative,' the man in the sunglasses told her. 'It'll knock you out for a few hours. You'll be quite safe.' Still Kelly wouldn't let the needle near her arm, kicking at the man whenever he came in range. 'Don't force us to use the stun gun again. I'm sure you wouldn't want that, would you?'

The masked kidnapper with the stun gun took a step towards her. She could see by his twisted grin that he'd like nothing more than to use it on her. She was in a no-win situation. She could go down fighting, or she could save herself a lot of unnecessary pain by letting them give her the sedative. Assuming it was a sedative. But she had no reason to doubt that. She didn't know why they'd taken her, but it was clear they wanted her alive.

Inner strength was more than just defiance. It was also knowing when to resort to common sense as a means of compromise. She slumped back against the wall and her face remained expressionless as she felt the needle break her skin. She closed her eyes and relaxed as drowsiness drifted through her. *At least it's a release from the bloody headache,* was her last coherent thought before she passed out.

The Secret Service, with the New York Police Department, had sealed off the Richmond Hotel for a block in either direction. Further security precautions consisted of a web of police roadblocks on every approach road, which would remain in place until the VIPs departed the following morning. Élite police marksmen were deployed on the surrounding rooftops and at least one police helicopter was nearby at any given time. The police manning the roadblocks had been given specific instructions not to admit anyone unless they had a valid security pass, a confirmed hotel booking or an invitation to the Vets' dinner. They had all been issued with checklists for added verification. There could be no mistakes.

The pot-bellied sergeant waited until the car had stopped in front of the wooden barrier then ambled across to the driver's window. 'Evening,' he said, without looking into the car as he tugged the checklist from the breast pocket of his pale blue shirt.

'Still eating too much fried knish, I see.'

The sergeant peered through the open window and his startled expression softened in recognition as the beam of his torch played over the driver's face. 'Well, I'll be damned. Ray Brennan. Long time no see.'

'Not since you transferred out of the Four-O last year,' Brennan said, putting up a hand to shield his eyes from the glare of the light. 'Get that thing out of my face, will you?'

'What brings you down here?' the sergeant asked, after he'd switched off the torch.

Brennan retrieved his ID card from the dashboard. 'I'm part of the security detail. You'll find my name on one of those sheets.'

The sergeant switched on the torch again to look at the list. 'Yeah, here you are. And Lou. You guys are a bit far from home, aren't you? Why're they drafting in cops from the South Bronx?'

'It's a long story, Morty, not that I could tell you about it even if I'd wanted to,' Brennan replied. 'Now, are you going to let me through?'

The sergeant gestured for the wooden barrier to be moved aside and Brennan drove to the hotel where an attendant waved him towards the two-tiered underground car park. He found a space on the lower level, clipped his ID card to the breast pocket of his tuxedo and crossed to the elevator. Two uniformed policemen were standing guard on either side of the doors. Their eyes went to his ID card but they said nothing. He rode the elevator to the lobby where he was challenged by a Secret Service agent and asked for his ID. It was passed under a scanner then returned to him.

'What was that all about?' Brennan asked, as he clipped the disc back on to his pocket.

'Every security card has a tiny microchip built into it, invisible to the naked eye,' came the reply. 'Each has a different serial number printed on it. The number on your card corresponds to the name we have on our checklist.'

'And if it hadn't?' Brennan asked.

'You'd have been arrested and taken into custody.' The Secret Agent stepped aside. 'Have a nice one, Detective Brennan.'

'Let's hope so,' Brennan replied, then went in search of Monks. He found him talking to a couple of Secret Service agents by the main entrance.

'Any news of Kelly?' Monks asked, after they were out of earshot of the two men.

'Nothing so far,' Brennan replied. 'I tried to get Jason to put together a photofit of the driver, but it wasn't much use. He was still looking at mugshots when I left. I don't hold out much hope, though.'

'Who's the primary on the case?' Monks asked.

'I don't know him. Jerry Richards. He was transferred to the Seven-Nine from LA Homicide a few months ago.'

'Can't say I know the name either,' Monks replied. 'So what did you tell him about Kelly?'

'What could I tell him? I had to be real careful what I said – kept shtum about Caldwell and Dixon. I guess he thought I was a complete dweeb. He's been great with Jason, though, and he's putting a guard outside the apartment until I get back tonight. I know it's unlikely the kidnappers would try and get at Jason – they could have done that this afternoon – but it still makes me feel a little happier. Richards said he'll take the kid back to the apartment once he's through at the Seven-Nine. At least it'll save Lisa going over there to collect him.'

'I gave her the spare key for your apartment before I left the house.'

237

'She's a good kid,' Brennan said.

'She's nineteen, Ray.'

'I can still remember her as a ten-year-old with pigtails,' Brennan mused. 'It's hard to believe she's grown up so quickly.'

'You and me both, buddy.' Monks spotted a figure approaching them.

'I heard about what happened this afternoon,' Chip Garrett said to Brennan. 'I'm sorry. I know that you and Kelly are . . . well, more than just friends. I realize how difficult it must be for you right now. Do you think Caldwell was behind it?'

'No.'

'You seem very sure of that,' Garrett said.

'As I've already said to Lou, even if he knew you guys were on to him – which I doubt, unless he has inside information – what could he hope to gain by snatching her? No, I still think it's more likely to be some con I've put in the slammer, and who's now out for revenge.'

Garrett put his hand on Brennan's arm and led him a few paces away from Monks. 'I'd fully understand if you wanted out tonight. You've obviously got a lot on your mind—'

'I think you should give *me* a bit more credit than that,' Brennan cut in sharply. 'Of course I'm worried about Kelly but I've got a job to do here and you can be sure I'll do it to the best of my ability. That means giving one hundred per cent. But if you think I'm going to be a liability, then say so now?'

'We should get down to work,' Garrett said, then beckoned Monks towards them and walked towards the corridor which led off from the lobby to the function rooms. He stopped in front of the archway metal detector and handed his standard issue SIG-Sauer 228 9mm Parabellum to one of the special agents. He walked through and the pistol was returned to him. Brennan removed his Smith & Wesson .357 and handed it to the nearest agent, together with his watch and car keys. He stepped through the metal detector. It remained silent. He was body searched, then the items were returned to him. Monks was subjected to the same procedure.

'All the guests will have to pass through the metal detector. They'll also be body searched,' Garrett said.

'So where do you want us?' Brennan asked.

'Right here, of course,' Garrett replied. 'You're still the only one who's seen Caldwell and Dixon. Frankly, I don't see how either of them could possibly slip through our security cordon, but we can't take any chances. If they do get this far, then it means they're in disguise – and a good disguise at that. You might not recognize them, but they'll recognize you. That's when they'll know we're on to them. It'll unsettle them – could force them to play their hand prematurely. If they do, we'll be ready for them. Not that they'd get past here. Not without an official invitation. Each name on the guest list was vetted personally by our Deputy Director before they were sent out by the White House.'

'Maybe they'll try to pass themselves off as waiters,' Monks said.

'Impossible. All the waiters are permanent staff, as are the kitchen personnel. And all have been vetted and given access badges. Also, the back door leading from the kitchen has been locked and it's being guarded by two uniforms. As is the fire escape. It's not just to keep intruders out, but also to keep the staff in, limiting them to the kitchen and the function room for the duration of the dinner. The only exception will be the room-service waiters, but there's already a man assigned to the service elevator to ensure nobody gains access to the kitchen from one of the floors.'

'Sounds like you've got it wrapped,' Brennan said, nodding in approval.

'It's standard procedure,' Garrett replied matter-of-factly, then picked up the two portable radio systems that lay on the table beside the metal detector and handed one each to Brennan and Monks. 'I guess you're familiar with this system,' he said.

'Yeah,' Brennan replied, as he attached the microphone to his lapel.

'All the radios – apart from mine – are tuned in to the same frequency, but only my mike will receive the signal – so all communications have to be channelled through me. I can assess each situation as it arises and relay my instructions to the rest of you. It avoids any confusion.' He looked at his watch: 6.15 p.m. 'The Vice-President and his wife are due to come down in about a half-hour. The first of the guests will start arriving around seven. I gotta go now – things to do. Call if you need me.'

'Let's hope we don't,' Monks replied.

'I wouldn't count on it,' Brennan said.

Garrett's eyes rested on Brennan for a few seconds then he headed off towards the set of open doors further down the corridor.

Caldwell parked the van in a semi-lit alley on Lexington Avenue, close to the intersection with East 54th Street, three blocks away from the hotel. He switched off the engine and killed the headlights. Then he opened the built-in sliding door, directly behind the cab, and climbed through it. After he'd bolted the door behind him he switched on the low-wattage overhead light. The back of the van was empty except for a 14-inch Sony television set, fitted with an amplified aerial to boost the signal, and a Sony video recorder. He switched on the television set – the screen was blank, and would remain so until Dixon activated his miniature camera. It had been Caldwell's idea to record the assassination on tape – it would be the focal point of any presentation to his future clients. For a million dollars a hit, they would expect more than just assurances that his plan would work. What better way of proving his worth?

His phone rang and he was quick to answer it. 'Noonan's taxi's coming up to the police roadblock at the junction of Fifth and West Fifty-fourth,' a voice told him. 'He should reach the hotel within the next five minutes.'

Without a word Caldwell cut the connection. Noonan had been followed from his house in Hoboken. The tail, who would have peeled off before reaching the roadblock, had done his part. The rest was down to Dixon. Caldwell took the remote control from his pocket and placed it carefully on top of the television set. Then he called Dixon at the hotel.

'ETA five minutes,' was all Caldwell said.

Dixon replaced the handset and as he turned away from the bedside table he caught sight of his reflection in the cheval-glass mirror in the corner of the room. He was wearing the same disguise he'd had on when he first arrived at the hotel that morning. Then he'd been masquerading as a company executive from Dallas, now he was the owner of a moving firm on Tenth Avenue. Not that the Secret Service would pick up on the deception: the entire day shift had been relieved at five o'clock that afternoon. He would be just another face in the crowd.

He crossed to the closet where he unhooked his tuxedo from the hanger and slipped it on. A wide-angled miniature camera was sewn into the lining of the lapel with a lens small enough to shoot through the cloth. All its components were non-metallic to deceive the metal detector. He brushed his palms down his lapels. The camera wasn't detectable. He pulled the plastic tab from the back of his lapel. The camera was on. He was ready to go.

He left the room and walked the short distance to the elevator. When it arrived it was empty.

'Good evening,' an automated female voice greeted him. 'Please state the floor you require.'

'Lobby,' Dixon said.

'Lobby. Thank you.' Within seconds the elevator had reached its destination. 'Have a nice evening,' the voice instructed him, as the doors glided apart.

'I'm sure I will,' Dixon said, then crossed to a spread of armchairs in a corner of the lobby. No sooner had he sat down, facing the entrance to monitor Noonan's arrival, than a waiter approached and enquired if he'd care for anything from the bar. Dixon shook his head and the waiter left. Shortly afterwards the bulbous figure of Clive Noonan stepped through the automatic doors and was challenged by a uniformed policeman. He produced his invitation and was allowed through. Dixon got up and followed Noonan across the lobby to the corridor where several guests were waiting to clear the metal detector. Both men joined the back of the queue.

It was then that Dixon saw Brennan. He was scrutinizing each guest as they passed through the metal detector. Not that Brennan's presence surprised him. He'd already known the detective would be there and it hadn't troubled him – until now. Much as he tried to convince himself otherwise, seeing Brennan had unnerved him. But he had nothing to worry about – or so Caldwell had assured him. The disguise was good. But was it good enough to fool Brennan?

'Are you alone too?'

Dixon turned to Noonan. 'I'm afraid so,' he replied, sliding effortlessly into his Texan voice. He was surprised at how easy it had been to switch into character, considering how jangled his nerves were.

'Maybe we'll be at the same table.' A hand was stuck out towards him. 'Clive Noonan. Twenty-fifth Infantry Division.'

'Same as the Vice-President,' Dixon said, shaking Noonan's hand. 'Did you serve with him?'

'*Under* him,' said Noonan. 'I was just a grunt. He was an officer.'

Dixon's eyes flicked to Brennan. He didn't know whether the man had seen him yet. He hoped he had. It would mean he hadn't been recognized. *There's no way he'd still be standing there if he'd recognized me*, he said to himself. *He won't recognize you, for Christ's sake. He only saw you for a few moments . . .*

'I didn't catch your name, partner,' Noonan said.

'Jordan. Miles Jordan,' Dixon replied, using the name on the invitation.

'What unit?' Noonan persisted.

'Twentieth Airborne. Special Forces.'

Noonan whistled softly. 'Green Beret, eh? You guys sure kicked some ass out there.'

'Yeah.'

'That accent of yours. It's southern, isn't it?'

'Houston,' Dixon said. 'I settled here a few years ago.'

'You like it up here in New York City, then?'

Dixon forced a quick smile. Noonan's incessant banter was becoming irritating, but he comforted himself with the thought that he wouldn't have to put up with it for much longer. His eyes settled on Brennan again. He didn't know how long he'd been watching him when he felt Noonan's hand on his arm.

'Are you OK?' Noonan asked.

'Sure.'

'Do you know that guy?' Noonan asked, pointing at Brennan.

Dixon wanted to grab Noonan's arm and pull it down before the fool drew attention on them. Fortunately it was obscured from Brennan's view by the couple standing in front of them. 'No, he just looks a bit like my brother,' Dixon said, saying the first thing that came into his head. 'He died in 'Nam. We were real close.'

'I'm sorry,' Noonan said sympathetically.

'It was a long time ago,' Dixon shrugged.

They both fell silent. But not for long. 'We'll be up next,' Noonan announced, as the couple in front of them reached the head of the queue.

Dixon wanted to look at Brennan. See if there was even the faintest flicker of recognition on his face. But his nerve held and he was careful to avoid eye contact.

The couple in front were cleared through. It was his turn. He showed his invitation to one of the special agents and the name was checked against the guest list. He was asked if he was carrying any metallic items and removed his watch, then took a set of keys from his pocket and placed them on the table. He was invited to step through the metal detector. His heart was pounding. The alarm stayed silent. He was given a thorough body search and felt relief surge through him when the camera remained undetected. As he slipped the watch back on to his wrist he looked around casually at the other guests and allowed his eyes to drift casually across Brennan's face. The detective was staring straight at him. Dixon's stomach churned, but he forced himself to hold Brennan's stare: avoiding eye contact could be construed as a sign of guilt. Then he looked down at his watch strap and snapped the metal clasp into place.

'A drink, sir?' a voice enquired beside him.

Dixon turned to find a waiter holding a tray of champagne and orange juice towards him. He knew he should stick to the orange juice, but his celebratory instincts got the better of him and he helped himself to a glass of champagne. He took a sip and glanced surreptitiously at Brennan over the rim. Brennan was no longer looking at him. Dixon put the glass to his lips again to hide his faint smile. It was all going according to plan . . .

'I can't go through there.'

'If you don't go through the metal detector . . .' the special agent paused to check the name on the invitation card '. . . Mr Noonan, you can't attend the dinner.'

'It's not that I don't *want* to go through it,' Noonan said, 'it's that I can't. Doctor's orders. I have a pacemaker. The doctor told me these machines can interfere with the frequency. Look, I'll show you the stitches.'

'Not here,' the special agent replied hastily, as Noonan was about to unbutton his shirt. 'You'll have to undergo a strip search in one of the empty function rooms. I'm sorry, sir, but it's the only alternative under the circumstances.'

'That's no problem, just so long as I get to meet the Vice-President again,' Noonan said cheerfully. 'He was my CO in 'Nam, you know. It'll be interesting to see if he remembers me after all this time.'

'I'm sure he will,' the agent replied, knowing that the Vice-President would have been briefed by his aides on any guests who'd served with him. Another member of the security team was assigned to conduct the search and Noonan was led away.

'Seems like a bit of a character,' Monks said, as Noonan and the agent disappeared into the room and closed the door behind them.

'Yeah, I guess,' Brennan muttered absently, without taking

244

his eyes off the line of guests still waiting to pass through the metal detector.

'Still nothing?'

Brennan shook his head. 'It could be any one of a dozen guys I've seen here tonight. Not that I think they'd both be here. That would be too risky. And if Caldwell's half as smart as I think he is, he'll have sent Dixon to do the dirty work.'

'You think they'll try something tonight, don't you?'

'Not if I can—'

'What is it?' Monks asked. No reply. 'Ray?'

'It's him, Lou,' Brennan said under his breath.

'Who – Dixon?'

Brennan didn't answer. Instead he switched on his lapel microphone and tilted his head down to get his mouth close to the device. 'Garrett, it's Brennan. Get over here now! No questions, just do it.' He cut the connection.

'Ray, what the hell's going on?' Monks asked. Again no reply. Then he saw Garrett negotiating a brisk path towards them through the guests.

'What is it?' Garrett demanded, when he reached them.

'The guy standing third from the back in the line,' Brennan said. 'Early fifties. Greying hair. His wife's wearing a blue evening dress. You see him?'

'Sure I see him,' Garrett replied. 'That's Jackson Frain, the Deputy Director of the Secret Service. He flew in with the Vice-President and his entourage. What about him?'

'The Deputy Director of the Secret Service?' Brennan said in disbelief.

'That's what I said,' Garrett replied irritably. 'Now what the hell's this all about, Brennan?'

'That's the man who met Caldwell at the ranch in the Amazon,' Brennan said, without taking his eyes off Frain.

'Are you sure?' Monks asked.

'Of course I'm sure,' Brennan snapped. Several heads turned towards him, startled by his raised voice. 'Of course I'm sure,' he repeated, in a lowered tone. 'I saw him get off the plane, shake hands with Caldwell, then Dixon drove them both to the farmhouse. That's him. No question of it.'

'Wait here,' Garrett said, then skirted round the side of the metal detector and walked up to Frain.

'Chip, good to see you,' Frain said genially, and extended a hand towards him.

Garrett shook it then nodded politely to the man's wife. 'Sir, may I have a word with you?'

'Fire away,' Frain told him.

'In private.'

Frain sensed the underlying tension in Garrett's voice and put a hand lightly on his wife's arm. 'Excuse me, darling. Duty calls, I'm afraid. I'll be back as soon as I can.'

'We can talk in one of the empty function rooms,' Garrett said, but was stopped by one of his own men when he tried to bypass the metal detector.

'You know I can't let you do that, sir,' the special agent said.

Garrett thought about pulling rank but decided against it. The man was just following orders. Orders *he*'d given him earlier that day. He handed over his weapon and stepped through the archway. Frain, who wasn't armed, followed him through without triggering the alarm. Garrett then led him to the nearest door, opened it and motioned him inside. He switched on the main light but when he turned back to shut the door he found Brennan barring in his way. 'I'll handle this,' Garrett said tersely.

'*We*'ll handle this,' Brennan replied, and closed the door behind him.

'Who's this?' Frain demanded.

'Detective Ray Brennan, NYPD,' Garrett replied.

Frain acknowledged Brennan with a curt nod. 'OK, Chip, what's this all about? I guess you've come up with something otherwise we wouldn't be going through this cloak-and-dagger routine. What have you got?'

'You recently attended a conference in Caracas, didn't you, sir?' Garrett said.

'Yes,' Frain replied, with a puzzled frown.

'Did you fly to Brazil while you were there?'

'Chip, I don't know what—'

'Just answer the question!' Garrett interrupted. 'Did you, or did you not, fly to Brazil while you were in Caracas?'

'How dare you speak to me like that?' Frain shot back furiously. 'Now if you'll excuse me, my wife's waiting for me.'

'She's going to have to get used to it,' Brennan said, and slid his hand under his tuxedo. He didn't draw his weapon but the inference was enough to halt Frain.

'I don't know what's got into you, Chip, but I can tell you now that you'll be lucky to remain in the Service once I've finished with you,' Frain said, glaring at Garrett.

'Under the circumstances, I'm prepared to take that chance,' Garrett replied. 'Now would you please answer the question, *sir*. And remember, all it'll take is one phone call to confirm whether you're telling the truth or not.'

'Yes, I flew down to Brazil,' Frain said irritably. 'We had a free day during the conference. I just wanted to get away from it all. The American ambassador loaned me his private jet. It's was all above-board, I can assure you. Certainly no misappropriation of government property, if that's what you're implying.'

'Where did you go?' Garrett asked.

'I flew down to the Amazon. I've always wanted to see it.'

'And where did you put down?' Garrett asked.

'I refuelled twice at Manaus. Once when I arrived and again before I flew back to Caracas. It'll all be documented at Manaus airport.'

'You didn't put down anywhere else?' Garrett said.

'I told you, I only put down twice,' Frain said in exasperation.

'What about the other time – at Lamar Zander's ranch where you met Tom Caldwell?' Brennan asked.

Incredulity flashed briefly in Frain's eyes, then it was gone but there was a tremor in his voice when he spoke. 'I don't know what you're talking about.'

'I saw you meet with Caldwell and Dixon. I can even tell you what clothes you were wearing at the time. Grey suit. Pale blue shirt, open at the neck. Dixon drove you back to the farmhouse in a white Mercedes.' Brennan knew he was on a roll, and decided to take a major gamble knowing it could just as easily backfire on him, but Frain was rattled and it had to be worth the chance to hammer the final nail into his coffin. 'I also memorized the number on the fuselage. Do you want us to phone the embassy in Caracas and ask them for the serial number on the ambassador's private jet?'

The blood had drained from Frain's face even before Brennan had finished. He knew the man couldn't have made it up. He had to have been there.

'All I'm interested in right now is preventing anything from happening to the Vice-President,' Garrett said. 'Is Caldwell here?' Silence. 'Dixon?' Still silence. 'Are either of them here?' No reply. 'You can either make this easy on yourself, or really hard on your family. Your daughter's in her second year of a law degree at Yale, isn't she? And doing well, by all accounts. Your wife owns one of the most prestigious catering firms in Washington. All the politicians hire her for their private functions, don't they? Imagine what's going to happen to them when this is splashed across the front pages of every paper in the country. But, then, if this assassination is more important to you than your own family, so be it. I just hope they can find it in their hearts to forgive you before you're executed. Death by lethal injection. That's the penalty now for capital murder in New York State.'

'Dixon's already here,' Frain blurted out, as he wiped a shaking hand over his face. 'But he's wearing some disguise. I don't know what he looks like. I swear I don't.'

'How's he going to assassinate the Vice-President?' Garrett demanded.

'He's not,' Frain replied. 'Caldwell will do it by remote control. He's not in the hotel. I don't know where he is. He never told me.'

'Remote control?' Brennan said. 'What is it, some kind of bomb?'

'You could say that,' Frain replied.

'Go on,' Garrett pressed, when Frain fell silent.

'Not unless you give me certain guarantees upfront,' Frain

248

said, trawling up the last of his faltering defiance, but there was no fight left in his voice.

'Considering that you're going to end up on Death Row if the Vice-President is assassinated here tonight, I don't think you're in any position to ask for guarantees, do you?' Garrett enquired icily. 'I'd suggest you tell us what we need to know before it's too late.'

His resistance broken, Frain explained how the assassination was to be carried out.

'Who's carrying the device?' Garrett asked, already heading for the door.

'His name's Clive Noonan,' Frain said.

'I know who he is,' Brennan said. 'I saw him at the metal detector a few minutes ago—'

'Then find him – and isolate him,' Garrett cut across Brennan. 'And do it discreetly. We'll have all-out panic on our hands if the other guests find out what's going on.'

Brennan slipped out into the corridor and went straight to the room where Noonan had had the body search. It was empty.

'What's going on?' Monks asked behind him.

'We've got to find the guy with the pacemaker who was taken in here. You remember him?'

'Sure,' Monks replied. Then he frowned. 'You're not going to tell me that was Dixon?'

'No,' Brennan said. 'There's no time to explain. If you find him, take him to the nearest empty room and leave him there. Then contact Garrett. Whatever you do, don't stay in the room with him any longer than is absolutely necessary.'

Although baffled, Monks knew there would be time for explanations later. When they split up. Brennan made for the entrance to the function room where the Vice-President and his wife were greeting the arriving guests. If Noonan wasn't there, at least he could intercept him before he reached his intended target. Brennan had the urge to run, brush aside anyone who got in his way, but he checked himself, remembering Garrett's warning about not panicking the guests. His eyes darted around him, searching for any sign of his quarry.

He couldn't see him anywhere. *Where the hell was he?* It wasn't as if there were that many guests milling around the corridor. Perhaps he'd gone to the bathroom. That would be the perfect place to isolate him. Brennan cursed himself for letting his thoughts run away with him. *Just concentrate on finding him . . .*

Then he saw him. Partially obscured by a cluster of guests who were waiting outside the main doors, Noonan was peering round the door like some mischievous kid. Then he disappeared. Brennan remembered the two men laughing together at the back of the short queue outside the function room and the woman reaching for another glass of champagne from a hovering waiter. It felt almost as if he were watching them in slow motion. There was no sound. Then the men stopped laughing. Now they were staring at him. All the guests were staring at him. Then the waiter was stumbling backwards, the tray spilling from his hand, the glasses tumbling to the carpet. The silence was shattered. A voice was shouting at the special agent who'd gestured Noonan forward to meet the Vice-President. Brennan suddenly realized it was his own voice. He was running and shouting at the same time. The guests were reacting to him. The waiter had been knocked aside by him.

He reached the door where the special agent, alerted by his warning, had already stepped between Noonan and the Vice-President. But in that horrifying moment Brennan saw that Noonan was close enough to the Vice-President for the gas to be effective. He hurled himself at Noonan, taking his legs from under him. Noonan hit the ground and Brennan pushed him face down on the floor, knowing that if the device was triggered the gas would be partially absorbed by the other man's bulk. Then he heard Garrett yelling at his team to get the Vice-President and his wife back up to their suite. Special agents encircled the couple and they were hustled through the function room and into the kitchen.

Brennan felt a hand on his arm and he was pulled off Noonan who was still lying face down on the floor. Then he heard the muffled explosion as the device was detonated in the man's chest. But by then Brennan was already holding his breath and rolling across the floor. He had to get away from the body. Get away from the lethal gas. Then he felt more hands on him, stopping him moving. He tried desperately to break free. He had to get as far away as possible from the body—

'Brennan, quit struggling, for Christ's sake.' Garrett's voice. 'You're safe now.'

'Is the Vice-President OK?'

'Yeah.'

Brennan looked across at Noonan's lifeless body lying in the doorway of the function room. A pool of blood was seeping from under it and spreading slowly across the pale blue carpet. 'Poor bastard. He didn't stand a chance.'

'At least we got the other guests away before Caldwell detonated the device. There's an extractor fan in the ceiling above the doors, so most of the gas will have been sucked out through it.'

Suddenly a woman screamed. The guests recoiled in terror from the man holding a Smith & Wesson to the side of Monks's head. Brennan didn't recognize him but knew it had to be Dixon. Four special agents were behind Dixon, their weapons trained on his back. Garrett gestured for the guests to be moved out of harm's way and they were quickly ushered out into the lobby.

'Tell them to throw down their weapons, Brennan,' Dixon shouted, pushing the barrel harder against Monks's head. He had already spat out the mouth inserts and the distinctive Alabama twang in his voice confirmed Brennan's suspicions. Yet he would never have guessed it was Dixon. The disguise was brilliant.

'They're not going drop their weapons, Dixon, and you know it,' Brennan said. 'It's over. Put the gun down.'

'Fuck you!' Dixon snarled.

'There's no way you're going to walk out of here with a hostage,' Brennan said. 'It doesn't work that way. Which leaves you with two options. You can either leave in handcuffs or in a body bag. It's your choice, Dixon.'

251

'We can still do a deal if you put the gun down,' Garrett told him. 'You give us Caldwell and tell us everything you know about the operation, and I guarantee it'll reflect favourably on your sentence.'

'Noonan's dead.' Dixon snorted. 'That's already put me on Death Row.'

'I said we can do a deal,' Garrett replied calmly. 'Just put the gun down and we can take it from there.'

'Even if I did cheat Death Row, I'd still be looking at twenty-five to life, wouldn't I? Fuck that. Brennan's right. There are only two ways out of here. I'll take the body bag.' Dixon shoved Monks roughly in the back, propelling him towards Brennan, then pressed the barrel of the Smith & Wesson against the roof of his mouth and pulled the trigger.

One of the special agents went through the formality of checking for a pulse. He met Garrett's eyes and shook his head. Garrett said, 'Keep the press away from here until I give the word. I want that passed on to all the uniforms at the roadblocks. And tell them if they screw this, I'll see to it they'll all be back on the beat by morning. Get to it.' He waited until the man had hurried away then beckoned a second agent towards him. 'None of the guests are to leave the hotel. Put extra security on the main door and make sure this corridor remains cordoned off. I don't want any unauthorized personnel in here. And that includes hotel staff.'

'Yes, sir,' the man replied, and went off to carry out his orders.

Garrett turned to Monks. 'What happened?'

'He panicked,' Monks said. 'Broke away from the others and tried to make for the lobby. I moved to stop him but he got me with a sucker punch to the ribs. That's when he stuck his hand under my tux and pulled the gun out the holster.'

'So Frain's now our only link to Caldwell,' Garrett said.

'Where *is* Frain?' Brennan asked.

'Still in the room where we left him. I've got two men watching him.'

'Where are you going to take him?' Brennan asked.

'It's your town. I was hoping you could tell me. Somewhere

quiet. I don't want his arrest made public until I've had a chance to speak to my superiors and find out how they want to play it.'

'How about taking him to police headquarters in the Civil Center?' Monks suggested. 'That way you'll avoid the press-hounds who hang around the precincts.'

'Can you set it up?' Garrett asked.

'I'll make a couple calls, see if I can clear it,' Monks said.

'Use my mobile.' Garrett removed it from his pocket and handed it over.

Brennan and Garrett returned to the function room where Frain was being held. He was sitting forlornly in the centre of the otherwise empty room, his arms resting on his knees, his head bowed. The two agents stood by the door. Garrett ordered them to wait outside.

'I want to ask him about Kelly before we go any further,' Brennan said to Garrett. 'OK, I know I said I didn't think Caldwell was behind the kidnap – and I still don't. But I've got to ask.'

'Go ahead.'

Brennan crossed to where Frain was sitting. 'Did you or Caldwell order the abduction of Kelly McBride this afternoon?'

Frain raised his head for the first time since they'd entered the room. 'I didn't even know she'd been kidnapped. I certainly didn't order it. And I doubt Caldwell did either. I spoke to him less than an hour ago. He never mentioned anything about it. What would be gained by it?'

The door opened and Monks peered in. 'It's been cleared for you to take Frain down to Police Headquarters.'

'Excellent,' Garrett said. 'Can you get an unmarked patrol car for us to get him there?'

'Sure,' Monks replied. 'Where do you want it to meet you?'

'Basement car park.' He grabbed Frain by the arm and pulled him to his feet. 'Monks, take him outside and wait for us there. I want a word with Brennan. In private.' He waited until Frain had been led away. 'Your quick thinking saved the Vice-President's life tonight. As he'll be returning to Washington tomorrow morning, I wanted to ask you if you'd like him to be told so that he can thank you personally for what you did. I'm sure he'd want to.'

'It's ironic, isn't it?' Brennan said. 'The man's politics are anathema to me. Yet I risked my life to protect him. Who knows, maybe I've saved the life of the next President of the United States. I only hope for this country's sake I haven't just made my worst mistake ever.' He crossed to the door then turned back to Garrett. 'As for meeting him in person, I think you already know my answer.'

There was a tap at the door and Monks's head appeared round it. 'The car's waiting in the basement.'

'Brennan, take Frain to the car. Wait for me there. I won't be long. Monks, I want you to stay here and liaise with Frank Lewis, my deputy. He'll assume command once I've gone.'

'What do we do about Caldwell?' Monks asked, once Frain had been led away, flanked by two special agents with Brennan bringing up the rear.

'We can't do anything until we find him. But I think Frain will give him up, providing he's offered the right incentive.' Garrett's eyes settled on the figure who slipped past the cordon of Secret Service agents at the mouth of the corridor and walked towards them. 'Ah, here's Frank now. Come on, I'll introduce you.'

If only I hadn't delayed . . .

Caldwell had lost count of the times that thought had reverberated like an echo inside his head. Yet his defence was always the same. How could he have known that Brennan would intercept Noonan? There had been no warning. Which had been Dixon's fault. He'd been in place, opposite the main doors where the Vice-President and his wife had been greeting their guests. Dixon had to have seen Brennan, judging by the way the policeman had tackled Noonan in full flight. Only the camera hadn't picked it up until too late. By then Noonan was flat on his stomach and the Vice-President and his wife were safely out of range of the gas. And that's when Dixon had panicked. Not that it mattered. He doubted that Dixon would have escaped even if the assassination had been a success. But, then, he'd always been expendable. Like Noonan. He'd had no qualms about killing Noonan. It had been necessary to ensure that the device didn't fall into the wrong hands. At least, not intact.

It had been a setback, sure, but not a catastrophe. He had influential contacts abroad who'd give him a base where he could regroup, using the money he'd been siphoning off the account Zander had opened to cover their expenses while they were stationed in the Amazon. He already had a ticket booked to Amsterdam where he'd be met by one of his contacts. The flight left in two hours' time. Then the cycle could begin again.

He switched off the television and the VCR, then unbolted the door, but as he pulled it open to climb back into the cab, he saw a police car parked across the entrance to the alley. There was a brick wall at the other end. He was hemmed in. His first thought was that the authorities were on to him. But that made no sense. The only person who'd known he was there was Dixon. And Dixon was dead. But even if Dixon had told them, which he doubted, then surely they'd have already sealed off the area and stormed the van? Or at the very least, called on him to surrender. It still left him with a dilemma. Should he sit it out, and risk missing his flight to Amsterdam? Or ask the officers to move their car? There was a third choice, but one he'd only resort to if all else failed: kill them, and move the police car himself. He had a revolver strapped to the side of the driver's seat, but shots would alert police in the area. No, diplomacy was his best bet.

But fate dealt its own hand. The passenger door of the squad car swung open and an officer climbed out, pushing a night stick into the holster on his belt. The dirver got out too, and they walked towards the van. Caldwell climbed into the driver's seat and secured the door. The alley was ill-lit and it was only when they got to within a few feet of the van that he realized the driver was a woman. Attractive. Good figure. Her partner was a tall man with a pock-marked face.

Caldwell wound down the window and smiled. 'Evening, officer. Is there a problem?'

'Not any more,' she replied, then raised the suppressed SIG-Sauer 228 automatic she'd had concealed behind her back. Caldwell was still clawing frantically for the revolver strapped to his seat when she shot him through the head.

'Kickin' shot, partner,' the man said, then pulled open the door and checked for a pulse. Finding none, he went through Caldwell's pockets to find the van keys. He handed them to the woman, then unlocked the partition door and got into the back of the van. Grabbing Caldwell's body under the arms, he dragged it through the door and laid it out on the floor. The back doors were unlocked from the outside then pulled open and the woman jumped nimbly into the van and placed her weapon beside Caldwell's body. She then took out the video tape. 'I'll dump the patrol car in the Bronx. It'll be nothing more than a burnt-out shell by the morning,' she said. 'You get rid of Caldwell and the van. Remember, he's got to disappear without trace.'

'Leave it to me,' he said, with a chilling smile.

'I'll meet you back at the hotel at say . . . ten o'clock,' she said, consulting her watch. 'I just hope they've got a good room-service menu. I'll be starving when I get back.'

'Home to Washington tomorrow,' he said, jumping out of the van after her. 'I'm looking forward to that. I miss my kids.'

'You've only been gone a couple of days,' she said, then locked the doors and handed him the keys.

'I'm a family man. What else can I say?' he replied, getting behind the wheel.

'See you back at the hotel,' she said, then began to whistle softly to herself as she walked back to the patrol car.

'Caldwell's dead.'

Frain was sitting in an interrogation room on the seventh floor of the new Police Headquarters in the Civic Center. The two chairs opposite were empty. Garrett was at the coffee percolator, preparing a fresh brew and Brennan was at the window, the top two buttons of his shirt undone and the constricting bow-tie in his pocket. He was staring across the bland concrete expanse of the Police Plaza spread out below. Raising his eyes, he could see the illuminated rooftops of the New York City courthouses a couple of blocks away in Foley Square. Familiar territory for him – particularly 'The Tombs', the nickname given to the criminal court buildings housed there. He turned away from the window, Frain's words still fresh in his mind, but before he could speak Garrett said, 'Dead? I don't understand.'

'It had been agreed at the outset that this operation would be a one-off to assassinate the Vice-President,' Frain said. 'Only Caldwell reneged on the deal. He wanted to go free-lance. The last thing we needed was a loose cannon out for personal profit. So it was decided that irrespective of what happened tonight, Caldwell would be executed before he could take the show on the road. I don't know what will happen to the body, except that it'll never be found.'

'How did you know he intended to go solo?' Brennan asked, resuming his seat.

'Dixon found out. He was my eyes and ears in Caldwell's camp. Not that Caldwell knew. He thought Dixon was a borderline psychopath. Dixon had a dark side, granted, but he was a lot smarter than Caldwell gave him credit for. Just as well, really. I doubt whether Caldwell would have taken it too well if he'd ever discovered that Dixon was spying on him.'

'Who killed Caldwell?' Brennan asked.

'I can't tell you that. They were merely carrying out orders.'

'How can you be so sure that Caldwell's already dead?' Brennan said. 'It's not as if you'd any contact with them since your arrest.'

'I was entitled to one call when I got here,' Frain said, with a faint smile of satisfaction. 'I've no use for a lawyer.'

'Clever,' Garrett said, placing a cup of coffee in front of Frain. 'And I suppose if we were to trace the number you rang, it would turn out to be a pay phone somewhere in the city.'

'Near the subway on East Fifty-third,' Frain replied. 'But I'm sure you'll check.'

Garrett handed Brennan some coffee then pulled up the empty chair and sat down beside him. 'Who exactly were Caldwell and Dixon?'

'Their real names wouldn't mean anything to you. Caldwell was a senior officer in the Special Forces. A Gulf War veteran. Dixon was a former marine.'

'You're going to have to disclose their names at some point,' Brennan told him.

Frain gave a disinterested shrug. Brennan was amazed at the man's transformation. At the hotel he'd been a sad figure but now his confidence was back, with a revitalized defiance that verged on arrogance. He was laughing at them. They may have thwarted the assassination, but Frain had been stringing them along all the way. Especially Garrett, who'd kept him informed of every development, allowing him to make the necessary countermoves to protect his operatives. Garrett wasn't to blame, yet Brennan had a feeling his superiors in the Secret Service wouldn't see it that way. If there was going to be a fall guy to satisfy the bureaucrats in Washington, it would probably be Garrett. Unless he could find a way of extricating himself from an increasingly desperate situation . . .

'Was Zander behind it?' Garrett asked.

Frain laughed then picked up the polystyrene cup and took a sip of coffee. 'Zander was the money, nothing more. He was well known for his outspoken views against the religious right within the Republican Party. I thought he'd be an ideal candidate to finance this project. He was also a personal friend so I knew that even if he hadn't agreed to help us, he certainly wouldn't have said anything to damage the operation. As it turned out, he was more than happy to put up the money.'

'*Us?*' Brennan said suspiciously.

'I was just the middle man. The assassination was being planned by a coterie of liberal-minded senators on Capitol Hill within days of the President being elected to the White

House. Not that *he* had anything to do with it. I want that made known right now. On tape. He knew nothing about the plot to assassinate the Vice-President. To understand the reasoning behind their machinations, you have to go back to the election race itself. As I'm sure you both know, the President's main support came from the centre and left of the party. But he didn't have the backing of the right. And within the last ten years the right's become a potent force in the Republican movement. Without their support, he'd never have been elected as the official Republican candidate to run against the Democrats. That's why he had to take the Vice-President on board as his running mate. There were a lot of political analysts at the time who claimed it was a clever strategy, but that wasn't a view shared by the bulk of the party. Their greatest concern was that if anything were to happen to the President once he reached the White House, the Vice-President would automatically assume control. And that could open the floodgates for the right. Like my colleagues, I've always believed that religion and politics should be kept well apart. What right have these fanatics to force their minority views on the rest of the population? And they will if they ever get one of their own into the Oval Office. Which is why the assassination was deemed necessary.

'Caldwell, who'd had a lot of experience with germ warfare in the Special Forces, was hired to devise a method of assassination that wouldn't point the finger of suspicion at anyone within the Party. The pacemaker was his idea. That's when Zander's personal cardiologist was brought in to help him. Between the two of them, they came up with a prototype which they tested extensively in the Amazon.'

'On the local Indians?' Brennan said, not attempting to hide his disgust.

'It was the only way to perfect the device,' Frain replied. 'The locale was carefully chosen for the project. Indians die in the jungle all the time and their bodies are never found. We knew there wouldn't be any comebacks, at least not from the local authorities. And that's all that concerned us. They

259

were able to carry out experiments on the Indians with impunity. It was the perfect arrangement.'

'You son-of-a-bitch,' Brennan snarled, but as he leapt to his feet Garrett grabbed him.

'That's enough!' he snapped. 'Now either sit down and conduct yourself properly, or leave the room.'

Brennan ran his hands through his hair, frustration apparent on his face. Then he banged his fist angrily on the table before reluctantly resuming his seat.

'I'm sorry if I touched a raw nerve, Mr Brennan,' Frain said dispassionately. 'It's just that the future of my country means a hell of a lot more to me than the lives of a few savages. Obviously you don't see it that way.'

'Which senators planned the assassination?' Garrett asked.

'I'll give the names to the President. Nobody else.'

'Now you listen to me—'

'No. It's going to be the other way round this time,' Frain interrupted, his hand raised to silence Garrett. 'I've co-operated fully with your investigation so far. But the names of my co-conspirators is the last ace I have up my sleeve. And I intend to play it to the best of my advantage.'

'The President's not going to grant you any favours, you know that,' Garrett replied.

'I'd hardly call it a favour, more a proposition. I'll need a secure line to the White House and complete privacy to talk.'

'I'll stay here if you want to set it up,' Brennan said, and noticed the uncertainty in Garrett's eyes. 'What do you think I'm going to do? Deck him the moment you leave?'

Garrett left the room.

Brennan switched off the recorder and leaned forward, hands clasped on the table. 'There's still one unanswered question which is more important to me than any of this political bullshit. Off the record. What *did* happen to my brother and how did he come to get mixed up in this in the first place?'

'From what I heard, the coroner's verdict was accidental death.'

260

'So what are you saying? You don't know – or you're not going to tell me?'

'From what I understand, he was approached by one of Caldwell's senior men. Someone who had access to these experiments. He offered to tell your brother what was going on at the ranch in return for money. They met twice and Donald was given highly incriminating information on both occasions. That's when Caldwell found out what was going on. A third meeting was set up but this time Caldwell and Dixon followed the man to the rendezvous. Your brother escaped. They gave chase with dogs. He was finally cornered and tried to escape by jumping into a river. That's when he got the head wound. So the coroner was right all along. Accidental death.'

There was silence until Garrett returned. 'I've spoken to the White House,' he told Frain. 'The President's agreed to talk to you. But I'm warning you, you'd better be on the level here.'

'I think the President will realize I am when I give him the names. I reckon he's already got a good idea who the conspirators are.'

Garrett beckoned Brennan to where he was standing by the door. 'You might as well go home now. There's nothing more to keep you here. I'll call you once I get back to Washington.' Garrett extended a hand towards him. 'You did well tonight. Thanks.'

'Maybe too well,' Brennan said, gripping Garrett's hand.

'Maybe,' Garrett muttered, as he watched Brennan head for the elevator.

Brennan let himself into his apartment and was surprised to find Lou Monks in the lounge. 'Where's Lisa?' he asked, dropping his tuxedo over the back of the nearest chair.

'I told her to go home,' Monks replied. 'She's got to be up early in the morning anyway. She's going upstate for a few days to a leisure camp with some of her colleagues from work.'

'When did you get here?'

'About a half-hour ago,' Monks said. 'There was nothing for me to do at the hotel. The Secret Service had it wrapped. I was too hyped up to go home so I came here. I thought I might relax a little if I was on my own for a while.'

'And have you?' Brennan asked.

'I guess so,' Monks said, then sat forward in the chair, his arms resting on his knees. 'I've been a cop now for over thirty years. I've lost count of the number of hostage situations I've dealt with. But this was the first time I was the hostage. The first time I had the gun to my head. And I tell you, Ray, it scared the shit out of me. I thought I was going to die. Sometimes I wonder . . .'

'. . . whether it's all worth it?' Brennan concluded, when Monks's voice trailed off.

'Is it?' Monks asked, staring pensively at the carpet. 'Marilyn's been at me for some time now to take early retirement. She's never been comfortable with me being a cop. My argument's always been that you guys are like a second family to me and if I did retire, it would be like walking away from a part of myself. But after what happened tonight, I figured maybe I've been overlooking a flaw in my own argument. That Marilyn and the girls – my real family – ought to come first. Ruth's already talking about getting engaged. In a year or two they'll want to get married. I want to give her away at the altar and I want to be around to see my grandchildren grow up. And tonight I thought that was never going to happen.'

'I hear what you're saying,' Brennan said.

'It's been simmering for a while now. I've always pushed it to one side but tonight brought it home to me. And now that I've had a chance to think about it, I know I've got some decisions to make about my future.'

'Maybe you should talk with a counsellor,' Brennan said.

'I don't need some shrink spouting a load of shit at me. No, this is something I have to do myself. It's my family. And my future.' Monks stood up. 'Well, I'd better get going. Marilyn will have heard about tonight's little incident on the

262

TV news and that means she'll be waiting to deliver her standard sermon – the one about her fearing for my safety and why don't I either request a permanent desk job or leave the force altogether and work as a security consultant. I've heard it so often I reckon I must know it word for word by now. So the sooner we get it over with, the sooner I can get to bed.'

'She only says these things because she cares about you, Lou,' Brennan reminded him.

'I know. I just wish she'd find another way of showing it. I really do.'

Brennan walked his partner to the door. 'Thanks for keeping an eye on the kid, Lou.'

'He's been no trouble. Lisa said he went to bed around eight. I looked in on him after she'd gone. He was fast asleep, clutching a football. I didn't try to move it in case I woke him.'

Brennan smiled as he opened the door. 'Say thanks to Lisa for me, will you? I'll arrange to have some flowers delivered to the house for her.'

'She'd like that, especially coming from you. But leave it a few days, though. As I said, she's going upstate tomorrow. See you in the morning.'

Brennan closed the door behind Monks, then helped himself to a cold beer from the ice-box and returned to the lounge where he sat down in his favourite armchair by the window. Even with the window closed, he could still hear the muffled beat from one of the nightclubs further down the street. It was strangely comforting. The music had life. And with life, came hope . . .

He felt as if he'd just opened a door into his subconscious, releasing all the fears and uncertainties he'd had locked away there for the past few hours. Not that he'd consigned them there out of choice. Rather out of necessity. It had been the only way to make sure his personal feelings didn't encroach on his professional duty. He tried to reassure himself that Kelly would have expected it of him. But it didn't ease the pain. Or the guilt. Yet he knew the guilt would have been far greater had the Vice-President been killed because of Brennan's inattention to detail. Had he allowed himself to become preoccupied with his own thoughts of Kelly, Frain might have appeared as just another face in the crowd and the assassination *would* have succeeded. How could he ever have reconciled himself with that? But all this was overshadowed by overwhelming frustration and helplessness: Kelly was somewhere out there, probably frightened and alone, and there wasn't a damn thing he could do about it. It went deeper even than that. Brennan couldn't forget that when Kelly had needed him most, he hadn't been there for her. Why hadn't *he* gone to the deli? Sure, he couldn't have known what was going to happen that afternoon – but that was an excuse. And excuses were only short-term answers. When it came down to it, he'd failed her. And if any harm were to come to her . . .

He couldn't bring himself to think about that. He reached for his beer. It was going to be a long night . . .

14

Kelly was on Brennan's mind from the moment he was woken by the telephone. He was still in his favourite armchair by the window. His back ached and so did his neck. Ignoring the discomfort, he sat up and lifted the receiver to his ear. 'Hello?' he said.

'Brennan?'

'Who's this?' he demanded.

'Chip Garrett.'

Brennan sagged despondently in the chair and stifled a yawn as he looked across at the wall clock. 'It's seven o'clock in the morning, Garrett. Why in hell are you ringing at this godforsaken hour?'

'We need to talk.'

'What about?' Brennan demanded.

'There've been some developments, but that's all I'm prepared to say over the phone. I wanted to tell you personally – before you heard it on the radio, or saw it in the newspapers. I think we owe you that. I don't have a lot of time, though. I'm due to fly back to Washington later this morning. Can I come to your apartment? We can talk there.'

'Sure,' Brennan replied, massaging the back of his neck with his fingertips. 'I guess you know the address?'

'*We* know everything.'

'Then you'll also know I'm out of milk. Pick up a carton for me on your way over, will you?'

The line went dead. Brennan went through to the bathroom and washed. In his bedroom he changed into a pair of jeans and a T-shirt. He was about to leave the room when he

265

noticed Kelly's gold bracelet lying on the bedside table. Maybe, he thought, it had come loose and fallen off her wrist. So why hadn't she replaced it, as she always did? Could she have taken it off deliberately? A new beginning, perhaps. He stroked the baggy T-shirt, which she'd folded neatly and laid on the pillow on her side of the bed. *Her* side of the bed? It sounded so natural. She was now part of his life. He couldn't imagine—

He pushed the thought from his mind, knowing where it was leading, went through to the lounge and slumped on the couch. He tuned in to CNN where a studio discussion was analysing the political ramifications of the attempted assassination on the Vice-President. The anchor was chairing the debate with two men: a lecturer in political science at Princeton and a respected elder statesman from the powerful right-wing Christian coalition. Brennan reached for the remote and switched it off just as he heard a knock at the front door. He went out and peered through the spy hole. It was Garrett. He opened the door and gestured him into the hall.

'Milk,' Garrett said, depositing the carton into Brennan's hand.

'Let's go into the kitchen. I don't want to wake the kid.'

Garrett followed Brennan to the kitchen, but remained in the doorway, his hands in his pockets. 'No news of Kelly?'

'No. And you didn't come here to talk about her,' Brennan said. 'So get to the point.'

'Frain's dead.'

'What happened?'

'He had a heart-attack in his hotel room last night.'

'Why was he released from custody?' Brennan demanded.

'He was never in custody,' Garrett said. 'At least, not officially, that is.'

'I don't understand . . .' Brennan's voice trailed off. 'Of course. A heart-attack induced by hydrocyanic gas. Right?'

'Right,' Garrett confirmed. 'A small glass vial, identical to the one in the device implanted in Noonan's chest, was found near the body.'

'How did he get hold of it?'

266

'He had it with him,' Garrett said.

'This has something to do with the call he made to the White House last night, hasn't it?'

'It seems he offered to make a deal with the President. The names of his co-conspirators in exchange for keeping his own name out of the investigation. It was the only way he'd be able to protect his family's reputation after his death.'

'So his own death was part of the deal?'

'It was the cornerstone of the deal,' Garrett answered. 'He knew he was finished. His only concern was for his family.'

'And the President went for the deal.'

'Not initially, from what I understand. I didn't have any contact with the President. I dealt with one of his senior aides, who told me the President only agreed to the deal after consulting at length with the Director of the Secret Service and the CIA.'

'What will happen to the other conspirators?' Brennan asked.

'The President will have a quiet word with them over the next couple of weeks. There's six in all. He'll offer them the choice of either resigning their seats in the Senate by the end of the year, or being discredited publicly with some scandal that would wreck their political careers anyway. I think you'll find they'll opt for the easy way out.'

'In other words, a cover-up,' Brennan said, sardonically.

'I'd prefer to call it damage limitation. It makes sense when you think about it. If this conspiracy were ever made public, the main casualty would be the President himself. His credibility would be on the line. It could bring him down, putting the Vice-President into the Oval Office. And even if he were able to ride out the storm, it would leave him weakened.'

'How much will the Vice-President be told about all this?'

'Nothing. He'll only know what he reads in the papers.'

'Which is?' Brennan prompted, when Garrett fell silent.

'That Dixon and Noonan were working together. Noonan smuggled a small explosive device past the security cordon and would have detonated it within range of the Vice-

President. It would have been a suicide mission. When the plot was uncovered, Noonan committed suicide before he could be questioned. No mention will be made of the hydrocyanic gas or of the device implanted in his chest. As for Dixon, his suicide will be reported exactly as it happened. Documentation will be released within the next few days linking both men with the right-wing white supremacists. Dixon was a known member of Aryan Nations in Idaho, and that can only add further credibility to the story. Naturally the white supremacists will deny any involvement but the documentation will be virtually impossible to disprove. That will help to further discredit them in the eyes of the public.'

'Where does Caldwell fit into the picture?' Brennan asked.

'He doesn't. He's already dead.'

'And the cardiologist?'

'He flew to Amsterdam last night with his wife, a psychiatrist, who was also involved in the experiments at the ranch. The CIA have picked up their trail.'

'Then what?' Brennan replied in horror. 'Bring them back here so they can start producing these devices for the CIA?'

'I really wouldn't know,' Garrett said. 'That's not my concern. And neither is it yours.'

'Is that a threat?' Brennan asked.

'An observation. I came here to tell you the truth before the sanitized version was released to the press. I felt I owed you that. The Director of the Secret Service wasn't so convinced, though. It took a lot of persuading before he let me come here this morning.' Garrett gazed thoughtfully at the floor before continuing. 'I don't like this any more than you do, Brennan. But you tell me another way of protecting the President, as well as keeping the Vice-President out of the Oval Office, and I'll gladly pass it on to the suits in Washington.'

'I'll leave that to you guys. You seem to have a natural flair for it.'

'I wasn't in on it,' Garrett said. 'I'm just a grunt, like you. The first I knew about it was when I was told to release Frain. Don't question it. Just do it. Those were my orders. It was only after Frain had committed suicide that I was filled in on

268

the fine print. And that's because I was threatening to make a few waves of my own if I wasn't told what was going on.'

'But you won't, will you?'

'And risk bringing down the President?' Garrett shook his head. 'They know I wouldn't do that. I've got too much respect for him.'

'What's to stop me rocking the boat?' Brennan challenged him.

'I don't believe you will. Not that you'd achieve anything even if you did. Believe me, the White House has every angle covered. It would be your word against theirs.'

'What about Lou Monks? How much does he know?'

'Very little. I'll leave it up to you to tell him what you think he needs to know. Not that I think he'd cause any trouble with his retirement not far away, do you?'

'No, probably not,' Brennan muttered, recalling his conversation with his partner the previous evening.

'Oh, there is one other thing. Last night the Director of the Secret Service contacted the Police Commissioner and it was agreed that any references either to you or Monks should be kept out of the press. It would only throw up a lot of awkward questions about why two detectives from a precinct in the South Bronx were working so closely with the Secret Service. We're not out to steal your thunder. Believe me, we won't be getting any credit for saving the Vice-President's life last night. It's our job. It's expected of us. What we will get is a lot of flak from the press, and from Capitol Hill, for allowing Noonan to get so close to him.'

'That suits me fine,' Brennan said. 'The last thing I want right now is to be hounded by the press. They'd be digging into my private life for some exclusive to splash across the tabloids and if Kelly's name were to come up, it could spook the kidnappers into doing something rash.'

'I've got to get back to the hotel now. There's still a lot to do before the Vice-President leaves for the airport later this morning,' Garrett said.

Brennan folded his arms across his chest. 'The Secret Service and the White House were very quick to cover the

President's back after what happened last night. How can you be so sure the President himself didn't sanction the assassination, and that this had been planned in advance to protect him in case it didn't work?'

'You heard what Frain said. The President knew nothing about it,' Garrett replied indignantly. 'Why would he have lied?'

'Why indeed?' Brennan said, then brushed past Garrett to open the front door.

'If the President was in on this from the start, then he would have known the names of the other conspirators, wouldn't he?' Garrett added. 'He didn't, until Frain told him.'

'You've only got Frain's word for that,' Brennan said. 'But, as you said, why would he have lied?'

Garrett's eyes lingered uncertainly on Brennan's face, then he turned away and hurried down the stairs. Brennan remained in the hallway until Garrett's footsteps had died away. Then he closed the door and went to wake Jason.

An hour later Brennan and Jason were walking through the lobby of Precinct 40. He waved at the desk sergeant as he passed and smiled when he noticed how pleased Jason was when the officer acknowledged them both by name. They went to the squad room. Monks was already at his desk. 'You get those books I wanted?' Brennan asked.

'On your desk,' Monks replied.

'Morning, Lou,' Jason said, pausing beside Monks's desk.

'Morning,' Monks said genially, then shot a reprimanding look in Brennan's direction. 'At least someone in the family's got manners.'

'Someone's a bit tetchy this morning,' Brennan said, wryly. 'I guess Marilyn went on a bit longer than usual last night.'

'We ended up having one hell of a row after I got back home. I was still wound up after Dixon . . .' Monks paused as his eyes fell on Jason '. . . not that I told her about it. I ended up sleeping in the spare room. I'd forgotten just how

270

uncomfortable that mattress was. I was tossing and turning for most of the night. I don't know how much sleep I got.'

'Not enough,' Brennan replied.

'Brennan!' a voice shouted across the squad room.

Brennan groaned. The voice was unmistakable: Captain Frank d'Arcy. 'Sir?' he called back.

'In my office. Now!'

Brennan patted the two battered books on his desk. 'Lou, will you start going through these mugshots with Jason? See if he can identify the van driver.' He got up and went over to d'Arcy's office, knocked on the door and entered. 'You wanted to see me, sir?'

'Close the door,' d'Arcy replied, and waited until Brennan had done so before continuing, 'I wanted to congratulate you on a job well done last night.'

'Thank you, sir,' Brennan said. 'I didn't realize you knew.'

'The Police Commissioner rang me this morning to bring me up to speed. Frankly, I think the whole thing sucks. You saved the Vice-President's life last night. That amounts to a commendation from the White House. Excellent publicity for a detective of your calibre. I reckon it would open a lot of doors for you. All you have to do is say the word, and the Police Commissioner will see to it that you're given the credit you deserve.'

'I know what you're getting at, sir, and I appreciate it,' Brennan replied. 'But with all due respect I don't want to end up behind a desk. It's not for me. I want to be out there on the streets with the other cops. It's where I belong.'

'Well, it's your decision. You've obviously made up your mind.'

'Yes, sir, I have.'

'That's all,' d'Arcy said, gesturing to the door.

Brennan returned to his desk. 'How we doing, bud?' he asked, leaning over Jason who was busy studying a page of mugshots.

'Nothing so far, Uncle Ray,' Jason replied, despondently.

'You just keep at it,' Brennan said, patting the boy's shoulder. 'I know most of the faces are the same as the ones you looked at yesterday, but sometimes a face slips through the net – and it's got to be worth a try.'

Jason nodded then squinted up at Brennan. 'I'm kind of thirsty, Uncle Ray. Can I have a soda?'

'Yeah, sure,' Brennan replied, then dug some loose change out of his pocket and poured it into Jason's cupped hands. 'There's a machine downstairs in the lobby.'

He waited until Jason had gone then crossed to Monks's desk, pulled up a chair and sat down. He leaned forward and spoke in a hushed voice, even though there was no one nearby. 'Garrett came to see me this morning. There's going to be a cover-up to save the President's credibility. I'll tell you what I know.'

'You put your life on the line last night, and this is the thanks you get.' Monks snorted in disgust once Brennan had finished.

'Don't you start as well,' Brennan replied. 'I've just had d'Arcy on to me about that. I'm comfortable with it, so that's an end to it.'

'This could be your ticket off the streets, Ray. I would have jumped at the chance to get my own command but I've never been command material. You've done your time in this cesspit. Stand up and take the credit for what happened last night.'

'I don't want a command. At least, not yet. Maybe in another five years I'll have changed my mind. Who knows? But right now I want to stay on the streets.'

'Maybe in another five years it'll be too late,' Monks said softly.

'It's a chance I've got to take, Lou,' Brennan replied, then looked round at the sound of pounding footsteps.

It was Jason. 'Uncle Ray! It's him!' He said breathlessly, stabbing a finger frantically towards the door. 'It's him! It's him!'

'Slow down, son,' Monks said, putting a paternal arm round him. 'Now take a couple of deep breaths.' He raised and lowered his hand to guide Jason's breathing. 'OK, now who is it?'

'The van driver!' Jason blurted out. 'He's downstairs.'

'Are you sure?' Monks asked.

'Yes, it's him.' Jason turned to Brennan. 'It *is* him, Uncle Ray. He's wearing those cheaters. With the cracked lens. *It's him!*'

'Where is he?' Brennan asked.

'In the lobby. I was standing at the soda machine when I saw him. He was talking to a policeman. A detective, I think, wearing a shoulder holster.'

'I want you to point him out,' Brennan said. 'But he mustn't see us.'

Monks pushed back his chair and followed them out of the squad room and to the staircase. They paused half-way down where the whole lobby was visible through the metal grille at the side of the stairs. 'Do you see him, Jason?' Monks asked, crouching down beside the boy.

'He was standing—' Jason stopped abruptly, and slowly raised a trembling finger. 'That's him. Over there. You see that detective by the door. The fat one. With the blue shirt.'

'I see him,' Monks replied.

'The man he's talking to, with the long hair and the scruffy clothes,' Jason replied. 'That's the driver.'

'Eddie Morrison?' Monks whispered in amazement. 'He's just a two-bit snitch. Are you sure?'

'A two-bit snitch who used to be involved with Noraid,' Brennan said to Monks. 'And who also collects "wanted" posters.'

'Yeah,' Monks replied hesitantly, not sure where Brennan's reasoning was leading.

'Kelly's father put out a contract on her after she'd helped to put her brothers away for murder. And you can be sure word of it would have reached these shores.' Brennan saw the puzzled frown on Monks's face. 'It's too long to explain right now. But I reckon Jason's spot on here. Kelly had a run-in with Morrison yesterday morning in the lobby. If her face was on one of his posters, chances are he recognized her. And if there was a reward on offer, you can bet he'll have snatched her to get his hands on it. It makes sense, Lou.'

'So what's our next—'

'He's leaving,' Brennan cut across Monks, bounded down the stairs and ran through the lobby, out of the main door and on to the steps just in time to see Morrison climb into the back of a yellow cab, which pulled away from the kerb. He hurried back inside, almost colliding with Monks. 'Get an unmarked radio car and bring it round to the front,' he told his partner, then rushed over to the detective Morrison had been talking to. 'Where's Eddie Morrison going?' he demanded.

'How should I know?' the man replied. 'He gave me a lead a few days ago. I owed him for it. He came in this morning to collect his money.'

'So he didn't say anything about where he was headed?'

'I told you, Ray, no. He said he was in a hurry. And so am I.'

Brennan watched him leave, then his eyes settled on Jason, who was still standing on the stairs. 'You did well, kid,' he said with a thumb's-up sign. 'Real well.'

'Do you know where Kelly is?' Jason asked excitedly.

'Not yet, but we'll find out soon enough. I want you to wait here. And don't get under anybody's feet. Sit at my desk if you want.'

'Will Kelly be with you when you come back?'

'That's the plan. Go on upstairs. I'll see you later.' Brennan asked the desk sergeant to call the squad room and ask the others up there to keep an eye on his nephew, then he left the building and waited impatiently on the sidewalk until Monks pulled up beside him in the unmarked police car. He climbed into the passenger seat.

'Where are we going?' Monks asked.

'Morrison's apartment in Union Port. Chances are Kelly's being held there.'

'This is crazy, Ray. The first rule they teach new recruits at the academy is never to get mixed up in a case if you're emotionally involved with one of the players.'

'I'm not some fucking choirboy fresh out of the academy!' Brennan shot back.

'No, you're an experienced cop who should know better.'

'If it means losing my badge – hell, they can have it for all I care. Just as long as Kelly's safe. That's all that matters to me, Lou. If we were to report this to d'Arcy, he'd call in a SWAT team. They don't know that area like we do. But if you want out, now's the time to say. I'd understand after what you said last night about taking early retirement.'

'I said I was *thinking* about taking early retirement. And I had a lot of time to do just that while I was tossing and turning in the spare bed last night. But it wasn't a difficult decision to make. Not with Marilyn's voice still ringing in my ears. So like it or not, you're stuck with me.' Monks slipped the car into gear and pulled away. 'Now, perhaps you'd care to tell me why Kelly's father put out a contract on her. And don't leave anything out.'

Monks parked out of sight of the rundown tenement block where Morrison lived. They got out, careful to keep their weapons concealed beneath their jackets. They didn't want to draw any unnecessary attention to themselves. Both kept a lookout for the snipers who regularly lay concealed on the rooftops of deserted buildings, with a panoramic view of the street below, ready to open fire on rival gang members or to fire randomly at anyone who happened to enter their sights. There was no race or gender discrimination in the South Bronx. Everyone was a potential victim.

Brennan was relieved to reach the entrance. He pushed open the door and found himself face to face with two black youths. He recognized one from a previous bust. The youths eyed the detectives coldly but chose against confrontation and disappeared out on to the street. Monks closed the doors behind them. 'Second floor, isn't it?'

Brennan nodded, then withdrew his revolver and walked cautiously up the garbage-strewn stairs. He paused at the top, his back against the wall, then pivoted round and fanned the deserted corridor with the revolver. With Monks watching his back, he went along the corridor until he reached Morrison's apartment. He took up a position on one side of the door. Monks pressed himself against the wall on the other side and nodded when Brennan indicated he'd kick open the door. Brennan stepped away from the wall, ready to go, but heard footsteps on the stairs. He grabbed Monks's arm and pulled him through the open door opposite Morrison's apartment.

They remained out of sight as the footsteps drew closer. Brennan could monitor a section of the corridor through the crack between the door and the jamb. A figure came into view and paused outside the opposite apartment. It was Eddie Morrison. Brennan remained rigid, fearful that any movement would give them away. Morrison knocked three times on the door. A pause. Twice more. Another pause. Twice more. Moments later came the sound of bolts being drawn back and the door was opened. From where he was standing, Brennan couldn't see who'd answered it. Monks tapped his arm and gestured for them to make their move. Brennan shook his head.

'You two can go now,' Morrison said. 'Come back again this evening. About nine. I'll have your money then.'

'You'd better be on the level, Morrison, or I'll cut out your fucking heart,' a second voice snarled.

'You'll get your money,' Morrison assured him. 'But I got to deal with this guy alone. Those were his conditions, not mine.'

'Nine o'clock. The money, in full,' the second voice said. 'Come on, let's go.'

Two sets of footsteps headed away from the apartment, towards the stairs. The door was closed and the bolt slipped back into place. Then silence.

'We had them, Ray,' Monks whispered. 'Now two of them are gone.'

'Let them go. You heard them. They'll be back. What if a couple of them had got back into the apartment before we could arrest them? We'd have had a hostage situation on our hands. Which is what we don't want. It's my guess Morrison's alone in there with Kelly. Two against one. Better odds, wouldn't you say?'

'How are you going in? You heard the bolts. It'll be like a goddamn fortress in there.'

'I'll knock like anyone else,' Brennan said, then stepped out into the corridor and told Monks to take up a position on one side of the door. Then he gave the coded knock. Three times. Pause. Twice more. Pause. Twice more. He heard Morrison curse behind the door, then the bolts being drawn back. As the door was opened Brennan hammered his foot against it, slamming it into Morrison's face. The man screamed in pain as one of the metal bolts opened a deep gash on his cheek and he was thrown backwards on to the floor. Brennan left Monks to cuff him and kicked open the door leading into the bedroom. Kelly was sitting in the corner of the empty room, her hands manacled to the pipe behind her, a strip of masking tape secured across her mouth. He hurried over to her and tore the tape off her mouth. 'Are you OK?' he asked anxiously.

'I will be once you get me out of these damn handcuffs,' she replied.

'Ray?' Monks called from the doorway and tossed Brennan the key he'd found in Morrison's pocket.

Brennan unlocked the handcuffs then helped her up. 'Did you get the other two?' she asked, as she massaged the red grooves on her wrists where the cuffs had dug into her skin.

'Not yet, but we'll pick them up soon enough.'

'What about Caldwell and Dixon? Have you caught them yet? And the Vice-President? Is he all right?'

'It's a long story. The Vice-President's OK. Dixon and Caldwell are dead. But I'll explain it all later.'

'Do you know why I was kidnapped?' she asked. 'At first I thought Caldwell might have been behind it, until I saw *him*,' she said, pointing at Morrison. 'He's the one who tried to steal my bracelet at the police station yesterday. At the time I just thought he was a petty thief.'

'That's exactly what he is,' Monks told her. 'A petty thief who makes a squalid living as an informer.'

'So why did he kidnap me?'

'You want to answer that, Eddie?' Brennan said.

'Please, Mr Brennan, I'm bleeding real bad,' Morrison whimpered. 'You got to get me to a doctor.'

'Where's the poster?' Brennan asked.

'Poster, Mr Brennan? I – I don't know what you mean.'

'The longer you keep jacking around, the longer it's going to take for us to call the paramedics,' Brennan told him.

'It's in the box in that cupboard behind you.'

'What poster?' Kelly demanded, as Brennan opened the cupboard and pulled out the cardboard box.

'This one,' he said, holding it up.

'My God,' she whispered in disbelief as she took it from him.

'Bring back a few memories?' Brennan asked.

'And then some. But this is ten years old,' she said in bewilderment. 'How did he get hold of it after all this time?'

'He's *had* it all this time,' Brennan corrected her. 'As Lou said, he's an informer. This is how he makes his living. Memorizing faces on wanted posters. He saw you at the Four-O and came up with this little scheme to net him the reward.'

'Do you recognize the phone number on the poster?' Monks asked her.

'No, other than it's a Belfast number.'

'Who did you speak to, Eddie?' Brennan asked.

'I don't know his name. When I rang the number I was told I'd be called back. I had to wait half an hour. It was another man. He wouldn't give his name. He said he'd pay me the money once he got here. I gave him this address. Then he hung up.'

'He's coming out here?' Monks said.

'He said he'd be here at dinnertime,' Morrison replied. 'Then he rang off.'

'So we're talking about . . . what . . . six, seven o'clock tonight?' Brennan said to Monks.

'Unless he meant British dinnertime,' Kelly said. 'Dinner is lunchtime back home.'

'Shit,' Brennan hissed and looked at his watch. 'That means he could be here within the next hour or so. Lou, get on to control. Tell them to send an ambulance for Morrison and a uniform to go with him to the hospital. Then call d'Arcy and tell him what's going on. We need the names of all the passengers on every flight out of Belfast in the past twenty-four hours.'

'Who exactly are we looking for?' Monks asked.

'My father, Seamus McBride,' Kelly answered. 'He swore ten years ago he'd kill me for giving evidence against my brothers at their trial. He won't send some flunky to do the job for him. He'll want to pull the trigger himself.'

'I'll get on to it right away,' Monks said. 'You know d'Arcy's going to hit the roof when he finds out what's happened.'

'He can do what the hell he wants with me – after Kelly's father's been stopped at the airport,' Brennan replied.

'That is, of course, unless he's already in the country and on his way over here,' Monks said.

'Then he's going to get one hell of a surprise when he gets here, isn't he?' Brennan said.

'I'll take him with me, and transfer him to the ambulance as soon it arrives,' Monks said, then led the handcuffed Morrison away.

'You never told me how you found me?' Kelly asked, once they were alone.

'You've got Jason to thank for that,' Brennan replied. 'He saw Morrison at the Four-O earlier this morning and recognized him from the cracked sunglasses he was wearing. That's not all, though. He tried to stop them taking you yesterday afernoon and took a punch in the face for his trouble. He's got a colourful bruise on his cheek this morning.'

'I knew they hadn't got him. Morrison told me. Jason's quite a guy, isn't he?'

'Yeah, you're right there,' Brennan said. He peered cautiously into the street when he heard the sound of an approaching engine but the car drove past the building and disappeared.

'You know he doesn't want to live with your mother, don't you?' she said.

Brennan turned away slowly from the window. 'Yeah, he told me that the other night. I got to say, I kind of like having him around the apartment but it's too early to start talking

279

about having him move in permanently. That's a hell of a decision to make. And one that would need a lot of thought.'

'Would you ever consider adopting him?'

'If I thought it was in his best interests.'

'Your mother wouldn't give him up without a fight, though, would she?'

'No, but a sympathetic judge might be swayed by what Jason wants, rather than by what my mother thinks is best for him,' Brennan replied. 'These days judges are far more inclined to listen to the kids' point of view than they were, say, ten years ago . . .' His voice trailed off when he heard footsteps. He got out his Smith & Wesson and motioned Kelly away from the front door. The footsteps stopped outside the apartment and the door was pushed open. He exhaled deeply and put away his weapon when Monks entered.

'The plane touched down at JFK an hour ago. The passengers have already cleared customs,' Monks said. Then his eyes went to Kelly. 'It's not your father. He died four years ago. It's your brother, Feargal.'

'That's not possible,' she said firmly. 'He's serving a life sentence at the Maze. It's obviously someone using his name. It's not Feargal. It can't be.'

'It is,' Monks said softly. 'Captain D'Arcy spoke to a senior officer in the RUC who told him your brother was released from prison two months ago. The RUC were against it, but the psychiatrists said he was a model prisoner and recommended him for parole.'

'I bet he was a model prisoner,' she shot back venomously. 'He's always been able to deceive people, obviously he's done it again. Is Patrick out too?'

'He was stabbed to death in the prison six years ago,' Monks replied. 'And, from what d'Arcy was told, Feargal never tried to avenge his death, even though he knew who did it.'

'I bet that impressed the psychiatrists no end,' she snorted.

'I've got an idea,' Brennan said, then looked at Kelly. 'It could be dangerous, though. You'd have to trust me completely.'

'You know I do,' she replied, her voice softening. 'So let's hear it.'

'And you're sure it'll work?' d'Arcy said, once Brennan had outlined the plan to him. The two men were standing in Morrison's bedroom, the connecting door closed.

'Yeah, I am,' Brennan replied. 'Right now we don't have jack shit on this guy. Sure, we could apprehend him when he turns up here. If he's armed, we could get him for UPF. But the unlawful possession of a firearm as a first offence? He'd get off lightly. That's not going to achieve anything. He'll just come after Kelly again. We need to nail this bastard. And the only way we're going to do that is by catching him in the act of handing over the money, which would then tie him in with the kidnapping. That's a felony. With his record, he'd be looking at a ten-year stretch at the very least. Probably more.'

'And you'll be Morrison?' d'Arcy said.

'He doesn't know what Morrison looks like.'

'OK, I'll go with it, but wear body armour,' d'Arcy said, after a thoughtful silence. 'And once this is over, we're going to have a little chat about breaking departmental rules.'

'Once this is over, you can skin me alive and hang me outside the precinct if you want.'

'Don't tempt me,' d'Arcy said. 'Now go and get Ms McBride. We've got to fine-tune this plan to ensure that nothing goes wrong. And I mean *nothing*.'

'You're late!'

'Sorry. I got caught in traffic in the Holland Tunnel. It's good to see you again, Feargal.'

Feargal McBride climbed into the passenger seat and tossed his holdall into the back of the car. 'Just drive, Johnny. I'm already late.'

'How was the flight?'

'Fine,' McBride replied irritably. 'Where's the gun?'

'In the glove compartment.'

McBride waited until they were clear of the airport and travelling on the highway before he opened it and removed the Browning Hi-Power 9mm. He checked the clip then pushed it back into place before slipping the pistol into the side pocket of his leather jacket.

'It was hard to get it at such short notice. There were extra costs. You know how it is.'

McBride removed an envelope from the inside pocket of his jacket and tossed it on to the dashboard. 'I think you'll find that more than covers any expenses.'

'It's not the money, Feargal, you know that,' the man said, palming the envelope and slipping it into his shirt pocket. 'It's about friendship. We go back a long way. We had some good times back home, didn't we? You, me and Patrick.'

'Patrick's dead.'

'I . . . I had no idea. What happened?'

'He's dead. Let's leave it at that,' McBride said. 'What do you know about this Eddie Morrison?'

'Small-time crook.'

'Does he carry?'

'Never. It's not his scene. Everyone knows that.'

Feargal McBride smiled faintly to himself. 'So how long before we get there?'

'Forty minutes. Fifty at most.'

'Let's make it forty, shall we?' McBride said.

'Sure thing.' There was an uneasy pause. 'Are you really going to kill Kelly?'

'I didn't fly all the way over here for a fucking family reunion,' McBride snapped.

'What about the guy who's holding her at the apartment? You think fifteen's enough to keep him quiet?'

'It's no wonder you never made it in the IRA. You're so fucking naïve at times. Do you really think I'm going to pay him? Two more bodies in the South Bronx aren't going to arouse suspicion. Not from what I've heard about the place. And I'll be back in Belfast long before the bodies are discovered. Sweet revenge, Johnny. Sweet revenge.'

The driver swallowed nervously as his eyes flickered uncertainly to McBride. 'You – you can trust me to keep my mouth shut, Feargal.'

282

'I know I can,' McBride replied, then leaned his head back against the seat, folded his arms and closed his eyes.

'You sure look the part,' Monks said, appraising Brennan's clothes after he'd fitted a concealed microphone under his partner's shirt.

'You sure smell it as well,' Kelly added, wrinkling her nose in disgust.

'Buying clothes off a vagrant in the street,' d'Arcy muttered, wisely keeping his distance from Brennan. 'That's going to look really good on this month's expense sheet.'

'Are you strapped?' Monks asked.

Brennan nodded and patted the concealed Smith & Wesson on his belt. Then d'Arcy's two-way radio crackled into life. He was quick to answer it. 'Vehicle approaching,' a voice announced. It was a member of the back-up unit, which was parked out of sight further down the street. 'Two males. Both Caucasian. Vehicle slowing. Should be within visual now. Over and out.'

Brennan moved to the window and tweaked back the curtain as the car pulled up outside the block. The passenger door swung open and a man got out. 'Cropped ginger hair. Pale complexion. Age, late thirties.'

'That sound's like Feargal,' Kelly replied, and Brennan saw the vulnerability in her eyes. Then it was gone.

'We'll be listening in on the wire from the opposite apartment,' Monks said to Brennan. 'Don't lock the front door in case we need to move in fast.'

'Yeah, yeah, Lou, we've been through all this before,' Brennan said, as he ushered them out of the apartment and bolted the door behind them. 'I won't let anything happen to you,' he said, with a reassuring smile as he brushed a loose strand of hair away from Kelly's face. 'I swear I won't.'

'I know,' she said softly. Then he placed a strip of masking tape over her mouth and she sat down on the floor and clasped her hands behind her back to make it look like she was tied to the pipe.

Brennan began to punch his fist into his palm as he paced

283

the room, waiting for Feargal McBride to arrive. He felt confident. But not over-confident. He wouldn't let Kelly down. He *couldn't* let her down. But he couldn't shake the uneasiness that had been building inside him ever since the car had pulled up outside.

He froze mid-step when he heard the knock at the door. The same code he'd used to gain entry. *Morrison never had much imagination*, he thought as he closed the connecting door. He moved to the front door, paused to take a deep breath, then drew back the bolts and opened it.

'Morrison?' Feargal McBride asked. Brennan didn't reply. 'We spoke on the phone,' McBride continued, then patted his jacket pocket. 'Fifteen thousand dollars. In used notes. As agreed.' Brennan stepped aside to allow McBride to enter the apartment. McBride closed the door behind him and slotted the bolts back into place. 'We wouldn't want to be disturbed, now, would we?' McBride said.

'Not much chance of that around here,' Brennan retorted. Now d'Arcy and Monks wouldn't be able to enter the apartment in a hurry. But there wasn't anything he could do without making it appear suspicious. It only strengthened his resolve to protect Kelly. He raised a hand as McBride took a step towards the bedroom door. 'The money,' he demanded, rubbing his thumb and forefinger together.

'You get it once I've seen the woman,' McBride said, then gestured towards the closed door. 'After you, friend.' Brennan led the way to the door and was about to push it open when McBride pressed the Browning into the small of his back. 'This is just a precaution, in case you've got someone behind the door, waiting to jump me,' McBride said in his ear. 'It's nothing personal. I'm sure you understand. Now open the door all the way.'

Brennan pushed hard on the door with the flat of his hand. It swung open and banged against the wall. He stepped tentatively into the room, the barrel pressed into his back. He noticed the concern in Kelly's eyes and, for one awful moment, saw her arms move, as if she were going to get up.

But she stopped herself and, as her eyes went past him the concern was replaced with intense hatred.

'Hello, little sister,' McBride said, then shoved Brennan away from him and shot him in the back. Brennan was punched forward by the force of the shot and landed heavily on the floor. McBride swung the Browning on Kelly before she'd had a chance to react, and shot her through the chest.

He looked round sharply when he heard the sound of a heavy kick at the front door. It rattled but the bolts held. There was a second blow. He'd walked into a trap. He looked down at Kelly and saw, to his horror, no blood on the front of her tracksuit. She was wearing body armour! The pounding continued relentlessly on the door. He had only a few seconds before they broke through. He swung the Browning on Kelly again. He aimed for a head shot. This time there would no mistake. He smiled coldly at the terror in her eyes as his finger tightened around the trigger.

The bullet hammered into his chest, slamming him back against the wall. Blood bubbled into his throat and seeped out of the corner of his mouth. His glazed eyes went to where Kelly was still lying on the floor. He knew he was dying. That didn't matter. But at least he'd have the satisfaction of taking her with him. Drawing on the last of his strength, he swung the automatic towards her again. The second bullet punctured his heart. The Browning slipped from his fingers and he toppled forward lifelessly on to the floor.

The door finally gave way. D'Arcy and Monks burst into the apartment, followed by two uniformed officers. They found Brennan lying on his back, the Smith & Wesson still trained on the spot where, moments earlier, Feargal McBride had been standing. Monks eased the weapon gently from Brennan's grasp then one of the officers crouched down beside McBride and checked for a pulse. Nothing. The other officer found a blanket which he threw over the body.

Brennan sat up. 'I had no choice, Frank,' he said. 'He only had one thought on his mind and that was to kill Kelly. He was going for a head shot. I had to put him down.'

'Not exactly according to plan, was it?' d'Arcy said, but

there was no anger in his voice, just a resigned acceptance. They'd come out of it in one piece, and that's all that mattered. He'd always stood by his men if he felt they'd been justified in their actions – and he was in no doubt that Brennan had been forced to kill Feargal McBride. There would be the inevitable enquiry into the shooting, but it would go down as justifiable homicide. He'd see to that.

Monks crouched beside Kelly. 'Are you OK?' he asked. She nodded then removed her tracksuit top to let him unfasten the body armour and lift it over her head. He held up the vest to see where the bullet had struck it. 'It looks like it would have hit you close to the breastbone.'

'Just here,' she said, touching the sensitive area on her skin. 'It smarts a bit.'

He helped her to her feet and she crossed to where Brennan was sitting, gingerly prodding the bruise on his back where the bullet had thudded into him. 'I had no other option,' he said to her. 'I'm sorry.'

'So am I,' she said bitterly. 'I'm sorry I couldn't have killed him myself.'

'Come on, you two,' d'Arcy said. 'Forensics are on their way. I want the place cordoned off before they get here.'

Brennan struggled to his feet and hovered uncertainly behind Kelly when she paused to look down at the outline of her brother's body underneath the bloodstained blanket. Then she left the room. He went after her and as he closed the door behind him she cupped her hand around the back of his head, pulling his face down towards hers, and kissed him. 'That's for saving my life.'

'Remind me to do it more often,' he replied, with a quick smile.

'Oh, you can count on it.'

'Brennan!' d'Arcy yelled, his voice booming the length of the corridor. 'Let's go. Now!'

'We can continue this later,' Brennan said, then opened the front door and disappeared into the corridor.

'You can count on that, too,' she said softly, and went after him.